**Ma** 

**by** 

*G000167728*

## *She was dying for him.*

Every flick of Drew's tongue against her breast sent bolts of delight downwards. Their lips met again in a hot, quick mating, and she reached for his belt.

When he leaned away, Tori whispered, "I want this," reassuring him as she reached for him again.

"Not now."

Tori froze. "You want to run that by me again?"

He closed his eyes and gave one hard shake of his head. "God, if only you knew how hard this is for me…"

"It's *hard* for *me*," she said, staring at his crotch. "I can *see* how *hard* it is for *me*."

A hoarse laugh that sounded more pained than amused erupted from his lips. "You're not ready," he finally said.

*Oh, she was ready, all right.* "Wanna bet?" she snapped. Then she proved it to him by grabbing his hand and pulling it down her body.

"Any *more* questions?" she asked.

# Really Hot!
## by Jennifer LaBrecque

ᘒ ᙭ ᘓ

### *She opened the drawer and pulled out a condom…*

"Oh, my God, Portia, this is like a fantasy come true," Rourke groaned, "but I'm not sure I'm up to it. Wait. What the hell am I saying? The sexiest woman in the universe is standing next to my bed, unwrapping a condom. Hell, yes, I'm up to it. You'll have to do most of the work, but still…"

It took Portia's hormonally oversaturated brain about a nanosecond to imagine herself pulling off her clothes and going for a ride.

She picked up an ice cube. "I'm making you an ice pack. For your back."

"Oh." Rourke lay there for a second, his eyes closed. It was suddenly incredibly hot in his room.

"You're a wicked woman, Portia Tomlinson." Rourke choked out the words. "But I wouldn't have you any other way…"

# Available in November 2005 from Silhouette Desire

*Terms of Surrender*
by Shirley Rogers
&
*Shocking the Senator*
by Leanne Banks
*(Dynasties: The Danforths)*

ᘒ ᔆᴕ ᘓ

*Best-Kept Lies*
by Lisa Jackson
*(The McCaffertys)*
&
*Wild in the Moment*
by  Jennifer Greene
*(The Campbell Sisters)*

ᘒ ᔆᴕ ᘓ

*A Bed of Sand*
by Laura Wright
&
*Principles and Pleasures*
by Margaret Allison

ᘒ ᔆᴕ ᘓ

*Make Me Over*
by Leslie Kelly
&
*Really Hot!*
by Jennifer LaBrecque
*(Getting Real)*

# Make Me Over
## LESLIE KELLY

# Really Hot!
## JENNIFER LABRECQUE

**DID YOU PURCHASE THIS BOOK WITHOUT A COVER?**
If you did, you should be aware it is **stolen property** as it was
reported *unsold and destroyed* by a retailer. Neither the author nor
the publisher has received any payment for this book.

*All the characters in this book have no existence outside the
imagination of the author, and have no relation whatsoever to anyone
bearing the same name or names. They are not even distantly inspired
by any individual known or unknown to the author, and all the
incidents are pure invention.*

*All Rights Reserved including the right of reproduction in whole or in
part in any form. This edition is published by arrangement with
Harlequin Enterprises II B.V. The text of this publication or any part
thereof may not be reproduced or transmitted in any form or by any
means, electronic or mechanical, including photocopying, recording,
storage in an information retrieval system, or otherwise, without
the written permission of the publisher.*

*This book is sold subject to the condition that it shall not, by way of
trade or otherwise, be lent, resold, hired out or otherwise circulated
without the prior consent of the publisher in any form of binding or cover
other than that in which it is published and without a similar condition
including this condition being imposed on the subsequent purchaser.*

*Silhouette, Silhouette Desire and Colophon
are registered trademarks of Harlequin Books S.A.,
used under licence.*

*First published in Great Britain 2005
Silhouette Books, Eton House, 18-24 Paradise Road,
Richmond, Surrey TW9 1SR*

The publisher acknowledges the copyright holders of the
individual works as follows:

Make Me Over © Leslie Kelly 2004
Really Hot! © Jennifer LaBrecque 2005

ISBN 0 373 60398 3

*51-1105*

*Printed and bound in Spain
by Litografia Rosés S.A., Barcelona*

Dear Reader,

Is there anything hotter than a gorgeous man who's so intelligent he doesn't even realise how sexy he is? Not to me there isn't. I just love the kind of guy who's so secure in himself that the question of how he looks never even enters his mind.

Drew Bennett is just such a man. Brilliant, driven, cultured, worldly and intuitive, the last thing he's worried about is whether or not women are attracted to his brawny shoulders or brilliant blue eyes. He considers the mind so much more important.

Such a man definitely needs a wake-up call, don't you think? And Tori Lyons is about to give him one. Tori's known a lot of men. The drag-racing circuit is full of them. But she's never met one like Drew, and she's willing to do anything—even give herself a complete cultural makeover—to get his attention.

I love reality shows. This one was such a ball to create. I really hope Tori and Drew...as well as all the rest of the crazy cast and crew...give you a few hours of reading pleasure.

Best wishes,

*Leslie Kelly*

# MAKE ME OVER
by
Leslie Kelly

To all the members of my incredibly supportive RWA chapters: CFRW, TARA and my home chapter, FL-STAR. I appreciate you all more than you'll ever know.

# Prologue

"IF YOU THINK I'm ever gonna work on the set of another reality TV show, you're whacked in the head, old man."

Jacey Turner stared at her father across his expansive desk in his highbrow Hollywood office, not believing he'd just asked her to take over as lead camera operator on his latest project. And definitely not believing *why* he was asking.

He was nearly broke. Burt Mueller, the king of TV in the 1970s, had backed a string of stinkers in more recent decades—everyone knew that. But she'd never thought he'd come to this. Losing his edge, his power, his "in"-ness.

Cripes…his *Rolls*.

"I'm serious. I need you, babe."

"Whacked," she continued, as if he hadn't spoken. "Or you've been popping some of those happy pills that got you through the sixties."

Daddy dearest tsked as he gestured toward his recently Botoxed face, which looked as if it belonged on a forty year old—not someone two decades older. "Do you think I'd spend *this* much money on trainers and plastic surgeons to go and poison myself with drugs?"

She cast a pointed look at the cigarette smoldering in the ashtray on his desk. Against policy in this no-smoking building, like every other building in L.A. these days. As if he cared.

Burt merely shrugged. "They're not hurting me on the

*outside*, which is more important to me than my lungs right now."

God, how could a man say something so completely shallow, yet manage to make it sound so sincere? She couldn't help chuckling. "Tell that to the wrinkles that are eventually gonna show back up around your mouth from constantly having a cancer stick clamped between your lips."

"You berate me because you care."

Yeah, she did. And he knew it. Leaning back in the chair, she put her boot-clad feet on his desk and crossed them, just to keep him guessing. She did not need the old man realizing she'd do just about anything for him. "Okay, be honest, how bad could it be? I mean, the residuals on *Paw Come Git Your Dinner* alone should keep you in Bruno Magli shoes until you're ninety."

"You're thinking like a Hollywood insider of *today*. Not of the seventies," he retorted, sounding weary. "Residuals? Ha. Ask me why stars of *The Brady Bunch* made so many bad reunion movies, until I thought we might soon see *Alice Does Dallas*. Or why Gilligan's gang had to be rescued by the Harlem Globetrotters."

Jacey, who recognized the shows by their eternal life on TV Land, merely waited.

"It's so Gilligan doesn't have to shine shoes at LAX and Cindy, Jan and Marcia don't have to work as Hooters girls. Everything was in the studio's favor in those days."

Okay, she'd heard that, but still found it hard to believe Burt could be so bad off. She was looking at the man who'd created six of the top ten shows of 1970. Who'd first seized on canned laughter to beef up audience response and sparked a revolution in sitcoms. Who'd earned ten Emmys, for piss sake!

"So you really think you can salvage a historic thirty-some-years career as a TV legend by jumping on the reality-show hysteria which hasn't died its overdue death? What a dumb idea."

He didn't take offense. Her old man never took offense at anything, except being called a has-been. And he certainly didn't get all fatherly on her. Why would he? Their relationship wasn't like that. He hadn't even known she existed until she'd shown up on his doorstep at age seventeen with a ratty backpack and a bad attitude, informing him he was her dear old dad.

Some Hollywood types would've kicked her to the curb. Burt Mueller hadn't. He'd taken her in, welcomed her, convinced her he'd never known of her existence, and given her a job.

Somehow, over the past six years, they'd become, well, if not exactly what you'd call family…at least friends. But there was only so much she'd do for friendship. And setting foot on the set of another reality show wasn't on the list. Not after the last one, *Killing Time In A Small Town*, where she'd worked as lead camera operator. Because getting fired hadn't been the highlight of her frickin' year.

Though honestly, she had to admit, the experience hadn't been *all* bad. And the show had done *really* well in ratings this fall.

She also had to give thanks because of what it had led to in her personal life. She, tough-as-nails Jacey Turner, had let down her guard and fallen in love.

Lord, she missed Digg. Missed him like mad. But coming here to California to answer her father's desperate call wasn't such a bad thing. The past couple of months, when she and Digg had tried to make their unconventional romance work in the real world—*his* world of fire stations and big Hispanic-New York families—had been tough. Particularly because she suspected all of Digg's friends and loved ones secretly looked at her as a sewer rat who'd glommed on to him for the million bucks he'd won on

*Killing Time.* She couldn't prove it, but she'd lay money his mother made the sign of the cross behind her back every time Jacey entered her house.

She'd been hiding her unhappiness at that—and at not being able to land a job with any studio in New York—for weeks now.

"It'll be a good break for you," Burt said, moving in for the kill. "A classy mansion in New England in the winter. Snow, skiing, hot chocolate."

"Gag me. I'm not an Aspen bunny. Remember? I skied on a skateboard in the aqueducts of South Central."

He chuckled. "Then do it because you need the money, too."

She raised a brow, but didn't ask how he knew. He knew everything. "What's this show about, anyway?"

He didn't gloat over being right, though he grinned as he filled her in. When he was done, she sighed. "Sounds boring. A social makeover show. Trashy girls get cash for class."

His brow shot indignantly up toward his bald head. "It's perfect. Like the musical, the one with Audrey Hepburn."

Jacey hated musicals. She could never get past how moronic a guy would look breaking out into a big song-and-dance number right in the middle of a gang war. If it happened in real life, someone would have Baker Acted the loser in two seconds flat. Those things made reality TV look realistic.

"You know the one," Burt continued. "He makes her over, she sings the song about how she coulda schtupped all night."

That made her snort a laugh, exactly as he'd intended. The old man was good. Because in spite of hating all musicals, she did have a soft spot for *one. My Fair Lady.* For the same reason she liked *Pretty Woman.* She enjoyed seeing the gutter girl fool all the rich snots into thinking she was all highbrow and stuff.

But she wouldn't give in so easily. "I still don't see the great angle. It's...ordinary."

Burt hated to be told that anything he touched could be ordinary. His scowl wasn't aimed at her, however; it was aimed at himself. Because even he had to see how dull the whole thing sounded. Put a bunch of uneducated girls in a house and teach them stuff. Whoop-de-fricking-wow.

"Well, *this* has certainly grabbed enough interest to land on the *Times* list," Burt finally said as he slid his rolling chair back and pulled a hardbound book off a shelf Jacey had assumed was merely for decoration. This book actually looked like it'd been opened. At least once.

She took it from him, studying the title. *Beyond Eliza Doolittle: Education vs. Genetics in Today's Society*. "Yawn."

"But it's not." Burt flipped the book over so she could see the large black-and-white photo of the author on the back. "Yum."

"Exactly. He's all the rage, and he's agreed to let us do a reality show based on the theories in this book, as long as we donate a large sum of money to educational charities."

Jacey hardly listened. She was too busy reading the bio on the author, Dr. Andrew Bennett. The bio didn't say much, but it revealed the most important detail. "He's single."

Burt tilted his head. "Interested?" The mild tone didn't fool her. He'd very much like to know what was going on with her love life. Heck, so would Jacey.

Shaking her head, she leaned back in her chair and crossed her arms, letting the creative juices really get flowing.

A fancy estate during the holidays. Bubbly hot tubs. Red wine in front of a fire. A bunch of busty bimbos in search of a little class-i-fication. And a hunky-as-heck brainiac doctor.

"I've got an idea," she finally said. "I think I just might have come up with a way for you to take this boring makeover show of yours and turn it into a *bona fide* hit."

Burt sat up straight, immediately interested. "How?"

"Well," Jacey replied smoothly, "it's simple. You don't make the women compete for money or to be named Grand Duchess of Poobah because her pinkie stays the highest during a tea party."

Her father huffed.

Leaning close to his desk, Jacey crossed her arms on its wood surface and met the old man's stare. Once she was sure she had his complete attention, she tapped the photo on the back of the book with the tip of her nail.

"You make them compete for *him*."

# 1

HE'D STUMBLED into a hooker convention.

Arriving at the Vermont estate to which he'd been directed, Dr. Andrew Bennett immediately suspected he'd made a wrong turn somewhere. Because this *had* to be a group of hookers raucously making themselves at home in the tastefully decorated library of a fabulous New England mansion. Either that or someone was filming an episode of *Girls Gone Wild*.

From the two brunettes and the redhead sitting on top of the bar doing shots—to the trio of blondes dirty dancing around a hapless waiter serving hors d'oeuvres—to the tall one lying on her back in the middle of the floor attempting to guzzle a yard of beer—to the petite, washed-out girl demonstrating pole dancing against the floor lamp, every woman in the room looked about as raucous, uncouth and outrageous as could be.

He'd asked for women with little education or social skills. Not the entire mud-wrestling team from Big Al's Slaughterhouse in Bangor.

Drew wished he felt elated to have such *raw* material to work with.

He didn't.

He wished he could muster some enthusiasm about the daunting task of overseeing the transformation of these, er, *ladies* of the evening into real ladies.

He couldn't.

He wished he'd turned around and left the minute he'd seen two of the women competing in a spitting contest into the fireplace.

He hadn't.

He wished there was some legitimate reason he actually *had* to participate in this reality-show nonsense, rather than just let his book be the basis for it.

There wasn't.

He wished he could change his mind.

Too late. He was stuck. Here. With the rollicking house full of…test subjects.

One-on-one he could have handled. Frankly, he would have relished the opportunity to show the world what he'd learned from his own research…from his own life. Genetics or upbringing didn't determine the capacity of a person's success. Education did.

Education. Resilience. A modicum of social ability… they could overcome nearly any hurdles mere birth could bestow. Hadn't his transition from homeless kid of a flighty mother to college professor illustrated as much? God knew, if he, Drew Bennett—former thief and con artist who'd once picked pockets in Miami Beach to feed his kid sister—could make it from the back seat of an ancient, rusty VW Beetle to the podiums of Georgetown University, anyone could.

A crash jerked his attention back to the women in the room.

"Wooo, girl, you're gonna have to pay for that!" someone shouted as a redhead giggled over the vase she'd just knocked off an end table.

"Maybe they'll take it out in trade," the pole dancer said, sounding weary and jaded.

Drew blew out a long, frustrated breath.

Why he'd ever thought this reality-show idea might actually do some good, he had no idea. Back in September when he'd first been approached by the TV people, he'd refused. Not only because it seemed a silly idea, but also because he simply didn't have the time to deal with such nonsense. He'd already had to take the semester off teaching anthropology and sociology at Georgetown because of the insanity of book tours and publicity associated with being an overnight bestseller. Throw in his next project—a trip to a university in Mexico to participate in an expedition to an ancient Mayan city—and he was completely booked.

Then they'd hit him in his weak spot, his Achilles' heel. The production company had offered to donate ten percent of the *gross* profits of the show—not *net* profits; even he, a total non-Hollywood type knew better than that—to A Book and a Dream, Drew's favorite charity. Few people knew Drew had helped found the organization, which taught reading to underprivileged kids. That they'd investigated him enough to track down the information showed how serious they were.

The biggest hitch came when they'd suddenly decided, last week, that *he* had to be on the set to oversee things and gauge the women's progress. But when the ten percent had gone up to fifteen, he'd allowed himself to be persuaded. He'd consoled himself over the decision by thinking it wouldn't be *that* difficult. He could transform anyone who had the drive and basic intelligence to succeed.

But not a dozen women at once.

Certainly not *these* dozen women, who looked much more up for a rave than a grammar lesson.

Sighing heavily, he turned to leave, thankful no one had spotted him, when suddenly his attention was caught by one woman who stood apart from the rest. Her back to the room, she faced a floor-to-ceiling bookcase loaded with leather-bound editions, completely oblivious to the cacophony behind her. She remained separate. Distinct. In a bubble of introspection over the books—a posture Drew could understand, having lost himself in research on many occasions.

From behind, she was, well, to put it in the most basic terms…hot. She was petite, likely the smallest woman here. Tight, worn jeans clung to a slim pair of legs and a quite delectable backside. They nipped in to hug a tiny waist, though not without spreading over some fine curvy hips.

Her heavy, red flannel shirt was too bulky to allow him to make out much of the rest of her figure. But the thick bunch of wavy brown hair cascading down to the middle of her back led him to suspect she had brown eyes and olive skin.

Suddenly, the most unusual sensation drew his attention to his hands. Prickly. They tingled—though not from cold. He soon realized why. His mind was overflowing with images of twining his hands in all that hair, testing its weight, its silkiness.

It was not his *intellect* that decided she was most likely sexier than anyone he'd ever known. That intuitive response had come from somewhere south of his brain. South of his belt, to be precise.

*Turn around.*

She didn't respond to his silent order, leaving him wondering about the face of the woman who seemed so separate from the rest of the group.

"Woo hoo! Look who's here! Hold me back, ladies, but hands off 'cause he's mine."

Blinking, he tried to pull his focus off the woman by the bookcase, who continued to run her fingertip down the spines of several books as she read their titles. The fifteen or so others had stopped their various lewd and possibly illegal activities and had focused every bit of their attention on him. Every pair of eyes in the place widened in stares that ranged from friendly to voracious. He managed to remain completely still under the scrutiny, though he suddenly began to empathize with those guys who stripped off their clothes for women in trendy nightclubs.

"Come join the party, sweetie," the one on the floor said, a bit of beer dribbling down the side of her face. Wiping it off with the back of her hand, she gave him a big smile.

"Yeah, don't be shy," said the pole dancer, who suddenly looked much more animated. Like a tigress confronting a wounded wildebeest.

"Don't mind me, ladies," Drew murmured, nodding to them all. "I'm simply here to observe."

A flurry of protests broke out from the women, all of whom were giving him lascivious looks usually found during mating rituals. Not in New England mansions.

He pulled back slightly, deciding he needed to track down Burt Mueller, or whoever was in charge, and try to end this thing here and now. Frankly, he'd rather be back in Bolivia searching for evidence of the ancient lost civilization of the Bodomoqua tribe—while dodging armed guerrillas and the military—than spend an hour in this place.

Before he could exit, however, something came flying through the air from the group at the bar. He tried to duck, to no avail. The thing landed right on his head, dangling down to block his vision, and he blinked in response.

It took less than a second to realize exactly what he was looking at: a pair of black-and-red thong underwear.

And suddenly, because the thing rested right against his face with nothing to cover his eyes, Dr. Drew Bennett wished one more thing.

That he'd been wearing his glasses instead of his contacts.

IF SHE LIVED TO BE a hundred, Tori Lyons was never gonna make another deathbed promise. Specially to somebody who up and got better afterward. Seemed to her if you didn't die, all bets should be off. Promises, too.

Not that she wasn't happy Daddy had recovered from the heart attack that had about given them *all* heart attacks last September. She was. She thanked the Lord and all his little angels for his full recovery. Now, just three months later, he was back to his cantankerous self, on and off the track.

But she hadn't counted on him holding her to her promise: to get some education. Criminy, when she'd made the durn promise, she'd figured he meant for her to take some shop courses at the tech school near home in Sheets Creek, Tennessee.

'Course, at the time, in the exam room of Doc Barnes's vet clinic—where they'd taken Daddy on account of the closest hospital was forty miles away—she'd figured she might not have to go through with it. In the back of her mind, over the sound of Aunt Teeny wailin' for Jesus to spare her brother, and Daddy's girlfriend of fifteen years tellin' him she'd skin him like a polecat if he died before he got around to marryin' her, she'd figured it was a long shot. Because what high-tech school like Rudy B's Garage of Higher Learnin' would have *her*, a high-school dropout who'd only taken her GED two years ago 'cause it was the only way she could get her youngest brother to take it?

She'd passed. He hadn't. Huh. Go figure.

Still, she'd made the promise, which she'da kept, if she'd been able to. Would've been a waste of time, of course. Tori'd been learning her trade since the age of five in the pits and garages of drag strips across America. Wasn't much she couldn't do with a torque wrench or a transmission. Or an engine that only ran the quarter mile in six seconds at Talladega and needed to be under 5.6 by Music City.

But yessir, she woulda tried to keep her promise to her dear old departed daddy.

Only, the stubborn old cuss hadn't departed. And to add insult to injury, he'd held her to her promise. Tori'd given in, if only so Daddy'd get some peace of mind knowin' that when he finally *did* go to meet Jesus, he could be sure his kin on earth were doin' what he wanted them to.

Just like they'd always done when he was alive.

She'd been fixin' to start up in mechanic's class come January. But noooooo, Daddy'd had some highfalutin educatin' in mind. It was her bad luck that he'd run into some fella in Kentucky who was lookin' for girls to be part of a big makeover thingamabob.

Which was how she'd ended up here. On the set of a hoity-toity, high-class reality TV show. When she should be home, not only helpin' Daddy get back onto the NHRA—National Hot Rod Association—circuit, but also gearin' up for Christmastime in Sheets Creek.

He'd never've asked one of her spoiled rotten brothers to do somethin' so senseless. Then she scowled, the thought of her middle brother, Luther, makin' her fingers curl up into fists. She'd like to land one of them on his fat nose.

The phone call she'd had from him last night at the hotel in Albany had repeated in her brain all night long. Stupid Luther and his stupid bettin'. That boy was too poor to pay attention, but he'd been runnin' with the big dogs out at the track. He'd really done himself in this time and had told Tori she *had* to win on the show to come up with enough money to bail him out of his troubles.

Not durn likely. She was gettin' outta here first thing tomorrow and headin' home to whack some sense into him, then to figure out a way to pay off his debt. Because the money she could earn if she stuck it all the way out to the end of this here reality-show thing *still* wouldn't be enough to pay off Joe-Bob Baker, the toughest bookie in Knoxville.

What Luther didn't know was that the big prize on *Hey,*

*Make Me Over* was a shopping spree for clothes and stuff. And to get all gussied up and go to some nose-in-the-air Christmas Eve party in New York City. As if she really wanted to go to a party—on Christmas no less—with the highfalutin folks who, right now, wouldn't spit on her if she was afire.

No, she needed to get outta here. Fast. Then she'd find a way to get the money to keep her ornery brother alive all right. At least long enough for her to whale on him like a rented mule. An ass-whuppin' was gonna come along with her help, that was for sure. The thought cheered her right up.

"Good evening, ladies, if you're finished with cocktail hour, perhaps you'd care to follow me to the dining room."

She looked up at the squeaky little butler, who was dressed like a penguin and looked stiff enough to have been dipped in shellac. His nose was always quiverin', like he'd caught a whiff of something rank. Put her right on edge.

Jiminy crickets, she didn't belong here. Not with a pushy butler, and cameras everywhere and expensive furniture that looked like it'd break if you took a real sit-down on it. Nossir, she was as out of place as a skunk at a garden party.

Except, she had to admit, with all the *other* women in the room. With them, she almost felt right at home.

"Whadda I gotta do to get myself kicked offa this thing fast?" she said under her breath.

One of the other contestants, a redhead named Sukie, replied, "Pick your nose at dinner."

Sukie and Tori had struck up a quick friendship when they'd arrived earlier today at this mansion in Vermont. Probably because the two of them had been so tickled by the way the butler came back every time one of 'em gave a pull on that cloth rope in the corner. Sukie and Tori had pulled the rope about twenty times today, until she thought Mr. Shellac was gonna take a pair of scissors to the thing.

Or to her and Sukie.

"I gotta be the first one gone, but I grew up watchin' my granddaddy dig for nose gold at the dinner table, and I don't think I could do it," Tori said. "There's gotta be another way."

"You'll think of something," said Sukie with a loud smack of her shiny pink bubblegum.

Sukie worked as a hairdresser in Cleveland and was so far Tori's favorite to win the grand prize. Anybody who could walk in those fancy, glittery four-inch-tall heels had the makins' of a real lady.

Blowing a big, juicy bubble and cracking it between her teeth, Sukie added, "And if you don't, you can always scratch yourself or start a food fight tomorrow. Tonight doesn't count, anyway."

Tori was glad've that much. Tonight was just a social gathering, a get-to-know-you party before taping got started tomorrow. So there wouldn't be no pressure to compete with anybody else, or time to worry where the cameras were hidden. But Tori believed in getting a head start. It was never too soon to make a bad impression.

Trouble was, she greatly feared even nose pickin' wasn't gonna make her stand out in this crowd, which included a trucker, a bartender—she'd been working the bar and, from the sound of it, making some wicked good hurricanes—some sales clerks, a stripper or two, a maid, and one girl named Ginny who had a huge set of knockers, which she'd gladly flashed at anyone they'd passed during the bus trip up from Albany.

"You don't really wanna leave already, do you?" asked Sukie as they turned to follow the other women—and the penguin—into the dining room.

"I sure do," Tori said. "I had to come 'cause I promised my daddy. That don't mean I gotta stay. If I get throwed off, he can't never say I didn't try."

*And then I'll have time to figure out how to help Luther.*

Then she sighed. Because truly, she wasn't sure of the best way to get tossed out—by being too bad…or by being too good? The fast-talkin' producer, Mr. Mueller, might be looking for girls who were the *worst* off to keep around. Making it funner for the TV folks. After all, Tori, herself, liked watching the real stinkeroos on *American Idol*.

But, since the whole show was supposed to be about one girl gettin' lots of class and manners and going to the society party in New York, they might be lookin' for the girls most likely to pull it off. Meaning they'd want the ones who were the *best* of the bunch.

So the question remained: should she be on her best behavior? Or her worst?

"I wouldn't mind staying if I get to find out who the hunky guy who got a face-full of Ginny's panties was."

Tori scrunched up her brow, not knowing what the other woman meant.

"You were staring at the books like none of us were even in the room," Sukie said. "And ooh, girl, what you missed! A hunka burning love standing in the doorway, all tall and sexy and looking like he stepped right off an underwear billboard."

"He was in his underwear?" Tori squeaked.

"Nuh-uh. I was imagining."

Tori frowned. "He got a pair of used drawers on his face?"

Sukie shook her head. "Ginny pulled 'em outta her pocket."

Tori didn't rightly wanna know why somebody carried underdrawers in their pocket. But since Ginny hadn't minded showin' every driver on the interstate her hooters, maybe she didn't go around wearin' her underwear, either, and just had 'em stashed nearby for emergencies. Like, hmm…goin' to church or climbin' a ladder or somethin'.

Before she could ask any more questions, they all had

to leave to follow the butler through the maze of halls. Shew, she'd seen hotels smaller than this place. More welcomin' too. Christmas was three weeks from today, but there wasn't one pretty red bow or as much as a sprig of holly in sight.

Christmas was Tori's favorite time of year. And she sure didn't wanna spend it in *this* place that was about as friendly as a huntin' dog with a burr up its butt. That made her even more sure she wanted to get herself thrown outta here as soon as possible.

To her surprise, dinner was a hoot. Much more fun than she'd ever expected. The girls had a ball squawkin' over the nasty stuff put in front of them. Finally, after all of them had downright refused to so much as *taste* the slimy-looking snails they'd been served, they got somethin' normal. Steak 'n' potatoes. It wasn't Granny Lyons's fried catfish, but it stuck to the ribs all right.

She had figured somebody official from the show would come and talk to them tonight, but the butler said they had the evening all free and clear to themselves. And tomorrow bright and early things'd get underway. So after dinner they were on their own.

Most everyone went to the game room or the fancy in-house theater, where somebody said they was gonna watch *Days of Thunder.* Tori'd seen that movie nigh on a hundred times, always wonderin' if drivers who looked like Tom Cruise really were on the NASCAR circuit—since they sure weren't on the NHRA. So she passed on the movie. Instead, she moseyed on through the quiet house, tiptoein' like, because she didn't want to bump into anybody. She wasn't gonna steal nothin', she just wanted to be alone. To enjoy the one thing about this place she might actually miss once she got herself thrown outta here tomorrow.

The library.

Shew-ee the room was full, floor to ceilin', of bookcases.

She'd never seen so many books in one place in her life. The only library Sheets Creek had was one'a them books-on-wheels trucks. Since the donated truck had once been driven by the ice cream man—an' still had the faintest smell of fudge pops on a hot summer day—it attracted the attention of a lot of dogs when it drove down the street. Not to mention the young 'uns who came scramblin' outside with their pennies and nickels, only to pitch rocks at the tires when they found out the driver had books and magazines, not fudgies and Sno-Kones.

Tori watched for the library truck though, since it was a good way to practice up on her readin'. She wasn't very good at it, but she sure did like it. Usually the truck only had picture books for the kids or magazines that'd been handled so much it'd make your fingers greasy to touch one. Tori didn't care. She gobbled up whatever she could find.

Only she'd never seen *nothin'* like this place. Rows and rows of shelves, all of 'em with nice pretty books…hardcover books without cracked spines or yellowed dog-eared pages. Ones that hadn't been handled by half the population of Kruger County.

Keeping the lights low, just in case the butler had been funnin' them about no cameras being in use tonight, Tori made her way to the shelf she'd been starin' at earlier. She pulled down the exact book she wanted…*Tom Sawyer,* and turned around to curl up on one of the leather couches.

"I see we had the same idea."

The voice startled her so much, she nearly dropped the book.

"I'm sorry, I didn't mean to frighten you."

A lamp on one of the rickety little tables clicked on, and Tori saw who'd been talkin' in the dim light.

A man. A holy-moly-save-us-Mary-and-all-the-saints gorgeous-lookin' man. He took her breath away, making it hard to even breathe, much less talk.

He had hair so dark it looked like fresh-laid blacktop. Thick and shiny with a bit of wave. Dark brown eyes stared at her from a face that looked like it should be on a movie screen. Lean cheeks, strong jaw, lips just the right size for suckin' on during a long, hot night of lovin'.

*Please let the rest of him match,* she whispered mentally before looking down. She almost sighed in relief, because the rest of him was as pretty as the top. All tall and lean. Not thick and bulky like so many of the boys she knew back home, who liked to get together and throw tree stumps to see who was strongest. The bulk'd turn to fat in five years, once those boys settled down.

No, this man was nothin' like that. He was perfect and sexy and hotter 'n Satan's housecoat.

And starin'.

With one of *those* stares. The kind men had been givin' her since she turned fourteen or so and started gettin' all bumpy under her jeans and baggy shirts. Hungry like.

Only, this time, for the first time in her whole entire twenty-three years, Tori felt ravenous-hungry, too.

# 2

DREW COULDN'T STOP STARING at the young woman who'd
crept in here so quietly he hadn't even realized she was
here until she'd taken a book from the shelf. It was the
brunette he'd been so captivated by earlier. He could tell
by the jeans and red flannel shirt. Not to mention the long
curly hair that rioted around one of the prettiest faces he'd
ever seen.

He'd been wrong about one thing. Her eyes weren't
brown. They were blue. Deep, beautiful blue, surrounded
by thick, black lashes. And as he stared into them, he felt
something shift.

The earth beneath his feet, maybe. Or just his per-
ception of it.

She watched him warily from a few feet away, saying
nothing, her eyes wide and her lips parted as she drew in
deep, even breaths. He half wondered if she was about to flee.
Because she looked…hesitant. As if waiting for something.

"I guess we both needed to get away from the madness
for a little while, hmm?" he finally managed to say.

She nodded.

A conversationalist she was not, leaving him more con-
fused about who she was. It seemed impossible that she
could be one of the women here to participate in the show.
Because, though dressed casually, she'd seemed so very
distant from the rest of the contestants earlier. Above it all,

somehow, not even deigning to turn around when he'd been so raucously discovered.

And now, from the tilt of her pert chin to the sharp intelligence shining through those amazing blue eyes, she seemed already perfect. Certainly not in need of any improvement on a ridiculous reality show.

"Where is everyone else?"

She merely shrugged.

He tried again. "What book did you decide on?"

She held it up and stepped closer, then closer, until she stood only a foot away. He was able to make out the title in the semidarkness of the room.

More importantly, he could make out every feature on her face, every freckle, the sparkle of gold on the tips of her hair. And he could feel her warm breaths touching his skin, and her clean, flowery scent filling his head so he could barely think.

He stared at her for a long moment, asking a million questions. Who she was. Where she was from.

Exactly how long she needed to know a man before she'd allow him to take her to bed.

Shaking off his momentary lapse into insanity—not to mention bad manners—he focused on the book. "Tom Sawyer." Clearing his throat, he added, "That's a good one."

She simply nodded.

Finally, crossing his arms, he peered down at her curiously. "Are you unable to speak?"

This time he got a shake of the head in response.

He had to chuckle. "Was that a no, you're not *unable* to speak? Or a no you can't speak?"

"I can," she whispered.

"Then why aren't you?"

She blew out an impatient breath and rolled her eyes. "Because I was hopin' if I kept quiet, you'd shut up, too, and get back to lookin' at me the way you was a minute ago."

Eyes growing wide, Drew just stared at her for a moment. The young woman was practically glaring at him, so her heavily twanged words didn't quite sink in. "Excuse me?"

"I said..."

"I heard you."

"So why'd you 'scuse yourself?" Then she nibbled her lip. "Oh, did you, uh, make a noise or somethin'?"

Startled into a laugh, Drew shook his head. "I'm sorry, maybe we should start this conversation again. Okay?"

"I guess."

"Hello," Drew said, extending his hand to shake hers. "I'm Drew Bennett."

She stared at his hand for a moment. Finally she extended her own, grasping his so hard he felt like he was meeting a linebacker. "Tori Lyons."

"A pleasure to meet you, Tori."

"Likewise."

"Now," Drew said, getting back to her original comment, "why did you want me to shut up?"

She visibly swallowed, then slipped her tongue out to moisten her pretty pink lips. An uncalculated move, it still hit him hard, somewhere down low, bringing forth a reaction that had everything to do with instinct and nothing to do with intellect.

"You was starin'," she finally replied, her voice husky.

"Yes."

She hesitated, then tilted her head back in challenge. "I kinda liked it."

"You liked me staring at you?"

"The *way* you was starin'."

"Were staring," he couldn't help murmuring. "Why?"

She raised one brow, giving him a look that dared him to deny he'd been looking at her with a great deal of visceral appreciation. He wouldn't deny any such thing. He just wanted to know why she'd...*liked* it.

"You was lookin' at me like you was a hound dog and me a rare, juicy steak."

Being compared to a hound dog amused him. Considering his primitive response to her, he probably deserved the comparison. "Perhaps I was. I beg your pardon."

"For what? You make another noise?"

"No, I beg your pardon for staring."

"I toldja I liked it. Kinda took me by surprise, because usually when a man stares at me like that, I wanna black his eye."

Considering the top of her head barely reached his chin, he questioned whether she'd be able to reach his eye. But he didn't want to tempt fate by asking her. "Well, you're correct. I was staring. My apologies. Your appearance here took *me* by surprise." Seeing she wouldn't buy that simple of an explanation, he admitted, "And you're very pretty."

"Thankee," she said with a tiny smile and a tinier nod. "So're you."

"So are," he murmured, even as he smiled inwardly at being called pretty.

"So are what?"

He realized he'd once again corrected her, not even realizing he was doing it. The teacher in him was easing in on this conversation, taking over for the hound dog. Not surprising, probably. Judging by her speech, she was, indeed, a contestant on this reality show. Meaning, his pupil.

He nearly groaned at the realization. Because this was not a woman he could pursue, by any means. So far, he'd gone through his entire professional career without ever even being tempted by a student. And he'd sworn he never would.

Which just about killed him since his whole body was still tight with the awareness of her sweet scent and soft breaths. Her heart-shaped face. That hair.

He quickly changed the subject. "Can I assume you're here for the, uh, reality show?"

Almost grunting her response, she plopped down onto the leather sofa, where Drew had been sitting until she'd arrived. "Ayuh."

He sat down beside her, not too close—not trusting himself to get within touching distance of her. His thoughts were too jumbled, his emotions too sharp as he spoke to this unusual young woman for him to risk physical closeness.

The wise thing, given his instant attraction to her from the moment he'd seen her earlier, would be to leave. Immediately. To go to his room and think about whether Burt Mueller had really meant it when he said he'd pull the plug on the whole show—and the charitable donation— if Drew didn't stay to participate.

Something, however, kept him here, in the secluded darkness of the quiet room, where he could hear nothing more than the soft tick of a mantel clock and her even softer breaths.

"You don't seem too happy about being on television," he murmured.

"How'd you like ta be a lab rat?"

Interesting. She wasn't here by choice. "So why did you come?"

"Deathbed promise."

He gave her a sympathetic look. "I'm sorry."

"For what?"

"That someone died. Someone you cared about?"

"He didn't die, the stubborn ole mule. But he held me to the promise anyway. Weren't fair."

"*Wasn't* fair."

"Do you know you keep repeatin' everything I say?" she asked. Then she leaned forward, dropping her hand on his knee. The contact was innocent, yet made warmth explode upward from there, flooding his whole body with awareness of her touch.

"If you got a problem or somethin', you know, with your talkin', that's okay. I've known people who repeated everything twice. 'Course, they was old... or, like my aunt Millie, they'd got kicked in the head by a mule or somethin'." Then she frowned in concentration. "No, come to think of it, Aunt Millie *always* repeats herself, on account of her havin' so many kids in her family nobody'd ever listen to her." Then she smiled. "I remember now. The time she got kicked in the head, she just started talkin' in Latin. Took her fallin' off the porch a few weeks later to get her speakin' natural again."

Amused by her story—and the way she told it—he could only grin at her. "You mean someone you know really began to speak a foreign language after a head injury?"

"Heck, pig latin ain't foreign t'anybody," she said with a snicker. "Every five year old knows it."

Pig latin. He sucked his lips into his mouth to prevent a laugh, liking her down-home humor more and more. "I'm sorry I've been repeating your words. I was automatically trying to correct your grammar."

"You a teacher or somethin'?"

He nodded.

"For real? I figured you was one'a them TV folks."

"I teach anthropology and sociology at Georgetown University in Washington."

She snorted. "Sociology?"

He nodded.

"Jiminy crickets, they got college classes for everything these days, don't they? As if a body needs to learn how to be sociable. Down in Sheets Creek, bein' sociable's about second nature, since neighbors gotta rely on each other most times."

"Sheets Creek?" he asked, more interested in where she was from than in explaining the much more boring details of his job.

"Tennessee. It's a teeny town, twenty miles from the nearest grocery store. There's a little shop inside the gas station for emergencies, but you can't never be sure if you're buyin' somethin' that's fresh or that's been settin' there for five years. So you gotta be sociable with your neighbors, because, if'n you run outta flour or sugar you sure don't wanna have to make a twenty mile trek right in the middle of baking day."

"I see. Do you like living there?"

She shrugged, glancing away, not meeting his eye directly for the first time since they'd sat down. "I s'pose. I get to travel a lot, so it's not like I ain't never seen the rest of the world."

"Not like *I've never* seen the rest of the world."

"You travel a lot, too?" Groaning, she shot him a glare. "Stop doin' that teacher stuff on me."

"I'm sorry, Tori, I don't mean to. It's…instinctual." Then he clarified. "Habit."

"I know what instinctual is," she retorted. "I ain't ignorant. It's like the way tub-a-guts Bubba Freeman always sucks in his belly and sticks out his chest whenever a pretty girl walks into the garage, even though that boy not only fell outta the ugly tree, he got beat on by the whole forest."

He supposed the analogy worked.

"Now, you were saying you've seen the world?" he asked.

She leaned back on the sofa, lifting her boot-clad feet to rest them on the coffee table. "Well, mosta the US of A below the Mason-Dixon line. I been ridin' the southern circuit with my daddy and my brothers for nigh on twelve years now, since Mama died."

"I'm sorry."

This time, she didn't question him. A brief nod acknowledged his expression of sympathy. "Daddy's driven in a few national races, so I even been as far away as San Diego, California."

"Races? Is your father a race-car driver?"

She nodded.

"And you…"

"I'm head of his pit crew. And a backup driver."

His jaw dropped in surprise. This tiny, lovely looking woman was a mechanic and a race-car driver? "You're serious?"

She giggled at his look of surprise.

"You drive small cars at high rates of speed on an enclosed track for hundreds of miles?" he asked, still trying to get his mind around it.

"Nope. NHRA." When he simply stared, she explained, "Hot rods." When he still didn't understand, she sighed deeply. "Drag racing. Not long distances, it's quarter mile. Get it?"

When he finally nodded, still speechless, she added, "Daddy's one of the top funny car drivers in the country."

Drag racing. So she drove even smaller cars, at even shorter distances…at even higher speeds. Somehow, that didn't make him feel better. "And your father—is he the one who elicited your promise to come here?"

"If your askin' did he use some chest pains to get me to agree to get some higher learnin', yeah, he'd be the one all right."

Higher learning. On the set of a reality-television show. He didn't begin to have the time to evaluate that contradiction.

Though he didn't ask, Tori must have seen the curiosity in his expression. Because she began explaining her sport to him, the history, the importance of air velocity and starting speed.

But all he could think about was her little body inside a tiny metal can hurtling at over two hundred miles per hour.

"Do your brothers work with your father, too?"

She snorted. "Not hardly what you'd call work. My oldest younger brother, Jimmy, he was backup driver, 'til he got hitched last year. His wife put her foot down about him bein' gone so much, what with her 'n' their three kids at home."

He didn't so much as bat an eye.

"My baby brother, Sammy, he works the crew, but he's pretty green still. More interested in chasin' the track hos than payin' attention to the art of draggin'.'"

Didn't bat one at that, either. He just smiled inwardly, liking her voice, the way she softened her words with that Tennessee twang. He also liked what she revealed about herself—her life, how hard she worked, her enthusiasm for her job—with every word she spoke.

"As for Luther…" This time, her whole body grew tense. Her fingers curled into fists in her lap, and Drew suddenly wondered exactly what poor Luther had done to inspire such anger in his sister. But she didn't elaborate. "Well, he's about as useless as tits on a boar hog around cars."

How…colorful. Still, a clear description. He began to understand her enmity toward her lazy brother Luther. "So you're your daddy's heir?"

She met his eye and nodded slowly. "I suppose."

Hearing the slight hesitation in her voice, he had to ask, "How do you feel about that? Is it what you'd choose for yourself, if you had a choice?"

Her gaze returned to her lap, where her fingers remained tightly clenched. "Sure."

She was lying. But he wasn't going to be rude enough to call her on it. "You're the oldest, with three younger brothers. No sisters?"

"Huh-uh. Jimmy's one year younger than me, Luther one year younger than him, and Sammy one step more. Except, three days outta the year, Sammy's the same age as Luther, because their birthdays are only three days apart." Then she shrugged. "We all have October birthdays, on account of January being cold. And it bein' off-season so Daddy didn't have nothin' better to do than be botherin' Mama."

It took him a second, but he got it. He couldn't help laughing. The fondness in her smile as she laughed along told him a lot about how she felt toward her family.

"You miss them."

She nodded. "But it won't be for long. I plan on skedaddlin' outta here tomorrow. Next day at the latest."

He stiffened suddenly, as the word *no* flashed through his brain. "You can't. The show…"

"Girls start gettin' kicked off tomorrow. I aim to be the first."

He couldn't explain the dismay that swept through him at her words. He'd only known her a short time, but he'd already realized something very important. Tori could be the one. She could be exactly the woman Burt Mueller—and he, Drew Bennett—had been looking for.

She was lovely and sweet. Funny and quick-witted. Her lack of education didn't diminish one bit from what he sensed was real intelligence behind her pretty blue eyes. And her spirit and tenacity hinted she would give herself wholeheartedly to something once she'd set her mind to do it.

Why she'd set her mind to leaving, he had no idea. But one thing was sure. He'd do *anything* to get her to stay.

TORI'D BEEN JABBERIN' ON about her life and her family and drivin' for over an hour, and she still couldn't focus on much besides the mouth of the man she was talkin' to.

She wanted to kiss Drew Bennett. To kiss him and kiss him and never stop. Well, maybe stop a little, so she could look up at him and see him starin' at her in the hungry way he had right at first. She'd been ogled by men from time to time. But that didn't feel nothin' like the warm, tingly way this handsome man had made her feel.

Not only handsome, he was also nice and smart and he smelled like somethin' salty and fresh. Like the ocean. He had the cutest little dent in his cheek when he laughed, and he listened real good, like he was interested in every word she had to say. And through it all, his dark eyes didn't hide what he was really thinkin'.

The same thing she was...about gettin' a *whole* lot closer.

He wanted her, too. Wanted her bad. There was only one reason he hadn't tried kissin' her yet and it had nothin' to do with her.

It was the show. This stupid reality show. There didn't seem to be no doubt he was here as some kind of teacher and that'd made him get all teacherly.

Shew-ee, if she'd ever had a English teacher who looked like this one, she mighta stuck it out for the rest of high school, insteada droppin' out when the readin' got too tough in junior year.

"You know," he said, after they'd been sittin' there in the near dark, jawin' for almost an hour, "I'm afraid you didn't get a chance to do much reading."

She shrugged. "Slow's I read, I'd probably still be on the second page, anyway."

He tilted his head and gave her one of the funny, intense-looking stares that made her go all a-quivery down in her belly. Like he wanted to crawl right inside her mind and settle down for a spell, gettin' to know all her secrets.

Well, she didn't want nobody inside her mind. But this here was one man she could honestly say she wouldn't mind havin' inside her body.

"Do you have trouble reading, Tori?"

"What?" she mumbled, havin' a hard time keeping up with the words when her mind was filled with all kinds of wicked pictures. Drew's mouth on hers. His hands windin' in her hair. His chest... Lord almighty, that body. Strippin' every piece of clothing off, down to his Skivvies.

"Wait," she said, snapping upright. "Are you the underwear man?"

His jaw about hit his chest it dropped so hard. Tori

scrunched her eyes shut in embarrassment. "Sorry, I didn't mean that. I mean, Sukie, one of the girls, she said a steamin' hunka man came in here earlier and got a pair of drawers thrown at him."

The man turned red. Blushed like a bride on her weddin' day. The sight made Tori grin.

"I thought I'd stumbled into a hooker convention," he muttered.

"With a pair of undies on your head, I can see why."

"I don't suppose they were yours?" He sounded almost hopeful.

"Nope. I didn't even know you was in the room."

"No, you were busy looking at the books."

That she had been. Imagine how different her dinner mighta been if she'd had Drew's handsome face to think on, instead of focusin' on the sliminess of the snails on her plate. He was a lot more appetizin' than *anything* they coulda served in this place.

How she could've missed him in the room, she had no idea. Them books must have spelled her or somethin'. Then she thought about what Ginny'd done, and how *she'd* feel havin' a pair of undies on her head. "They weren't used," she said, hoping that'd make him feel better. "In case you were, you know...wonderin'."

"Excuse me?"

This time, she knew what he meant, but gave him a saucy grin, anyways. "Another noise?"

"Tori..."

"I was just joshin'. I mean, Ginny, the girl who threw the scanties, she didn't pull 'em off herself or nothin'."

"Thank heaven for small favors."

"She pulled 'em outta her pocket." She grimaced. "I been tryin' to think why somebody'd need spare drawers in her pocket."

"Perhaps she was afraid her luggage would get lost."

He said it in so dry a voice, she knew right away he was funnin'. She chuckled, likin' this man's delivery. "Maybe." Then, thinkin' on it, she added, "I got a cousin who'll shimmy outta hers right under her dress and toss 'em to her boyfriend whenever she wants him to hurry up and take her home from the bar." Then she shrugged. "'Course, that's only when she's walkin' on a slant. She's a good girl when she ain't drinkin'. Works as one'a them cosmetologists puttin' makeup on the dead people down at Franklin's Funerals and Exterminatin'.'"

Drew just shook his head, a cute hunk of hair floppin' down onto his forehead. "Did you say a funeral parlor *and* exterminator?"

"Sheets Creek's kinda small," she explained. "Not much buryin' business around, but they sure is a lotta bugs. So when he ain't haulin' a body around, ole Mr. Franklin hitches up a sprayer onto the back of his hearse."

Drew nodded. "You know, I think I might someday have to make a visit to Sheets Creek. It sounds as interesting as many of the ancient civilizations and societies I've studied."

It did? Shew, Tori figured Sheets Creek was about as normal and boring as any other town in America. Then she thought on the word he'd used. "Society," she repeated, soundin' it out, thinkin' on what he'd said earlier about his job. "That have somethin' to do with…what was the word you used…sociology?"

A little twinkle in his eye told her she was right.

Tori wanted to sink right through the couch onto the floor. She musta sounded like a fool prattling on about people bein' social. He didn't teach nothin' as dumb as how to get along with people. He taught about history and stuff. People from the past. Like them disco dancers from the seventies.

But Drew quickly distracted her from her fit of embarrassment. He reached over and put his hand on hers, until, suddenly, Tori couldn't think of nothin' but the warmth of his fingers. And how close he was. So close...but not close enough.

She scooted over a teeny bit, real casual-like, until their legs almost touched. Then she sighed, wonderin' if somebody'd turned up the radiator, or if this man was the one puttin' off all that sudden heat.

"Forget about it," he said softly. "You'd obviously never heard of what I did. But you figured it out...right quick."

The teasing smile on those lips of his told her he was pokin' gentle fun. Not being mean. He was tryin' to talk on her level, to put her at ease. She liked him for that, she surely did.

"Drew?" she asked, nibbling her lip as she worked up her nerve to get the subject where she really wanted it. "Since I'm leavin' and all tomorrow, can I ask you a favor?"

"Don't leave tomorrow."

"I gotta...."

"No, you don't." He turned a little, facing her. "This is perfect for you, Tori. You're smart and you're quick and you're obviously bored with the life you've been living. You could improve your reading— I could help you."

Her eyes popped and she opened her mouth t'tell him he was crazier than a bedbug. But she couldn't. Because, dangit, the man was right. Wouldn't she love to get better at readin'. And she had been bored lately. Awful bored. Restless and wantin' somethin'...though she couldn't have said what.

Not until she stood right here in this very room earlier tonight. And set her eyes on all those books. All that learnin'.

Deep down, she hadn't been able to admit the truth, even in her own brain. A part of her had *wanted* to fulfill her promise to Daddy to get some education. Not mechanic'ing, not learnin' how to be all ladylike on a dumb-ass TV show, but *real* education. Ever since a few years ago when she started practicin' real hard to get better at readin'—good enough to pass her GED by the skin of her teeth—she'd wondered what it might be like to go back to school.

"I can see the hunger in you," Drew continued. He still had his hand on hers, and he started doing funny things with his fingers, runnin' 'em up and down softly, until her whole hand started to shake a bit. She wondered how fast he could make the rest of her body shake with that soft touch.

Probably faster than she could drive the quarter mile at Music City Raceway.

"Give yourself a chance to experience this, Tori. I think something special could happen for you here, in this house. It's just a few weeks out of your life."

My, but he sounded convincing. So reasonable, but strong. He nearly had her forgettin' how impossible it was. *Nearly.* She closed her eyes and grimaced as she pictured Luther's pretty, lazy little face all squished up and bruised. Sighing, she shook her head. "I cain't. I gotta get home and clean up a mess."

"I'm sure any mess in Sheets Creek will still be there in three weeks."

Yeah. She was pretty sure he was right. Knowin' Luther, there'd *always* be a mess.

He pushed her. "You know I'm right."

"You might be," she bit out, still looking at their hands, then at his khaki pants, so close to hers they overlapped onto her tight jeans.

"So you'll at least think about it?"

Unable to resist either the thought of learnin'…or the thought of *him* bein' the one teachin' her…she gave one short nod. "I'll think on it." Then she looked up at him and took a deep breath, for luck. "But in case I do get kicked outta here tomorrow, there's somethin' I gotta do, or I'll kick myself forever."

He waited, looking curious, apparently having no clue what she had in mind. Which made it that much easier to leap onto him and kiss the daylights outta the man.

She didn't give Drew a chance to say yes or no. She wanted a kiss from him, just one kiss to take with her, so she'd always remember at least once in her life she'd kissed a man who actually liked readin' more than the lotto numbers, the funny papers and the occasional verse outta the Good Book.

He gave one little grunt of surprise when she landed on his lap. Then he caught her in those big strong arms of his, pullin' her tight as their lips met.

Tori moaned a bit, she couldn't help it, he tasted *so* good. He had soft lips and sweet-tastin' breath. When she opened her mouth on his, he didn't get all sloppy and slobbery like every other man she'd ever kissed. No, his tongue met hers real gentlelike, as if he had to taste her, not swallow her whole.

He shifted a bit, keepin' her on his lap and droppin' one arm over her hip. Tori couldn't help feelin' every bump and bulge down there. Big bumps and bulges, truth be told.

That made her quiver even more.

"I've been wanting to do this since the moment I saw you," he said, real soft, against her lips.

She thought he meant kissin' her, which was what she'd been thinkin' about since the first second she set eyes on the man.

Then he showed her what he meant. He cupped her cheeks, kissin' her again; sweet, wet kisses, while slidin' his fingers into her hair. He wound it round his hands, playing with her curls.

Tori had never felt so…so…*cherished* was the only word her brain could think up. He treated her plain old hair as gentle and reverent as Tori treated her great grandma's antique linen tablecloth, the one she only took out at Christmas and Easter. Like it was precious and special.

He kissed her exactly the same way, sharin' breaths and soft nips and gentle thrusts of his tongue. Until she wanted to cry at how good she felt, down to the tips of her toes. Especially low in her belly. And lower, where she hadn't wanted any man to touch her in ages, not since she'd made the mistake of lettin' Billy Grayson do it to her in the back of his Camaro when she was twenty.

This wasn't nothin' like that. Billy'd been an overgrown kid, impatient and speedy on the trigger. Drew...oh, not only was he a man, he was a man who knew what to do to a woman. Because his kisses and his touches were sendin' her right outta her mind. She didn't expect this man would have to be apologizin' to a girl for it lastin' less time than it'd taken for Tori to unhook her bra.

When he stopped kissin' her, pullin' away so they could regain some distance, she wondered for a second if she was gonna die of disappointment. Oh, Lord-a-mercy did she wanna keep kissin' on and on and never stop.

A sucked in, shaky breath told her she was still among the livin'. Working up her nerve, she opened her eyes and found him starin' at her, a little smile on his lips, like someone who'd opened a pretty present.

"Thank you," he murmured.

"Welcome." Then, suckin' in a deep breath, she hopped off his lap. Shakin' her head in disappointment, she said what she knew was true. "Now I *gotta* go. That was a hello an' goodbye kiss. Just, you know, for my memory box."

"You have a memory box for kisses?"

She tapped the tip of her finger on her head. "In here. Where I keep all the special times tucked away."

He nodded, like he understood and had a memory box of his own. Before he could say anything, though, Tori figured the time had come for her to get away. Before she went and did somethin' even more stupid, like, oh, say, strippin' off her clothes and beggin' him to kiss her whole nekkid body the way he had her mouth.

"Bye, Drew. It was sure nice meetin' you. If you ever do decide to do some social studyin' down Tennessee way, look me up, okay?"

Then, not waiting for his answer, she dashed out of the room.

# 3

DREW WOKE UP VERY EARLY the next morning in the room he'd been assigned, after a long, restless night.

*Tori.* He'd thought of her through every waking moment, and she'd filled his dreams during what little sleep he'd managed.

Damn, but the woman got to him. And not just physically.

Yes, there had been an instant sexual attraction between them. She'd caught his eye at once and he'd been reacting to her on almost a primal level. After their kiss, that attraction had flared from a spark into a raging inferno.

But even more, he was attracted to her mind. To her wit. To the potential he saw in her. Because if there had ever been anyone ripe for learning and self-improvement, it was Tori Lyons. The enthusiasm in her voice and the innate sparkle in her eye told him so much about her. She not only needed it…she secretly *longed* for her life to change. He knew it like he knew his own ambitions, and he admired anyone who went after their dreams.

Well, usually. That philosophy had backfired on him at least once in the past, so Drew should know better than to even think of getting involved with someone with an uncertain future. He frowned as a less-pleasant memory surfaced. He hadn't thought of Sarah in a long time—months, at least—even though she'd once occupied his every waking thought.

Tori and Sarah were *nothing* alike, so his former fiancée shouldn't have intruded on his pleasant thoughts. Still, he supposed the woman he'd once planned to marry would never be completely erased from his mind. Not because he still cared for her, but because she'd made him look at every woman he met with a more jaundiced eye.

But not every woman was like her. Not even *most* women. And certainly not Tori. About the only thing they had in common was that they'd each faced real changes in their lives, the chance to reach for something more. Tori was about to reach for education.

Sarah had reached for money. Someone else's. She'd landed herself a rich plastic surgeon when she'd gone to Hollywood to pursue her dream of acting, putting her engagement to Drew on hold to do so.

"Forget her," he mumbled. Truthfully, he nearly had. Once she'd left, he knew it'd been for the best. He'd been practically a kid, just young and stupid, wanting what he thought he'd missed out on in his childhood—a real home, a family. Now, with his whirlwind life of world travel, well, he couldn't even fathom being settled down with a wife and kids somewhere.

That didn't mean he was immune to women. Especially not to Tori Lyons. Her unaffected charm and all her energy appealed to him, to the deepest part of Drew that few people really knew. They saw the college professor. The author. Not many people saw the wild kid who'd once had a similar sparkle and enthusiasm about everything in life. Or the man he became when he was away from the academic world, tromping through the jungle in South America or interacting with tribes in Africa.

That's probably what had appealed to him so much about Tori from the very beginning. She'd called to the part of him he kept so carefully contained in his daily life. The adventurer. The wanderer. The risk taker.

They were a lot alike, though she probably wouldn't believe it. He didn't let the world see the rough kid he'd once been. And she wouldn't let the world see the eager-for-knowledge woman lurking inside her, begging to be brought into the light.

He wanted to help her, encourage her, watch her become the incredible woman he sensed was beneath her rough exterior. Though he had to concede, she hadn't been rough all over.

*Don't go there*, he told himself, knowing he couldn't afford to think anymore of how soft and perfect she'd felt in his arms.

Tori might like to think she'd "stolen" a kiss for her memory box, but Drew knew better. He'd been surprised she'd made the first move—so very *forcefully*, which had delighted him—but she'd only done what *he'd* planned to do. He couldn't have gone back to his room last night without learning if she tasted as sweet as she looked, if she felt as delightful as she sounded.

She had. She'd surpassed every expectation, until he felt like he was stumbling into something new and rare. Then she'd left. He'd had to watch her walk away when all he wanted was to pull her back down and let her feel what she'd done to him.

His groin tightened. Again. Just at the thought.

Calling himself an ass, he got out of bed and headed for the bathroom adjoining his suite. A cold shower. That's what he needed. *Or her warm body.*

No. It couldn't happen. He'd been strong enough to let her go last night, when he knew, with a few words, they could both have been naked and panting on that couch.

One thing had stopped him. No matter what Burt Mueller and his crew said about the show not kicking off officially until today, he wouldn't put it past the man to have had cameras already up and running last night.

Bad enough to be caught kissing one of the women he was supposed to be helping the very first night. If he'd made love to her, he'd have humiliated her completely. And ruined any chance he had of getting her to stay—for the *right* reasons.

After his shower he dressed quickly, then left his room to seek out Mr. Mueller. They had some talking to do. He was going to stay here and see this thing through, but only on one condition. That his number-one pupil stay, also.

If Tori went, so did he.

Which was *exactly* what he told Burt Mueller when he tracked him down in the enormous dining room. The producer was talking with the director, a man named Niles Monahan, whom Drew had met last night. Monahan was a quiet, nervous type, who barely said a word when the effusive producer was around. He quickly made himself scarce, apparently hearing the curtness in Drew's tone.

Just as well. Monahan had no power. Mueller planned to leave today or tomorrow, but he'd most certainly call the shots in this production, even if from a distance.

"Tori Lyons..." Mueller said, his brow pulling down in concentration.

"The race-car driver," someone murmured.

Drew glanced at the lead camera operator, who'd been introduced as Jacey Turner the evening before. A slim, pale-skinned brunette dressed all in black, the woman had huge brown eyes that dominated her face. And she always seemed aware of everything that was happening around her. A listener, that one. She'd be the one who'd expose any and all secrets taking place in this house over the next few weeks. No doubt about it.

Now she was standing on a chair, setting up a camera shot over the expansive dining room table, apparently listening to every word they said.

"Exactly. She has the potential to really make this work,"

Drew explained, striving to remain detached and not let them see how much he, personally, wanted Tori to remain.

"You know this after a short glimpse of the women yesterday afternoon?" Mueller asked, his stare pointed.

Drew managed an even nod.

"Or because of your conversation in the library last night?" Jacey's voice was deceptively light.

"Sonofabitch," Drew muttered.

"Ahh, ahh," Mueller said with an all-too-innocent smile. "You knew the house was wired."

"You said the cameras were off until today."

The man simply shrugged. His camera operator gave Drew a sympathetic look. "Everyone associated with the show signed a release stating they knew they might be filmed any time from the minute they arrived." She paused. "Including you."

"I see. So it was my error for actually *believing* what you said." Drew gave a humorless laugh. "I forgot the type of people I was dealing with. A mistake I won't make again."

Jacey's eyes widened. She and Burt exchanged a quick glance, a look Drew recognized. Same old story. People saw the credentials or his polite manner and assumed he was some kind of damn pushover.

They had a lot to learn. A whole lot.

"As I recall," Drew added, remaining calm in spite of his inner fury, "I stipulated in the contract we both signed that I would be taped in any common areas of the house, but *not* in my private quarters." He stared at Mueller, hard, until the man's eyes shifted away and his face flushed. The pink color crept all the way up his forehead onto his bald pate.

"I'll be returning to my room in one hour," Drew bit out. "If there are any cameras in it, I will consider you in violation of our written contract. I will leave these premises immediately and will be calling my attorney."

Then he looked at Jacey, who continued to watch, wide-eyed.

"I know what you're thinking, Miss Turner. That you're rather adept at hiding small electronic devices." Her eyes flared a bit, but she kept still. She was better at this than her boss, he had to give her that much.

With a tight smile, he added, "But believe me, if I can find a shard of three-thousand-year-old pottery buried in the side of a South American mountain, I can surely find any type of camera or microphone you've planted in my room."

Drew didn't bother adding that when he was twelve, he, his mother and his sister had lived for weeks in a basement storage room of a shopping mall. He'd become quite familiar with electronic security equipment. How to spot it. How to avoid it. How to disable it.

He sensed they wouldn't believe him, anyway.

He turned his attention back to Mueller. "I trust I'm making myself clear?"

The man nodded once, obviously not liking being bested.

Well, neither did Drew. Not in anything.

He turned to leave the dining room, but before exiting completely, he said over his shoulder, "And by the way, about Miss Lyons? I mean it. She's the best shot you've got at making this thing work. You'd better hold on to her, no matter what it takes."

He didn't even turn around, or wait for a reaction. As he strode out of the room, he heard Jacey Turner mumble to her boss, "I think we might have underestimated him."

Stalking down the hall toward the front door, where he planned to get in his car and drive off his rage for an hour while they cleared his room of bugs, he nodded in agreement.

Yeah. They had underestimated him.

But they wouldn't again.

TORI WOKE UP, AS USUAL, with the sun. Her roommate, Sukie—thank the Lord she'd ended up with *her* and not Ginny the flasher or one of the other wild girls—was still sawin' logs, even though it was nigh on seven in the mornin'.

Tori hated to slug-a-bed. So real quiet, she got up and gathered her clothes. She knew the cameras went on today and didn't trust the TV people not to have the little spy doohickeys every which place. So she planned to do *all* her undressin' in the bathroom. They'd put that much in writin'—no bathroom stuff. Guaranteed.

If she stayed around, she'd probably spend a fair amount of time in here. The big tub looked nice and comfy... She sure could do some readin' in it. But, she reminded herself, she *wasn't* staying around.

She'd kept her promise to Drew and thought on it all night. She just couldn't come up with any way around it. She had to bail her brother outta his troubles, no matter how much she wanted to stay. Which, to her genuine amazement, she *did*.

Sukie still wasn't up by the time she came back out, but Tori was ready to start her day, anyway. So she left her room, countin' doors down the hall, tryin' to remember how to get back to her own. Hopefully, she'd be comin' back soon to pack up and go home.

"It's for the best," she whispered, thinkin' about Luther and his problem. But boy, it sure did hurt for some reason. Part of her got all tight and achy when she thought about leavin'.

*The horny part.*

She shushed the little voice in her brain. Because yeah, she sure wouldn't mind spendin' some more time with Drew Bennett...between the sheets. Or on the sofa. Or the big fancy piano, or the dinin' room table or any old place.

But there was more than that. She'd liked him. Dangitall, why'd she have to go and meet a man who made her all shivery inside, and also made her mind start doin' leapfrogs with all the ideas he put in her head? Like about her readin' better. Learnin' about places, and…*societies*… like he did.

She didn't just want to learn from him. She liked talkin' to him. Liked listenin' to him. Lookin' at him get all energetic when he'd tried to sweet-talk her into stayin'.

He made her want—*more*. To sound like him. To think like him.

*To get nekkid with him, girl, that's all this is about, so forget about it right now!*

She wasn't about to start arguin' with the voice in her head. Because it usually won.

Needing some alone time before breakfast, Tori beelined for the front door. They couldn't have wired the whole yard with cameras. Leastwise, she hoped not!

She grabbed her heavy coat from the front closet and tugged it on over her sweater, fastening it up tight. Good thing, because when she stepped outside, the cold mornin' air made her breaths turn to icicles in her lungs. It stung a bit. But a good kinda sting…the kind that reminded a body it was still alive and kickin'.

Shoving her hands into her pockets, she curled her fingers tight. Too bad she hadn't thought to buy some gloves during the overnight stay in Albany. "No matter," she told herself. "You'll be home before you woulda been able to get any use out of 'em."

Somebody'd done a good job shovelin' all the snow off the front walk, but Tori was mindful of overnight ice as she walked down it. Then she mulled it over, realizin', suddenly, that she'd known all along where she wanted to go. She didn't have the right shoes on for a tromp through the snow, but she figured her work boots were at least a little bit waterproof.

Veering off the walk, she headed for the building she'd spied yesterday on the way in. It was a strange-lookin' thing—all glass walls, shiny and sparkly in the sunlight. She'd seen the reflection of it this mornin' from her bedroom window, which had gotten her curiosity all riled up again.

As she got closer, she realized what it was. "A greenhouse," she whispered, her breath making misty clouds in front've her face. She never knowed people had such things in their own yards, and had only ever seen them on TV commercials for plant nurseries.

This one was glassy and huge, steamy water coverin' the walls, probably from whatever plants were growin' inside. She wanted to see them. Wanted to see green plants and springtime in this place that was covered with a pretty— but lifeless—blanket of snow.

Tori had a green thumb. Some of her earliest memories were of pullin' weeds with her mama in their vegetable garden. On days when she needed to be alone—away from family and the track and the feelin' she was missin' something—she liked nothing better than to spend hours in the garden. She'd kneel down in the dirt, her fingers in the earth as she coaxed the little sprouts of peas or green beans, and she'd forget her troubles for awhile.

"Wonder if they got weeds in greenhouses?" she muttered, thinkin' she had a lotta troubles she'd like to forget this mornin'.

It was worth a look-see.

Opening the door, she stepped in almost sideways, keepin' her back to the inside and her face to the wall. She wanted to see everything all at once, not just bits and pieces as she came in. So after carefully pushin' the door shut, she clamped her eyes closed. She kept them that way as she swiveled on her heel to face the room.

Her skin reacted right away to the difference in the inside air, so odd after bein' outside. It felt thick and wet, heavy as it went down her windpipe. And *hot*. But it also smelled so sweet, of earth and flowers, that she couldn't help just standin' there, suckin' it in for a spell.

Finally, when she was almost light-headed with the deep breaths of earthy air, she opened her eyes.

And froze.

"Jeezum crow," she whispered.

Her jaw dropped open as she stared around in wonder, feelin' like a little kid lookin' at pretty wrappin's on a roomful'a Christmas presents. All ablaze with lights and colors and shiny, glittery decorations.

Lordy, she'd never seen a prettier sight. Huge clumps of green plants filled the place. Row after row of palmy lookin' things, graceful and slim, almost bowin' to each other under a soft breeze comin' from an overhead fan.

And the flowers… "Oh, mercy," she whispered, entranced by the brilliant hues. Red and orange and a yellow so pure it looked like the petals had been dipped in sunshine.

Nothin' simple like daisies or roses, these flowers were all jaggedy and strange but still perfect. Bloomin' in exotic shapes and points, but so darn lovely, they took her breath away.

"My, oh, my, it's like God's own garden," she whispered.

"It is, isn't it?"

Almost leaping, she blinked and peered around the corner of a big old plant with spiky-lookin' orange flowers that almost looked like birds' heads. Her heart tripped over itself, flutterin' all inside her chest, when she saw who'd spoken. "It's you."

"We've got to stop meeting like this," Drew said with a wide smile.

"Let's don't."

He chuckled. "I see I wasn't the only one who got an early start today."

"I can't stay abed once the sun's in the sky," she replied,

wonderin' if fate had brought her out here this mornin' so she could see him one more time before she left.

Drew stepped out from behind the plant, until he stood next to her. He'd taken off his jacket, it was so warm in here, and had it slung over his shoulder. A tiny bit of moisture—sweat, or humidity—shone on the sunken-in part of his throat. Tori suddenly had the strangest feelin'. Her mouth went dry, wonderin' how that little spot of wetness would taste if she leaned over and licked it right off of his skin. Salty, she'd bet. Salty and sweet and absolutely delicious.

She finally got her attention off the shiny skin and forced herself to look around the greenhouse. Unfortunately, the flowers weren't near as nice to look at.

"I never seen so many beautiful plants," Tori said.

Drew stared around, too, and nodded. "I haven't, either." Then he turned his attention solely to her. "Why are you out here? Shouldn't you be getting ready for breakfast?"

"I could ask you the same question."

He shrugged. "I wasn't invited."

"That ain't very polite."

"I don't mind. The director wants to talk to all of you. I'm not an active part of the show."

Feeling much warmer herself now, Tori slipped her coat off her back and draped it over a tall pile of unused planter boxes. "What is your part on the show, anyway?"

Drew's coat joined hers. He was again wearing what he probably thought was casual, comfortable clothes. Back home, comfortable and casual meant jeans. She'd like to see this man in a pair of sinful tight jeans. But these dressy pants, loose where they needed to be but right snug across the front—where it *really* counted—were nice, too.

"I'm not entirely sure. I'm supposed to be some kind of overseer. To gauge everyone's progress and help where I can."

"You're not, like, the celebrity host or something?"

"Good God, no," he said with a shudder. "I didn't want any active part in this at all, but allowed myself to be convinced. Believe me, I *hate* having any part of my personal life exposed on television for public consumption. I value my privacy and intend to stay as far out of camera range as possible." Then he gave her a serious look. "Tell me you're staying."

She sucked her lip into her mouth, hatin' to disappoint him. And knowin' he would be disappointed, though they hadn't known each other but for one day. "Sorry," she mumbled. "I can't."

His face went frowny. "You said you'd think about it."

"I did. All night." A yawn came over her then, just to prove the point.

He smiled. "I didn't sleep well, either."

"Was it them snails?"

Shaking his head, he stepped a bit closer. "No, it was our kiss."

Oh. *That.* "Well, uh, that was one'a them…instinctual things," she mumbled.

"See a man, kiss him?" His voice held an edge.

She slowly shook her head. "Huh-uh. See a dead-sexy man, talk to him a spell and find out he's got brains to go with the looks and a smile to make you forget all your troubles. Figure you ain't never gonna see him again so you better take your shot." She shrugged. "*Then* kiss him."

He nodded, lookin' like he was thinkin' things over, before coming even closer. "Funny," he said, real softlike, "but you telling me you're leaving has suddenly aroused the same instinctual reaction in me."

But before Tori could figure out what he meant, he put his arms around her and pulled her close.

Then he showed her.

DREW HADN'T INTENDED to kiss Tori. But the thought of her leaving—of never seeing her again—got to him. Especially because of her explanation about why she'd kissed him…because she'd sensed there was something special between them and it was never going to be explored.

He felt the same way. She was beautiful. Funny. Smart. Had an irresistible smile.

And was leaving.

That, more than anything, made him pull her into his arms and press a hot, languorous kiss on her lips. She parted them immediately, licking at him, sucking his tongue into her mouth. Curling against his body, she moaned a little. Or maybe he did. He couldn't be sure.

Kissing her suddenly didn't seem enough. He wanted to feel her smooth skin beneath his fingers. Unable to resist, he slid his hands to her waist, easily moving under the bottom hem of her sweater, and lightly stroked her bare skin.

Just as soft, supple and appealing.

He groaned, allowing Tori to pull him even tighter against her, until not a sliver of humid air could come between them. The place was steaming hot and rapidly becoming more so. All he wanted was to take off his clothes—and hers—and make love to her right here in this heady-smelling place.

Reason reared its ugly head. *You can't do this.*

He slowly—ruefully—ended their kiss and stepped back. Then he looked around, wondering just how desperate Burt Mueller was. Would he really risk expensive camera equipment by outfitting this greenhouse? Doubtful. There wasn't one corner of the room that wouldn't get misty. Besides, there were no unexposed hidden spots to conceal a camera.

So *this* kiss, at least, should remain private.

"Wow…you can say goodbye to me anytime you want," she whispered, sounding a little dazed.

He slowly backed away, trying to regain control of his

brain and his impulses. "I don't want to. Tell me why you have to leave."

And suddenly, to his great surprise, she did. He listened to her explanation, eyes widening in disbelief. When she'd finished, his jaw stiffened and he frowned. "So you're telling me you're going to give up something I know damn well you want..." Her eyes flared, but she didn't deny his words. "So you can go bail out your spoiled brother who needs to grow up and learn to solve his own problems?"

"When you put it that way, it don't sound too smart."

"What's the matter with letting your father—Luther's *parent*—help him get himself out of this mess?"

Seeing the quivering of Tori's beautiful lips, he suspected what she'd say. She *felt* like a parent, though, if he remembered the yearly sequence right, she was only two years older than Luther.

"Never mind. I understand," he muttered. And he meant it. Sweeping a frustrated hand through his hair, he explained, "I have a sister who's three years younger than me, and I started feeling responsible for her by the time she was old enough to walk. Still do, really."

There could have been a long explanation. Anyone else might have asked a million questions. About whether he'd had a father around. If he'd had a normal childhood. Why a little boy would feel responsible for his baby sister's welfare.

Tori didn't ask a thing. She simply...got it. A slight nod told him she completely understood. Because she'd been there herself.

"Don't leave, Tori," he found himself saying, his voice low and intense. "You can't return to your old life and step back into that role because you'll never break out of it if you don't take your shot now." Trying to lighten his tone, he continued. "This is just a silly show on the outside. But it's a start. I'll work with you on your reading, and you'll have other teachers with you day and night. You can come out of this ready to tackle any kind of future you envision for yourself."

She met his stare, her blue eyes shining. With the moisture from the air? Or her unshed tears? He couldn't tell. But sensing he had the advantage, he reached out and touched her hair, brushing it off her face until he had her full attention.

"If you leave you'll regret it for the rest of your life."

Thinking of the similar choice he'd been forced to make—when his aunt and uncle had taken him and his sister into their home, demanding nothing more for their love than that he give everything he had into turning his life around—he knew he was right.

Finally, after a long, silent moment filled with expectation and uncertainty, she offered him a tentative smile.

"I'll stay."

BREAKFAST WAS a whole lot quieter than dinner had been the night before. Tori figured all the girls were on their best behavior, mindful of the cameras and crew. Not to mention the frowny-faced, sniffly little director guy.

She'd made it back from the greenhouse just as the rest of the girls came downstairs. Nobody seemed to have missed her, thank the Lord. Drew hadn't come in with her, sayin' he figured it'd be best for them not to come back together. She didn't see what difference it made, but figured somebody might accuse him of givin' her extra help.

He'd been givin' her *somethin'* in the greenhouse, but that was nobody else's business.

They tried to feed 'em some fancy breakfast food, but Tori wasn't havin' any part of that smoked fish stuff and stuck to the fruit and rolls. While she nibbled it, she looked around the room at the other fifteen girls, wonderin' which of them would be gone by tomorrow mornin'.

"You decided not to pick your nose?" someone whispered in her right ear.

She looked over and saw Sukie smilin' her big smile and crackin' her gum between her teeth.

"I think I'll stick it out for a spell."

"Good," Sukie said. "'Cause I don't want anybody else for a roommate." She looked around the table at the other women and lowered her voice even more. "Ginny said Robin was snoring all night, loud enough to wake the dead."

Tori snickered. "Ginny shoulda just pulled her knockers on either side'a her head to block out the noise."

Sukie snorted and barked a laugh. A couple of girls glanced over, and Tori shoved a piece of banana into her mouth, suddenly feeling a little bad. Good thing they'd been whisperin'—nobody else could hear them.

She didn't like catty women and didn't consider herself one of 'em. Bein' around men all the time, she was glad for the chance to talk to *any* livin' female. That'd be another bright part of stickin' around this place. There were lotsa females to make friends with.

Deciding to watch her sassy mouth from now on, she glanced around and met the eye of the dark-haired camerawoman. She was laughin' beneath her breath, and when her stare met Tori's, her eyes twinkled. The other woman's grin told Tori she'd been overheard.

*Dang them microphones.*

"Ladies, may I have your attention, please?"

The producer, Mr. Mueller, tapped his spoon on the side of his glass to get their attention. Tori put down her fork and looked at him. So did everyone else.

Mueller looked just exactly what she'd expect a Hollywood type to look like. Fancy suit with a bit of a shine in the material. Smooth face that'd been under the knife once or twice. Big ole white teeth. Bald and shiny head, kinda big for his shoulders. Yep. He somehow fit the Hollywood she'd always imagined.

"As you know," he was sayin', "you're all about to undergo an intensive crash course in…socialization." He smiled his big white smile. "We will be breaking you up into smaller groups and rotating you through lessons throughout the day, as outlined in the information packet you received weeks ago."

Yeah. Tori remembered. Classes from everything on how to talk good, to which fork to use at dinner. Even how to walk.

She couldn't care less about that. But she did look forward to the grammar and real book-learnin'. Not just because she really wanted to learn those things, but because Drew would most likely be the one teachin' them.

"What you *don't* know," Mr. Mueller said, "is that we have another agenda. A secret agenda, for all of you. One that could make someone in this room very, very wealthy."

The girls all sat up straight, ears open as big as their eyes now.

Mueller shared a look with the camerawoman in black. Then he turned his attention back to them. "You see, we've decided to truly up the stakes in this transformation game. Now, you're not only competing for a chance to attend a society gala in New York during the holidays, as well as the wardrobe and jewelry for the trip." He paused, and all the girls around the table almost held their breath, waitin' to hear what the man was getting at. "One of you ladies might leave this place at the end of the month with a cool million dollars."

Tori's jaw dropped. Sukie muttered a swear word. Ginny whooped. A few others started askin' questions and gigglin'.

Mueller gave them all a couple of seconds to mull it over, then he held up his hand, askin' for their attention again. "I know you're all curious about what might be required of you. In fact, it's very simple." He pointed to a big screen hangin' on the wall just behind him. Nothin' was showing yet, but one of his tech guys was fiddlin' with a computer.

While they waited for the picture to flash up there, Mueller looked around the room, nodding to himself. Then, actin' all calm and quiet in spite of the twinkle in his eye and the way he almost was bouncing in excitement, he dropped the bomb. "All you have to do to win the million dollars," he said with a broad smile, "is get someone to fall in love with you."

A bunch of whispers started again, while the computer guy flicked a switch and a big giant computer page appeared on the overhead screen.

"It might sound unusual, but if you look at the target you will certainly agree it shouldn't be a hardship," Mueller said softly, pointin' to the image.

Everyone froze, watching a picture appear.

Tori felt a flutterin' in her stomach. She didn't have the second sight, like her cousin Peachy, who'd been born with a caul over her face. Still, sometimes she had a little shine. Intuition or somethin'.

Right now, hers was screamin' that she knew whose face she was gonna see any second.

"Ladies," Mr. Mueller said, "here is your objective. To win the money, get the man pictured right there to tell you he loves you, before the lady of them all is announced on December twenty-second."

Tori scrunched her eyes shut, not wantin' to see. Around her, the girls all started jabberin' and oohin' and aahin'.

Finally, she took a deep breath and slowly opened her eyes. And saw his face. His dark-as-pitch hair, those shiny eyes. That dent in his cheek from his big ole smile.

She wanted to cry. Because for the next two-and-a-half

weeks, every woman in this place was gonna be competin' for *him*.

Drew Bennett.

# 4

TO DREW'S GREAT DISAPPOINTMENT, he didn't see Tori much at all the first few days of taping. He told himself it was only because of her busy schedule, but had to wonder if she was avoiding him. If their unexpected attraction to each other had scared her off, instead of intriguing her, as it had him.

Still, he had to give thanks for small favors: she hadn't left.

On the first night, the sixteen women had been reduced in number to twelve. The four least-promising subjects had been whisked out of the mansion, under guard, not exchanging a word with anyone. Drew hadn't been part of the team doing the choosing, to his surprise, and he'd had a few tense moments worrying about Tori. But she'd been fine.

Late that night, he'd mulled over the four names, wondering if Mueller had intentionally eliminated the four least attractive of the women, or if Drew was being jaded about Hollywood these days. As if there was any time it *wasn't* okay to be jaded about Hollywood.

The following morning, the dozen had been divided into four groups of three and each group had begun a rigorous schedule of training. Drew, himself, taught a current events class designed to aid the women with conversation in social settings. But Tori hadn't shown up with her group. Not yesterday or today. Though she'd claimed to be sick, Drew had questioned that. Because she hadn't missed any of her *other* classes.

Mueller had brought in several instructors—including a former English teacher, a dance instructor, a hair, makeup and wardrobe professional, a maître d'. Even a woman who wrote a column called "Auntie Etiquette" for a New England paper. And Tori had been right there working with every one of them, looking earnest and intent every time he'd walked by an open door and seen her. But she'd blown *him* off. Which was really unsettling.

Even worse than not wanting to see him with her group, she hadn't made any effort to seek him out alone.

Unlike just about every other woman on the set.

"Come on, Professor, don't ya want to see what you've got to work with?" asked a blonde named Teresa. Teresa, who'd seemed more interested in Hollywood gossip than current events during his class, was the woman he'd dubbed the pole dancer thé day of his arrival.

"Thank you, but no," Drew murmured, wondering how she'd managed to trap him, alone, in the sunroom, when he'd taken such pains to avoid letting anyone see him enter. It seemed wherever he went in this place, one of the women always managed to find him. He could accept it from the crew, who kept track of everyone with their cameras. But the female contestants on the set seemed to have built-in radar to his location every minute of the day.

Drew had never lacked for female company whenever he desired it. And sometimes when he didn't. He'd certainly been on the receiving end of a lot of come-ons from his students over the years, and he'd heard a lot of Indiana Jones comments. The women in this house, however, were acting like a nuclear holocaust had taken place and he was the last male on the planet.

Which needed rapid repopulating.

"You know yōu wanna see what I got," Teresa said as she reached up and ran her fingertips across his cheek.

"No, I really don't."

She chuckled, running her hand down his neck. He leaned back, his body language doing the talking.

She didn't listen to that, either. "Watch, now, I'm gonna give you the kind of private show guys usually pay a hundred bucks for."

Drew frowned. "I'm sure your dance instructor will be happy to review your skills before he begins teaching you…uh…" *Something other than a bump and grind.* "Ballroom dancing."

"*Watch,*" she said, obviously not taking *no* for an answer. Since she stood between Drew and the only exit, he didn't have much choice.

Teresa began to hum a low, thrumming tune, and started to gyrate like a she-wolf in heat. He supposed the expression on her face—eyes half-closed, lips pursed—was meant to represent orgasmic ecstasy. Instead she merely looked like she'd eaten something unpleasant.

"Teresa, I really have to go. And so do you. You're late for something, I'm sure."

"Wait, it hasn't even started getting good!"

She reached for a floor lamp.

*Okay, that's it.* Time to make his exit.

"Ooh, baby, yeah," she moaned, licking her lips.

Men actually paid money to see this? He began to feel sorry for the owners of this house, who'd rented their place to Mueller for the month. They were going to have to pay someone to come in and disinfect all of their lamps. At least the ones in the rooms Teresa had inhabited.

"Oooh, you know you love it," she was saying through heavy breaths as she did mildly obscene things to the poor brass light-fixture.

"Nice," he muttered.

She obviously didn't hear his sarcasm. "I'm just gettin' started." Still holding the lamp with one hand, she lifted her other to unzip her dress.

"Whoa," Drew said, wondering if Burt Mueller was spiking the women's food with some kind of aphrodisiac. "Sorry, but I'm not interested in…uh… any more of your dancing."

While her hands were occupied, he moved smoothly around her and out the door.

"Hey, Professor, wait," she called. "It's just getting good."

Hearing a crash, he cringed over the loss of the lamp. The poor thing had probably thrown itself to its death to get out from between Teresa's well-used thighs.

Ducking down a hallway, which would put him out of sight-range of Teresa when she exited the sunroom, he paused to get his bearings. The house was huge. But it wasn't big enough to give him any privacy whatsoever. The only time he'd been alone since yesterday morning was when he was firmly ensconced in his room. And considering the way four of the women had felt free to stroll right in, he'd had to start locking the door!

"This is crazy," he muttered aloud.

Very crazy. The whole thing. He was supposed to be overseeing some lessons. Not having to hide from a bunch of amorous women who wanted to get a little extracurricular with the teacher.

His frustration was made worse because he'd been unable to see the only person in this asylum whom he really *wanted* to see. Tori.

Glancing at his watch, he noted it was nearly four. He'd checked the posted schedule this morning and knew Tori's group was, at this time, supposed to be in the kitchen getting lessons in food appreciation and table manners.

Hopefully that would prevent any more food fights, like the one this afternoon at lunch. Drew had been dining with Group B, and had made the mistake of complimenting one of the women—a very tall redhead named Robin—on her knowledge of cutlery.

Robin had ended up with a face full of cold soup, courtesy of Ginny. Then it'd turned into a free-for-all. Even after grabbing a quick, midday shower, Drew still smelled the lingering, cloying sweetness of key-lime pie in his hair.

*Pie. The kitchen. Tori.*

He didn't hesitate and began striding down the hallway, determined to see her and find out why she'd been avoiding him.

Another of the contestants, however, had other ideas.

"Hey there, Professor," a tawny-skinned woman said as she stepped out from an inset doorway. It almost felt as if she'd been lying in wait for him.

"Aren't you supposed to be in your speech class?" Drew asked absently, trying not to slow down.

She planted herself right in front of him. "I'm already very good at speaking," she said, licking her lips. "Come here and I'll whisper something special in your ear." She smiled, her sharp teeth white and glistening.

He'd sooner put his ear next to an open flame.

"Uh, Simone, I'm not even scheduled to conduct the first evaluation until Friday. There's really no need for you to display your...skills." He shook his head, seizing on what seemed to be the only logical explanation. "All of you seem to be under the mistaken impression that currying my favor is going to aid you in some way."

"It's not your favor I'm after," she said, putting her hand flat on his chest and batting her heavily made-up eyes.

"I'm your teacher," he snapped.

"I can teach you a few things."

"*Goddamn* it," he muttered, suddenly having enough of this, "have you all completely lost it?"

Simone pouted, obviously not realizing she'd pushed him too far. "Chill babe, let me help you work off some of that frustration."

"Look," he said, trying to maintain his calm, "you're

here to learn. To gain some polish, some social skills. Not to get laid."

"How do you know?" she countered.

Drew merely gritted his teeth, gave her the kind of withering stare that had intimidated every obnoxious student he'd ever had, then strode past her.

He wished he could confront Mueller, but it was too late. The man had left, whirling onto his next big project, leaving the soft-voiced director, Niles Monahan, in charge. And Monahan had about as much chance of getting a dozen horny women to behave as Drew had of sprouting wings and flying out of this madhouse.

Shaking his head, he drew in a few deep breaths, trying to regain his calm, rational mood. It'd somehow deserted him in the past few days.

He should go to his room or his car—the two places where he could lock himself in, away from the cameras and the women.

But he didn't. He headed straight for the kitchen.

Tori had been tryin'—try*ing*—to figure out how to handle things ever since Mr. Mueller had dropped his bomb Sunday at breakfast. She'd fumed about it and even, to her mortification, cried about it, but couldn't figure a way around the truth.

Drew was the stakes and a million smackers was the prize.

Her first instinct had been to leave. She'd tell the director she'd changed her mind and skedaddle on home. Because this silly competition stuff just made her feel…nasty.

Drew Bennett would *hate* bein' some kinda prey for the women on this here show. *Being* she reminded herself, mindful of the way the snippy-faced English teacher had made Tori repeat the phrase *ing* about a half a gajillion times over the past few days.

For sure, Drew would blow a gasket when this romance

competition came to light. He'd said as much before, telling her he planned to stay out of camera sight as much as possible, to keep his private life private.

She was tempted to tell him herself, only, the contract she'd signed might get her into trouble if she did. She remembered a buncha legal mumbo jumbo in there, but one thing stuck out—if any part of the so-called secrecy agreement got violated, she had to pay back every penny they'd put into her, including her airfare, her food, her education expenses and who knew what all.

Her next instinct had been to break her promise and get herself kicked out. Because she liked him too much to stay and watch what these greedy, horny women were gonna do to him.

But she *wanted* him too much to leave and let them do it!

There was no denying it, she wanted him for herself. Not because of any cash prize—because, while she knew for sure he was interested in her, she didn't for one second believe a handsome, wealthy college professor was gonna go prostrating himself with love for *her*.

No, money didn't factor into it. *He* did. It was all about Drew Bennett. His smile and his laugh and his brains. Not to mention the way he'd made her feel from the first minute she'd set eyes on him: hungry and empty and wanting and needy.

And very special.

"Special," she whispered under her breath, feeling a little shivery when she said it.

Because he had. From the first word he'd said, the first look he'd given her, he'd made her see herself differently. Not as rough-edged Tori who'd beat up a man soon's look at him. But as a pretty woman with a brain and a real chance to do something with her life.

Why, oh *why*, had Mueller gone and ruined things by turning this simple makeover show into a manhunt? She might actually be enjoying herself if he hadn't gone and changed the rules. Though it'd been hard work, she really liked the stuff she was learning from the English teacher. She was even beginning to correct herself in her own thoughts, which oughta count for something.

But ever since the real point of this show had been announced, she seemed to be the *only* one interested in learning a darn thing.

"I don't get why we still have to do this stuff like knowing whether to drink white wine or red with dinner, now that we know what the real object of this game is," said Tiffany, a young blond girl from California. Tiffany had more hair than brains. And less clothes than Britney Spears.

Tori coulda told her Drew Bennett would never fall in love with someone who wouldn't even try to use the smarts God'd given her. She wasn't, however, that charitable. Let the wolves figure it out themselves; she planned to stay right out of it.

Only, she couldn't, could she? Her mind might not want to do something as low-down dirty and rotten as compete for the man for money. But her body wanted him. Wanted him bad.

Which was why she'd done her best to just steer clear of the man. Leastwise until she could figure out what to do.

"Well, what I don't get is why you can't always drink pink wine no matter what you're eating, and forget about it," Sukie muttered, glaring at the glasses spread out in front of them on the big butcher-block kitchen counter.

Tori was with Sukie. Made sense to her.

"Because," a smooth male voice said, "if you order the wrong wine at *some* restaurants, you'll end up getting lousy service from a snotty waiter who thinks he's smarter than you."

Tori's—everyone's—gaze shot to the doorway, where a smiling Drew Bennett watched them.

Oh, my, he looked good to her. His dark hair gleamed and his sexy smile made her shake right in her boots. And made dollar signs light up in the minds of every other woman in the room.

*Shoot me now.*

"Oooh," Tiffany said, practically cooing as she stuck her lips out. Not to mention her chest. "I never thought of it that way. Maybe we could go to a nice restaurant sometime to get something…" she licked her lips and lowered her voice, "to *eat.*"

Tori rolled her eyes. Was there anything more nauseating than a blond bimbo trying out tricks on another woman's man?

*Whoa, there, girl. He ain't yours.*

No. He wasn't hers. She might want him to be, but he was fair game. Literally, thanks to Mr. Mueller, who'd made him the birdie and this here duck season.

"I'm sure you'll have lots of chances to practice right here, Miss Myers," he said to Tiffany, his voice all cool and even. Tori hadn't heard that tone before. It didn't sound nothing…*anything*…like the way he talked when they were alone.

"Professor?" Sukie straightened in her seat and tapped her finger on the countertop, waiting for his attention.

He turned toward her. "Yes, Miss Green?"

"Well, I wanted you to know that I've been thinking all afternoon about the little problem in the Middle East that we're supposed to talk about in class tomorrow."

Little problem? If that place had a little problem, Tori figured World War II musta been a friendly spat.

"Oh?" Drew said, sounding a bit more polite and interested as he gave Sukie his full attention.

"Uh-huh. I think the answer is to make them all become Scientologists."

Tiffany snorted, sounding just like the pet hog Tori'd

had when she was a kid. "How many hairdressers do you think one country needs, especially since the women all have to wear those veils?"

*Hairdressers.* Tori rolled her eyes, thinking Tiffany had got whacked with a stupid stick one too many times in her life.

Sukie glared. "It's a religion, you...you...blonde!" Then she looked at Drew. "Then they wouldn't have anything to fight over. And John Travolta could go visit them and teach them to dance, because people who dance together don't usually want to kill each other afterward. Especially with as good a dancer as John Travolta."

Tori lowered her head so Sukie wouldn't see her laugh. She liked Sukie a lot, but dang, sometimes the girl didn't make a lick of sense.

Drew kept a straight face. "Interesting idea. Maybe we can talk it out as a group tomorrow."

Then he cleared his throat.

Tori didn't look up. She knew he was staring at her, heck, she practically felt the burning of his eyes on her face. But she couldn't meet that stare, not without flinching and blushing and letting him and the whole TV world see every thought going on inside her head.

"Tori," he said, stepping closer.

She could see the tips of his brown shoes beside the feet of her stool and felt the brush of his hip against her side.

*Lord gimme strength.*

"I heard you were sick earlier," he said. "Are you feeling okay now?"

She nodded. "I'm fine."

"Good. Then maybe you can give me some time so I can catch you up with the rest of your group."

She peeked up. He didn't even give her a chance to answer, he just looked at the woman teaching the class—who was watching him all wide-eyed with interest, even though she didn't have a million-dollar bone being dan-

gled in front of her face. The man probably caused that reaction in every woman he met. He sure was handsome
enough to.

"I'm sure you won't mind if Tori cuts out of this lesson a
few minutes early. I think I can catch her up before dinner."

Tori gulped, very aware of the stares of the other contestants. Not to mention the one of the dark-haired camerawoman, Jacey, who seemed to follow Tori around
everywhere these days. "I don't mind...."

He didn't give her time to argue. Or give the kitchen
lady time to answer. He just took her by the arm and practically hoisted her off her stool.

Which was when she figured out he was mad. Darn
mad. At her.

"Why have you been avoiding me?"

Drew frankly didn't care about the cameras or anyone
who might be watching as he practically hauled Tori out
of the kitchen, toward the front stairs.

"I dunno what you mean."

"Like hell you don't."

When she almost stumbled, he slowed down. But his
steps remained deliberate. "Why?"

"I ain't been avoiding you."

"Haven't," he snapped as they reached the staircase
and began to ascend it.

"Haven't what?"

"*Haven't* been avoiding you."

"I never said you had."

Drew almost groaned. Then he saw the sassy sparkle in
Tori's eye and the grin dancing about her pretty lips, and
knew she'd been playing him. His anger started to ease away.

"Where we going?"

"To someplace where we can be alone to...work."

Work. That's *all*. He was going to work with her. Not kiss

her. Not throw her down onto the nearest flat surface and torture her with every sensual trick he knew until she admitted why she'd been avoiding him. Even though that's exactly what he wanted to do.

A thumping sound behind them reminded him why he couldn't. Looking back, he saw Jacey the camerawoman, strolling up the stairs, her camera on her shoulder. Drew glared at her, at the camera, at the television viewers who didn't even exist yet, but who were already getting in his way.

He considered taking Tori to his room, since it was the only place he felt pretty sure wasn't bugged. Then he thought better of it. Like it or not, they were on the set of a television show, and their every move was up for interpretation. If he hauled her into his bedroom right now, in a few months the entire television-watching public would be making up their minds about what had happened behind the closed door.

He couldn't do it to her.

"Come on," he said with a shake of his head, turning left at the top of the stairs, rather than right.

At the end of the hall, past the last bedroom door, the carpeted corridor widened into a small sitting area. It was somewhat secluded, overlooking the foyer through a railing on one side. The other was dominated by a window with a vista of the expansive east lawn. Two chairs stood in front of the window.

Leading her to one of the chairs, he dropped into the other one. He pulled it closer, until their knees almost touched. Jacey hadn't quite caught up yet so he leaned close and kept his voice low. "This isn't as private as the greenhouse, but it's the best we can do right now."

She nibbled on her lip. "About the greenhouse…"

"Yes?"

She looked over his shoulder, obviously spying the camerawoman. Jacey couldn't join them in the sitting area, it was too tiny. But she was taping them from a few feet away.

"Nothing," Tori muttered.

He followed her lead. "Good. You didn't lose the *g*."

"Pardon?"

"Did you make a noise?"

She laughed, a bright, joyous sound that spilled across her lips and washed over him like something sweet and clean. He began to relax for the first time all day.

"You're bad," she said. "Saucy."

"I think the saying 'it takes one to know one' might be appropriate here."

And it did. They were very much alike. He'd sensed that since the very beginning, even if she still hadn't realized it. "By the way, I was complimenting you on finishing the *ing* at the end of your word."

She grimaced. "Mr. Halloway, he's the kinda teacher who'd probably kept a switch in his desk back a hunnert years ago when he was teaching." Then she shook her head. "I mean a *hundred* years ago."

He noted the way she corrected herself, not a bit surprised at how quickly she was adapting to the changes in her daily life and dialect. "But you're doing well."

She nodded.

"And the rest of the classes?"

She shrugged, looking bored. "I suppose if Queen Elizabeth ever invites me over, I won't shock her by using my soup spoon to stir my tea."

The smart-alecky tone had returned to her voice, so at odds with the subdued way she'd behaved back in the kitchen.

"So what's the real reason you didn't come to my class?"

Her eyes shifted down, her half-lowered lashes concealing them from view. "Maybe I don't feel smart enough for current events yet."

"Yesterday," he said, his tone dry, "you missed a sparkling conversation on the Brad and Jen rumors. And today was even better, with everyone bringing up at least one topic they'd seen on a news program they were asked to watch last night." He couldn't help adding "I never knew *Entertainment Tonight* had such hard-hitting stories."

Her lashes came up. Those laughing blue eyes appeared again. "Are you going crazy yet?"

"Yeah. You?"

"Not so much. But we haven't really started doing a lot of the hard stuff yet."

He was almost afraid to ask. "What's the hard stuff?"

"Wearing fancy dresses."

Her grimace and tone would have been appropriate for someone who'd been invited to dine on monkey brains.

"I'll probably break my ankles if they make me wear any shoes higher than an inch."

"You found your *g*'s. You'll find your high-heel ankles."

Hearing a sound, he looked over his shoulder and saw Jacey capturing every word with her camera. She had a smile on her face. Not, he was surprised to note, a predatory one. But a rather nice one. As if she enjoyed Tori as much as he did.

He made a mental note to drop his dislike of the woman down one notch.

"Are you ready to get to work?" he asked Tori, trying to forget they were on camera.

"I didn't watch *Entertainment Tonight* last night." She nibbled her lip, looking almost guilty and tentative.

"No?" Then, knowing without a doubt what she had been doing, he leaned back in his chair and crossed his arms over his chest. "Okay then. Let's talk about *Tom Sawyer.*"

# 5

JACEY TURNER HAD BEEN around enough to know attraction when she saw it. She might've had to have her *own* romance pointed out to her by Digg—who'd told her she was falling for him even before Jacey realized it herself—but she didn't have much trouble seeing it in other people.

And there was definitely something to see between Dr. Drew Bennett and race-car driver Tori Lyons.

"I'm telling you," she told director Niles Monahan, "Tori Lyons is the one."

The crew had gotten together for a week-one wrap meeting very early Sunday morning to discuss the latest round of cuts that had left them with nine contestants.

The director, a pale-faced whiner who had this really irritating, watery sniff after every third word he spoke, rolled his eyes. "You must be joking. She has such an awful twang."

"It's getting much better."

"She wore work boots beneath the Vera Wang gown we had her try on."

Jacey was with Tori on that one. She shot Niles a glare, ignoring the rest of the crew, who simply watched them argue yet again. Old news at this point. "You ever worn spike-heeled do-me shoes?" she asked.

His eyes bugged out and he sputtered a bit.

"They're agony." Jacey leaned back in her chair and crossed her legs, tapping her own black engineer boots, which she wore under her long, black wool skirt. "I'm sure as hell not going to criticize anybody else who doesn't wanna wear them, either."

Niles stared at her for a minute. She held his gaze until he finally looked away. She knew what he was thinking... He was wondering why he had to put up with an opinionated lead camera operator who his producer insisted be an active part of any decision making.

Niles didn't know Jacey was Burt's daughter. Which was exactly the way Jacey and Burt liked to keep things.

"That Ginny, she's looking good in her new wardrobe." This came from Spike, one of the guys on Jacey's camera crew, who had way too much testosterone and way too little intelligence.

"You mean you actually see her wardrobe? I thought you always pictured her naked," Jacey said with a roll of her eyes.

"I personally see the most potential in Robin," said Bernice, the makeup woman. "You know, she does her own face beautifully, and did from the day she walked in the door. I couldn't teach her a thing, if I were one of the instructors."

Personally, Jacey thought Robin wore so much makeup her whole face was being held together by it. If the layers of foundation ever came off, there might be a Kermit the Frog face under there. But she didn't want to offend Bernice, the only other woman on the crew, by saying so.

"It appears the field is wide open," Niles said with a nod, as if everyone else's comments validated his lame opinions. "Of the nine women left, I'd say Tori Lyons isn't even in the top five in terms of her potential as lady of them all."

It was all Jacey could do not to yank her hair out by the fistful. "Are you all forgetting why we're *really* here?"

They all went silent, staring at her from around the meeting-room table where they'd ensconced themselves with coffee and bagels before the contestants came down.

"It's not about who *you* like the best. It's about who Dr. Bennett likes the best."

And that, Jacey knew without a doubt, was Tori Lyons.

"Well, I don't agree, but since three more have been eliminated, it will be easier to see his interaction with each of the women," Niles said, still sounding so superior.

But at least he was on the same wavelength, finally. "I've begun feeling him out about the necessity of inter-acting with the women in social settings," Jacey said. "And so has my f—Mr. Mueller, who called and spoke with him last night. That will be the perfect excuse to send him on dates." *Without him ever knowing he was dating.*

It was only fair to give the other women some one-on-one time with the hunky doc. Because so far, only Tori had had that chance, though, Jacey believed she was the only one on the set who knew Drew Bennett was sneaking out to meet with his star pupil every morning.

An early riser, Jacey had been making use of the tread-mills in the fitness room of the house—a poor substitute for her morning run, but all she could manage. Yesterday and the day before, she'd seen Tori slipping out just after dawn, only to be followed by Drew. Both times, he'd had a book in his hand.

The Hollywood pessimist inside her speculated on what they were *really* doing together in the greenhouse. But the woman who saw the tender way he'd been helping Tori read some old book the other day suspected they were up to something altogether different. Which was why she hadn't ratted them out.

Not that it would matter, really, if she did. Because they met in the greenhouse—their blessing, but a camera's curse. Even if she had informed the snotty little director, what could he have done about it? If she or any of the crew showed up with a camera—after equipping it for the extreme moisture— Drew and Tori would likely stop their lessons altogether.

So she left them alone. Probably, she had to admit, because of the slight tinge of guilt she felt over her involvement in this whole thing. It had been her idea, after all. A part of Jacey felt a teeny bit bad about setting the good doctor up like this, even though the TV-insider part of her loved it.

Deep down, she'd also had a completely unexpected reaction, one Dr. Bennett—or her father—probably wouldn't believe. One she wouldn't have believed a few weeks ago, before this all began. But it was true. She'd gone all sappy and stupid because she saw something in Dr. Bennett's relationship with Tori that reminded her of her own. With Digg.

Jacey had been the wildly different outsider with the handsome, stoic fireman. She'd been where Tori was now. So a part of her wanted to see if Drew and Tori could possibly make it work. Because if they could, it might give her a renewed sense of faith for her own up-in-the-air romance. The one that, in spite of several tender long-distance phone calls this week, still seemed tenuous at best.

So as the meeting broke up and the crew separated for the day, she didn't even think of pointing Niles Monahan's attention toward the large window over the sideboard. She even intentionally blocked it with her body, to be sure nobody else saw what she'd just seen.

Drew and Tori, entering the greenhouse.

OF ALL THE ACTIVITIES that had filled her every waking moment for the past few days, Tori's favorite were these quiet mornings with Drew. They hadn't meant to do anything secret or sneaky, and she sure wasn't trying to get him alone so she could do any women's tricks on him. Unlike most of the other girls in the house.

He'd offered to help her with her reading. And she'd said yes. That's all there was to these daily meetings in the greenhouse.

*Big fat liar.* Yep. She was. Because that *wasn't* all there was to it. How could it be when she grew more and more attracted to him as each day passed?

She was changing. Not only in her speech—due to hard classes with frowny-faced old Mr. Halloway, who'd moved from getting her to pronounce her *g*'s to eliminating the word *ain't* from her daily speech. Not to mention doing whatever he could to soften up her accent. Shew, she hardly recognized her own voice sometimes.

The changes in her had sparked something else—a change in how she viewed *him.* Drew. Because every time she saw him, every time she spoke or displayed some of the knowledge she'd been picking up all week, he was there to look on in approval. Interest. Anticipation. As if he was, well, *waiting* for something. She only wished she knew what.

Their tutoring sessions were friendly and whatnot, but as every day passed, she was more and more aware of this tension building between them. How could she not be when they were in this hot, humid place filled with moisture and heavenly smells? How could she possibly think of anything but having him kiss her again…and *more*… when they were together on a big, squishy, soft blanket they'd brought out from the house?

She told herself the blanket—which they hid in the storage closet each time they left—was so inviting only because it protected them from the ground. Not because it felt so wonderful to sprawl out here, lying on her stomach, right beside him.

Their bodies were just a few inches apart. Since he was sitting up, leaning against the storage closet, his legs right beside her, she was almost face level with his hip. Whoa, boy, had *that* given her some distracting moments. She sure would like to land in his lap again someday, like she had the night they'd met.

Forcing her thoughts away from the man's hard body, she tried to focus on the novel lying on the blanket in front of her. Propped up on her elbows, she read aloud from what was becoming her favorite book. "Is there really a book about Huckleberry Finn I could read after I finish this one?" she asked as she reached the end of the chapter.

"Yes. It's darker, lots of deeper themes about prejudice and hatred. But a good one. You'll be ready for it in no time."

"You keep teaching me tricks like the *i* before *e* one, or the one about two vowels going walking and the first one doing the talking, and you might be right."

He chuckled. "Tori, I'm sure you heard those silly rhymes in first grade."

"I didn't listen much in first grade."

"*That* I can believe."

She raised a brow. "You calling me a troublemaker?"

His wide-eyed expression looked innocent. "Oh, no. Why on earth would anyone think you're a troublemaker? Just because you led a hunger strike with your teammates to demand pizza for dinner Friday night instead of steak tartare."

She wrinkled her nose. "I'm supposed to be the one without social know-how, but I sure know better than to eat raw meat!"

He met her eye, laughing with her, but the laughter slowly faded. He kept looking at her, his dark eyes full of interest. Warmth. Steam. That coulda been the steam from the greenhouse. But she honestly didn't think the heat was coming from anywhere except him, this hot-as-blazes man.

The heavy moment was interrupted by a ringing sound. Drew reached into his pocket and withdrew a cell phone. Lucky him. Hers had been confiscated when she arrived on the set.

"Do you mind if I get this?" he asked after he checked the ID on the screen. "It's my sister."

She merely shrugged, then turned her attention back toward the book while he talked. She only heard his part of the conversation, but it wasn't hard to tell he doted on his sister. He was sweet and playful with her, teasing, the way Tori sometimes did with her baby brother Sammy. Then he grew more serious and began to frown.

She couldn't tell what was going on, but Drew didn't seem pleased with whatever he was hearing. Finally he said, "It's okay, Jill, I'll call him. He can't flunk you for that. But don't do it again."

After he'd disconnected the call, he dropped the phone back into his pocket. Feigning nonchalance, Tori asked, "Everything okay?"

He sighed heavily. "She finally went back to school, but she's been missing a lot of classes. One of her professors is threatening to flunk her out."

Tori nodded, still gazing at her book, not at Drew. Then she said evenly, "So you're gonna bail her out, huh? Seems to me if she's an adult she ought to be able to get out of her own problems."

That was all she had to say. A long moment of silence followed, before Drew laughed softly. "Okay," he admitted, "so we're both suckers. Maybe I won't call her professor and bail her out of this one."

"Good plan," she said, liking this additional proof that they were a lot more alike than she'd ever have expected at first.

"So tell me," he said, suddenly sounding more serious, "what have you heard about these *outings* we're supposed to have?"

She stiffened, unable to help it. She'd heard about what he called "outings." The director had called them "dates." Only none of the girls were supposed to tell Drew.

This was killing her, and she hated being reminded of why she was really here. For an hour or so every morning, here in the greenhouse, she was able to forget about everything else. Forget that inside the house were eight women ready to do just about anything—except maybe pop out of a cake naked—to get Drew's attention. And even the cake thing didn't sound too far-fetched for *some* of the girls, like Ginny and Teresa.

"I've heard," she mumbled, hating to have to keep the director's dirty little secret.

"Are you looking forward to them?"

She'd rather get a root canal than watch Drew Bennett walk out the door with one of the other women on his arm. If he kissed one'a them, she'd… she'd…well, she didn't know *what* she'd do. Probably punch something. Or somebody. Maybe even him.

"Are *you* looking forward to them?" she asked.

"Well, you know I don't want to be dragged on camera any more than absolutely necessary. I want as little to do with *Hey, Make Me Over* as possible." Then he shrugged, a tiny smile playing about his lips. "But I have to say, I don't mind the prospect of a few of them."

Tori had no experience playing coy, so she came right out and asked. "The ones with me?"

"Yeah."

"How come?"

He looked surprised by the question. "Well, it's a chance to be alone with you, outside of this place."

"With cameras and millions of TV viewers watching."

"We'll ignore them."

*Impossible.*

"I'm looking forward to dancing with you."

Her jaw dropped. "Dancing?"

"Of course. We're attending a holiday party at a local country club."

Tori scrunched her eyes closed and groaned. "I can't dance."

"Sure you can."

"No," she said, finally opening her eyes again. "Even the dance instructor is ready to declare me the two-left-feet girl."

"You can move your hands and feet in a race car with perfect precision, Tori. You're not clumsy."

Shrugging, she rolled her eyes. "That's natural."

"So's dancing," he said. "If you have the right partner."

"Meaning you?" She wondered if he heard that hopeful sound in her voice.

He nodded.

"I'll step all over your feet."

"You can't weigh much." His boyish grin didn't make her feel any better.

"I'll look stupid."

He brushed some hair off her face, his fingertips lingering on her cheek. "You'll look beautiful."

Gulping, she managed to whisper "I won't know what to do. The only dancing I know is line dancing in the honky-tonks. Or else slow dancing, which's more an excuse to make out while standing up than anything else. Girl's arms are around his neck, and the guy's hands are on her tush, and they just sorta stand there rubbing up against one another in time to the music."

Instead of replying, he rose to his feet, then bent down to offer her his hand. Tori put her fingers in his, letting him pull her to stand before him. She raised a brow, not sure whether he wanted to fold up the blanket to leave, or…something else. Then he drew her into his arms.

"What're you…"

"Dance with me," he murmured, holding her close.

Any protest she might have made faded right outta her mouth. She was back in his arms, exactly where she'd wanted to be for days. And oh, my, he felt wonderful.

The warmth in the greenhouse had made them both dress a little lighter for their mornings together. So now

Tori wore a tight T-shirt with her jeans; Drew, a golf shirt. Tori had never considered her arms erogenous zones, but the brush of her bare skin against his had her rethinking that idea.

"There's no music," she murmured, not caring, hoping he didn't care, either.

"Sure there is," he said, lacing his fingers with hers, while his other hand, splayed against the small of her back, pulled her even closer. Until she gasped at the contact.

This, she realized, might be even *better* than the dancing she saw other couples doing in the darkness of the honky-tonks back home. He was still close, but it almost seemed proper, as if they were satisfying all the proprieties, but secretly flouting them at the very same time. She could enjoy this in public, she surely could. "Drew?"

"Shh. Close your eyes and feel it."

She closed her eyes, focusing on the warmth of his hands. The press of his firm chest against her nipples, which were taut and hard against her shirt. Never having a whole lot up top, Tori was in the habit of going without a bra, so the contact of her cotton shirt—not to mention his body—was especially sweet torture.

She couldn't help it. A teeny sigh escaped her lips as she fell into step with him, catching his rhythm as he moved to some unheard music. And suddenly, unbelievably, she almost *did* hear it. The hiss of the equipment, the whir of the overhead fan. The swish of the palms swaying under that breeze. Her heart provided a steadily pounding drumbeat and a bass note sounded with her every inhaled breath.

"There *is* music," she said, her eyes still closed as she turned her face to rest her cheek on his shoulder.

Their legs brushed against one another. Their hips moved together in about as intimate a touch as a body could have while clothed. But she didn't *want* to be clothed. She wanted to dance like this, upright, then, there on the blanket, without a bit of clothing between them.

He stopped moving. Tori slowly opened her eyes to see that smooth, hot skin of his neck so very close. She had to taste it. Without a word, she rose on tiptoe and pressed her lips to a vulnerable spot just below his ear.

He hissed. He didn't, however, pull away. Which left her free to explore a little with her mouth. She pressed soft kisses down toward his shoulder, then moved to the front, licking a bit at the hollow of his throat.

"Tori," he groaned.

"Kiss me, please," she whispered, her voice sounding breathy and full of need.

And he did. Lifting her chin with the tips of his fingers, he lowered his lips to hers, catching her mouth in a slow, wet, hungry kiss. A deep sigh came from her throat as he licked her tongue, tasting her with delicate precision. Achingly slow and so intimate she felt as if she was being appreciated like some of that fancy wine she'd been learning about all week.

Then he started to move. To dance again. To slide his hard form against hers while both his hands dropped to her hips. She didn't protest when he slipped them below the bottom of her shirt and lifted it. Didn't even breathe when he tugged it all the way off and tossed it aside. Thought ceased altogether when he ran those big, strong hands of his up her sides to tease the bottoms of her breasts.

He finally pulled away, just far enough to look down at her, his eyes filled with dark desire. "You're gorgeous."

She didn't answer. Instead, she reached for his shirt. He helped her pull it up and off. "So're you."

Then their mouths met again and their dance continued. Only now, their upper bodies touched, slid against each other and aroused Tori to the brink of insanity. The heat and humidity caused a sheen of moisture on their skin, reducing friction. Raising awareness.

"See? Dancing's easy."

"Think anyone'll notice at that fancy party if we dance naked?" she asked with a sigh.

A low rumble of laughter was his only reply. But his hands were busy, cupping her, teasing her, tweaking her nipples with his fingertips as they continued their sultry dance.

Tori held her breath as he bent lower to taste the skin of her neck, down to her collarbone. When he dropped to his knees in front of her, she couldn't help swaying into him, until he encircled her thighs with one powerful arm. He tasted her belly, her torso, until Tori was whimpering with the need to have his mouth on one of her begging-for-attention nipples.

"Drew," she wailed, bending toward him practically ordering him to give her what she hungered for.

He finally took pity and covered the tip of her breast with his lips. One strong pull and she cried out, having to rest her hands on his bare shoulders to support herself on suddenly shaky legs. She felt the sensation rushing through her body, almost not recognizing it because it'd never been so powerful before.

She was dying for him. Just *dying*. Every flick of his tongue against her breast sent bolts of delight downward, until the throbbing between her legs was almost unbearable. When he moved his mouth away, she immediately dropped down to her knees, right in front of him. Their lips met again in a hot, quick mating, and she reached for his belt.

He said something, leaning away. It took a second for her to realize what it had been.

"Tori, no...."

"I want this," she whispered, reassuring him even as she nipped and sucked at his neck.

"So do I."

She went for the belt again.

"But not now."

She froze, her fingers just barely brushing the front of his pants, where his visible erection strained against the fabric. "You wanna run that by me again?"

He closed his eyes and gave one hard shake of his head, as if trying to knock some sense back into it. If he continued with this crazy talk, he was gonna get some help.

"God, if only you knew how hard this is for me."

"*It's* hard for *me*," she insisted, staring directly at his crotch. "I can *see* how hard it is for me."

A hoarse laugh that sounded more pained than amused erupted from his lips. "You're not ready," he finally said.

Oh, she was ready, all right. "Wanna bet?" she snapped. Then she proved it to him by grabbing his hand and pulling it down her body. Down over the front of her jeans.

Right between her legs where the fabric was hot and damp.

He shuddered, cupping her, his eyes closing as a groan of male pleasure eased from his mouth. Tori shook a little, arching into his hand, desperate to have him touch her naked skin, but also loving the anticipation and friction caused by her jeans.

"Any more questions?" she asked, not needing an answer. Reaching up, she laced her fingers into his hair and tugged him close for another slow, wet kiss, knowing he couldn't claim she didn't really want him when her own body insisted she did.

Then he pulled away. Both his mouth, *and*, dangitall, his hand. "We can't."

"Argh," she groaned, "how could I be any more ready?"

"Okay, *I'm* not ready for this."

This time she reached for the front of *his* pants. "News flash, Professor. I got a fistful here that calls you a liar," she managed to say between harsh breaths as she closed her hand over him. All of him. Sakes alive, every hard, throbbing bit of him.

His jaw started clenching as the pulse in his temple pounded. But when she caressed him, leaning up to kiss him at the same time, he turned his head away.

"This can't happen, Tori. Not now."

She'd seen that look on his face before. That stern, hard look, so different from his usual friendly self. And she finally realized he meant what he said.

Disappointment flooded through her as she dropped to sit on her bent legs. It was followed by a quick flash of anger. "There's a name they call women who do what you just did."

He gaped. "You're calling me a...tease?"

"Uh-huh."

He sat back, too, thrusting a hand into his hair, then looking up in the air as if somebody up there had answers she wasn't privy to. Then he met her eye, his jaw clenched still, making it clear he wasn't at all calm. "I didn't mean to tease you. It went too far." Sighing deeply, he added, "If it's any help, I'm suffering, too. I want you so much I'm going to have to take a cold shower after we leave here so I can get control of myself."

His confession didn't help. "Well, in case you didn't know it, Mr. Professor, cold showers don't work so great for women." Reaching for her shirt, she let her tongue rush ahead of her brain. "I ain't exactly the type to take care of business on my own. Even if I were, I sure don't have the privacy of my own bedroom, with no cameras. So I'm gonna be walking around for the next two weeks dying to come and not able to do it."

Tori paused, her blood rushing to her face as she realized what she'd just said. She'd never once, in her life, talked to a man about something like...that. She'd hardly ever *done*...that. Touching herself.

Realizing she'd said it out loud—put those thoughts, those images, in both their heads—she dropped her shirt and clenched her hands together. Closing her eyes, she bit her lip and waited, praying she'd hear the opening—and closing—of the greenhouse door. *Go, just go.*

She didn't hear anything for a long moment, only the pounding of her heart and the deep breaths she inhaled to try to calm herself.

"Well," he finally said, his voice thick and hoarse, "we can't have that, now can we?"

DREW HAD WANTED TORI from the first moment he saw her. Maybe back then, he would have gone for something more physical if he'd had the chance—without cameras present. But now, he was falling for her. More interested in her than he'd been in anyone for a long time. Which had instantly sent up warning flares in his brain.

He couldn't help thinking of his long-ago engagement. Of how his former fiancée had changed overnight from the girl next door, who wanted to marry him and have babies, to the pouting wannabe-actress who'd flown to Hollywood and hitched up with the first millionaire she'd met.

He wouldn't say she'd broken his heart, but she'd put a dent in it. One he was reminded of now, with Tori. Because, he sensed, he really *could* care for her, in a way he never had about anyone else.

So he couldn't act on his desire for her. Not until she knew what she wanted, where she was going, and where he might fit into the picture. Not until she was ready for it, in every way.

She might be *physically* ready now. Oh, God, yeah, she was physically ready. His whole body nearly shook remembering how hot and damp and needy she'd been.

But in every other way, she was far from it.

He couldn't become her lover until she recognized and

dealt with the changes in her life. Tori hadn't yet grasped what was happening here. She hadn't realized she was doing a hell of a lot more than competing for some new clothes and jewelry. She was striding forward into a new future.

Soon, as she continued to gobble up every bit of knowledge she could, as her hungry, bright mind strove further and further toward new experiences, she'd reach a point of no return—when she came to understand she couldn't return to her old world. Not entirely. Nor would she *want* to go back to it.

Who knew what new world she'd want. Hell, for all he knew, it could be one in Hollywood, with oily plastic surgeons.

So no, better to keep at least some kind of distance between them. At least for now, until she figured out for sure that she wanted a *lover,* not just a hot sexual encounter. And that she wanted a real future, not a step back into her small-town world where she couldn't even read a book in peace.

When she reached that moment, he planned to be by her side to help her deal with it. And *then* to act on the hot desire he'd felt for her from day one. When she was ready—*really* ready—he was going to make love to her until they'd both die from pleasure.

But now? No. He couldn't take her now, couldn't bury himself inside her and lose his mind, not when Tori had no idea who she'd be—or what she'd want—next week.

He *could,* however, give her some relief, temporary though it might be.

"Drew?" she asked, confusion in her voice.

"Shh," he said, staring at her, drawing in a few deep breaths to be sure he had control of himself. He couldn't touch her until he did. So instead, he simply waited. And stared.

She was glorious. Her body damp and misty from the

humid air and the passionate heat they'd made each other feel. Sitting just a few inches away in jeans and nothing else, she looked almost pagan, with her long, curly hair curtaining one breast. The other was completely bare, and his mouth went dry, remembering how she'd tasted, the little coos she'd made when he'd sucked her pretty, taut nipple.

Finally, reminding himself that a cold shower and his own hand would do him okay later on, he moved close to her again. "I'm not going to have sex with you right now."

She opened her mouth to protest, but he put his hand up, palm out, stopping her. With a wicked grin, he promised, "But I *can* give you lots of nice things to think about... until we do."

Her eyes flared a bit and her pink tongue slipped out to moisten her lips. Drew needed no further invitation. He dropped his mouth to hers, open and hungry, licking her, nearly devouring her.

"Lie back," he ordered.

She instantly complied.

Drew kissed her again, making love to her mouth with deep, steady thrusts of his tongue, while his hand roamed over her. Cupping one breast, he caught her nipple between his fingertips and teased it until she began to whimper.

"Please..."

She didn't have to ask twice. Kissing his way down her body, he covered her breast with his mouth, then sucked deep. At the same moment, he dropped one hand between her legs and cupped her through her jeans, the pressure of his palm hitting her at just the right angle.

She bucked up against him, crying out again. "Touch me, touch me," she began to murmur. "Closer, please."

Though he'd hoped to keep the physical barrier of clothing between them, his own pants would have to do. Because he could no more deny her than he could stop drawing short choppy breaths into his lungs. She took the matter out of his hands, literally, by reaching down to unfasten her own jeans and push them down over her hips.

Drew tasted his way down her body, with kisses and light nips of his teeth, until he reached the top of her tiny panties.

"Up," he murmured as he slid his hands beneath her bottom to lift her. She helped, making it easy for him to tug her jeans farther down and out of the way. Then he swept her panties away in one smooth stroke, pausing for a second to appreciate her secret, feminine beauty.

Her body was lean and smooth, her skin a perfect creamy color, soft and supple. She had a tiny little birthmark on her right hip, and he ran his fingers over it, wanting to taste her there. Everywhere.

She arched up, rising toward him, knowing what was coming and *wanting* it.

With a helpless groan of pleasure, Drew dropped his lips over her, tasting her sweet hot flesh. Her warm scent filled his head, until he only vaguely heard her cries of pleasure. Her body rocked, finding its rhythm, which he matched with his tongue. And, unable to resist, his fingers, which he sunk inside her.

He groaned at the sensations battering him. Glorious. She was absolutely glorious. Wet, soft, welcoming around his fingers and beneath his mouth. The urge to unzip his pants and plunge into her, to lose himself in that tight warmth nearly made him lose his mind. Not to mention his control.

Thank God Tori had nearly lost hers. Her cries of pleasure pierced the haze of lust in his brain, giving him the strength to proceed with *just* his hand and tongue.

"Yes, Drew, yes," she cried, her voice shaky and trembling.

"Come now, Tori," he growled as he picked up the pace,

knowing he had to take her up and over the edge soon or risk going over it with her.

And finally, perfectly, she did.

# 6

AFTER THEIR INTERLUDE in the greenhouse, Drew no longer trusted himself to be alone with Tori—at least, not unless they were within sight of a camera. If he allowed himself to be *completely* alone with her again—without a video chaperone—there would be no stopping. Not until they'd both achieved the kind of shattering climax he'd been able to give her Sunday morning. He'd completely lose the thin thread of control that'd kept him from making love to her then.

So it was time to end their reading lessons in the greenhouse.

Tori seemed to understand, without him having to say a word. Since that morning, she'd been subdued around him, quiet and watchful. As if waiting for him to decide what he wanted. That was a no-brainer. He wanted her. In any way he could have her. Preferably in *every* way he could have her.

*Not now, asshole,* he reminded himself, trying to remember exactly why his stupid intellect had been in control over his body Sunday when she'd so obviously wanted more.

Then he remembered. It was because she was changing. Growing. Emerging like a butterfly from a cocoon every single day.

The twangy southern accent was smoother now. Still detectable, but softened, until her voice sounded nearly lyrical. Her eyes still sparkled, but those raucous witticisms didn't fall off her pretty lips as often. She wore the same casual clothes, but wore them a little better—because her chin was high and her shoulders straight. She looked more confident, that was the only way he could describe it.

Confident. Beautiful. Nearly irresistible.

He'd also been fascinated to learn Tori had an amazing memory. Now, with her newfound confidence, she'd reached the point where she debated with him about current issues during their daily classes, nailing names, dates and details with almost photographic precision. The other women in the group just watched, wide-eyed and wide-mouthed while the two of them shot different opinions back and forth.

There was no question: every day brought her closer to the new woman she was going to be. A new woman who might not even *want* to get involved with him. So he waited it out, missing their private time together, wondering how the hell he'd ever thought a cold shower and his own hand were going to be enough to sate the incredible want.

He was about to lose his mind from sexual tension. God, Tori merely had to walk into the room in her tight jeans that hugged her pert little ass and he reacted as predictably as Pavlov's dog. He'd taken to keeping books, newspapers or papers in his lap whenever he knew she was about to show up. He could only hope some eagle-eyed old lady out in TV land didn't notice and lodge an indecency complaint with the network. He could see the tabloid headlines now: Man Unable To Keep It Down. And below: Passes Out On National TV From Lack Of Oxygen To The Brain. His picture would be right next to the one of the latest martian robot clone who looked just like Richard Simmons.

"Get your mind outta your pants, man," he whispered aloud as he sat in his room Thursday morning. "Mind over body."

That basic philosophy seemed to have deserted him. His emotions had twisted him up inside, and his intellect seemed to have abandoned him as he got wrapped tighter and tighter in this reality-show noose.

Though Tori was the cause of his most basic problem—an overactive libido—she was also the only pleasure he had in this madhouse. He wanted her like crazy, but he also truly *liked* her. He liked spending time with her, and her presence was just about the only thing he looked forward to every single day. So he put up with the sensual torture if only to gain the emotional relief.

They hadn't stopped the reading lessons altogether, they'd simply moved them indoors. For an hour each day, they sat together in the open area in the upstairs hall, where they'd sat the first time they'd read *Tom Sawyer*, in full view of the camera and the crew.

It hadn't taken long for the other girls to find out he was giving Tori private lessons. It seemed to annoy them for some reason, because suddenly he was being asked to help Ginny with her geography and Robin with her world politics. And he'd probably soon hear from Teresa who'd say she needed to learn…well, probably whatever she could about poles. North, south or brass.

As long as it wasn't *his*, he really didn't care.

The women's nonstop attention had gone beyond tiresome to outright annoying. Drew liked women. Hell, he'd been crazy about a few of them in his life. But he preferred to choose his own, *not* have them chase him down like he was the fox to their hounds. He'd seen less-determined grad students.

As the week went on, it became harder and harder to leave his own unwired room without stumbling over one of them clad in a skimpy robe, or another asking him to help her fix something in her room. Like he was stupid enough to get himself trapped in a bedroom with one of them? Christ, he'd be safer pulling up a chair next to a vampire than letting one of these women get him alone.

Which was why he was spending nearly every spare minute he had locked inside his room, like now, as he sat by the window looking outside, counting the hours until he could get out of here. A soft knock interrupted his contemplation of the snowy lawn, and made him stop wondering if he could make snowshoes out of tennis rackets and escape on foot.

"Yes?" he asked, knowing better than to actually unlock the door again. Last time, he'd ended up with a face full of Tiffany's breasts, barely covered by a skimpy bikini. She'd asked him to join her in the hot tub. He'd told her he was allergic to water.

Somehow, he couldn't even claim too much surprise that she'd believed him.

"Drew? It's me. Tori."

Her voice got his immediate attention. He undid the lock, opened the door and drank her in with his eyes. She'd started dressing differently, due to the influence of the show, he suspected. He liked the pale pink sweater draping softly across her curves, and the beige slacks that emphasized them even more. But the naughtiness in her eye—that hadn't changed a bit. She was still the saucy, outrageous woman she'd been on the day of her arrival.

Thank God in heaven.

"I need your help," she said. "Can I come in?"

Come in. Into his bedroom. Where there were no cameras. But there *was* a bed. A big comfortable bed.

And him with the same hard-on he'd had for going on four days now.

No. She definitely could *not* come in.

But somehow, his upper brain lost control over his vocal cords. Because it was surely the one below his belt that answered, "Sure."

TORI COULD HAVE COME UP with any number of excuses to see Drew over the past few days, but she hadn't. The man had made it very clear he needed his space. Needed to figure things out before they went any further. She had to give him what he'd asked for, even if it nearly killed her since she was dying for more of the same wicked delights he'd shown her Sunday.

But today, she really did need his help. A few more orgasms would be dang nice, too, but she wasn't one to be greedy.

"I've been worrying about Luther," she explained as she stepped into Drew's room. She glanced around in curiosity. This was the first time she'd come into his room. To her knowledge, it was the first time *any* of the women on the set had been allowed into his room, which made it easier for her to sleep at night.

"Your brother?" Drew asked as he shut the door, then turned to face her.

Tori nodded. "We're not allowed to contact anyone in the outside world. But ever since I saw you talking on your cell phone Sunday, I've been thinking maybe the rules didn't apply to you."

Drew crossed his arms and leaned against the doorjamb, looking sexy as all get-out. He hadn't shaved yet, and his face had a bit of a morning shadow. And he wore—lord have mercy—jeans. Tight jeans that hugged those lean hips and rode below his flat belly. His pullover shirt was long-sleeved, but not loose and baggy. Nope, it was tight, accentuating every inch of his broad chest and his thick arms.

But it was his bare feet that made her legs start to wobble. Lord, this man had it all. From the top of his tousled hair to the bottom of his sexy feet, he was temptation walking.

Tori gulped, then turned her attention toward the window.

"You want to borrow my phone?" he asked, apparently not noticing the look of dumb lust washing over her face.

She shook her head. "No, I don't wanna cheat." She said that part for the cameras because, truly, if she could call home herself, she would. "But I was thinking maybe *you* could call for me."

She heard him step closer, but still didn't turn around. "And say what?"

"You don't have to say noth—anything. Just dial the number, ask for Luther, and see if he's there. If they say he's in the hospital or the morgue or something, I guess I'll have my answer. Or if he gets on and sounds like he's talking through a buncha bandages or a busted-up face, I'll know, too."

Her flip tone didn't hide her worry. She realized he'd heard it when he put a hand on her shoulder. "I'm sure he's fine. And I thought we made a pact not to interfere with our siblings who need to grow up."

"I'm not interfering," she said, "I'm curious, is all." She ducked away, still not turning around. My, oh my, her whole shoulder felt hot where his hand had rested on it for that brief second. She probably had a glow-in-the-dark red handprint there, right on her sweater, for all the TV world to see. "I'd feel better if I knew for sure." Clearing her throat, she raised her voice. "But I sure don't aim to cheat."

Drew paused. During the moment of silence, Tori nibbled her lip, then slowly turned around to peek at him through half-lowered lashes. He was smiling, a small secretive smile. "You think there are cameras in here, don't you?"

Rolling her eyes, she fisted one hand and put it on her hip. "Well, duh."

Raising his arms to his sides, he gestured around the room. "It's clean. I know how to spot hidden cameras.... Why do you think the pictures are off the walls and the grates for the heating vents are missing? My deal gave me complete privacy behind that door. My private life is off-limits." Crossing his arms, he added, "But I'm not stupid. I check *every* time I come back in this room."

They both glanced at the door. The firmly closed door. And the tension in the room ratcheted up. Tori drew a shaky breath into her lungs as she realized the implications. They had complete privacy. As in, she could strip off her clothes and jump up and down naked to get his attention, and nobody else would ever know.

He must have seen the thought dash through her brain because he took a tiny step back. "That doesn't mean…"

"Yeah, I know," she muttered, shaking her head in disgust. "Forget it. I didn't come in here for that, anyway. I came to ask you to call Luther for me." Then she remembered what he'd said. "But if there's no cameras, maybe I could use your phone after all."

He shook his head. "No." Then he reached for a pen and paper on the table next to his bed. "But if you write down the number, I'll call and see if he's able to come to the phone. That'll tell you something. Will that satisfy you?"

She snorted at the way he put that while she wrote down the number. "Satisfy me? Huh. You should know better than anyone what satisfies me."

Drew closed his eyes. She could practically hear him counting to ten, and almost regretted taunting him again. She definitely regretted it when he responded with a throaty whisper. "If that's all it takes I'm gonna have a great time satisfying you over and over again until you can't even remember your own name."

Tori gasped. She hadn't expected such a sexy reaction.

He gave her a pitying little smile. "But not now."

She wanted to throttle him. "Right. You're still not gonna finish what you started Sunday morning. Same old story."

He quirked a brow and frowned. "You calling me a tease again?"

She merely shrugged. He was the one who'd put the name on it.

"Because, if I'm not mistaken, you were the *only* one who walked out of the greenhouse Sunday morning feeling any sort of...relief."

Heat flooded her cheeks. Darn the man for saying it out loud, as if it wasn't already embarrassing enough to think about the fact that he'd seen her most private parts—pretty close up—and she hadn't seen him with so much as his belt unbuckled.

She could, however, remedy that.

"Ahh, ahh," he said with a shake of his head, as soon as she began reaching for him.

"Maybe I was going for your phone," she snapped.

"Maybe you were going for my zipper." His half smile dared her to deny it.

"Maybe a *normal* man would wish I was."

His eyes flared a bit, and his smile tightened. A funny throbbing started in his temple and she knew he was gritting his teeth, trying to hold on to his casual laughter and his laid-back attitude.

Her respect for him went up a notch. Not one other man in Tori's life had ever been very successful at keeping control of his temper. This one was.

"Don't ever doubt I'm a normal man, Tori," he warned, his deep breaths and tight tone the only indications of his anger. "I've been picturing you naked and open to me every minute of every day this week."

Her heart tripped a little in her chest.

"I see your face when I close my eyes at night and I dream of burying myself inside you, making love to you until you have to scream at how good it feels." He stepped closer, lifting her chin with the tip of his finger to make good and sure he had her attention. As if she was capable of tearing it away from his husky voice and the wicked word-pictures he was painting.

"I want to *devour* you again."

*Oh, mercy.*

"I've never tasted anything as sweet and wet as your body and I've been hungry for more," he whispered, sounding like a starving man. "I want to feel your mouth on me, too, and I want us to do every erotic, wicked thing we can think of together."

She drew in a jagged breath, turning her face in his palm until she could press a kiss against his warm skin. Her tongue flicked out to taste him, just a tiny bit of him. He moved his hand, tangling his fingers into her hair and tilted her head back. "Oh, Tori," he muttered, as if unable to help himself. Then he kissed her, his mouth consuming her, giving and taking until, as he'd threatened, she couldn't even remember her own name.

When he pulled away, she had to keep her eyes closed, trying to bring the world back into focus as she swayed on unsteady legs. Finally, when she felt capable of thought, she managed one word. One single word. "When?"

He hesitated for a moment, until she opened her eyes and looked at him. The stark, raw want on his face mirrored her own.

"When you can tell me you understand exactly *why* I waited."

Then he turned toward the door and walked out of his own room, leaving her there, alone.

"You ready to go, Professor?" Drew heard as he stood by the front door, ready to go on another of these ridiculous "outings" Saturday night. This time, he was escorting a small group of the women—Tiffany, Sukie and Robin—to the ballet.

So far, none of the outings had been one-on-one. Which suited him fine. At least, until Sunday evening when he was supposed to escort Tori to the local country club for a holiday dance. Then, if disaster struck and two of the girls came down with mysterious ailments, leaving just him and Tori, he wouldn't complain a bit. Because in spite of the agony of being alone with her while unable to make love to her, he missed her too damn much to stay away from her.

She hadn't shown up for her private reading lesson yesterday or today. After Thursday's interlude in his bedroom, he hadn't been entirely surprised. The only time they'd talked was very briefly before the other women had arrived for their current events class, when he'd told her about his call to Luther.

Tori had been relieved to hear her brother hadn't sounded bandaged, drugged or in pain. Not that Drew had engaged him in a conversation or anything. He'd simply asked for the man, gotten him on the line, then offered him a subscription to *Ladies' Home Journal*.

Tori's brother had hung up so fast, Drew's ear had stung.

"Professor?"

"I'm ready," he said as he watched the three women descend the stairs.

They were all dressed appropriately—courtesy of Evelyn, the hair, makeup and clothing instructor. Still, in this case, the clothes definitely didn't make the women. With these three, he had to wonder what the evening had in store. They'd probably be lucky not to land in jail, though, that was less likely since Ginny wouldn't be along to flash anyone. And Teresa wouldn't be there to gyrate against any light poles.

"So this ballet, it's called *The Nutcracker?*" Tiffany asked.

Drew nodded, already dreading the evening ahead. He hated the ballet. Really, truly hated it. But he hadn't been given much choice. Apparently all the instructors were going on public outings with the students, who'd been narrowed down to six yesterday morning.

One interesting thing to note—he and all the other instructors appeared to be completely in agreement on which women were doing the best with their "makeovers." The women Drew had ranked the highest had all advanced into the next round of play. They were falling faster now. By Monday, there would be four, and Wednesday would reveal the final two. These little "tests" and the women's performance in their daily classes would determine the winner in this *Pygmalion* game.

He had no doubt who would win. Tori was thriving, practically glowing with energy and light. Her speech was beautiful, her manners graceful. Sure, she had a few rough spots, but she, more than anyone, had made the most dramatic change in the past two weeks.

He tried to remain impartial and had to admit that Robin had done pretty well, too. And Sukie had tried awfully hard. As for the rest? Well, he doubted any of them would be around come Tuesday.

It was just his bad luck he'd drawn the ballet outing. He'd have much preferred taking the women to a ball game or even a singles' club…a place where they could get their kicks making plays for *other* men for a change.

Because *he* was getting damned tired of it.

"Drew?" Tiffany prompted. "We're going to see something called *The Nutcracker?*"

"Exactly."

"And it's a Christmas story?" Sukie asked.

This time Robin answered. "Haven't you two ever heard of *The Nutcracker?*"

"Is it anything like the *Terminator?* Because, I really liked those movies, I think they'd make great dancing shows," Tiffany said.

Drew closed his eyes. *God give me strength.* "No, Tiffany, it's nothing like the *Terminator.*"

"Well, who's the nutcracker? Is she a superhero or something? Or a cop? Does she really crack the nuts of the guys on stage, or is it just pretend, like WWE wrestling?"

"I'll explain it on the way," he murmured, shaking his head in tired resignation as he led the ladies out to the waiting car.

He only hoped that whatever Tori was doing this evening would be more interesting than what he had in store.

"TURN OFF THE CAMERA and get drunk with me."

Tori watched a smile curve Jacey Turner's lips up at the corners. The camerawoman looked younger—nicer—when she smiled. Not nearly so goth, with her black clothes and pale skin. In fact, Tori realized for the first time, Jacey was probably only her age, younger than she'd originally thought.

"I really shouldn't," Jacey said, sounding regretful.

"Oh, criminy," Tori muttered as she stalked across the library to the bar. "We have the place to ourselves. It ain't…it's *not*…like you're going to have to catch every minute of somebody batting her eyelashes or shaking her tail feathers at the professor."

She couldn't prevent a frown at that one. Lord it was driving her batty to watch the women in this place throwing themselves at him. And Drew, God love the man's soul, had thrown every one of them back, untouched, so far.

Except her. Tori. Her he'd touched. And kissed. And tasted. And stuck his tongue into….

*Enough of that*, she reminded herself with a hard shake of the head. She couldn't go there, not even in her own mind. Not without getting all weak and shaky remembering those wildly erotic moments Sunday and the intensely sexual conversation they'd had in his room Thursday morning.

"This place is empty, isn't it?" Jacey admitted.

It was. They were pretty much alone. Drew had, to

Tori's complete annoyance, taken a trio of women out to the ballet. Tori and the remaining two—Teresa and Ginny—were supposed to go on a shopping trip with Evelyn, who was teaching them all about beauty and fashion. Tori had played hooky, pretending she had a stomachache. Tori didn't suppose she'd mind, since Evelyn had latched on to Robin as her most promising pupil. That was probably because Robin knew more about women's makeup than Mary Kay. And had more of it.

"You're not sick, are you?" Jacey asked, still not putting the camera down.

Tori stuck her tongue out at it. "Nope. You gonna tell on me?"

Chuckling, the other woman hit a switch on her camera and the lens came out a little bit. Tori stuck her tongue out again, this time not only at Jacey, but at all of the TV-watching public, who might be seeing this moment on close-up in a couple of months.

"You just confessed in front of half of America."

"Yeah, well, as long as Miss Evelyn doesn't find out till I'm long gone, back in Tennessee, I don't much care." Tori poured herself a shot—some good Kentucky bourbon—and raised a glass, not to mention a questioning brow. "You in? You know you do deserve a break once in a while."

Nodding, Jacey turned the camera off and lowered it to her side. "Straight up."

"My kinda gal," Tori said, pouring another neat shot of bourbon. Handing it to Jacey, she lifted her own for a toast. "To getting that camera out from in front of your pretty face."

Jacey snorted a laugh. "To stomachaches and an empty house."

"And no more lame-ass reality shows," Tori said with a disgusted sigh. Then she lifted the glass to her lips and drained it. The warmth fell into her belly, then spread out all through her body, bringing instant—if short-lived—calm. "Good."

"Very," Jacey said.

"I wonder if Mr. Mueller has to pay the owners of this house for this stuff."

"Serves him right if he does," Jacey said. "It's the least he can do since he took off, leaving the rest of us here to suffer."

Tori poured them each another shot. "So," she asked, "you like your job following people around trying to catch 'em at their worst for the sake of ratings?"

Jacey raised a brow and took her drink. "I like what I do. Reality TV is just part of it."

"The hellacious part?"

Snorting, Jacey nodded, then sat down on one of the cushy leather sofas. "This one has been pretty bad. But the last one…well, it had its moments."

Seeing the secretive smile on the other woman's face, Tori chuckled. "I can picture what kind of moments."

Jacey lifted her feet onto the coffee table, tugging her long, thick skirt out of the way. "Murder, mayhem, love, sex, lots of fun stuff."

Tori gaped. "You serious?"

As the other woman nodded, Tori whistled a little. Then she figured it out. "You were on the set of *Killing Time In A Small Time,* the murder-mystery show, weren't you?"

Again Jacey nodded.

"Wow," Tori mumbled. "The right guy won for a change." Then, thinking about who the winner had been, she asked, "Is Digg as much of a hottie in real life as he is on TV?"

Jacey didn't answer right away. Instead she drained her glass, then stood and approached the bar to help herself to another. Finally she muttered, "He is."

There was a story there, but Tori wasn't about to pry to

get at it. Prying in other people's business left them feeling a mite bit too free to pry into her own. And as much as she was enjoying Jacey's company tonight, she wasn't about to forget the woman's job was to try to find out every little bit of information she could about Drew Bennett and any potential lovers.

Of course, they weren't lovers. Not technically, anyway. Though, she honestly had to say that any man who'd had his tongue where *his* had been had probably earned the right to be called a wee bit more 'n a friend.

"Ready?" Jacey asked, holding the bottle up.

Tori shook her head. She might have joined Jacey in another drink, but, truly, Tori didn't have much of a head for bourbon. So instead, she moved right to club soda, which she sipped and nursed for an hour or more. As they talked, she began to really like Jacey. The other girl was caustic, with a kind of pull-no-punches wit that Tori had always admired in others. Though on the surface they had nothing in common, she found herself thinking she and Jacey could become good friends. Jacey even talked her into getting back to doin' some drinkin', and Tori was working on a nice little head buzz after another shot.

"So," the camerawoman said after they'd discussed everything from their childhoods to the best—and worst—of the reality-TV craze, "tell me how you think it's going."

"What's going?"

"This show. How will it go down in the annals of reality-TV history?"

Tori grunted. "No brainer. As a big lust-fest with an audience who hates every woman in this place and roots for the professor to tell all you TV folks to take this show and shove it when he finds out the truth."

Jacey stared, her mouth dropping open. "Well, gee, don't pull any punches. Tell me what you really think."

"I call 'em like I see 'em."

And she did. She wasn't exaggerating one bit. She hoped when it came right down to it, and Drew learned he'd been misled and lied to, that he'd walk out of here without a backward glance for any one of them.

A twist of pain in her gut called her a liar, since she suspected she'd want a lot more than a backward glance. Tori chalked it up to the bourbon, refusing to allow herself to dream there was any possibility of a future between them.

"You really want him to walk away without falling in love?"

"He ain't gonna fall in love with any of these women," she muttered, dropping back into her Tennessee accent. "He's smart and he's well traveled and he's drop-dead gorgeous. What's a single woman on this set have to offer a man like that?"

Jacey stared her directly in the eye, her smile fading away. Then she leaned forward in her seat, dropping her elbows on her knees. "How about a great woman who's funny and smart and brave as hell. One who makes him laugh and makes him hot and will make anyone with a brain and two good eyes root for her to succeed?"

It took Tori a second to realize who the other woman was talking about. When she did, she snorted. "Not a chance."

"Yes, there is."

"Uh-uh," Tori said, shaking her head in disbelief. "Drew Bennett's got about as much chance of falling in love with me as I got of being named lady of them all in some real-life fairy tale." Tori flung herself back in her overstuffed chair, her legs sprawled out in very unladylike fashion in front of her. Miss Evelyn would likely have a conniption. But tonight, Tori just plum didn't care. "Besides which, even if he did start caring for somebody, me or Ginny or you for that matter, the minute he finds out he's been lied to and made a fool of on national TV, those feelings'll die pretty fast."

Jacey's brow pulled down in an obvious frown. She thought it over, then perked back up. "That might be his first reaction. But the hero always comes around when true love is involved."

The words *hero* and *true love* didn't seem the type to fall too easily off Jacey's lips. That's how Tori knew the girl'd had one too many shots.

"Believe me," Tori said, rolling her eyes at the romantic picture Jacey painted, "Drew's no Prince Charming, and I'm sure no fairy-tale princess. I'd never *want* to be. I wanted to smack Snow White when I saw that movie as a kid. Imagine taking an apple from someone who looked like that old witch. Girl didn't have a lick of sense in her purty little head."

Jacey nodded, understanding perfectly. "I wanted Sleeping Beauty to march herself right to her parents and tell them off for dumping her on three fairy godmothers in some godforsaken cabin. Cripes, they were the frickin' king and queen. Couldn't they have at least sent her to some fabulous boarding school on the Mediterranean?"

The two of them giggled as they continued to trash fairy-tale princesses. Tori figured Walt Disney had to be rolling over in his grave, right there along with those Grimm brothers. As they talked, she thought again about how much she and Jacey had in common...right down to the belief that the happily-ever-after stuff shouldn't just be reserved for the pretty, nice, perfect princess types.

What was wrong with the wicked stepsister landing the hottie prince once in a while? Or maybe the less pretty girl who lived next door to Rapunzel, who *had* to have fewer split ends, at least. And didn't come saddled with some possessive witch who obviously wasn't so sure of her sexual preferences since she kept a young girl all boarded up for her own viewing pleasure.

"I tell you the truth, you can keep your Prince Charmings, with their white horses and their proper manners," Tori said. She shook her head, hard, trying to focus on Jacey's face, which suddenly seemed to have duplicated itself, as had everything else in the room. Then, with a wicked smile caused by an even *more* wicked memory, she added, "As far as I'm concerned, I'd rather have me a nice, smart man…who can lick his eyebrows."

Jacey shrieked with laughter, and Tori giggled, wondering whether it was the alcohol or Jacey's company that made her feel more comfortable than she'd ever felt with another woman in her whole entire life. She almost voiced her question, when suddenly she saw Jacey's eyes grow round. As the sound of their laughter evaporated, Tori was able to hear a funny choking-coughing sound from behind her. A *male* funny choking-coughing sound.

*Oh, criminy, no.*

She scrunched her eyes shut, then slow as she could, turned toward the door. Because fate was meaner than a miser with his last nickel, someone stood there in the doorway. Watching. Listening. Obviously having heard every word she'd just said.

And because if she didn't have bad luck, she'd have no luck at all, that someone happened to be Drew Bennett.

# 7

DREW REMAINED FROZEN, as stiff as a statue, while he stood in the open doorway of the library. After saying goodnight to his ballet-inept students, he'd come in here looking for some privacy. Not to mention a drink.

Only, the room had been occupied, by two laughing women. One of whom had just complimented him on his oral-sex prowess. At least, he *thought* she had. Never having tried to lick his eyebrows, he couldn't be entirely sure.

Her red face and wide eyes—and the way her mouth opened up but no sound came out—confirmed it. She'd been talking about him. Referring to the incredibly erotic moments they'd shared last Sunday. He almost sighed at the pleasant memory.

"Good evening, ladies," he murmured, almost laughing at the look of panic on Tori's pretty face, in spite of his own embarrassment. Realizing Jacey couldn't possibly know who Tori was thinking about made it a little better, anyway.

"If you're back, that means everyone else is, too, huh?" Jacey said.

He nodded, fully expecting her to stay—to pick up her camera, turn it on and go right into spy mode. Instead, the woman rose, grabbed her gear and headed toward the door. She swayed just a tiny bit. "It's late," she mumbled. "And I'm beat. Don't do anything major without me, okay?"

"As if we'd forget the cameras hidden in this room?" Drew said, his voice holding an edge.

"I obviously did," Tori said with a groan. She dropped her face into her hands, her shoulders slumped.

"Don't worry," Jacey said, "those tapes are going to get lost bright and early tomorrow morning. Monahan's not going to want to show footage of a contestant mingling with the help, anyway." She gave Drew a steady stare. "I know you don't trust me. But I give you my word. Tonight's off the record. I figure I owe you that much since your first night here was *supposed* to be." Then she was gone, leaving him alone with Tori in the silent library.

"So I guess your secret's safe from the TV audience," Drew murmured as he walked into the room, closing the door behind him. Leaving the two of them completely alone.

She looked up. "My secret?"

"You know. Your criteria for the perfect man." Smiling evilly, he moved to the bar and poured himself a drink. "I believe it had something to do with his, hmm, shall we say, tongue mobility?"

"Jiminy crickets," she wailed, throwing her hands over her face again. This time she also threw herself back on the couch, until she was completely flat. "You *did* hear everything."

He poured the drink. "Uh-huh. Let me ask you something. When did you develop this, uh, standard?"

She didn't even move. "As if you don't know."

"Just checking," he said with a shrug. "I mean, I wasn't sure if I *set* the standard or merely measured up to it."

Slowly sitting up, Tori said, "Well, since you're the one and only man who's ever done that to me, I'd say you set it pretty gosh-darn high." Then her mouth fell open. "Oh, my Lord, do you suppose Jacey's going to lose the tapes for the *entire* night, or only the parts before she left?"

Drew nodded. "I have a feeling she meant the whole night. In fact, I'm pretty sure she did."

"So no evidence to be used against us. Does that mean I can leap on you and kiss your lips off, if only to make you forget what you heard when you came in?"

"I'm afraid not. I might need them." He gave her a suggestive look. "It's not *all* in the tongue, you know."

His wicked words surprised a burst of laughter out of her. "You're bad as can be, Drew Bennett. You just hide it better than most." Her eyes sparkled with good humor.

Drew sat down on the sofa, watching her, trying to figure out why he hadn't fled from this risky situation and gone up to his room. Then he figured it out. He needed to spend some time with her, to rid himself of the memories of his horrendous evening. Even if it did put him right back on that sexual precipice he'd been trying to avoid all week.

"So how was the ballet?"

"Dull."

She nodded. "How were the girls?"

"Raucous," he admitted with a heavy sigh. "Tiffany wolf-whistled at all the men in tights and Sukie wanted to know why they don't serve popcorn at the ballet."

Her lips curled up into a tiny smile. "They don't?"

She was in an odd mood. Teasing. Glowing, almost. Then he saw the empty shot glass. *Tipsy.* "Did you have a good time with Jacey?"

She nodded, curling up on the end of the sofa. "I did. She's a lot like me, believe it or not."

He raised a brow. "Do you have vampire tendencies I should know about?"

When Tori's jaw dropped open, Drew pointed to a corner of the ceiling, where a tiny camera was recording every word they exchanged. "Gotcha," he said, knowing full well Jacey would be going over every second of this tape tomorrow morning, before she destroyed it.

"This is kinda hard, isn't it?" Tori asked from a few feet away. Her eyes said so much, told him that she felt the few feet separating them as much as he did. They might as well have been a mile, for all the emotional—or physical—closeness they could risk. Still, this was the first time in days that they'd been completely alone, without one of the giggling women down the hall, or the ever-present camerapeople spying on their reading lessons. "It's like the story with Big Brother—not the TV show, but the old story. Somebody always watching."

"That was called *1984*."

"They didn't have reality TV in 1984, did they?" she asked.

"I think it was called MTV."

She snickered. "Jacey just came from the set of *Killing Time In A Small Town*. That was actually a pretty good one."

"I have to confess, I've never watched a reality show."

Her jaw dropped. "Never?"

He shook his head.

"Not even *Survivor* or *American Idol?*"

Another shake of the head. "I've seen enough real survivor situations. Don't really need to watch the made-up variety."

"*Joe Millionaire?*"

He grimaced. "The one where some man lied to try to get some desperate, greedy women to fall in love with him? No. Definitely not. Talk about TV at its *worst*."

She cleared her throat. "Why does that sound a little personal, like you're very offended by that."

She'd seen that so easily, he hadn't realized how obvious his feelings on the subject would be to her. "It's an old story."

"I've got young ears."

Unable to resist the gentle warmth in her tone, he gruffly explained, "I was once seriously involved with someone who, well, let's just say if it were a case of love or money, she'd go for the money."

"That was a reality show, too."

He grunted, somehow not surprised. "How on earth anyone could really fall in love with a person who'd lie and deceive them—for money—and all for the viewing pleasure of American TV audiences, is beyond me."

"Oh," she said softly, staring at the carpet as if it had suddenly developed magical flying abilities. She didn't say anything for a long moment, then, finally, shook off the moment of introspection. Turning on the couch until she faced him, she said, "Get back to the *Survivor* stuff. I want to hear about some of your adventures. Tell me a story."

He shrugged. "You'd be bored."

"No, I wouldn't."

Glancing at the camera, he said, "Well, *she'd* be bored."

Tori followed his stare, then gave a little wave at it. "Then she can just burn this whole thing *now.*"

Drew didn't suspect Tori's not-so-subtle hint would make Jacey stop watching at this point. Still, one could hope.

"Tell me."

So he did. Somehow, maybe because she was so truly interested and asked thought-provoking questions, it was easy to share some of his experiences with her. He wasn't in a glamorous field, he didn't dig for grand tombs filled with gold in Egypt, or discover new species of dinosaur. Instead, as he told her, he followed the trail of evidence that let him know about the day-to-day lives of people long since gone.

"In the future, your job'll be kind of obsolete, won't it?" she asked at one point. "I mean, all anybody in the year 2952 will have to do is watch copies of our old reality shows and they'll know exactly how we lived."

Drew groaned. "Good God, you mean Ginny and Tiffany will represent modern women?"

She matched his exaggerated shudder with one of her own. Then she said, "But look on the bright side. Everyone in the future will think men of 2004 were all brilliant, gorgeous gentlemen." She gave him a sideways glance from beneath half-lowered lashes, adding, "With the sexual restraint of monks."

"I'm no damn monk," he snapped, wondering how on earth she could think him restrained when he'd been hauling her into his arms—almost against his *own* will—practically from the first time they met. "Which I'll prove to you about a dozen times over the very *first* day you figure out where you're going from here and what it is you want out of life."

He hadn't meant to say that, but, as usual, his emotions overruled his intellect when it came to Tori. She stared at him for a long moment, her eyes narrowing as she tilted her head.

"Oh, boy," she whispered, "that's it, isn't it? That's the reason you've been staying away from me."

"I don't appear to have done a very good job," he said, a rueful smile on his lips.

She wouldn't be distracted. "You think I'm going to be a completely different person when this is all over with. As if, somehow, changing the way I talk or the way I dress is going to change what I *want*."

"Well, isn't it?"

She shook her head and met his stare, her eyes clear, her expression somber. "Not when it comes to you."

He studied her face, searching for answers to unasked questions. "It's only a TV show, but you're still starting something that could change your whole life," he said softly. "Now's not the time for you to make any big decisions."

Tori slid closer, then closer, until there was no room on the couch for him to back away. "This *isn't* a tough decision, Drew. I want you to be my lover. Whether it's just for tonight, or for the next week. Whoever I turn out to be at the end of all this, I will never regret taking whatever I can get for as long as I can get it."

Leaning up, she brushed her lips against his. Asking. Demanding. Questioning. Offering.

And he was no longer able to resist.

Drew sunk his hands into her hair and held her tight to deepen the kiss. Languorous and wet, their tongues met and danced in lazy, sultry intimacy.

When they drew apart, Tori said, "Was I right? Do I understand why you've been trying so hard to not let things go too far?"

He gave one slow nod.

"My God," she said with a laugh, "I feel like Dorothy in *The Wizard of Oz*, when the good witch tells her she always had the power to go back home. She just needed to learn it for herself."

"You gonna click your heels together?" he asked.

She licked her lips and eyed him hungrily. "Only if I can do it while my legs are wrapped around your hips."

TORI KNEW BY THE LOOK on Drew's face, and the groan he couldn't contain, that he had reached the end of his rope. Her wicked words had helped him, which was, of course, exactly why she'd said them. The mental picture of her bare legs wrapped around his lean hips while he thrust into her until she lost her mind brought instant warmth—and moisture—to her body.

She wanted him desperately. Now more than ever.

Lord love him for being a decent enough guy to wait until she was really ready, in every way, including emotionally. Physically, yeah, she'd been wanting him since day one.

But emotionally? Well, maybe he was right. She was already a different person than she'd been two weeks ago when she'd flown up from Tennessee. And she knew she'd have to face those changes in herself once she left here. How perceptive of him to know that.

Most men wouldn't have thought twice about taking what she'd offered. Drew Bennett, however, wasn't most men. He was different. Wonderfully, perfectly different. Smart and sexy, kind and thoughtful. Sassy and dry-humored. Everything she'd ever fantasized about having in a man but never believed she'd ever really find. All wrapped up in a gorgeous package that was hers for the taking.

Hers. For tonight at least.

For the first time, Tori felt a tingling of concern run through her body. Because she couldn't fool herself into thinking she only liked the man. Drew wasn't the kind of man you simply liked, or lusted after.

He was the kind who stole hearts. Maybe even hers.

"Tori?" he said, his voice thick. He was watching her, waiting for whatever was going to happen next.

No doubt about that. No matter what happened tomorrow, or next week, for tonight, Tori Lyons was gonna get her man. Whoever that fool woman was who'd chosen money over him oughta have her head examined because this was about the most desirable man she'd ever seen in her life.

Swiveling her body, she slid one leg across him and sat on his lap, facing him. He didn't look a bit surprised that she'd landed on his lap—again.

"Kinda like the night we met," she murmured, wriggling a bit as she moved her face closer until they were nose to nose. Then she leaned in and licked his lips, daring his tongue to come out and play.

He groaned again, rising up a little so she could feel just how affected he was.

"Oh, my," she whispered. Because he was very, very affected. "I feel like I'm gonna die if I don't have you." Her voice seemed breathy, even to her own ears.

"Ditto."

He licked at her, teasing her, nibbling on her lips.

"Your room is too far away."

"Yeah, it is. But we can't stay here. Even if she destroys the tape, I don't think either one of us wants to give Jacey any kind of private show tomorrow."

She giggled, glancing over her shoulder at the camera, hoping Jacey was not watching any of this. "I'm sure she won't sit there and watch the whole thing. I bet she won't get past our conversation about the ballet."

"Maybe not," he murmured as he lightly kissed her jaw, then the sensitive skin beneath her ear. "But do you really want to risk it?"

Sighing deeply, she put her head back, wanting him to move his mouth lower, down her throat. "I think I'd risk anything if it means I can finally have you."

Her words seemed to inflame him because suddenly there were no more teasing words, no more little nibbles and smiles. Drew slipped his hand in her hair, tangling it around his fingers. Then he tugged her close for another one of those hot, wet kisses that sapped every bit of strength from her body.

"Come on," she said when the kiss ended. "We gotta get outta here before I say to hell with Jacey and her cameras and just rip your clothes off."

She leapt off his lap and tugged at his hand, nearly desperate to get somewhere private. Really private.

Drew let her pull him to his feet, but he was shaking his head. "I trust Jacey to kill the tape from this room. But once we get out of here, it's not just Jacey we have to worry about. Every other camera in the house is going to be taping us once we walk out that door, and we're fair game."

She nibbled her lip, not liking the reminder.

"There's no way you won't be seen coming into my room," he added. "And I don't want to do that to you on national television. Thursday morning was bad enough, but at least you were only there for a few minutes."

She appreciated his concern. At the same time she wanted to bash him in the head for realizing they couldn't go to his room.

"This is so unfair," she wailed. "I can't go one more night without you." To prove it, she rose up and put her arms around his neck, pressing every inch of her body against his as she pulled him down for a kiss.

He licked at her, devouring her, putting his arms around her waist to draw her even tighter. Then he pulled away and looked over her shoulder. "Come on," he growled.

Tori almost stumbled as he grabbed her and pulled her toward the French doors leading outside. "It's freezing."

He paused only long enough to grab a lap blanket, which was draped across the back of the couch. Wrapping it around her, he strode out the door into the snowy night, pulling her after him.

And suddenly she knew where he was taking her. "Perfect," she whispered, her word causing a cloud of icy cold mist to envelop her face. She shivered a little. From the cold. From the heat. From the anticipation that had been welling up inside her for weeks.

Drew didn't even seem to notice the frigid air. But he did notice her slip a bit on the icy patio. Before Tori knew what he was doing, he'd bent down and swept her up into his arms.

"Good Lord," she sputtered, even though she was starting to feel a bit like a fairy-tale princess, "put me down."

"No."

He bent his head to kiss her again, sweeping his warm tongue into her mouth as if he couldn't wait the few more moments it would take to get to the greenhouse. They shared a breath in the cold night air. Then he strode across the snowy lawn, his steps never faltering, his strong hold on her never weakening.

When they reached the greenhouse, Tori reached down to open the door. He carried her inside, then kicked the door shut behind them. They didn't need to turn on the light. The spotlights on the corners of the house provided plenty of illumination. She could see all the undisguised want in his eyes, that was for certain.

"Oh, this is perfect," she whispered, the hot, steamy air bringing instant relief to her cold face and hands.

He lowered her to stand on her own in front of him. "Thank goodness our host likes hothouse flowers."

Then they didn't say anything. They merely fell into each other, kissing like they needed each other's mouths to survive. Tori loved how he tasted, how he felt pressed against her. With frantic hands, she pushed his suit coat off his shoulders, then reached for his tie. Her cold fingers fumbled a bit, so he helped, yanking the thing off, then pulling at the buttons of his dress shirt.

She had to taste every bit of skin as it was revealed. His hard shoulder, that sharp corner of his collarbone. The hollow of his throat where dark, spiky hairs tickled her skin. Lower. Oh, Lord almighty, lower, down the man's rock-hard chest, sprinkled with more of that wiry hair. She licked and nibbled her way down his rippled belly, until she was kneeling in front of him, grabbing at his belt. The lap blanket from the library was beneath her knees, providing a slight cushion.

"I've been wanting to taste you since the last time we were here," she said through hoarsely indrawn breaths.

He didn't try to stop her, thank heaven. Tori made quick work of removing his pants, while he kicked off his shoes. Then she carefully pulled his boxer briefs out of the way. When she saw him—all of him—thought deserted her and pure hunger took over. She licked her lips, instinctively knowing what she wanted. She'd never done such intimate things with a man before, but hungered—absolutely starved—to take him into her mouth. So she did.

"Oh, God," he groaned when she covered all that pulsing, hard flesh with her lips. "Tori, you're so hot, so sweet," he muttered.

So was he. But her mouth was too full to tell him so. Instead, she showed him how much she liked his taste by drawing him deeper and deeper, sucking and licking as much of him as she could take. Still following some ancient, womanly instinct that told her what to do, she began to move, to draw deep, then pull away. The heat in the room ratcheted up and a sheen of sweat grew visible on his body. His muscles were tense, straining, and suddenly he dropped his hands on her shoulders and pushed her away.

Tori opened her mouth to protest. But before she could do so, Drew had dropped down to kneel in front of her on the blanket. "I'm not gonna come in your mouth our first time," he growled against her lips as he kissed her again.

"I did," she said through choppy breaths.

He laughed hoarsely, even as his hands continued moving frantically over her body, one sliding across her breast, her waist, then lower. Then he added, "Maybe so, but I'm gonna come *here*." He punctuated the promise by grabbing her between the legs, his fingers warm through the fabric of her slacks. Tori almost howled at the barrage of sensation.

"Then *do* it," she ordered, yanking at her sweater and pulling it off.

He helped her, reaching for her bra, unfastening it before she'd even pulled her hair free of her sweater. Then he was kissing her breasts, suckling her, feasting on her with his mouth, while he unbuttoned her slacks. Her legs went weak and the rolls of pleasure began to wash through her body. She arched against him, needing more...more pressure, more intensity. And he gave it to her, working his hand into her open zipper and under her panties. When his fingers dipped into her, she shuddered and shook, her orgasm washing over her almost immediately.

She'd barely begun to recover from it when Drew pushed her pants all the way off, dropping them with the rest of their clothes. They knelt again, facing one another on the small blanket as they touched with heated, frenzied strokes.

Had her fingers ever moved across something as warm, as hard, yet silky smooth as his body? And lordy, how could she stand any more of this sensual torture; the kisses, the fleeting caresses, when what she wanted was him driving into her hard and fast, punching up the pace the way she punched the gas pedal at the start of a race?

"I need you," she mumbled, lifting one leg. She wanted to wrap it around him and pull him down on top of her, needing him now. *Right now.*

But he wouldn't let her. Pulling away, he opened the cabinet, where they'd stashed the fluffy blanket they'd used for their reading lessons.

"Oh, yes," she murmured in approval.

He paused only long enough to toss the thing to the floor, then he was pushing her onto it. Moving over her, he pressed kiss after kiss onto her mouth, her neck, her breasts, until Tori was begging for more. "Please, *please* give it to me," she said, her voice almost a whimper. She parted her legs, inviting him, rising up to him.

He smiled at her, a wicked smile that said he knew exactly how mad he'd been driving her. "One more second."

"No, now!"

Though she tried to yank him down, he leaned away, toward his clothes. "I've walked around with one of these in my pocket since the night we met," he admitted as he retrieved a condom.

Criminy, Tori hadn't even though of that. Hadn't spared

one second to consider birth control, he'd had her that hot and frantic. She watched him sheathe himself, nibbling her lip as the excitement built again.

To be honest, this slow torture was thrilling her beyond belief. "I love looking forward to things," she whispered. "The anticipation of getting something good used to keep me up all night Christmas Eve. Looking forward to what's coming is as good as getting it."

He chuckled and lowered himself close enough for her to feel that thick weight of his erection against her curls. "Gee, does this mean you want to look forward to it, more than you want to get it?"

"No!"

"You're sure?"

"Do it now, Drew, or I swear to God, I'll bash you with one of those planters," she growled, even as she arched up to him, trying to take what he wasn't giving her.

He waited one more second, taunting her, driving her utterly mad. "I only hope after you get something good, you keep wanting to get it."

"Oh, I do...."

She couldn't say anything else because he plunged into her. Deep. Hard. Fast. Tori howled. Truly cried out at the bliss of it as he stroked her, way inside, with intense, body-rocking thrusts.

"Yes," she moaned, almost sobbing with relief at the sheer perfection of it.

As if afraid his weight was too much for her, Drew rolled onto his back, taking her with him. Tori hissed, feeling the incredible sensations battering her. She'd never done *this*, either, and absolutely loved feeling so in control.

"You're so deep," she whispered brokenly, closing her eyes and savoring the way he felt buried so far inside her body.

He held her hips and thrust up, wringing another cry

from Tori's lips. "I figured you might like being in the driver's seat," he said with a wicked smile.

"I *do*," she replied. Then she began to rock against him. "I definitely like being in control of the...stick."

He caught hold of her hips, catching her rhythm and met her in an erotic give-and-take that seemed to go on forever. She rode the wave until it brought the first of several shattering orgasms, one after another, that made her entire body shake and shudder.

Her legs felt weak, and her breaths turned into pants until she had to drop down to lie on his chest. That, too, provided incredible friction. Though thoroughly sated, she *still* wanted more. Moaning, she ground against him, not believing how many wonderful, erotic things she was learning, all in one night. She fleetingly wondered if it was possible for a body to OD on sexual pleasure. But didn't much care at this point.

"You okay?" he asked, before pressing a slow, sweet kiss on her parted lips.

She nodded. "I'm a short-track driver, in case you, uh, forgot. Don't know if I've got it in me to take on these long distances."

With a low chuckle, Drew instantly rolled her over. "Well then, honey, I'll be happy to take over."

He did. Superbly. Sublimely. Until finally, when she thought she couldn't possibly come again, she reached yet another peak. And this time, she took him with her when she flew over the edge.

# 8

TORI DREADED THE THOUGHT of attending the country-club
dance with Drew, Ginny and Teresa Sunday night. She
looked forward to it about as much as she looked forward
to getting a tooth filled. Or pulling ticks off her dog Ralph
in the summertime.

Ticks. Fat bloodsuckers. That seemed appropriate.

Bad enough seeing the man-eaters in this house trying
to catch Drew alone so they could try their tricks on him.
She'd even heard Teresa whispering to Tiffany the other
day that she was going to climb from her balcony to Drew's
during the night and sneak in through his open door.

Tori had been tempted not to tell the woman Drew was
unlikely to leave his balcony door open in twenty-frickin'-
degree weather. But in the end, her better nature won out
and she did.

Too bad Teresa hadn't gone for it anyway. Then maybe,
she'd be sick in bed with pneumonia or something so Tori
wouldn't have to watch while the woman flirted with
Drew. He'd have to dance with her and Ginny, pay attention to them, and interact with them in a public place.

It'd been bad *before* he'd become her lover—in every delicious sense of the word. Now, however, she felt damn
near territorial about Drew Bennett.

He was hers. Last night had proved it beyond a doubt,
at least in her mind. She was crazy about the man, falling

head-over-heels in love with him. She'd never have predicted it, but it'd still happened. She'd certainly been more intimate with him than anyone she'd ever known in her entire life.

And she was about to go on a date with him with two other women. Which made her want to scream. This reality show had never made her feel more helpless and frustrated than she did at this very moment.

She'd almost convinced herself to work up another realistic-sounding stomachache, which shouldn't have been too difficult since she'd felt sick about the dance all morning—when she learned something very surprising.

"We've decided to step things up a bit," Mr. Monahan said to the six remaining women Sunday morning at breakfast. "Dr. Bennett isn't going to fall in love with *anyone* if he doesn't get some alone time with her." He glanced at Tori. "So tonight will be the first of the individual dates."

The other women around the table groaned, even as Monahan and Jacey exchanged a long look, which Tori noticed.

A mix of confusing emotions rushed through her. Relief, of course. Excitement. Even a bit of resentment. Because she knew without asking that this change in plan had been Jacey's idea.

Part of her wanted to be angry that Jacey was so obviously setting Tori and Drew up for some good air-time, which, due to her promise, she'd been unable to take advantage of last night. She'd confirmed as much this morning, whispering to Tori that she'd watched as far as the ballet discussion and had then destroyed the tape.

Tori tried to remember where the oral-sex part of the conversation had taken place but was too embarrassed to ask.

Another part of her, however, was blissfully happy about the chance to get out of here and be alone with Drew for any reason. It'd been hell not greeting him with a sensual kiss this morning, after the amazing night they'd shared.

She still got all shaky when she thought about it. They'd stayed in the greenhouse for a few hours, curled up together on the blanket as they kissed, and whispered, and made slow, languorous love again. Drew had somehow managed to get her to open up and reveal more about herself than she'd ever have imagined.

Like the fact that she really *had* wanted to come here. That she *did* want to learn. That she wasn't sure what her future held or where it would take her.

Voicing the words made them real in her mind, and even after she and Drew had exchanged a soft kiss goodnight before slipping back into the library, she'd been mulling them over in her head.

She'd been so excited to finally get Drew to agree she was ready to progress to the more steamy stuff in their relationship, that she hadn't thought too hard on her own realization. She was changing. And her future did look different now. Different and confusing.

Whether this completely unexpected, passionate affair with Drew lasted beyond next week or not, she had some thinking to do about the direction her life would take from here.

"So you get the hunky professor all to yourself tonight. Guess that'll be fun," someone said as Tori sat alone in the sunroom, staring out at the snow-filled clouds hanging heavy in the sky.

Looking up, she saw Robin and offered the other woman a smile. Though quiet, Robin was one of the nicest of the women left in the house, the other one being Sukie.

"I guess so," Tori replied, wondering why Robin couldn't read the wicked truth all over her.

*I had headboard bangin' sex with the man all night last night, you're dang right it's fun to be alone with him!*

"Would you like me to help you pick out something to wear?" Robin said as she strolled into the room and sat on the edge of the other wicker love seat. She lowered herself into it so gracefully. Good to see those etiquette lessons had rubbed off on somebody around here. "Or I'd love to help you do your makeup."

Tori gulped. Because one thing that *hadn't* rubbed off on Robin were the makeup lessons. The other woman still wore inches of the stuff on every exposed bit of her face and neck. Tori suspected Robin must have a bad skin condition or something, because Ginny, Robin's roommate, swore she even wore the makeup to bed every night.

Too bad, really. Robin wasn't exactly a beauty, but she was nice and ladylike. Not pretty, exactly. More like what her old granny would call a handsome woman. Regal. Tall and commanding respect. Plus, she had that sexy throaty voice most men liked, and a good sense of humor.

Not for the first time, Tori wondered why on earth Robin had decided to appear on this TV makeover show. Because as far as she could tell, Robin hadn't needed much making over from the minute she walked through the door.

Finally, seeing the look of expectation on Robin's face, Tori remembered her offer. "Uh, thanks anyway, but Evelyn's going to do it." She rolled her eyes. "I don't 'spect I'll even be allowed to choose my own underwear."

Robin nodded in commiseration. "Too bad. But I'm sure she'll pick out something nice." Then she leaned close to whisper, as if afraid the cameras and microphones would overhear—which they *would*—"Just make sure you go over your makeup again after she's done. She goes way too light on the eyes."

Tori bit the inside of her cheek to keep from laughing as she stared into Robin's eyes, which were accentuated by a thick black, chipmunk eyeliner ring and the longest, fakest-looking lashes she'd ever seen. "I'll remember that."

"Sukie and I are so excited for you," Robin said with a big toothy smile that dominated her lean face. "We know you're the only one who might actually have a chance with Dr. Bennett, given how...close...you two seem to be."

Tori's jaw dropped open. "What?"

Robin waved an airy hand. "Don't act so surprised. We've seen how he looks at you. And how you look at him. You're not in this for the money, are you?"

Shaking her head, Tori remained silent.

"We could tell. It's so romantic." Then she laughed. "Of course, on the practical side, a million dollars *would* provide a very nice honeymoon."

A million dollars. The prize for getting Drew to say he loved her by Wednesday. Tori had nearly forgotten about it. She'd been so focused on the other women trying to get her man that she'd lost sight of *why* they were trying to get him.

"The money isn't important."

Robin gave a sad-looking nod. "I know. That's what makes it so funny. You're the one who's got a real shot at it, and you don't care about the prize. While everyone else wants nothing but the money and he won't give them the time of day."

Tori noticed an obvious omission. "What about you? What are you after?"

"Not him," Robin said quickly.

"Good," Tori said, feeling slightly relieved that at least one woman here wasn't after Drew. "But that makes you the only one."

Robin reached over and covered both of Tori's clasped hands with one of her own. "It's okay, sweetie, he has never once looked at anyone else here with the pleasure he always shows when you're around."

"Thank you," Tori said, genuinely touched by Robin's niceness and support.

Robin squeezed her hands, then pulled away and sat back in her own seat.

"So," Tori said, "what do you want from this experience, if not the big prize?"

Robin crossed her legs and draped one long, elegant arm across the back of the small love seat. "I'm after exactly what I was after when I first came here, before we learned anything about the secret agenda and the bonus."

Tori raised a brow. "You mean, you really just want to be named lady of them all and go to some party?"

Robin nodded. "Just because they added Dr. Bennett as a carrot doesn't mean the original prize is no longer up for grabs. And I want to win it."

Judging by the sincere expression, Tori had to believe she meant it. "I guess you would get some really nice clothes and jewelry."

Robin waved that off. "The acknowledgement would be enough for me, even without the prizes. I was always the weird kid in school, looked down on, never attractive enough. Picked on. This would change all that."

Tori didn't think being called a lady by a bunch of TV people would suddenly make crappy high-school memories go away, but she didn't want to burst Robin's bubble.

With a throaty laugh, Robin added, "Though to be honest, the jewelry would be nice, too."

"Not to mention the Manhattan shopping spree," Tori pointed out.

"Exactly."

They both laughed together, and Tori realized this was the third woman she'd met here in Vermont whom she actually liked. Funny. She'd always assumed she just wasn't the type who could get along with other women—or that she needed to—since she'd never had any real girlfriends growing up. Or in her adulthood. She'd assumed the choice had been hers and that she wasn't missing anything.

Now she had to wonder if she'd been wrong. Maybe being surrounded by men—at home, at work, on the circuit—had made her the one hardened to female friendships. Perhaps she'd been unapproachable, too rough and rowdy for women to reach out a hand in friendship to for fear of being rejected, ignored. Or slugged. A few weeks ago, Tori *would* likely have ignored such a gesture, or not even recognized it. Now she feared she'd greatly miss these friendships when she returned home.

Her eyes were suddenly opened in yet another area of her life. Another experience she'd never missed, having never known it, but now knew she didn't want to lose. She liked having friends. As much as she liked learning, and dressing a little nicer, and using her brains instead of her hands for a change.

Which brought her full circle to the mental debate she'd been having before Robin had entered the room. Who, exactly, was she going to be next week when she left here?

More importantly, who exactly did she *want* to be?

Before she could give the matter any thought, she saw Robin rise from her seat, looking over toward the door.

She knew without asking who stood there. The smile on the other woman's face clued her in. But so did Tori's own physical reaction. The air grew thicker. Warmer. Her skin started to tingle. Only one man had ever made her react like that.

"Hi, Professor," Robin said, "I was just leaving."

And, God love her, she did.

"Hi," he said softly after Robin had left the room. He walked over and took the seat the other woman had just vacated.

"Morning," she said softly, not quite able to meet his eye.

They'd been so incredibly intimate just hours before. This man was her lover, for heaven's sake, he'd touched her in ways she hadn't been sure were possible, much less legal. He'd given her more pleasure in a three-hour period than she'd ever had in her whole entire life.

Yet now, she couldn't even look at him.

*It's the cameras.* Yes, the fact that those little peeping eyes were watching their every move had her completely on edge. Because if she gave him her full attention, no way could she hide her feelings, her reactions, her longing for more. Not from him. Definitely not from TV-watching America, who she was ready to send straight to hell by this point.

"Tori, is everything okay?" he asked, leaning forward in his seat to drop his elbows on his knees.

She nodded.

"What are you doing?"

She shrugged.

"This somehow seems familiar. Are you waiting for me to shut up for any particular reason this time?"

Finally looking up, she saw a twinkle in his eye and knew he was referring to their very first conversation. That night in the library, when she'd wanted him to stop talking and just keep looking at her. All hungry and handsome and fascinating.

A reluctant smile curled her lips up. "No, I just find I get a little tired of watching every word I say because of the cameras."

He followed her pointed stare, then frowned. "I have a feeling these tapes will be edited before they air on television."

"They'd better be," she said with a definite roll of her eyes. "Unless Mr. Mueller wants to pay a lot of fines to the TV government people. That Janet Jackson thing can't hold a candle to the way Ginny's been letting them fly the past two weeks."

"Fortunately, I've missed most of those incidents." His deep chuckle brought a warm sensation to Tori in spite of the chilly morning. Lordy she liked being with this man.

Teasing him, she said, "Most men wouldn't mind so much."

"I'm not most men, in case you haven't noticed."

"Oh, I've noticed." She met his dark-eyed stare. They looked at one another for an endless moment, saying a thousand things, each one of them answered. They relived last night, every second of it, all in a heavy silence that the camera crew could interpret any way they wanted.

It was torture, really. A morning-after in front of the whole bloody world. But as the moment lengthened, Tori almost began to enjoy it. She got a little shivery thrill, sharing this secret with him, the rest of the world be damned.

"So have you been doing anything interesting the past few days?" he asked, giving her a look of such innocence it nearly made her burst into laughter. That was likely what he'd intended, to playfully torment her, knowing she couldn't respond.

She could play his game. "Oh, not what I'd call interesting, really."

His brow shot up. "No? Nothing enlightening or exciting going on? I can't imagine that."

"It's been terribly dull."

*"Dull?"* He practically wore his offense on his face. The man was fun to tease, if only to give the naughty part of him more chances to come out and play.

"Shew, I've had more fun changing out a tranny in the pits than I've had around this place." Giving an exaggerated yawn, she stretched her arms out to her sides, knowing the move was pulling her turtleneck sweater even tighter against her body. He noticed. She saw him swallow visibly. But that was his only reaction.

"Well, I can imagine working on cars is exciting for you." Then he lowered his voice. "But maybe not as exciting as racing. Being in the driver's seat, in complete control." An evil smile warned her one second before he added, "Handling the *stick*."

Oooh, the wicked man. Her body shook, from top to bottom, at the mental pictures his words put in her head. Her tummy started rolling over, and heat dropped down to rest between her legs. She throbbed there, her corded slacks suddenly feeling too tight. Uncomfortable.

If only to get even, to make him sweat a little, too, she replied, "I'd say that depends on the stick. Some of them don't have the right feel." His eyes flared but he remained silent. "It has to be the perfect size, just thick enough to fit into my…" She licked her lips provocatively before concluding, "palm."

Drew's face reddened as he mentally substituted the word she wanted him to imagine. *Mouth.* How perfectly he'd fit into her mouth. She never could have imagined how much she'd like doing something so blatantly carnal and her whispered words told him so.

He drew in a deep breath. She watched his hand, resting lightly on the seat beside him, curl into a fist as his muscles visibly tensed. Oh, yes, she was definitely getting to him.

But he, apparently, wasn't crying uncle just yet. "Hmm, I never thought about it that way. About it fitting into your…palm. Seems to me there should be other criteria for how well it works. Maybe making sure it has stamina. Staying power. And that it's *long* enough."

She sucked her bottom lip between her teeth, almost groaning, almost laughing. "Oh, yes, length and breadth are both important. But it's the smooth movement of it that matters more than anything else."

Nodding thoughtfully, he murmured, "That makes sense."

She thought they were done torturing each other, that they'd both scored a few hits and would stop this sensual torment. She should have known better.

"So I guess you have to keep it really well lubricated," he said, his tone light. "To make sure it moves smoothly."

Tori coughed into her fist as she choked on her own breath. Oh, she was going to get him for this. Definitely get him. Closing her eyes briefly, she managed a nod. "Yes. Right. Absolutely. Lubrication is important." Then, raising a brow she added, "As, of course, is having an expert in the driver's seat."

His jaw clenched. "You saying you're an expert? That'd take a lot of experience, with a lot of…equipment… wouldn't it?"

"Not necessarily a *lot*."

"How much?"

"Enough."

"*Dozens* of sticks?"

Dozens? Criminy, did he think she was some kind of track ho? "No."

"Tens?"

She shook her head. Finally, showing mercy, she admitted, "Maybe it only takes one or two for someone to find the perfect match."

He stared into her eyes and she didn't flinch, letting him see the truth she was trying to convey. No, he hadn't been her first, but he hadn't been much beyond that, either.

Finally, a pleased look softened his expression. "That sounds reasonable."

"Glad you approve. Not that it's, you know, really up to you."

"Correct," he admitted. "As long as you acknowledge that now, having found the perfect ride, it'll be the only one you ever want to race again."

WHEN SOMEONE KNOCKED on his bedroom door late Sunday afternoon, Drew's thoughts immediately turned to Tori. He'd been ready to strangle her, or jump on her, when she'd so playfully taunted him earlier in the sunroom. Even the presence of the cameras might not have been enough to keep him from touching her. But Sukie and Ginny's arrival had been. He'd barely given Tori his not-so-subtle hint that he might not have been the first man in her life but he was damn well going to be her last, when they'd burst into the room.

Drew had made a quick excuse and left, praying none of the women—or the camera—noticed that his tailored trousers didn't fit quite so neatly across his crotch as they were supposed to.

Hoping to see Tori's smiling face, he answered the knock without even asking who was on the other side of his door. So he had to smother his quick sigh of irritation when he opened it to find Niles Monahan instead.

"I'd like to speak with you," the man said.

Drew crossed his arms and leaned against the doorjamb, not inviting the other man in to sit in the small sitting area adjoining his room.

Something about the director really got on his nerves. He was a sneaky little bastard, you could see it in his nervous eyes and his constantly moving hands. Drew wasn't risking going off-camera with this guy. He trusted him as far as he could throw him and wanted everything *on* the record.

"Okay, talk."

Monahan sniffed. "I thought you should know, there's been a change in plans for this evening."

Drew immediately tensed. If Tori had backed out, he'd find a reason to, as well. She was the only reason he wanted to go on this ridiculous country-club field trip. Frankly, he couldn't care less about what happened on the set of *Hey, Make Me Over*, and could barely muster any interest in helping to judge the remaining contestants. His life had come into brilliant, startling focus last night, and he had a hard time spotlighting his attention anywhere other than on her. On what had happened between them. What else was going to happen between them.

A lot. Definitely a lot. Maybe a life-altering amount.

After his first botched engagement, Drew had stopped thinking about settling down with a wife, kids and a house. None of that stuff seemed as important as his career and his travels, and he'd never met anyone else who'd made him think that would change.

Now, however, he was beginning to see the possibilities. Because he'd finally found someone he thought he might truly want to come home to.

"So what's this change in plans?" Drew asked, returning his attention to the director.

"We're so close to the end, and we feel it's imperative to really put the ladies to the test. To see how they function in a social setting, one-on-one."

Drew wasn't listening too closely, he was still too focused on his thoughts of Tori. Of *them*. So he mumbled, "Good idea."

Like he cared. His heart had never been in this game, and now his mind wasn't, either. He just couldn't wait to get it over with.

Funny, he'd come here for two reasons—to raise money for his charity and to see his theories put to practical use. Not to lose his mind over a woman he'd only known a few weeks. Not to give in to the most powerful sexual urge he'd ever experienced on the floor of a greenhouse.

Certainly not to fall in love.

But that, he very much suspected, was what had happened. He was in love and in lust and out-of-his-mind crazy about sassy race-car driver Tori Lyons. Everyone else in this house could do whatever they wanted with this TV nonsense. All he wanted was to get it over with and get on with his life with Tori. Because one way or another, she *would* be in his life.

"I'm glad you agree," Niles said. "Because we've decided an appropriate test would be for the ladies to each go on a mock 'date.'"

Date. Date? His jaw stiffened. This little pissant wanted to send Tori out on a date with some other man?

Over his dead body.

"Forget it," he snapped. Then he realized, instantly recognizing the problems with Monahan's idea. "It's not like there's anybody around here for her…for *them*…to go out with. Unless you're going to hire someone, and I don't think the network people are going to want their lady fair escorted by some gigolo male escort."

Miles smiled thinly. "Of course you're right. Which is why, you see, we've come up with the perfect solution."

Drew waited, sensing he wasn't going to like what he was about to hear.

"You're a well-spoken, well-dressed bachelor. And you'd be in the perfect position to judge their performance. It's truly in everyone's best interest."

Drew was already shaking his head before the man even finished his sentence. "No. No way."

"You wouldn't be going on a real date, you'd simply be continuing the 'outings' one-on-one. Think of it as a private tutoring lesson—I hear you don't mind giving *those*."

Drew's eyes narrowed. "You insinuating something?"

Monahan sniffed again and drew a hand to his chest as he protested his innocence. "Of course not. Your efforts with these women are both admirable and remarkable. This show is going to do exactly what you hoped it would. The extreme social-makeover hit of the season."

For the sake of the charity—and book sales, he had to admit—Drew hoped so. But there was still no frigging way he was going on a date with one of the women on this show. No way.

"Your first outing will be this evening," Monahan said, still ignoring Drew's refusal. "You can go to the country-club dance, as scheduled."

Drew shook his head again, but Monahan pressed on. "With Miss Lyons."

And suddenly, Drew realized, the idea wasn't such a bad one.

Not bad at all.

# 9

As SHE'D EXPECTED, Tori was given absolutely no choice about what she'd wear, how she'd do her hair, her makeup, her shoes, criminy, even her underwear. But as she stood in front of the floor-length mirror in her room early Sunday evening, she couldn't bring herself to care. "Is that really me?" she murmured, unable to believe her own eyes.

In her regular life, Tori was used to wearing jeans, flannel shirts and engineer boots. She had one plain black dress for funerals, and a blue one that did okay for weddings. The highest shoes she ever wore were one-inch pumps. But now… "I don't even recognize myself."

The dress was gold. Simple and perfect, a long straight, tight sheath that was held up by tiny sparkly spaghetti straps at the top. It glistened all the way down to the floor, where her painted toenails peeked out from strappy matching sandals. She resembled one of the long, shiny gold Christmas ornaments she sometimes saw in fancy mail-order catalogs.

"You look beautiful, Tori." Sukie was staring at her in the mirror, smiling like a proud mama sending her baby out to prom.

Tori'd been riding the circuit for more than a year by the time she would have had her senior prom. She'd never felt the loss much. Until now. Now she had to wonder what *else* she'd missed out on, never even realizing she was missing a thing.

"Thanks, Sukie. And thanks for being so nice about this. I thought Teresa and Tiffany were going to rip my hair out when they found out."

"Pfft on them," Sukie said with a toothy grin as she cracked her ever-present bubblegum. No matter what the teachers had tried, Sukie wasn't giving up that habit. "They're just jealous because they know they don't have a chance at getting the professor. But you do."

Chance? She'd had more than a chance at bedding him, that was for sure. But as for him falling in love with her? Well, Tori still found that part debatable. Not to mention disturbing, in light of this whole contest thing.

Because even if by some miracle of miracles Drew did fall in love with her, how long would he *stay* in love with her if he found out she'd been lying to him about this stupid competition since day one?

"You do look quite lovely," said Miss Evelyn, who'd supervised every minute of Tori's transformation like a Nazi general. Tori had been half-afraid the woman was going to come into the shower with her to make sure she shaved her legs right. "Thank heaven we tamed those wild brows of yours."

Tori winced just at the memory of the plucking she'd endured earlier.

"But I do wish you'd let me go a bit heavier around the eyes," Evelyn added with a frown.

"No, thank you," Tori said, hiding a grimace. Goodness, if Miss Evelyn thought she needed more eye makeup, she could only imagine what Robin would have to say.

"No, she doesn't need anything else," Sukie said. "Tori, that gold shadow glitters just perfectly, like your dress. You don't need any more color than the bright blue of your eyes."

Tori gave her a grateful smile.

One of the other instructors, Suzanne, who wrote some kind of etiquette column for a northern paper, entered the room, which might as well have had a revolving door for all the privacy it held. "Very nice," she said to Tori with an approving nod. "You do remember everything we discussed? Waiting for the valet to open the door, letting him help you out...."

"If he helps me out, he might smear up my cheat notes," Tori said with a naughty wink at Sukie. That was pretty much how Tori had made it through geometry in tenth grade, with all those silly theorems and whatnot.

Suzanne's eyes widened and she grabbed Tori's hands, lifting them for inspection to ensure nothing was written on her palms.

"Just joshing," Tori admitted, looking at her own spick-and-span clean hands.

Behind her, she heard a laugh. She'd almost forgotten Jacey was in the room, her camera stuck to her face like always. Turning around, she gave a little mock-curtsy for the TV audience. "Think I'll do?" she asked.

"America says yes," Jacey replied.

Her comment would most likely be edited out, but Tori appreciated the vote of confidence. Then, still feeling very saucy, she retorted, "America can kiss my fanny tonight. I'm out to have a good time."

Jacey gave her a thumbs-up, even as Miss Evelyn and Suzanne groaned.

"There better not be any fairy princesses at this shindig. My elbows might go flying if we start doing some line dancing."

This time, they didn't just groan, they actually fell into one another, grimacing in horror. Meanwhile, Jacey's eyes danced with humor and Sukie snorted with laughter.

"Wish I could be there to see it," Jacey said.

"I'm surprised you won't be," Tori said, still wondering why Jacey, as lead camera operator, wasn't the one going to the club with Drew and Tori.

Jacey shrugged. "It's better this way."

Then Tori realized the truth. Jacey had intentionally backed out, probably because she, Tori and Drew all realized Jacey had lost some of her objectivity toward them. Jacey probably didn't trust herself not to give them some privacy if Drew and Tori had a chance to slip away. Last night was the only blatant help she could give them.

Tori gave her a slight nod of understanding and Jacey met her stare evenly. Though the woman was part of the crew and couldn't show any favoritism, Tori knew in her heart that Jacey was rooting for them. Not just for the sake of ratings. And not, she believed, just for the sake of friendship, either. Jacey seemed to have something more personal at stake in this, though Tori couldn't imagine what.

Finally as ready as she'd ever be, Tori exited her room and made her way downstairs to the foyer. As she walked down the sweeping, curved staircase, she saw Drew standing there at the bottom, gazing up at her.

Her heart started rolling around in her chest. Oh, the man was glorious. Dressed in a black tux, freshly shaven, his hair still slightly damp from his shower, he was like a fantasy man out of a magazine. The kind Tori had never in all her days expected to meet, much less *have*.

But the best part was the look on his face. The hungry, appreciative look that she'd loved from the minute they'd met. Again, directed solely at her. Tori thought she could live her whole life on that look, if only she had the chance.

"You're beautiful," he murmured as she reached the bottom of the stairs.

She took his arm. "Thank you." Then, lowering her voice to a whisper for his ears alone, she added, "You looked like Rhett Butler staring up at me from the bottom of the stairs. All wicked smile and wickeder eyes."

"Speaking of wicked, I hope you know I had to go take

another one of those rotten cold showers this morning after I left you in the sunroom."

"You started it."

"Yeah, I plan to finish it, too."

"Gonna bribe the cameraman?"

"Maybe we could drug him."

"Or just run like hell?"

His low laughter caught the attention of the camera operator, who immediately stepped closer and zoomed in. He'd obviously noticed them whispering.

"Well, Professor, I'll try not to say any more silly things like that when we're out in public. I don't want to embarrass you," Tori said, speaking loudly for the audience's benefit. Of course, for all she knew, there were microphones hidden in the flower pots that probably caught every naughty word they'd said.

"Tori, you could never embarrass me," he replied, his tone almost stern.

Again, she figured, for the audience's benefit. But it was still awfully nice to hear.

WHILE WITH ANY of the other women from the show tonight might have been an agonizing chore, with Tori, the evening was remarkable. Perfect. From the moment he drew her long, borrowed cape over her beautiful bare shoulders, until now, three hours later, when they stood swaying together on the dance floor, using the soft lighting and the music as an excuse to keep their arms around one another, they'd been inseparable.

Tori seemed to have grown more beautiful as the evening went on. She was easily the loveliest woman in the place. The changes in her over the past two weeks had never been so markedly noticeable before. She'd always been pretty, but her newfound confidence and elegance put her above any other female here.

She held herself proudly, yet smiled with genuine warmth whenever she met someone new. The soft Tennessee twang in her voice merely accentuated her charm, and she chatted easily with everyone from the chauffeur and the valet to the club president who'd come over to welcome their celebrity guests upon their arrival.

Tonight was like a perfect first date between two people who were wildly attracted to each other. Even though they'd certainly already progressed far beyond first-date stuff *physically.*

For her part, Tori seemed utterly delighted to see evidence of the fast-approaching holidays. The club was bedecked with greenery and red velvet bows, and an immense Christmas tree stood in one corner of the ballroom. It twinkled with lights and sparkling ornaments, none of which, he realized, were as dazzling as Tori's dress.

Drew hadn't given much thought to Christmas, since the estate where they were taping showed no evidence of it at all. Probably because the show would air in February, during sweeps, long after the festive season was over. People would be thinking about Valentines, not gingerbread men—except, of course, for the grand finale episode, when the lady of them all would attend her Christmas Eve ball in New York.

The delight in Tori's eyes and the way she nearly bounced on her toes as she talked about her favorite holiday traditions merely made the entire night that much more perfect. It was almost too easy to forget the cameraman, or the interested people all around them, who knew full well that a reality show was taping in their midst.

"I wonder what on earth all these people are thinking," Tori said softly as they danced, as if she'd read his thoughts.

Then again, considering they were being whispered about by practically every person in the place, maybe it wasn't so surprising. "I have no idea. Maybe they're thinking that we're a runaway royal couple, mingling with the commoners for an evening."

She rolled her eyes. "No fairy-tale princesses for me, thankyouverymuch."

"You look like one," he said, staring into her eyes to convince her of his words.

"Maybe Cinderella."

"She was my favorite."

"Mine, too." Smiling, she tucked her head back onto his shoulder, and her body even tighter against his, letting him lead her.

Drew wasn't much of a dancer. He'd certainly never had lessons. As a kid, food had been much more of a priority for him and his sister than Boy Scouts, sports, dance lessons or anything like that. And the biggest social events he'd attended in recent years had been around huge bonfires with tribal leaders in foreign countries. The dancing hadn't much resembled this.

Somehow, though, he and Tori made it work. They were perfectly in sync, every turn, every dip, every step.

Like making love while fully clothed.

"We have an audience," she said after the music changed, segueing into another slow, sultry number that kept them there, swaying, alone in the world they'd created.

"Uh, no kidding," he said with a chuckle, glancing at their ever-present chaperone, Sam, the cameraman.

"I meant *other* than the camera."

Following her stare, he noticed many of the other partygoers watching them from around the dance floor. Then he shrugged. "They know we're part of a reality show." Rolling his eyes in disgust, he added, "They probably think it's one of those ridiculous dating things where perfect strangers try to make other people fall in love for the sake of money or greed. That's the absolute dregs of the reality-show world."

Tori shivered a little, and Drew noticed someone had opened a door leading to an outside patio. He drew her closer. "You okay?"

She nodded, not saying anything, just burrowing closer to him. He kissed her temple, for once not giving a damn what the TV audience would make of it two months from now. "You warm enough?"

Another nod. Then after a long pause, she took a deep breath and looked up at him with a smile.

"What's on your mind?"

"Dancing. I had a feeling I was going to like your kind of dancing in public."

"My kind of dancing?"

"Uh-huh. Proper and acceptable. But still kinda wicked, like making out while upright, only without the kissing."

"I was just thinking the same thing," he admitted. Then, remembering their impromptu dance lesson last Sunday in the greenhouse—as she obviously was—he added, "I'd like to try your kind of dancing sometime, too."

"Maybe you'll come visit me in Tennessee and come to the honky-tonk with me some night."

Drew pulled away slightly to stare down at her. "Tennessee? You really think that's where you'll be?"

He was asking her more than that—much, much more. Judging by the sudden confusion in her eyes, she knew it, too.

"I don't know," she said softly. "I don't know much of anything these days."

"You'll know. And I'll be right there beside you when you figure out where you want to go when you leave this place. It'll be forward, I have no doubt about that. You're too strong to take a step back."

"I don't feel very strong." She nibbled her lip, not even looking at him as she added, "Besides which, you and I are so different, from different worlds. I don't think we should even think about where we'll be a week from now. Anything can happen before then." She frowned, looking troubled as she added, "Who knows how you'll be feeling about me when this is all over with, everything finished and in the open."

Drew didn't understand her, but he certainly heard the concern in her voice and felt the tension in her suddenly stiff body. "That's ridiculous. And our worlds are not as different as you seem to think. I'm not who you think I am." He hadn't confided in her yet about his own childhood, which had probably been every bit as rough as her own. Now didn't seem the time or the place for that. They would, however, have the conversation soon. Once they were out of the TV business.

Tori said something else, in a low voice that he almost didn't hear. "Maybe I'm not who you think I am."

He tilted her chin up, forcing her to look him in the eye. "Tori, what are you trying to tell me?"

Her mouth opened, but no sound came out.

"Is there something I need to know about? You can tell me anything…unless it's that you're a guy in drag or something." He'd been teasing her to make her smile, but she didn't. "Uh, I was joking. Now talk to me."

She hesitated again, but this time, took a deep breath, as if about to speak. But before she could say a word, they were interrupted by Sam, the camera operator, who stepped so close with the camera he nearly hit Drew's arm.

Drew shot him a glare, watching him exchange one long look with Tori. Then he stepped back. And the moment was lost. Whatever she'd been about to say, her lips were tightly closed now.

TORI'S EVENING HAD BEEN pure magic, every minute of it, right up until they'd started talking about the reality show. For a few hours, in his arms, beneath the Christmas garland and the wreaths and the mistletoe, she'd been able to forget how they'd met, why they'd come together. Even Sam's presence hadn't distracted her too much until that moment, that one moment when she'd been ready to admit the truth to Drew. The words had spilled up to her lips before she'd even had a chance to think about the repercussions. She wanted him to know that *he* was the target of one of those schemes he'd been talking about in disgust.

Now more than ever, she knew he was not going to react well when he found out the truth. Burt Mueller would be lucky if Drew only sued him…. He'd probably be tempted to get violent on the man. How he'd feel about *her*, she didn't even want to think about.

But it appeared she had longer to think about it. Because Sam had obviously overheard and realized what she was about to do. His pointed stare had warned her not to, and the opportunity had been lost. The evening hadn't presented another one. Oh, okay, it *might* have, but Tori was too chicken to really look for it.

She didn't want this to end. Not now. And she very much feared that when she told Drew the truth, it would end. Maybe not entirely, but she'd sure as heck kill any trust the man might have in her. He'd been burned once by a woman who wanted money, which might make him not forgive her at all.

So for tonight, she planned to take what she could. To build up lots of pleasant moments for the memory box in her head. Just in case that was all she ever had.

Later in the evening, as the party began to get a little more raucous and filled with holiday spirit…or spirits, at least…Drew went over to the bar to get them each a drink. Tori saw him slip the bartender some money and then tip a waiter. She watched curiously as the bartender made a drink—adding a liberal amount of alcohol—and handed it to the waiter.

"What are you up to?" she asked Drew when he returned and handed her a glass of red wine. Tori wasn't much of a wine drinker, but this dark red stuff tasted pretty good. Put her in mind of Christmas, too, with its rich burgundy color, and that was fine with her.

"Just thinking Sam might need to wet his whistle," Drew replied easily. The twinkle in his eye gave him away.

"You trying to get the cameraman drunk so he won't follow us?"

"That's the fourth drink I've had sent over to him."

Bringing her hand to her mouth to cover her giggles, Tori asked, "So where exactly do you plan to go once he's passed out…uh, *distracted?*"

"You'll see."

As it turned out, she didn't have long to wait. Sam, a large man who'd already broken out in a sweat in this stuffy room while he lugged his heavy camera around, downed the glass shortly after the waiter handed it to him. Five minutes later, while Tori and Drew sampled a bit of heavenly cheesecake, they saw Sam put his camera down on an empty table and lower himself into a chair beside it.

"Nearly midnight," Drew said, not hiding his amusement. "Took less than I'd expected, given his size."

"You bad man, you."

"Come on."

He took the small plate out of her hand, but Tori managed to snatch another bite of cheesecake with her fingers. She popped it into her mouth, licking her fingertips. Drew noticed, of course, and gave her a mock frown. "Suzanne would be fainting right about now."

"Suzanne needs to get a life," Tori retorted. "Or get laid."

Fortunately, the music was as loud as the laughter, so no one overheard as they made their way around the edges of the dance floor. As they reached the exit, Drew glanced back at the cameraman. "Still down," he murmured approvingly.

Once out of the banquet room, Drew took Tori's hand

and hurried her down a long carpeted corridor. A few people stood outside the coat check and he slowed his pace, nodding pleasantly as they walked by. They might have been touring the place…if not for the sexual energy snapping so strongly between them she felt sure they were going to start a fire.

As if reading her thoughts, he paused long enough to pull her into his arms. She threw hers around his neck, holding him tight as he lifted her right off the floor to kiss her until she couldn't breathe, couldn't think, couldn't move. She just hung there, letting him support her while he kissed the living daylights out of her.

Voices farther down the hall finally made him pull away. He lowered her to her own two feet, slowly, so her whole body rubbed against his during the long, sultry slide down.

"Oh, God, I want you so much," she whispered, letting him hear her urgency. Her frenzy.

Taking his hand again, she started pulling him along, heading for the ladies' room, which had a nice big, comfortable lounge area, including a sofa.

"The ladies' room?" he asked, laughing but also looking hopeful.

"Wait here." He did as she asked while she went inside and scoped the place out. It was completely empty, silent and cool—and even a little bit eerie with its black fixtures and black-and-white tiled floor.

Best of all, the entrance had a lock. One that locked from the inside. Opening the door, she found Drew standing right outside, gazing up the hall on the lookout. Tori grabbed his lapel and yanked him in, kissing the surprised laughter right off his lips.

A quick snap secured the lock. A quick yank undid his bow tie. A few flicks of her fingers and his shirt was coming off. A few more and his pants followed.

"You've been making me crazy all night," he said hoarsely as he reached around her to unzip her dress. Though urgent, he was careful when lowering it, protecting the delicate fabric. In spite of the consuming want driving her every move, Tori was still coherent enough to appreciate that sweetness about him.

He was a gentleman.

But right now, the last thing he needed was a lady.

"Take me, Drew," she whispered as her dress fell away.

He stared at her, from her hair—which had loosened and fallen from its elaborate do—down her throat, her shoulders, over her bare breasts. Farther, to the tiny gold panties, then the thigh-high stockings.

The hunger on the man's face made the first moments after they'd left the house—when she'd thought her private parts were going to freeze off—completely worth it.

He lowered his mouth to hers again, this time slowing the kiss, tasting every surface; the softness of her tongue, the sharpness of her teeth. She moaned, low, deep inside, tilting her head farther so their tongues could dance and mate.

"Wait," she whispered against his lips, stepping back to separate their bodies by an inch or so. Far enough for her to work the panties down her hips and let them drop to the floor.

The stockings—and the high-heeled gold sandals—she left on.

"You are utterly stunning," he said through a tight-sounding throat. "As pagan and seductive as any tribal goddess I've ever imagined."

Oooh, she liked that image. Liked him gazing at her with that appreciation—and hunger, while looking very much the adventurer she imagined him to be in his travels.

Then his hunger faded. He dropped his head back with a moan and ran one hand through his hair in frustration. "Oh, my God, I didn't stock these pockets."

It didn't sink in at first. Then she realized what he meant. He hadn't brought any condoms.

"I don't suppose this is the kind of place that provides them in the men's room," he added.

"Wanna dash across the hall real quick to find out?" she asked, eyeing him and wagging her brows.

He moved closer, towering over her as he growled, "How can you find this funny?"

Tori nipped at his chest, toyed with one of his flat nipples until it puckered between her fingers. And until he hissed. "Maybe," she finally replied, "because I *stocked* my purse?"

He looked up. "There *is* a God."

Tori had dropped her tiny handbag on the sofa. As she reached for it, she sent up a mental thanks to Sukie, who'd made her take a handful of condoms…just in case. Tori had never expected to need them, but she'd left one in her bag…again, just in case.

Drew didn't need any more urging to continue. She barely had time to reach into the bag and pull out the little packet when he picked her up and lowered her to the sofa. He kissed her, long and sweet, as his hands moved over her body, bringing her to rapturous peaks of pleasure.

He seemed to like the feel of the stockings, because he took delight in stroking her thighs, rising higher and higher, toward the elastic. And above it. But only to tease her, to scrape his fingers across her curls until she clenched and shivered in anticipation, only to move away again.

"More, please," she whispered.

"There are no planters handy for you to bash my head in with," he said as he lowered his mouth to her breast. His tongue flicked out to scrape across her nipple, and she arched her back, giving him more access. He did as she silently demanded, sucking it deep into his mouth until the sensation traveled throughout her body, increasing the throbbing between her thighs.

"I don't feel the need to threaten you tonight," she managed to whisper between choppy breaths. "But you should remember, I do believe in an eye for an eye." Giving him only a second's warning with one evil grin, she pushed him over and moved on top of him. "And a torment for a torment." Then she began to move her lips and hands over his body, delighting in tasting his skin, feeling his strength and his warmth.

"I love doing this with you," she murmured as she kissed a trail across his chest, tasting the ripples of muscle with her tongue.

"That makes two of us."

Finally, unable to take any more, she pulled away and tore the condom open. Drew watched with fire in his eyes while she sheathed him, probably expecting her to keep control. But she didn't want it. She wanted him to ride her this time, slow and deep and strong.

Lying back, she pulled him on top of her, parting her legs and whispering, "Make love to me now."

He did, sliding into her slowly, carefully, again building that pleasure until she could only purr at how good it felt. He continued his leisurely pace until buried completely inside her, kissing her deeply all the while.

They continued like that. Giving and taking. With wet kisses and languorous strokes. Tori whispered things. How much she loved what they did together. How amazing he made her feel. How she never wanted it to end.

He whispered something back. As the passion overwhelmed them and they rode out their climaxes together, she had a hard time focusing on what he'd said. But her heart kept telling her she already knew. His words had imprinted themselves somewhere on her subconscious. *I've fallen in love with you, Tori.*

Her body soared, spiraling with pleasure like she'd never experienced and all her emotions sparked in reaction to what she felt and what she thought those whispered words had been. But her mind got the full picture. And knew she'd now reached the end.

His words meant a million dollars. But she also realized that in the long run they meant losing *him*.

# 10

As Drew could have predicted, Teresa and Tiffany were both eliminated Monday morning. That left Robin, Sukie, Ginny and Tori in the house, the final four competing for the grand prize.

He didn't have any doubt that Tori would win it. Everyone last night had been amazed by the change in her. Even Monahan had approached him Monday night, telling him he'd gone over the tapes from the dance and had been amazed by Tori's grace, beauty and the way she'd charmed everyone she'd met.

He also asked where Drew and Tori had disappeared to during the brief time Sam had lost sight of them. Drew had simply said Tori'd needed some air. Not caring what Monahan made of the fact that it had probably been only ten degrees at midnight. Nor that when they'd returned to the party, Tori's hair was down and loose around her shoulders. Not to mention that she looked like a woman who'd just been well and truly *done*.

The curiosity among the crew, and the rest of the cast, didn't bother him a bit. But it appeared to bother her. Tori had gone back to avoiding him, not showing up for their private lesson, not even coming to his current events class. And when they did run into one another, she'd avoided his eye.

He really needed to do something about that—to convince her she had nothing to be embarrassed about. So they'd made crazy, loud love in a public restroom. And so there'd been a couple of wide-eyed old broads waiting in the corridor when they'd finally unlocked the door and come out.

None of that mattered. Not compared to what they shared. What they felt.

At least, what *he* felt. To his best recollection, he'd been the only one making any serious statement of feelings. He'd told her he loved her. Yeah, it'd been in the height of sexual pleasure, and some men would have blown it off as the heat of the moment. Drew, however, had been prepared to admit it in the cold light of day. But Tori hadn't even asked. Never mentioned it, not there while they lay naked on the sofa. Nor while they dressed. Not during the rest of the dance or the limo ride home.

Even more surprising, when he tried to broach the subject, to assure her he hadn't just been blowing smoke because of their physical relationship, she'd changed the subject. Not too discreetly, either.

It was as if she didn't want to know how he felt about her.

"Ridiculous," he told himself Tuesday morning as he came downstairs for the day. She wanted to know, just not publicly. He could understand that, and was fully prepared to wait until they were out of here before confronting her about his feelings—and her own, which he suspected were the same.

She'd hinted at her concerns over their differences, their backgrounds and lifestyles. He could understand that; after all, he hadn't had a chance to convince her how very much they did have in common. The loss of a parent as a child, instability, lack of money. But they'd talk about that soon.

"Professor, I'm afraid we have a bit of a problem," Niles Monahan said as he spied Drew at the bottom of the stairs.

Drew stiffened, knowing from past experience he

wouldn't like hearing about any of the director's problems—or solutions. "What is it?"

"Well, it is snowing hard out there. You were supposed to have private dates…." The director swallowed hard, rushing to clarify. "I mean outings, with all the remaining contestants. But since Sukie was too sick last night, we're already one behind. We'd planned for you to have lunch out with one and a dinner with another tonight. But that still leaves one out. We discussed adding an intimate breakfast with the fourth girl tomorrow, but we really want the elimination to the final two to take place before that so the last day of taping will be devoted entirely to you and the last two girls."

The man was talking fast, as if nervous, and Drew could figure why. No matter what the hell the director called it, these little "outings" looked like dates, smelled like dates and were, for all practical purposes, dates. That and the way the director had said the last days would focus on the girls and *him* really put his back up.

Then he looked out the window and saw the snow falling, steady and thick, and realized the director did, indeed, have a problem. Drew smiled, not about to complain if snow forced the cancellation of all of these final dates, since he'd thought the idea a ridiculous one to begin with. He'd gone on the one he wanted to—with Tori. Which suited him just fine.

"Gee, sorry to hear about that, buddy," he said. "That stuff's falling so thick, I bet the plows won't be out for hours."

Niles nodded in agreement, then said, "We have thought of something else."

Drew grimaced.

"If you would spend just an hour alone with each lady today, tutoring, dining, taking a sleigh ride, however you want to spend the time, we feel that would be sufficient for us to capture moments with each one of them handling herself with a man."

Didn't sound *too* painful. But he didn't want to let the sweaty little bastard off the hook too quickly. "You're sure the others will be okay with it, since Tori did come to the party with me the other night? She was the only one who got to go off-site, alone."

Monahan smiled his thin little smile. "Oh, I think everyone understood how unique that evening was for her, especially since Sukie and Robin did go to the ballet with you. But to make up for it, we thought we'd let the four ladies dress for dinner this evening and make a special night of it right here in the house."

Him with four dressed-up, aggressive women? "Not a chance."

Niles seemed to have anticipated the reaction. "It won't be *just* you. We'll have all the instructors right there in the reception room. This will be a major test, with all of you casting your votes for which two contestants will proceed to the final round." He crossed his arms and nodded. "Should be much more dramatic this way, anyway, rather than having secret voting."

Okay. A roomful of people. That didn't sound so bad. "I suppose that could work."

"But you'll spend some time alone with each of them today, as well?" Niles prodded.

Drew hesitated, letting the man sweat, then replied, "All right. One hour each."

TORI DIDN'T MIND SO MUCH that Robin got to sit in the sunroom having a private, hour-long breakfast with Drew. Particularly since the woman told her afterward they'd talked primarily about the weather, the house and South American cultures.

She also didn't mind that Sukie spent an hour with him

in the library. Sukie, who seemed to have realized Robin and Tori were the most likely to move on to the next round, had used her hour to pick Drew's brain about what she should do with the money she earned for making it into the final four.

Ginny, however...

"Relax, would you?" Sukie said that afternoon as she lay on her bed, bringing her legs straight up into the air and pointing her toes. Sukie was bored. She exercised when she was bored. She'd been exercising a lot lately, especially since she'd run out of gum and Miss Evelyn had refused to let anyone give her any more.

"They're having a nice little lunch together," Tori muttered.

"Lunch. That's it. Not hot monkey-sex on the dining room table."

Tori snorted. "I think as ladies we're supposed to say, 'Having relations.'"

"I have relations," Sukie said, rolling her eyes. "And they're all going to be hitting me up for money as soon as I get home."

Tori laughed for the first time all day. Sukie was good at brightening her mood.

So was Drew. Drew, the guy currently on a date with a wannabe Playboy bunny out to win a million bucks, who wasn't afraid to use her assets to win.

Tori trusted Drew completely. He was much too decent a guy to sleep with her Sunday night then do anything with Ginny today. Still, Ginny had to know her chances were slipping away. And desperate women... "What if she strips naked and puts those hooters of hers right in his face?"

"Then he'll suffocate," Sukie quipped. "But he won't touch 'em."

That made her feel better. She gave Sukie a smile, watching her move from leg-lifts to sit-ups.

They both watched the clock. For some reason, Sukie was now as anxious as Tori to see what would happen. She suspected Sukie had figured out something had gone on between her and Drew the other night at the party. Tori sure hadn't told her anything, but she wouldn't put it past her new friend to do some condom counting. Ever since then, Sukie had been practically bouncing in excitement, saying she was certain Tori was going to waltz out of here a millionaire.

Tori hadn't had the heart to burst her bubble. Because waltzing out of here a millionaire was the *last* thing she wanted to do. Oh, sure, the money would be nice. Nice, hell, it would be *fabulous.* But whoever the old guy was who'd said money couldn't buy happiness had been on to something. Because money couldn't buy Drew. And Drew, she truly believed, was the key to her future happiness.

It was like that Lady and the Tiger story they'd been reading in the literature and grammar lessons with Mr. Halloway. She didn't have to choose a door, but rather a path for her future. And whichever way she chose, she was taking a big risk.

"Here she comes," Sukie hissed. They both heard someone stomping down the corridor outside their room. Leaping out of the bed, Sukie dashed to the door and pulled it open to peek out. "It's Ginny all right. Ooh, she looks mad. She's slamming—"

She didn't have to finish her sentence. Tori heard the door to the next bedroom slam shut.

"Whew," she whispered. Obviously things hadn't gone however Ginny had wanted them to.

"Now it's your turn," Sukie said. "You ready?"

Tori nodded, looking down at her thickly corded slacks, her bulky sweater and the long black coat Evelyn had produced for her. "I've never been on a sleigh ride. Shew, I've hardly ever seen snow before this trip."

"You'll love it. The only trouble is you can't get naked and do the nasty out in the snow in this weather. Something's liable to freeze off."

Sukie's sassy good humor hadn't changed a bit from the day they'd arrived, and Tori had never been more glad of it. Though she'd never reached out to hug another woman who wasn't kin, she couldn't help grabbing Sukie and yanking her close. Sukie grunted, then threw her arms around Tori's shoulders, hugging her back. "Have fun."

"I will."

"Oh, wait," Sukie said, letting go to dash over to her dresser. She drew out a pair of thick gloves. "You said you didn't have any." She held them out, and watched as Tori put them on.

"You're a very nice person," Tori whispered. "I'm going to miss you when this is over."

"They have airports in Tennessee?"

Tori nodded.

"Then you'll be seeing me."

With a little wave, Tori left the room and went downstairs to meet Drew for their sleigh ride. He was waiting for her at the bottom of the stairs again. But this time, he looked more like the abominable snowman than Rhett Butler.

"You in there?" she asked, seeing only his face beneath the hat and behind the scarf.

"It's cold as hell out there," he said, taking her arm as she reached the bottom of the steps.

"Hell's hot, from what I hear."

"Okay, it's cold as...as..."

"As a well-digger's butt in January," Tori declared, the old southern expression coming easily to her lips.

"That works."

Taking her gloved hand in his, he led her outside. In front of the house, an old-fashioned looking sleigh waited. Tori'd never seen one, except in movies, and she smiled, thinking how perfect it was for this time of year. Christmas was this Saturday, and she was *finally* beginning to feel the spirit of the season. "I feel like one of Santa's helpers."

"Only with horses instead of reindeer."

"And with a human driver instead of an elf," she agreed, watching the driver hop down from his seat to help her up.

Once inside the sleigh, Tori scooted over to make room for Drew on the crushed red-velvet seat, then moved closer to him to share the warmth.

The driver placed a lap rug over their legs. "Snow's died down enough. Should be a beautiful ride. My name's Anthony, and I'm wearing earplugs." Smiling a big, toothy smile that revealed a gold cap on one front tooth, he added, "Of course, that little tiny camera ain't."

"We're used to it," Tori said, staring at the hated device carefully mounted near the base of the sleigh, protected from the elements by a decorative ledge and some Plexiglas.

"Careful not to kick it, now," Anthony said with a broad wink. Then he hopped into the front seat, clicked his tongue and tapped the reins.

Riding in the sleigh over the new-fallen snow was almost like flying. That was the only comparison Tori could make. They didn't go too fast, but they glided over the ground like a bird gliding over water, just skimming the surface and following the waves. Free and clean and fresh. Her breaths misted in front of her and snow landed softly on her face and eyelashes. She licked them off her lips, laughing at the simple pleasure of it.

"I love this," she said with a happy smile.

Drew took her hand beneath the lap rug. "I'm glad."

"I think I might actually miss the snow when I go back home. We don't get much in my part of Tennessee."

He turned in the seat a little, so their eyes met. "You really plan to go back?"

"Well, sure, what else would I do?"

His brown eyes stared into hers, serious and intense, saying a million things that couldn't be said aloud over the whistle of the wind…and into the powerful microphone of the camera. Finally, though, he murmured, "You can't go home again. I mean, of course you'll want to be with your family for Christmas."

Oh, if only he knew how she really wanted to spend Christmas. This one and every one after.

With him.

"But after that, you can't just step back into your old life, as if you'd never left. You know that, don't you?"

She said nothing.

"I mean, you're not the girl you were a couple of weeks ago. You can't go back to a life with no books and no education prospects except the Garage of Higher Learning."

Lowering her gaze, she dropped her lashes to half shield her eyes. Whatever happened, whether she stayed or left, Drew deserved to know she'd at least begun thinking about a different kind of future for herself. Beyond what she'd always planned. She had drive and ambition and hunger.

He'd given her those, too. As well as a full heart.

"There's a community college about an hour away from home," she admitted.

"That's a start." Then he squeezed her hand beneath the rug. "But there are lots of community colleges. Lots of them up north, too."

Oh, lordy, he was saying so much, without saying a thing. Almost asking her to say, but not putting it into words for the rest of the world to hear and chew over two months from now. It was so hard, so intrusive and voyeuristic. But, she reminded herself, she was the one who'd chosen to remain here. To open up her most private life to the TV world.

She'd just never imagined she'd be opening up her *heart*, too. Especially not now, when it was nearly broken, knowing she wasn't going to get her fairy-tale happily-ever-after. Not once Drew found out she'd been lying to him. He'd see nothing but the money. The competition. And he'd never forgive her.

She could stay to see that condemnation in his eyes, and fight to make him understand why she'd done it. Or she could go now and cut her losses, praying he'd forgive her over time and track her down in Tennessee.

Right now, at this moment, she honestly didn't know which she'd choose. "I didn't say I wanted to go to college," she said, forcing the words out of her mouth. "I might think about it. But I like what I do."

"Driving? Being a mechanic?"

She heard the disbelief in his voice. Of course he wouldn't believe her, she didn't even sound convincing to herself. But she pressed on. "You ever think I might like my world? Okay, so I wanted to learn. I can do that without having to change everything about myself. I like my family and I like racing and I like Sheets Creek." Gulping, she told the biggest lie of them all. "I'm ready to go back to my world. I don't know that I want to be a part of this one."

He just stared, saying nothing. The wind picked up, whistling a little as they sped by. The scrape of the sleigh's rails cutting through the new snow faded away, drowned out by the sound of Tori's own heart beating. Her blood pulsing through her veins. That voice in her head telling her she was making a mistake trying to push him away now.

"Tori," Drew finally said, keeping his voice low and intimate. "I don't want you to leave."

Oh, this was so unfair. So wrong. She wanted the moment to be private and special. Intimate. Just for her. Not for the whole cable-TV-watching public. "Don't," she said, glancing at the camera.

He shrugged, obviously not caring. "To hell with them. My private life isn't anybody else's goddamn business. They can edit this out because this stupid TV show has nothing to do with *me*. With us." He glanced down at the camera. "You hear me, Mueller? I agreed to teach here, I didn't agree to become a monkey in this damned circus." Then he turned his stare back at her. "Tori, I mean it. I know you care for me. You don't want to go. That's just…fear talking."

She stiffened. "You're calling me a coward?"

"Will you stay and prove me wrong if I do?" Then he tightened his hold on her hand. "Forget I said that. I know you're not a coward. But you're facing a choice here, one you didn't even know you'd be making when you came here just a couple of weeks ago. It's not unusual for you to have misgivings." He leaned closer, so he could brush his lips lightly across her temple. "You just can't let them drive you away. Not from me. I lo—"

"Look, a deer!" Tori squealed, desperate for a distraction. She could not let Drew say those words. Could not let him whisper he loved her. Not when that camera and the powerful microphone would pick up every word.

God in heaven, he'd just flat out said this TV show had nothing to do with him. The man had no more of a clue today than he did on day one that the show was *all* about him. And when he found out, he was going to look like a fool. In front of the world. How cruel a trick to play on a man so filled with honor and goodness and dignity.

She was so disgusted with herself she could barely breathe.

"Tori…"

"I swear it was a deer," she said, pulling away from him to sit at the very edge of the seat. She wouldn't turn around, wouldn't look at him. She couldn't, not without bursting into tears or telling him the truth herself.

Even if she did, it wouldn't matter at this point. The damage was done. There were tons of footage of him being stalked by every woman in this house—they'd get their show, and he'd still be at the center of it.

She had to convince Drew that he meant more to her than a million dollars. Had to make him truly believe she'd really fallen in love with him, for all the right reasons and not for any financial ones. Maybe, if she could make him believe that, if she could prove it beyond all doubt, he could forgive her for the rest.

And as far as Tori could see, there was only one way to prove it.

Which she intended to do. Tonight.

AS SOON AS THEY GOT BACK to the house, Tori disappeared, still refusing to talk to him. To listen. To look him in the eye, for God's sake. She'd removed herself mentally from him and nothing he could say or do was going to bring her back. Until she was ready to admit what was wrong, to face her insecurities and decide what the hell she wanted out of her life, he was completely helpless.

He paced a lot that day, and skipped dinner altogether. More than anything, he wanted to march down the hall to her bedroom, bang on the door and drag her out of this house. Maybe away from the cameras, from all the prying eyes, she'd have a chance to get her head together. To figure out she did love him, damn it. And would let him admit it out loud, too.

By eight o'clock that evening, when the cocktail party was set to begin, his mood had grown even darker. He hadn't expected her to fly into his arms and say she'd forget about her father and her brothers and her whole life for him. Still, for the first time ever, he'd tried to tell a woman he truly loved her, and she'd practically thrown his declaration back into his face before he'd even been able to voice it.

Dressed in a suit and tie, since the evening was supposed to be an elegant one, he made his way downstairs to the large reception room. The owners of the house apparently entertained a lot, for there was another bar in here, even larger and more well stocked than the one in the library. The comfortable furniture was arranged in small groupings around the perimeter, with the large center area available for dancing, should the occasion demand it.

"No dancing," he told himself as he walked into the place. It was already loud, brimming with conversation and excitement. Everyone on the crew was here. Every one of the instructors—right down to a frowning Mr. Halloway, who watched them all with blatant disapproval even as he sipped from an enormous martini.

Ginny, dressed in a low-cut black cocktail dress, stood chatting with one of the camera operators. Judging by the way she kept bending closer, she knew he was staring down her dress and she didn't care.

Drew somehow didn't suspect she was going to be named lady of them all.

Sukie and Robin spoke quietly with the director, while Jacey and Sam circled the room, getting shots from every angle possible.

The only person missing was Tori.

"Where is she?" Drew asked Jacey as soon as she came within earshot.

"Who?"

He just stared until she shrugged, admitting, "I haven't seen her come down yet."

She'd better not stay in her room. If she chickened out on this event, he'd go up and drag her down here by the hair. Because in truth, she would only avoid tonight to avoid *him*.

At half-past eight, just when he thought he was going to have to march upstairs and kick her door in to get her to face him, he heard a rumble of conversation roll across the room. He was standing near the fireplace, sipping a gin-and-tonic, barely paying attention as the party continued all around him.

"Hey, y'all!"

That got his attention. That loud, twangy voice definitely interrupted his thoughts.

"Sorry I'm late. Shew-ee, I had a hell of a time finding my long underwear. Somebody musta hid 'em on me and it's too dang cold to go around without 'em. My ass about turned numb today on that sleigh ride."

Drew closed his eyes. He didn't have to turn around, didn't have to see, to know exactly what was happening. Her strident tone and heavy accent were proof enough. Not to mention the shocked silence that had descended in the room.

"Didj'all save any good food? I ain't had me a decent meal in days. Mr. Monahan, if ya only ordered finger food or some'a them slimy-as-snot snails, I might have to tan yer hide."

Finally, his eyes still closed, he slowly turned on his heel. Then, sending up a silent prayer that he'd misheard, he opened them to see Tori. Not the Tori they'd all come to know and love as she transformed into the elegant woman he'd escorted Sunday night. But the rough-edged, loud and gruff Tori who'd shown up here two and a half weeks ago.

She wore faded jeans and her scruffy black boots. Her flannel shirt hung down over her hips and was not only slightly dusty, but also misbuttoned. Her hair was slung up in a casual ponytail and her face completely bare of makeup.

And her expression was pure evil.

On any other occasion, he would have loved seeing this wild, exuberant side of her again. He'd wanted her from first glance, when she'd been exactly the girl appearing here tonight. Her clothes, her speech, her attitude—none of them made any difference to how he felt about her. He'd take her however he could get her...on any other night.

But not tonight.

*Tori, what are you doing?*

Even as he wondered, he suspected he already knew the answer: Tori was throwing the game.

She'd listened to what he'd said today, looked at her future from every angle and decided which one she wanted. Fear, uncertainty and lack of confidence had convinced her to go back home to Tennessee. To go back to the life she'd never thought she'd leave. This was how she'd chosen to do it.

He'd never taken her for a coward, so the disappointment flooding his body landed as hard as a punch in his gut. A pounding began in his head, the pulse throbbing in his temple. His jaw clenching, he met her stare over the crowd, not even trying to hide his anger and disappointment.

She didn't so much as flinch. She met that stare evenly, telling him without words that her decision was made.

Well, so be it. If she'd chosen to step back, to run away, he wasn't going to stand in her way. Which was why, at the end of the evening, he voted along with all the other instructors on who would leave. Ginny, of course.

And Tori Lyons.

# 11

THROUGHOUT THE EVENING, while Tori had done everything she could to deliberately destroy her chances to proceed to the final round of *Hey, Make Me Over* by being as obnoxious, uncouth and unladylike as possible, she'd kept her mind on Drew. On her feelings for him, and his for her. And their future. Because if she'd thought about tonight, she might have just sat down in the middle of the floor and cried. The anger in him...the disappointment in his eyes...well, the weight of them had nearly crushed her, *nearly* made her give in. But she didn't.

*He'll understand tomorrow,* she kept telling herself.

He'd understand, and maybe even find it in himself to forgive her for not being honest with him from the beginning. That was her hope, anyway, the one hope she'd held on to while she'd belched and spilled and slurped her way through the party.

Sukie had cried. Robin had been shocked. The only one who'd looked like she understood was Jacey. The camerawoman had stared at her good and hard, then, never saying a word, had given her one slow nod of encouragement.

That nod had been like a life ring thrown to a drowning person, and Tori had held on to it for as long as she could, using it to remind herself she was doing the right thing.

Nobody else on the crew seemed to think so. Mr. Monahan had looked like he wanted to strangle her for ruining things for him…which, she had to concede, she had. Viewers wouldn't be happy if there wasn't some romantic happily-ever-after. But she didn't care. The only way she was going to get her *real* happily-ever-after was by destroying her TV one.

But it sure didn't feel like any happily-ever-afters were coming her way as she and Ginny shared the lonely limo ride from the mansion down to a local hotel where they'd be staying for the night. Thank God the snow had stopped this afternoon and the roads had been plowed for traffic. Because if she'd had to stay in that house, if she'd had to face him, she wasn't sure she could have survived it without completely breaking down.

"You okay?" Ginny asked softly, patting Tori's hand in the darkness of the back seat.

Tori nodded, sniffing and blinking her eyes to stop the tears that had been threatening to fall since the minute the car door had shut in her face.

"You did it on purpose, huh?"

"How'd you guess?" Tori asked, her question sarcastic.

Ginny obviously didn't quite get sarcasm. "Well, you didn't much act tonight like you did all last week. At first I thought you had stage fright, like some actress or something. Then I saw Sukie and Robin crying, and I figured it out. You fell in love with the professor for real, and you know he's going to be pretty upset about this game, huh?"

"That's it," Tori admitted, not really wanting to talk about it, but unable to get away.

Ginny sighed deeply. "I've seen it in movies and read about it in books, but I never in my wildest dreams would have believed somebody would walk away from a million bucks for a man."

Tori stared straight ahead into the darkness of the glass separating them from the driver. Speaking almost as much to herself as to the other woman, she told them both the absolute truth. What was in her heart. "He's worth it."

Ginny didn't say anything for a while. Then she patted Tori's hand again. "I just hope he someday understands that *you're* worth it, too."

"So, Professor, you happy with the last two prospects for Grand Poobah lady of them all?"

Drew paused as he stood behind the bar in the library, pouring himself a drink. He certainly needed one after the evening he'd just had. Voting Tori out of here had been so hard, so bloody hard.

But it was what she'd wanted. What she'd practically demanded.

"Frankly, Jacey," he said, bringing his drink to his lips, "I don't give a damn."

The camerawoman closed the doors behind her and sauntered into the room. "Pour me one?"

Retrieving a glass, he made another gin-and-tonic and slid it across the bar to the woman who watched him in silence, her dark eyes assessing. Almost judgmental.

"What?"

She shrugged, sipping her drink.

"You have something to say?" he snapped.

Jacey lowered her glass to the bar and wiped her mouth with the back of her hand. Darn but she was a feisty little thing. Like Tori, only without the down-home sweetness.

"Why'd you let her go?"

Drew's eyes narrowed.

"Why'd you vote off the one woman who actually deserves to win this thing? Who's actually transformed herself in front of all our eyes into a damned amazing woman?"

Walking around the bar, Drew dropped into the nearest chair and stared at her. "It was her choice to go."

"She said that?"

"God, Jacey, did you not see the way she was dressed? The way she acted?"

The woman plopped onto the sofa sitting across from him, and waved an airy hand, as if his words meant nothing. "An act."

"Well, of course it was an act. She wanted to get out of here."

Jacey just stared. "And why, do you suppose, did she want that?"

Leaning back in his chair, Drew extended his legs out in front of him and crossed his ankles. His whole body felt weary. Drained. As if he'd just run a long race only to come in a split second behind the winner.

Defeat. That's what this felt like.

"I think she was afraid," he finally admitted, knowing Jacey still awaited his answer. "She realized her entire life was going to have to change, and in the end she didn't have the guts to go for it."

Snorting, Jacey began to shake her head. "You're whacked. That girl's got more guts than any ten guys I know."

"Well, what other explanation is there? What possible reason would she have for doing what she did?"

Jacey put her drink on the coffee table and leaned forward to drop her elbows onto her knees. Her expression troubled, she said, "Can I ask you a personal question?"

Warily, he replied, "Depends on the question."

"Did you tell her you love her?" Then, looking up at the camera watching silently in the corner of the room, she threw her hand up, palm out. "Wait, don't answer that."

He hadn't planned to.

"Do you care for her?"

"And this is your business because…?"

Jacey sighed deeply, running her hand over her brow, then rubbing at the corners of her eyes with two fingers. Finally, as if reaching some difficult decision, she looked up at the camera and said four words that made absolutely no sense to him.

"I'm sorry, old man."

"What? Jacey, if you know something about Tori, I wish you'd just come out and say it."

Returning her attention to him, she blurted out the last thing he expected to hear. "She did it for you. Because she loves you more than she loves the million bucks she could win if she stays long enough to get you to admit you love her on-camera."

Drew's jaw dropped. So did his heart. It took him a long moment to come to grips with what she'd said.

Jacey didn't elaborate. She didn't have to. Everything, the whole scenario, unfolded in his brain with perfect clarity. The women. The aggression. The dates. The romance.

Christ, he'd been completely set up. This was just another variation of the classic romance reality show, only, this time, he was the sucker who wasn't in on the gag. The makeovers, the lessons, none of it mattered. The only agenda was to put him in a house with a bunch of attractive women and try to make him fall in love, with the women using every sexy weapon in their arsenal.

His fingers clenched so tightly on his glass that he feared he'd break it. Needing to, he flung it toward the fireplace, watching as the remaining alcohol sent the flames shooting even higher and the shards of glass disappeared beneath the ash.

"I'm gonna kill that producer," he growled.

"No, you're not," Jacey said evenly, "because he's my father, and you owe me one for telling you the truth now."

He didn't even stop to analyze that tidbit. He could focus only on Tori. "She knew this? From day one? From the minute we met?"

Jacey shook her head. "No. None of the women found out until that first Sunday morning at breakfast."

The first Sunday. The morning after they met. *After* their first time in the greenhouse when he'd asked Tori to stay…and she'd agreed. That, at least, was some comfort.

Jacey continued. "The women all thought they were part of a social makeover show, and they still are. You were just a…side benefit."

The glare he shot her would have made some women back away. Jacey swallowed visibly, but rose from the couch and stepped closer to him, anyway. "You're supposed to be a smart guy, Professor."

His teeth were clenched so tightly together, it was hard to get words past them. "Your point being?"

"Meaning, stop being all pissed off long enough to think it through." Her voice lowered and her expression softened. "Really think it through, Dr. Bennett. Why Tori left and when she did it."

"She probably left so she wouldn't have to look me in the eye when I found out I'd been duped and deceived by her and every other person in this house of lies."

"By which point," Jacey continued, "she'd have been a million bucks richer. Or are you going to deny that you tried to tell her something *very* important during your sleigh ride this afternoon?"

That made him pause. A million dollars. For a declaration of love. Which he'd not only been about to offer her today during their ride, but he'd *also* said to her Sunday night. Out of camera range, true, but he'd said it. So when you came right down to it, Tori had already won the game, she'd only had to prove it by getting him to say it again. On tape.

But she'd stopped him today. Given up her chance.

It made no sense. If she'd stuck around for the money, why the hell would she have thrown it away, walked away when it was within her grasp?

"Are all men totally stupid, or just the smart ones who

analyze things too much?" Jacey said, sounding impatient and disgusted.

"Oh, my God," he whispered as the truth dawned with all the warmth and brilliance of a morning sun. He felt like someone had thrown him in a blender, spun him around for a couple of weeks, then tossed him out, only to learn he'd been transformed into something good. Something amazing.

A man in love. A man who was loved in return.

She'd thrown away her chance at a million dollars—a huge sum of money that could have done wonders for her and for her family. And she'd done it because she'd known that if she'd stayed, if she'd won the money, Drew would never know the truth.

That she really *did* love him.

He thought he was right. He *hoped* he was right. But there was only one way to be sure. Only one person who could tell him.

"Where is she?" he said, already striding toward the door.

Jacey hurried after him. "At a hotel in town. But it started snowing again an hour ago, really heavy. I just heard the roads closed back down because the plows can't keep up."

Drew's whole body tensed in frustration. "There's got to be another way."

Suddenly, he thought of one. Pausing only long enough to give Jacey a slight nod, he said, "I'm going after her. I'll say thank you for telling me now, but that doesn't mean I'm forgiving you for what happened here."

She nodded, her eyes suspiciously bright. That hint of brightness gave Drew pause. His curiosity getting the better of him, he asked, "Why'd you do it? Why'd you tell me tonight and ruin the big TV moment?"

Jacey shrugged. "Maybe because I've been where she is. And I want to believe the stepsister or the girl-next-door sometimes does get the happily-ever-after."

There was more, he knew it, he could see the emotion on Jacey's face. She was hurting, too, for some reason, and he sensed she had her own romantic battles ahead.

But that was for Jacey to deal with. Right now, he cared only about his own. So with one more nod of thanks, he stalked to the foyer, grabbed his heavy coat, then stormed out the front door. Heading directly toward the stables. And the sleigh.

Once he was gone, Jacey just stared at the door for a long moment, until she heard footsteps racing up behind her. She looked around in time to see Niles Monahan, panting and out of breath. "I just saw you talking to Drew, and he ran out of here. Where's he gone?"

Jacey smiled. "To get his fair lady."

TORI SAT UP LATE into the night, watching the thick snowflakes hit the window of her hotel room. They gathered at its base, rising higher and higher, until she had to stand to look outside, unable to see from her chair.

The snow was peaceful. Soothing on this silent night. Appropriate for a few nights before Christmas. She'd had a few white Christmases, when they'd gone up to visit family in the mountains for the holidays. But not any in a while.

She wished she'd have this one. Wished more than anything that she could stay here, anticipating the holiday with Drew. They wouldn't need prettily wrapped presents, not when they could give each other the gifts of love and emotion.

*And sex.*

Yeah, that, too. She didn't think she'd ever be able to make love with anyone else again, not after having something so perfect with Drew. He'd been joking, but he'd been right the other morning when he said she'd never want any other *ride.*

She sniffed a little, replaying that conversation—every

conversation, really, that they'd shared over the past few weeks. She was going to miss him terribly.

"Please, Drew," she whispered, "please realize why I did it and find me. Soon." Then, clasping her fingers in her lap, she added, "Lord, if you can help him make it by Christmas, that'd suit me just fine."

At that moment, the jingling of bells interrupted her little prayer. If it had been Christmas Eve, she would have thought a mama or a daddy was playing a sweet-natured prank on their little ones, jingling the bells as Santa landed on their roof.

The jingle bells grew closer, louder in the silent night. She doubted anyone who was asleep would be wakened by them, but for her, probably the only soul not sleeping in this hotel, they filled her head completely.

Curious, she rubbed a spot away on the glass and peeked out. Just in time to see the sleigh come into view. It resembled the one she and Drew had ridden in earlier that day, which made her heart clench up again.

When the sleigh drew closer to the streetlight, and she got a better look at the smiling driver, she gasped. There'd been a flash of gold in that smile. "Anthony!"

Her heart went into overdrive, beating rapidly until her pulse drummed in her ears. Almost holding her breath, she peered harder, mentally urging the sleigh to move closer so she could see if it held any passenger. One specific passenger.

Then the sleigh moved.

And she saw it did.

"Oh, *thank you*, Lord, that was the fastest-answered prayer I've ever heard of," she muttered even as she grabbed for her coat and pulled it on over her pajamas. She yanked her boots on, too, not bothering to tie them, then raced out the door onto the second-floor balcony.

"Drew!" she said in a whisper that masqueraded as a shout.

He looked up immediately. Met her stare for the longest moment Tori had ever experienced in her whole entire life.

Then that mouth widened into a smile. And everything was right with the world again.

She ran for the steps, tripping down them two at a time while he approached from the bottom. When they got close enough, Tori launched herself down, landing with an *oomph* in his arms. Then those arms closed around her and he hauled her close, covering her mouth with his for a sweet, wonderful, hungry and loving kiss.

When they parted, she gazed up at him, wanting to ask a bunch of questions, not quite knowing where to begin.

He beat her to the punch by answering the most important one. "I know about the show."

She watched him warily.

"I know you were all supposed to try to get me to fall in love with you."

"Sukie?" she asked.

He shook his head. "Jacey."

That surprised her for only a moment. Then it made sense. Frowning in concern, she asked, "Are you okay?" Not waiting for his answer, she hurried on. "Of course you're not okay. It's awful and embarrassing and humiliating and I'm so sorry I ever had anything to do with it."

When she'd finished babbling, he said, "You could have won."

She nodded.

"You walked away."

Another nod was all she could manage.

"Because you love me."

He wasn't asking. The man was stating a fact. Relief flooded through her whole body and she smiled, wanting to jump up and down and shout loud enough to wake up the whole hotel.

He understood. And miracle of miracles, judging by the loving way he was looking at her, he believed.

"I do," she finally said, her voice breaking with emotion. "I love you so much, and I'd never in this lifetime want you to think you were nothing but a dollar sign to me."

"A million dollar signs," he pointed out.

"Don't remind me," she said with a light groan. Then she cupped his cheek in her hand. He instantly covered her cold fingers, protecting her skin, warming her.

"You're worth it, Drew. I wouldn't risk losing you for every penny on this earth. I love you with all my heart."

Lowering his mouth to hers again, he kissed her deeply, hungrily, as if wanting to taste the words she'd just said. When they finally parted, sharing a few icy cold breaths, he whispered, "I love you, too, Tori Lyons. Sassy race-car driver and lady of them all, I love you for everything you are."

Smiling gently as tears rose in the corners of her eyes, only to freeze there, she said, "And that is the most perfect Christmas present I will ever get."

"It's not Christmas yet."

"Soon."

"Will you spend it with me?"

She nodded. "Have anything special in mind?"

"Oh, yes. Very special. In New York."

She suspected she knew what he meant. He wanted to walk into that ball on Christmas Eve with her on his arm. To let the producer and the director and the TV crew— and all those *watching*—that what they'd found, what they'd learned, had risen above everything and everyone around them.

The TV show couldn't cheapen their relationship ever again.

She could think of nothing more wonderful—more perfect—than to spend the evening with the love of her life, and the wonderful friends she'd made. Sukie. Robin. Jacey.

They'd be there, she felt sure. The final four contestants had been invited to attend, to watch the winner be crowned. The rest of the world could think whatever they wanted. Those who knew her would understand completely if she arrived with her *real* prize. Drew.

"That sounds like a perfect way to spend Christmas."

"And you'll spend every one hereafter with me, too?"

"Was that some kind of proposal?"

"A lousy one," he admitted, his voice starting to shake with the cold. "But if I drop to one knee I'm afraid my pants will freeze to the steps and I'll never be able to get up."

She giggled, realizing that in spite of being warmed by love, it was frigging *frigid* out here.

"I'll give you a proper proposal when you're ready. After you figure out where you're going and what you want to do."

Grabbing a fistful of his coat, she pulled him close. "Just don't you stop making love to me in the meantime, mister big-shot professor." Kissing the tip of his icy nose, she added, "And my future is with *you*." Almost unable to contain her excitement, she rattled off all the plans and dreams that had been spinning around in her head for days. "I want to go to school, and live with you, and make babies with you, and be a mechanical engineer, and teach our little ones to read, and marry you, and go on trips with you to the Amazon, and see every museum and art gallery in Washington, and learn how to speak French and…"

"All at the same time?" he asked, laughing and shaking his head at the same time.

"In whatever order it suits us."

She shivered a bit, but not from the cold. It was from the possibilities rolling out in front of her. In front of them.

Endless, glorious possibilities.

Seeing her shiver, he looked down. His eyes widened when he saw her pajamas under her unbuttoned coat. "My

God, Tori, you're going to freeze to death before you can learn one French word, much less make any babies." He immediately started to button her up.

"So come upstairs and keep me warm, big man," she said with a teasing grin.

"I think my entire body is frozen from the neck down."

"I think I can thaw certain parts of you out pretty quickly," she promised with a saucy toss of her head.

"I'm counting on it," he retorted, his eyes glittering and hungry. "But until my legs rise fifty degrees back to room temperature after that sleigh ride, you might have to do the driving." His tone was just as suggestive.

"I'm a good driver," she teased.

"I've heard that about you."

She walked faster, the excitement warming her as she thought of the long, sensuous night to come. In a bed. A real *bed*.

"Tori?" he said, as they stopped in front of her door, still open from her dash outside. Good thing, since she hadn't grabbed a key.

"Yes?"

"Will you do something for me?"

"Anything."

He caught her fingers and brought them to his mouth, pressing a gentle kiss there. And suddenly, she began to feel a bit like that lady fair.

Finally, with love shining in his eyes, he whispered, "Don't ever change."

# 12

JACEY HADN'T BEEN BACK to New York in a few weeks, so when she called Digg to let him know she'd be in town for Christmas Eve, she honestly wasn't sure what to expect. Would he welcome her? Be angry that she'd left? Be ready to end things, or ready to start all over again? Whatever the case, she was going to meet with him, face to face, and start working on the problems in their relationship. She loved the man, and he was worth any concessions she had to make to work things out.

Tori Lyons had just given up a million dollars for the man she loved, for cripe's sake. Jacey oughta be able to put up with a disapproving future mother-in-law. But she was still nervous. Because she'd left pretty suddenly and she and Digg hadn't seen each other since.

The Lady of Them All Ball was being held at a new ritzy Manhattan hotel that catered to the rich and tacky. It wasn't one of the old-school elegant establishments, which would be much too highbrow to allow camera crews from a reality show into their midst. But this one did just fine. It was gaudy and glittering, just right for reality TV and everything it entailed.

To her great surprise, her father had flown in to attend. She wasn't sure he'd even be speaking to her after what she'd done on the set of *Hey, Make Me Over*. He'd said a few words on the phone after the show had wrapped—and he'd gotten a full report from a furious Niles Monahan—but he hadn't blown his stack. When he met up with her in the lobby of the hotel, a few minutes before the ball was to start, she figured out why.

"I've got the most fabulous idea for a new show," he said, his voice nearly bellowing, as he kissed her on the cheek in greeting. "The last one might not have had the romance we wanted, but we will still crown our lady fair. And we'll get the romance next time. I've signed a former actress to be a damsel and I'm going to have men compete in physical challenges for her favor."

"Sounds stupid," Jacey said, rolling her eyes, though secretly glad he wasn't holding a grudge. She hadn't had the heart to tell him that a romance really *had* developed on the set of this show. It didn't seem the right time, besides which, she hadn't even heard from Tori or Drew since he'd taken off after her in that blizzard Tuesday night.

"I dunno, sounds pretty smart to me," a voice said. "Some women need to be *convinced* they're loved."

Digg. Oh, God, it was Digg. She'd know that smooth, slightly accented voice anywhere. Turning toward him, she saw his familiar handsome face, his dazzling white smile that had captivated half the women in America on TV last fall. He looked the same, all except for the classic black tuxedo, so different from his usual casual Hispanic firefighter look.

She'd never seen anything that looked better. Sucking in a deep breath, she threw herself into his arms. Hugging him tightly, she said, "I'm sorry I left. We have a lot to talk about. I've learned so much. I know I can't blame you for what's wrong if you don't even know what's happening."

He kissed her softly, cupping her face in one hand to stare at her with those deep brown eyes. "Welcome back. And we do have some talking to do. You won't be running out on me again anytime soon, will you?"

Burt, who'd been standing there watching them with a

knowing smile on his face, stepped over and clapped Digg on the back. "Well, you know I'm counting on my daughter to be part of my next few projects. I need her help...in a few areas."

For the first time, Jacey noticed a troubled frown on her father's face, but she didn't have time to evaluate it. Right now she had to introduce him to the man she loved.

After she did, they shook hands and Digg murmured, "I don't know if I can take these long separations. We might have to do something about that."

Jacey was distracted by the arrival of some of the girls from the show, so she didn't have time to question that funny twinkle in Digg's eye, or the way he and her father exchanged a secretive look. Swinging her camera up and into action, she focused on Sukie and Ginny, who'd arrived together and were being escorted by two studs Burt had hired for the evening. Judging by the way Ginny was rubbing the arm of hers, there might be some romance here tonight, after all.

"Is our lady fair here yet?" Burt asked, whispering softly.

Jacey shook her head, zooming in on the girls as they entered the ballroom and oohed and aahed over the decorations. There were already a number of people here; invitations had been sent out all over the place and a lot of New Yorkers who'd have otherwise spent the holiday home alone had ventured out for a festive Christmas Eve.

Sukie didn't seem to mind not having won. Jacey figured she'd been shocked just to make it into the final two. They *all* had been, once Tori had removed herself from the running.

In the end, the crown had gone to Robin, by a five to one vote. Only old Mr. Halloway had gone the other way, mumbling something about not entirely trusting Robin. Since Robin was one of the few Jacey had actually liked, she'd ignored the old man's mutterings.

"Ahh, here she is," Burt said, clapping his hands together as Robin came in on the arm of yet another stud.

She looked beautiful, tall and slim and so elegant in her long sapphire-blue gown. It was tailored to de-emphasize her rather broad shoulders and flatter her slim waist and hips. And she looked so happy, Jacey almost wanted to clap for her.

This reality show thing had been pretty stupid. But it had had its moments. This was shaping up to be one of them.

As the party progressed, Robin met with some of the members of the press who'd been invited. She did on-the-spot interviews, and agreed to make the rounds on some network morning shows. Then, at close to midnight, Burt took the stage and cleared his throat to make the final announcement about Robin's triumph.

The writers had written his speech, so it went off like clockwork, including his grand flourishing bow as he concluded, "And now please welcome the lady of them all, Miss Robin Calvin."

Robin was blushing, tears streaming down her face as she walked toward the small stage set up on the dance floor. She continued to cry, causing her makeup to smear down in thick black streaks as she was escorted up the steps.

"Please accept this as a token of our very high esteem, Miss Calvin," Burt said. He extended a velvet box, which Jacey knew held a sapphire necklace worth a cool ten grand.

Robin accepted it, kissed Burt on the cheek, then turned to face her clapping audience.

It was like a frigging beauty pageant, only, this time, the winner hadn't been trained from birth to always wear a plastic smile and parrot ideas about world peace and freedom. She was a real woman. A genuine, down-to-her-toes American girl who'd worked hard to improve herself to *earn* this moment.

"This is pretty good stuff," she murmured to Digg, who

stood right beside her, watching, a quiet, soothing presence as always.

"Nicely done," he replied. "Congratulations."

Burt had left the stage and reached them in time to hear Digg's comment. "Thanks." He clapped his hands together, rubbing them in glee, adding, "This is perfect, absolutely perfect." Then he shrugged. "Okay, not perfect. An engagement would have been perfect. But this is pretty damn good."

Jacey smiled and continued to tape, sending up a silent little Christmas prayer that somewhere, Drew and Tori were celebrating an engagement tonight.

"Ladies and gentlemen, I can't begin to tell you how much this means to me," Robin said into the microphone. The crowd's applause died off in anticipation of her remarks. "Ever since I was a teenager, I've dreamed of wearing a beautiful gown and glittering jewels and being among all you elegant people, feeling like I truly belonged somewhere, at last."

"Schmaltzy," Burt whispered, "but good."

Jacey ignored him, holding the shot steady.

"Tonight is especially sweet, for another reason," Robin said, giving the crowd another huge smile. "Because not only can I celebrate it on my own behalf, but I can share it, with all those others out there like me, who were unfortunate enough to be born in the wrong bodies."

Jacey stiffened, not quite sure she understood what Robin was getting at. It wasn't like there had been any plastic surgeries on *Hey, Make Me Over*, it wasn't *that* kind of makeover where women got the perfect bodies with liposuction or tummy tucks.

Then she gasped, as did much of the crowd, when Robin reached up to the top of her head and pulled her own hair.

Off. Right *off*.

"Oh, shit," Digg whispered, sounding stunned.

Jacey could only nod in agreement, but there was no frigging way she was taking the camera off Robin. No way.

Because she was starting to understand.

"Ladies and gentlemen, thank you so much, but please, do allow me to accept your accolades under my real name. It's *Rob*. Rob Calvin. And I consider tonight a triumph for transvestites like me everywhere in this great nation of ours." Fresh tears rose in her...*his* eyes. "This is for you, my sisters! Celebrate your individuality. Express yourself. Be the lady deep within you and the world will be at your feet!"

The entire room fell into a long moment of absolute silence. You could have heard an eyelash fall as the crowd—the audience—absorbed the grand finale.

The lady of them all was a dude.

Then everyone spoke at once. Gasping, chattering, shooting questions at Robin. Rolling with the punches as only good old New York could.

Jacey couldn't help it. She started to laugh. And laugh. Until the tears rolled out of her eyes, blurring her vision, making it impossible to see through the camera lens. "Oh, my God," she said as she almost snorted.

"Lady's a guy," Digg said with a casual nod. "Neat twist."

Finally Jacey worked up the nerve to look at her father, who was staring, goggle-eyed, at the scene unfolding on the stage. His face was red, his mouth open but no sound was coming out. Then finally he managed to whisper, "Ruined. I'm ruined."

"Don't be overdramatic. It's a great twist."

"Which no one will ever see," he replied, still keeping his voice low as the shock kept him frozen in place. "The network will never air this. The entire production was an exercise in futility." He began to shake his head, mumbling, "No lady fair, no romance, no happily ever after, no millionaire. It's a flop. A total flop."

Jacey was about to offer comfort to her father, although she did see his point. His prediction might very well come true, the way the lame-ass networks reacted to every slightly controversial thing that came along these days. But then Digg touched her arm, whispering, "Who's that?"

Giving him a questioning look, she saw him nod toward the dance floor. She tried to follow his stare, but her view was blocked by the crowd of people, who'd surged forward to surround Robin…er, Rob. She—he—continued to hold court onstage, with a supportive Sukie on one side and Ginny on the other.

Then the crowd shifted. Jacey sucked in a breath as she saw them. The two of them. Dancing there on the floor, oblivious to the cacophony, to the mania, to the hysteria.

The small orchestra was playing the Christmas Waltz, and beneath the soft spotlights, Drew Bennett and Tori Lyons slowly danced. Swayed. Loved. As blatantly and obviously…and *beautifully*…as anyone ever had before.

Tori wore a stunning burgundy gown, velvet on the top, with layers upon layers of lace, cascading to the floor, so she resembled nothing less than a fairy princess. A perfect Christmas angel, dancing with her tuxedoed Prince Charming.

Their eyes never strayed from each other. Their smiles were intimate, their whispers for no one else's ears but their own. They didn't see anyone else, didn't hear anyone else. All around them the party went to hell, but the professor and his lady fair danced on.

They probably could have danced all night.

"Dad," Jacey murmured, sensing Burt was about to walk away in dismay to cry over his ruined show. "Look."

Burt paused, probably at first over his shock at what she'd called him. He followed her stare, then gave her a questioning look. Finally, he appeared to recognize who was dancing. "Is that…"

"That's them. We might have our happily-ever-after yet."

Ever the slave to her craft, Jacey swung her camera up to her face and began to tape them, to capture the moment. But *not* up close. Only from afar. She wouldn't dream of intruding on their privacy—she merely let the world get a glimpse of a true fairy-tale ending. Like opening a cherished Christmas card to get a peek at what was inside, then closing it again, secure in the good tidings it had brought.

Slowly, with Digg's hand on her shoulder, and her father beginning to smile by her side, she sent a silent Christmas wish for many years of happiness to the oblivious couple, spinning away on the dance floor.

And then she faded to black.

\* \* \* \* \*

*If you enjoyed* Make Me Over, *don't miss*
Getting Real, *the ultimate reality TV anthology,*
*available in January 2006.*

Dear Reader,

A look across a crowded room…the flight of butterflies in your tummy…the slow tingle of awareness down your spine…the sizzle of the briefest touch. This is chemistry, the magic elixir of romance, the inexplicable, undeniable blossom of attraction between two people.

That's what finally happens to Rourke O'Malley. What a guy! The proverbial Mr Tall, Dark and Handsome, and a nice guy to boot, Rourke had hero written all over him. Unfortunately, the heroine of the story, Andrea Scarpini had other ideas…

But a potential hero is a terrible thing to waste. How could I just let this awesome, sexy guy walk away? There was only one thing to do…find him some chemistry. And what better way than to give this hottie his own reality TV show, complete with a bevy of beauties to choose from? Only, the woman he wants is "don't go there" associate producer and single mum Portia Tomlinson.

I hope you enjoy reading Portia and Rourke's story as much as I loved writing it. The only thing I like better than writing is hearing from readers. You can look me up at www.jenniferlabrecque.com or drop me a note by snail mail at PO Box 298, Hiram, GA 30141, USA.

Happy reading…

*Jennifer LaBrecque*

# REALLY HOT!
## by
## Jennifer LaBrecque

To Leslie Kelly, Julie Elizabeth Leto
and Vicki Lewis Thompson, talented writers
and extraordinary people, and the chemistry behind
GETTING REAL.

# 1

"ROURKE O'MALLEY is an orgasm waiting to happen," Portia Tomlinson read aloud. She rolled her eyes and scrolled down the screen, following the postings on the fan site for *The Last Virgin*, the latest reality show she'd worked on as associate producer. "Give me a break. Some women don't have good sense."

Rourke had been the favored contestant, but the show's bachelorette hadn't picked him. He had, however, captured the hearts of female viewers around the world and they were in a veritable lust frenzy. Amazing. She swung around in her office chair.

"You mean you don't think he's an orgasm waiting to happen?" Sadie Franken, an administrative assistant, asked.

More than once, Rourke O'Malley had intruded on Portia's dreams, but she wasn't about to make that public knowledge. And she wasn't happy about it, either. Portia shrugged. "He's okay. Great face, great body, but that's nothing new in Hollywood. Of course, this—" she gestured over her shoulder toward the computer screen "—should mean great ratings for our new show." This time around, they'd signed Rourke on as their star bachelor and lined up twelve wealthy single women for him to choose from. She'd read an article citing that the latest trend among the twenty-something idle rich was to push their parents' buttons by putting themselves in a controversial spotlight. They had twelve young women who were living proof. Portia, however, was the lucky duck saddled with baby-sitting Rourke, the star, through production. She eyed the petite redhead. "Obviously you've joined the legion of women ready to drop at his feet."

Sadie raised her hand. "Guilty as charged. I've enjoyed several orgasms with him lately. I just crank my vibrator, close my eyes and Rourke O'Malley and I have a grand time."

Brash and uninhibited, Sadie usually left Portia laughing. "*That* was so much more information than I *ever* wanted to know. Please feel free *not* to share in the future."

Sadie arched a brow. "Can you honestly tell me you've never fantasized about him after working with him and seeing him day after day?" Portia opened her mouth but Sadie cut her off before she could utter the denial. "You've never thought about kissing that fabulous mouth? Never imagined that hot bod naked and sweaty and getting down? Never imagined him touching you, you touching him?"

*Enough.* "No, no and no. I haven't." But now thanks to Sadie, she had. A warm flush spread inside her and she mercilessly exorcized the erotic imagery.

"Well maybe you should—"

"Not." Portia cut her off and finished the sentence. "I should not."

"A little fantasy never hurt anyone."

"I don't have time for fantasy." And if she craved the time, reality lurked right around the corner. The stark contrast between the two proved too painful. Portia lived in the here and now.

She'd found out nine years ago where fantasy got you— single, pregnant and shattered. The ensuing reality had been waiting tables, changing diapers, several long years of night school and working her butt off to get ahead and make a better life for her and Danny.

Sadie shook her head. "A woman without time for fantasy. That's just not right."

Portia grinned. "Sorry, toots."

"When's the last time you had a date?"

She shrugged and lied. "Not that long ago."

"Ha. Name the day, place and man."

Sadie was fun and they laughed together, but she'd just crossed into *nunya* territory, as in none of your business. Portia'd had one date in the last nine, almost ten, years. She had neither the time nor the inclination. Guys thought single moms were easy marks, desperate for sex. Thanks, but no thanks. The only thing she was desperate for was more hours in the day and a good pedicure.

Portia smiled to herself. Poor Sadie'd really be wrecked if she knew Portia hadn't had sex since the last time she'd slept with Mark, Danny's dad—wait, Mark hadn't been a dad at all, make that sperm donor—just before she found out she was pregnant. Sweet-talking, pretty-boy Mark, who'd promised to love her forever, had dumped her before the word *pregnant* was out of her mouth. And he'd turned out to be one rung lower than a deadbeat dad. The last she'd heard, he was a crackhead shacked up in East L.A.

"You're not going to answer me are you?" Sadie asked.

"Nope." Portia smiled to take the sting out of it.

"Well, okay. Don't date, don't fantasize. I'll handle all of that for both of us." Sadie nodded toward the computer screen crammed with fan postings. "Me and the other women without good sense."

"Good deal. You can drool enough for both of us."

"What a wasted opportunity. It's not fair you get to spend a couple of weeks shooting this new show with him. Fourteen days in a romantic setting with those blue eyes, that black hair, those chiseled features, that body…I've got chills just thinking about it."

"I know." Portia heaved a dramatic sigh, fluttered her lashes, and cooed in a falsetto voice. "Just me, him, the moonlight, the hot tub…" Portia lost the simpering tone and added dryly, "…a dozen poor little rich girls and a production crew. Cozy, intimate."

"Go ahead, make fun. I'd be content just to breathe the same air he does."

"You need to breathe a little more air *now* instead of waiting on O'Malley. Obviously your brain isn't getting enough oxygen." Portia glanced out the window. "Are we on red alert today?"

Actually, she thought the Santa Ana winds had blown through and temporarily cleared the wretched smog that smothered the city so badly that they issued breathing codes.

"Very funny."

"I was just reminding you that even if I were remotely interested in Boy Toy O'Malley, and I think we've established that I'm not, he's there to pick from a bevy of wealthy beauties and I'm a drone, there to produce a show that'll pull in ratings."

"Drone? That has such an ugly sound to it."

"Ah, but apropos." And nothing was going to stop her. This was her proving ground. One last two-weeker away on location. If she did well, she'd been promised a studio position. No more long stretches of time away on location, when Danny had to stay with her parents and her sister. He loved them and they loved him, but the poor kid only had one parent as it was. He deserved to have her around a little more. Yeah, she'd still work brutal hours, but she *would* be home every night and he'd wake up to her there every morning. She had high stakes riding on this assignment.

"I WANT to have your baby!"

Rourke ducked into the elevator and watched in horror as the woman chasing him brandished a pair of purple thong panties and almost lost a few fingers in the closing door. "I love you," she yelled, dropping the panties and yanking her hand out at the last minute. "Call me."

He slumped against the wall, relieved the stranger, nutso or not, wasn't an amputee because of him. "The whole world's gone insane."

"Nah, man. Just the female portion. And, yeah, they're all crazy about you," his baby brother Nick said.

"I'm pretty sure I'm crazy agreeing to do this show and all of…this." He gestured at the undies on the floor. No way. A piece of paper with a phone number was pinned in the crotch. Totally looney.

"You're a good brother. You know I appreciate what you're doing for me." Despite his words, Rourke wasn't sure whether Nick realized exactly how close he'd come to jail time. Embezzlement was a constant and serious temptation when you handled large quantities of money on a daily basis, and it had been a temptation his baby brother hadn't resisted. If Nick returned the money, his employer had agreed not to press charges, preferring his money back to bad publicity. "Although choosing from twelve beautiful women with more money than God…I don't know how much of a hardship that'll be, bro."

Nick really was clueless. "When people have that much money, they think they *are* God," Rourke said. He knew. He worked with them on a daily basis.

"Okay, sorry I sounded like an ingrate. Ya know, I can't thank you enough for helping me come up with the money." The elevator door opened. Rourke checked out the hallway for any other lingerie-wielding women. Coast was clear. He stepped over the purple thong. With a shrug,

Nick scooped the panties up and shoved them in his pocket. "And you were right about not telling Ma and Da, it would've killed them."

Paul and Moira O'Malley had worked hard all their lives for a neat little house and yard in Quincey and an almost-comfortable retirement. They took pride in hard work, their home and their kids. If they knew how off-track Nicky had gotten…the shame of embezzlement and prison would indeed damn near kill them. Not to mention they wouldn't hesitate to impoverish themselves trying to help him out of his jam. And Rourke wouldn't see that happen, or he'd die trying.

As an investment banker, he made decent money. *Investment* being the key word—most of his money was tied up. Ready cash simply wasn't that ready. Nick had pointed out that reality-TV winners could bring in big bucks. It had seemed like a longshot, but more palatable than a loan shark.

It was too bad Nick couldn't have been the one on the show. Nick had good looks and the charm to go with it. Having all those women acting crazy about Rourke was just testimony to the power of suggestion and slick PR hype. In the last twelve years, his braces had come off, he'd filled out a hell of a lot and traded in pop-bottle glasses for contact lenses, but Rourke knew he was a geek beneath it all. And he still found mixing and mingling difficult. He could talk financial investments all day, but outside of that, he was pretty much at a loss. He'd heard himself referred to as the strong, silent type, which made him feel even more like a fraud because he knew he was the quiet, I-don't-know-what-to-say geeky type. The truth of the matter was, women sort of scared the hell out of him.

But here he was, having blown the first opportunity to cash in on reality TV, moving on to round two, a sure thing to bring in the cash and keep Nick out of prison.

He unlocked his apartment door and Nick followed him in. He'd lived here two years and still loved the view from his place, the mix of modern skyscrapers, pre-Revolutionary redbrick buildings and Boston's legendary harbor.

"Thanks for looking after my place while I'm gone. Watson'll be much happier at home this time." Hearing his name, the miniature schnauzer jumped down from the recliner he shared with Rourke and trotted over to him. Rourke bent down to scratch him behind the ears. "We'll go for a walk in a minute." He straightened and Watson walked over to sit patiently at the door. "You know Mom and Dad aren't really dog people."

Watson had stayed with his parents during the taping of *The Last Virgin*. Not only had poor Watson lost the comfort of his recliner, he'd been relegated to the yard. This time around, Nick was staying at Rourke's place and dogsitting.

"It's cool. Wats and I are buds, but I hate scooping up the crap when he goes for a walk." Nick shuddered, wearing a look of disgust.

Rourke laughed with something close to incredulity. Nick could be so damned self-absorbed it amazed Rourke. "Probably not nearly as much as you'd hate being some tattooed felon's prison bitch. Keep that in mind while you're cleaning up after Watson. It'll put all the crap in your life in perspective."

Nick winced. "Where's a poop-scoop bag? Bring it on."

Rourke grabbed Watson's leash and passed the requested bag to Nick. Case in point, Rourke thought as he laughed with genuine amusement, it was impossible to stay angry with Nick.

"I'd love to trade places with you," Rourke said as they headed back out the door, Watson leading the way. He shuddered thinking about the next couple of weeks. It hadn't been so bad on the last show, a bunch of guys and one woman. And he and Andrea, the bachelorette now known around the world as The Virgin, had actually become friends. If they'd been on the set a bit longer he thought he might've become friends with the Goth-clad lead camera woman, Jacey, as well. Jacey was a bit of an odd fit and he'd instinctively known she wouldn't mind if he was a geek. But this time, it was only him and a legion of spoiled, high-maintenance women. And Portia Tomlinson.

He'd had mixed emotions when the studio listed her as associate producer. Portia fascinated him. Despite her friendly, easy demeanor, she had a way of looking at him with a trace of disdain, as if she'd judged him and found him lacking in some way. Perhaps if she got to know him better….

He'd thought about asking her out after the last show but they'd immediately offered him this upcoming show. And then there was the matter of him living in Boston and her living in LA. And those were both nice excuses. The ugly truth was he'd figured she'd turn him down so fast it'd leave his head spinning. "Trust me, I'd rather clean up after Watson than be hounded by those pampered princesses."

They got on the elevator.

Nick, who ran through women the way a slots addict in Vegas runs through a bag of coins, shook his head. "You are seriously warped, Rourke. Like, maybe you need some therapy. I can't say I understand it, but I appreciate your sacrifice." Nick punched him on the shoulder. "Who knows? A dozen hot women, you might find your own true love."

Maybe he did need therapy. Twelve women and he was half smitten already with a woman who wasn't available. "Yeah."

"I don't want to step on your toes or anything, but I could give you some pointers. You know, I do okay with women," Nick said. *That* was an understatement.

Rourke wasn't exactly hitting any home runs on his own. Portia had treated him as if he were a piece of furniture, a prop, on the last show. And he didn't want to humiliate himself by bombing with the twelve women. Best possible scenario would be to drag Nick along, a modern version of Cyrano de Bergerac, but that was impossible. He supposed the next best thing would be pointers. "I think I can use all the help I can get."

The door opened and Rourke was relieved to find the lobby empty. Nick shoved the poop bag into his pocket and grinned, "Welcome to Women 101."

PORTIA SCHLEPPED her suitcase along the service hallway of the mansion set high in the hills overlooking Hollywood. She grinned to herself. One of the first of many differences between a drone and a princess. Drones carried their own baggage.

"Can I help you with that?" The low, rich baritone slid across her skin, leaving a trail of gooseflesh in its wake. That voice belonged to the man who had haunted her dreams and left her discontented and frustrated the last couple of nights. O'Malley.

She pasted on a smile and glanced over her shoulder without breaking stride. "Thanks, but I've got it."

Oh. Those startling blue eyes were right over her shoulder. He was closer than she'd thought.

"It's no trouble," he said.

She bit back the comment, *save it for the princesses, pretty boy, they're gonna run you ragged*, reminding herself O'Malley was her star and it was her job to keep him happy. If he wanted to schlep for her then who was she to stand in his way? She stopped. "Well, thank you then, if it's no trouble."

She relinquished her suitcase, his fingers brushing hers

in the exchange. A slight tremor ran through her and the hallway suddenly seemed narrow and confining. His broad shoulders took up an inordinate amount of space and his subtle scent surrounded her.

Since the filming and subsequent airing of their previous show, *The Last Virgin,* the seemingly impossible had happened. Rourke O'Malley looked even better than he had before. Portia's gaze stopped on the top two buttons of his golf shirt, which were unbuttoned, revealing a smattering of dark hair and tanned skin. She glanced up. For a second his eyes held hers and something passed between them that Portia didn't want to acknowledge. Drawing a deep breath, she turned away from him. "It's this way."

"I'm following you," he said.

They started back down the hall and Portia scrambled to dispel the awareness that lingered between them, to get things back on the friendly, light footing she maintained with all her co-workers. He was just another cast member and the good-looking guys never tired of hearing how…well, how good they looked. "You're looking great. Obviously the adoration of thousands agrees with you." She offered a smile.

O'Malley shook his head and looked embarrassed. Not the faux embarrassment so many handsome men adopted, but genuinely loosen-his-collar embarrassed. "The whole thing is crazy." They turned a corner. "A woman chased me onto an elevator this week to give me her underwear…with her name and number pinned in the crotch."

It was both funny and slightly erotic. Portia couldn't choke back her laughter. O'Malley shot her a censoring look. "I hope she wasn't wearing them at the time and I hope they were nice."

He shook his head again, a glimmer of a smile in his startlingly blue eyes. "She had them in her hand. Purple thong. She offered to have my baby."

He wasn't boasting. It was more as if he were still reeling from the weirdness of it. It just confirmed Portia's earlier assertion that some women had lost it over this guy.

"Well, the burning question is, did you call her?" Portia couldn't resist teasing him.

"No. I didn't call her," he said, indignantly. Then he looked rather sheepish. "But you already knew that, didn't you?"

"Yeah, I did, but I'm glad you confirmed it for me," she said, stopping at the room door marked on the site map as hers. Go figure, the mansion was so huge, they'd armed the production crew with maps. And all of a sudden, she realized she'd been as relaxed, but still aware of O'Malley as a man instead of just a cast member, as she'd ever been. Which effectively dispelled any lingering camaraderie.

"Well, this is it." She opened the door and turned for her suitcase, "I've got it. Thanks so much."

O'Malley acted as if he hadn't heard her and brought her luggage into the room. He glanced around at the single dresser and unframed mirror, the ladderback chair, uncarpeted concrete floor, his gaze finally settling on the narrow bed that was little more than a cot. "This is…minimalist."

It was positively Spartan.

"You and the pri—" she caught herself in the nick of time, she had to stop thinking of the contestants as princesses "—contestants are housed in guest rooms. The crew, except for Lauchmann and Daniels—" the producer and director "—well, the rest of us get the slave quarters."

Like a change in the wind, the atmosphere between them shifted. O'Malley flicked his eyes over her and heat seared her. "It's hard to imagine you as anyone's slave," the husky note in his voice fired her imagination.

"I don't take orders well. Do you?"

"It depends on what's being asked of me," he said. His

glance slid over her. "And who's doing the asking. Speaking of… How does our relationship work?"

"Our relationship?"

"During the filming."

Of course. "Well, I need you to cooperate. If I ask you to be somewhere or do something, if you could accommodate that? On the other hand, it's my job to make sure you're satisfied—" that didn't sound right "—that your needs are met—" oy, that sounded even worse, next he'd think she'd be offering her underwear with a phone number "—if you need anything, please let me know."

"Anything?" He quirked a dark eyebrow and her heart knocked hard against her ribs.

"Within reason." She squashed his suggestive note.

"I'll try to keep my requests…reasonable."

"I appreciate that. And I don't think you'll find me too demanding." What was wrong with her? Why did *demanding* seem fraught with sexual innuendo?

"I'm more than willing to accommodate any of your demands. Just let me know." Rourke hefted her suitcase to the bed which didn't give an inch. "This bed is like a brick. Do you like it hard?"

It'd been so long she couldn't remember…and that was *so* not what he meant. He'd awakened some sexual energy she'd thought was long gone. But obviously she wasn't immune to drop-dead gorgeous O'Malley standing by her bed asking her if she liked it hard. The thought alone made her shiver inside. "I'm sure it will be fine."

"This hardly seems fair compared to our rooms."

"Oh, come on. Could you imagine Tara Mitchells in here?" Tara's father was an oil mogul. Or was he the real estate mogul? All the fathers were moguls, it merely varied by industry. "Or maybe one of the gaffers bunking down next to her?"

"Okay. You've got a point."

"Plus, we've got security in place that rivals Fort Knox. If some looney or terrorist group decided they wanted some ready cash, they could pick up twelve hostages, whose families' combined wealth is more than that of some small nations, in one fell swoop."

Rourke nodded. "I'd thought about that too. The studio's taking some pretty big chances on *Pick a Date with the Rich and Beautiful*."

Portia's surprise must've shown through.

"What?" Rourke asked.

"You're one of them."

Rourke laughed. "Not by a long shot. I'm not rich. I do okay, but I'll never be in the same league as any of their wealth—"

"Unless you marry one of them."

"Nobody said a word about marriage and I read the fine print on my contract. But even if I went there, it's still not my wealth is it? And as for being beautiful, the panties and all of that, it's just media hype. I know what I look like."

"And so do the women of the world. You're an incredibly handsome man, O'Malley, but then I have a hard time believing you don't already know that." She said it dispassionately, impersonally, as if she were observing the weather. In Hollywood, good looks were a commodity.

He shook his head. "My brother got the looks in the family."

There was another O'Malley that looked *better* than him? "God help the women of the world." And she mentally made a note to pass the info along to PR.

Her cell phone rang and her mother's number flashed on caller ID. "Excuse me. I need to take this call." She turned her back to him, dismissing him and the sexual energy he exuded. She flipped the phone open. "Hello."

"Hi, Mom," Danny said.

"Hey, you." She walked over to the small window that overlooked the back kitchen entrance.

"Are you busy?" He'd learned always to ask if she was tied up on the job. Every time she left home for a location, he called the first day or so. Poor guy. He was amazingly flexible and resilient, but it was an adjustment for him every time she traveled. It'd be nice to move into the studio job.

"No, I'm not too busy. What are you doing?" A white-jacketed cook stepped out of the kitchen door and lit up a cigarette.

"Nothing. I just wanted to make sure you got there okay."

"I did. This house is cool. You'd love it."

They talked for a minute about his day and she assured him she missed him before she ended the call.

"Love you, Danny. I'll call you tonight."

She snapped the phone shut and turned around, surprised to find O'Malley still by her bed.

"Oh, I thought you'd left," she said.

"I just had one more question for you." He shifted his weight to his other foot and nodded toward her phone. "Boyfriend?"

Portia shook her head. "The love of my life." Her private life was her own business and let him make of that what he would. And maybe that would block this energy, this awareness, that seemed to flow between them.

"So you don't need to go on a TV show to find someone special?"

They couldn't pay her enough. "No. I have someone special waiting at home." This was much better. Now if she could just get him out of her room before she found herself mired in more inappropriate thoughts. "Thanks for bringing my suitcase. I'll see you at the briefing."

She all but pushed him out into the hall and closed the door behind him. She blew out a deep breath and realized O'Malley'd never asked the question he'd waited around to ask. Too bad, so sad. She'd needed him out of her room. He had a way of invading her space, getting under her skin, unnerving her.

She opened her suitcase on the bed. O'Malley's scent lingered—or was it all in her head? *Do you like it hard?* She felt flushed. God help her, but her nipples hardened just thinking about the lazy challenge in his deep-blue eyes. Her hands shook slightly as she unpacked her underwear.

She had a feeling this was going to be a very long two weeks.

ROURKE WANDERED BACK through the mansion, fascinated by the architectural details in the house and disquieted by his encounter with Portia Tomlinson. She was pleasant, complimentary even, but he still had the feeling she disliked him. No. That wasn't exactly true. It was something between dislike and dismissal. She'd told him how handsome he was and even with her dispassionate tone, it'd meant more than all the crazy rantings Nick had shown him on a Web site. Pathetic really. When she'd laughed and teased him over the purple panties, she'd been different— more accessible, not so distant—which only accentuated the other.

And the change in her when she'd taken that phone call—there'd been a softness about her. What kind of man brought that look to her face? She'd deemed the caller, Danny, the love of her life and Rourke had felt a stab of something akin to jealousy. Which was ridiculous because she was clearly off-limits. He was about to meet twelve beautiful women who were here because they were interested in him. So what if, every time he was in the same room with Portia, his gut knotted and he felt as energized as he did when he was about to close a big deal?

And obviously he hadn't listened closely enough to Nick's pointers. For God's sake, he'd been in her bedroom... But then again, her boyfriend—nah, the love of her life—

"Hello again," said a female voice directly in front of him.

He stopped. He'd almost plowed right into Jacey.

"Sorry, my mind was somewhere else." He shook his head to clear it of Portia. He was delighted Jacey was here. He grinned at her. "It's good to see you. I'm glad you're going to be the person behind the camera on the set."

She returned the grin. "Yeah, it's a regular old home week."

"No kidding. I just ran into Portia," he said.

"Her room is next to mine. We're staying in the servants' quarters," Jacey said. "Tells you something about our jobs, doesn't it?"

"Is it really that bad?" he asked.

"Nah. There are worse ways to make a buck."

"How'd you get started in this business? Have you always been interested in cameras?" he asked, genuinely interested.

Jacey glanced at him suspiciously, as if he couldn't possibly be curious. He laughed aloud at her dark look. "I really want to know. You sort of remind me of my younger brother."

"He's into Goth?"

Rourke laughed aloud at the mental image of Nick decked out in Goth attire. He'd have to be drugged or dead first. "No. He's into Ralph Lauren, but you both say what you think."

Jacey relaxed, and began outlining her work history. The transformation was incredible. Finally, she gave a self-conscious laugh. "Probably more than you bargained for there."

"No. I think that's really cool."

"Have you ever looked through a studio camera?"

"I've never had any exposure to TV before this."

"I could show you sometime. Like maybe after taping or something. If you wanted to. But you don't have to."

"That'd be awesome. I'd love it. You just tell me one day when you have time."

"It's a deal then. The camera brings this clarity to things…" she caught herself. "Whoa, there I go again."

"It's obviously more than a job with you. More like a passion."

"Pretty much." She cocked her dark head to one side and looked at him. "You know, you sort of remind me of Digg. You're real."

"Thanks. I'm extremely flattered. He seems like a great guy." It hadn't been rocket science to figure out that Digg and Jacey were an item. An unlikely item, but an item nonetheless. Although, after chatting with Jacey they didn't seem as unlikely a couple as before.

"He's okay." Her smirk belied her tone. She checked her watch. "Holy shit. You've got a briefing and I've got camera checks in ten minutes. Portia'll have my ass if I'm the reason you're late."

"Really? She's a task master?"

"Not really. But she's punctual."

"She's sort of hard to get to know. What does she do for fun?" Rourke shamelessly pumped Jacey for information about Portia.

"Laundry? Seriously, I don't know. She keeps to herself. Hey, what's with the interest in Portia? Twelve rich girls aren't enough selection for you?"

"Of course not. I mean, of course they are. I was just curious about her since we'll be working together. I'm not interested in her that way."

The minute the words left his mouth, he realized they were patently untrue.

# 2

"HERE ARE the dossiers on the women you'll be meeting this evening at the predinner cocktail party. You'll find a variety of blondes, brunettes and redheads with varied interests. They do have three things in common. They're all women," Portia joked. Well, only sort of joked. The "female" contestant on *Make Me Over* had surprised everyone when she'd revealed that "she" was a "he." "They're all beautiful and they're all wealthy. You're the most envied man in America."

O'Malley took the booklet and leafed through it.

Portia watched Terry and Jeff, sound techs, check out the wiring and test the sound nearer the divan. They'd planned the meet-and-greet cocktail party in this room. Reminiscent of a Moorish castle, the entire house was a masterpiece of intricate tilework, carved wooden doors, arched doorways and a maze of high-ceilinged hallways that led to private quarters and a central Turkish bath that boasted live palms. The mingled scents of almond, sandalwood, frankincense and myrrh perfumed the air. It was opulent, with more than a hint of decadence, and a most fitting setting for a handsome man and his harem. Actually, and this twist delighted Portia, the house had originally belonged to a 1930s actress infamous for keeping a retinue of lovers on hand, a reversal of the classic male/female harem roles.

This room, the salon, was particularly lavish, with rich fabrics, low sofas, muted lighting and a high ceiling painted to resemble a velvet night sky alight with hundreds of stars. Doubtless these very walls contained the echoes of pleasure, perhaps with more than one lover at a time.

Was it her conversation with Sadie, the sensual setting, or the totally gorgeous bachelor beside her that had forbidden images teasing at the back of her mind? Images of her supine, being pleasured on that low divan by a tall, broadshouldered, dark-haired man who bore a striking resemblance to O'Malley were inescapable.

Ruthlessly, she swept aside the mental picture. Any pleasure given or received in this room, at least of the carnal nature, wouldn't involve her. Portia's delight would be in the subsequent ratings. One of the twelve women and O'Malley would play out that love scene. And it was her job to see that it happened. Sex sold. Sex pulled in viewers. And ratings meant she'd done her job well.

O'Malley finished thumbing through the photos and bio sheets. "You're right. They're all women." He grinned, which notched up his sex appeal to a devastating level. "They're definitely attractive and they all have that monied look about them. Have you met them? Were they nice? What do you think?"

Portia squashed the tingling response that slid down her spine and reminded herself that Rourke O'Malley was just another pretty face.

She'd met them. *Nice* and *money*, while not mutually exclusive, certainly didn't go hand in hand. Nor did money ensure good taste and decent conduct. All the women had massive egos and she could foresee more than a little jealous bickering. And that would make for good footage. Portia smiled. "I've met them and I think you'll find this very interesting. And very gratifying."

"Good." O'Malley shifted the papers into his other

hand. "I know where this question is going to get me, but I've got to ask anyway."

Here it came. The inevitable twist question. The "winner" had been promised her own TV show. It was weird, but hey, it had worked. Any of the women's fathers could probably buy a network, but they all wanted to compete for their own TV show, which should, once again, translate to good footage as they all tried to show how outrageous and at home they could appear on the camera. Of course, she couldn't reveal this to O'Malley. Terry and Jeff moved to the other side of the room, checking the audio cables running along the baseboards. Must be a snafu. She'd better check with them when she wrapped this up with O'Malley. "Go ahead. Ask away."

Anticipating his question and distracted by potential sound problems, she didn't really listen to the question, she just answered what she expected him to ask. "Even if I knew, I couldn't tell you."

He quirked one dark brow. "You can't tell me why you don't like me?"

He'd asked why she didn't like him? A flush crept up her face. Portia had realized early on that one of her greatest assets was her ability to get along well with pretty much anyone and everyone. She had a knack for putting people at ease. People found her easy to talk to. The fact that she never offered personal information in return usually worked to her favor. Mostly people wanted to talk about themselves. "I thought you asked about the twist."

He waved his hand in dismissal. "I never expected that you'd tell me anyway. I know I'm not a virgin, so that's out the window." His blue eyes twinkled devilishly and Portia wasn't sure whether he was making fun of himself or flirting with her, or perhaps both.

But she did know a slow heat seeped through her at the

visual supplied by her recently activated imagination—
O'Malley naked, thrusting between a woman's naked
thighs. "I'm sure. Many times over."

O'Malley shrugged. "*Many* is a relative term. I'm not a
player. And I can only hope you don't slip in a transvestite like on that other show." He grinned, and Portia smiled
in return. Most drop-dead gorgeous men took themselves
far more seriously than O'Malley.

"No surprises there." The production crew had managed to save that show, but afterward the executive director, Burt Mueller, threatened to can the entire screening
crew if another transvestite revealed him- or herself on
one of his shows. In typical Burt Mueller fashion, he'd declared he wouldn't become known as the Transvestite
Forum Network. She reassured Rourke again. "They're all
real women."

"For certain?"

"For certain."

"That's good to know," he said.

She bet it was. Portia'd seen a few looks pass between
some of the male crew that clearly said they didn't want
to think about the point when a guy might figure out the
"woman" carried the same equipment they did.

"You still haven't answered my question. Why don't
you like me?" Despite his easy smile, his eyes were serious.

"I don't dislike you." And she didn't. Not exactly. She
was wary. When he'd been on the set of *The Last Virgin*,
she'd dismissed him, categorizing him the way she did all
narcissistic men. But O'Malley refused to be dismissed or
categorized and that wasn't a good thing. His low-key
charm and good looks raised Portia's red flags. It was akin
to instinctively knowing a pretty red berry you found in
the woods might look good and taste good but wasn't necessarily good for you. However, she was supposed to be

working with him and keeping him happy. She reiterated her earlier assertion. "I don't dislike you at all."

"I think you're splitting hairs."

O'Malley was more discerning than she'd given him credit. "I have a job to do. I can't allow myself to get too close to our cast members."

"I just feel like you know everything about me and I know nothing about you."

She shook her head. "Contestants pretty much agree to open their lives up to the public. It's the price of celebrity. But there's the difference. You're a participant. I'm behind the scenes. And I like it that way." She personally thought anyone who agreed to come on to one of these shows wasn't dealing with a full deck anyway, which was statistically frightening when you considered the staggering number of applicants flooding the screening sites. Andrea and Zach from *The Last Virgin* had been exceptions. She'd heard through the studio grapevine that Sarah Donovan and Luke Richards from *Surviving Sarah* and Charlie Cuesta and Sam Ryan from *The Great Chase* weren't flakes either. Thank goodness, though, for all those other quirky people in the world because it meant she had a job.

"You're here for a love fest. I'm here to make sure it goes well for you. End of story." She smiled, but they both knew she meant it.

Honestly, if she hadn't known better, she'd swear hurt flashed in his eyes before he answered her smile with his own. "You're absolutely right. I apologize for overstepping boundaries."

Now she felt even more awkward, as if she'd extracted an apology that wasn't owed. "Don't worry about it." She checked her watch, relieved to see it was time to end this. "Okay, I should let you get back to your room to shower and change."

How many times had she said that to a man in similar circumstances and never thought a thing about it? What was wrong with her that she suddenly had a disturbingly erotic image of O'Malley naked, dripping wet, surrounded by a thick cloud of steam? And found it totally, inappropriately arousing.

She glanced back down at the clipboard in her hands, not because there was anything important there, but because it gave her somewhere to look other than at him. "Wardrobe will be along to your room in an hour or so. And I'll meet you there in an hour and a half to go over any last-minute questions."

O'Malley's smile held an edge. "Ah, yes, so you can expertly orchestrate my—what was it?—love fest." He gave her a nod of dismissal and walked away.

Portia stood in the middle of the room and watched his broad-shouldered retreat, until the door closed behind him.

"So, are you the newest member of the fan club, Portia?" Terry called from across the room, his voice teasing.

Startled, she almost dropped her clipboard. Damn, she'd been so caught up in watching him walk across the room, she'd forgotten about Terry and Jeff.

"You boys know better than that. I don't do fan clubs."

Bottom line. She orchestrated. He participated. And that was that.

"HOLD STILL for one more second…" Cindy from wardrobe tugged his black tie into place. She stepped back and surveyed him with a critical eye. A knock sounded on his bedroom door.

"Come in," he called over his shoulder. Portia had said she'd arrive in an hour and a half. She was punctual. Behind him, his bedroom door opened and closed.

He knew without turning that it was Portia. Yeah, she was scheduled to be here, but he could feel her. Tiny hairs stood up on the back of his neck and adrenaline surged through him.

Cindy tweaked his tux jacket and smiled. "Your mama will be proud and those women don't stand a chance." Cindy, with her cheerful attitude and nonstop chatter, rather reminded him of his mother. "Honey, you are yummy." She winked outrageously at him and looked over his shoulder. "Makes you wish you had a spoon so you could eat him up doesn't it?"

Laughing—how could you not laugh at such outrageous hyperbole—and she was obviously teasing him rather than flirting—he turned to face Portia.

Her answering smile struck him as a bit forced. "He's lucky I left my spoon in my room."

Her cool gaze flickered over him, having just the opposite effect on his temperature. Forget a spoon, he mentally urged her. His body tightened and his heart pounded at the thought of her mouth against his skin, her scent mingling with his. What was it about her that drew him to her? She wasn't beautiful in the accepted sense of the word, but she was arresting, exotic, intriguing, frustrating—and she got under his skin.

Cindy's two-way radio went off. Tamsin, the lead makeup artist, came across after the initial squawk. "Cindy, Ms. Freeman needs you ASAP."

Rourke had skimmed through the dossiers again, after his shower and before Cindy arrived. Lissa Freeman was heiress to a mind-boggling real-estate fortune, who'd spent the last year hanging out in Europe. What the dossier didn't include, but the media had more than adequately covered, was the havoc Lissa had wrecked along the way. She was a dark-haired, petulant time bomb given to explosions when things didn't go her way. Of course, he as well as anyone knew you couldn't and shouldn't believe all the media hype.

The radio clicked again. "I don't need you ASAP, I needed you five minutes ago."

Okay. Maybe you could believe the media. That peremptory tone could only belong to Ms. Freeman.

Cindy headed for the door, smirking. "Bet she doesn't have a clue you heard *that*. Bet she'll use a different tone with you."

Rourke chuckled. "No doubt."

The radio clicked again. "Are you on your way? I don't have all night."

"Okay, I can't resist and she deserves it," Cindy said to Rourke and Portia. She clicked the two-way. "I'm almost finished with Mr. O'Malley and then I'll be right there."

"Oh. Take your time. There's no hurry." Butter wouldn't have melted in Lissa Freeman's mouth this time around.

Cindy laughed and shook her head. "Take care of him," she said to Portia. "We're putting a guppy into a tank full of sharks."

A guppy? He laughed to cover his sudden nervousness. Him, patently incapable of small talk, among twelve socially adept women. Right. "I object to being called a guppy."

Cindy waved her radio. "You know what I mean. Take care of him, Portia."

"I have the utmost confidence he'll be fine," Portia said. He was glad one of them did.

The minute the door closed behind Cindy the mood shifted and Rourke was aware of being in his bedroom alone with Portia Tomlinson, a woman he found both bewitching and aggravating.

He was aware of the bed with its massive carved headboard and gossamer curtains tied back with silken cords, the lush carpet underfoot, the sensual suggestion of the entwined couple in the gilt-framed reproduction of Gustav Klimt's "The Kiss" adorning the wall, the copy of the *Kama Sutra* on the bedside table, the muted lighting, the sheer elegance of Portia's upswept blond hair, her no-nonsense suit paired with sexy designer shoes, and most of all, her scent.

Rourke spoke to fill the space with something other than the sexual tension strumming through him and permeating the room. "Lissa Freeman just narrowed my choices down to eleven."

"You should meet her with an open mind. She's probably got a bad case of PDS, predate syndrome," Portia said.

"Would you talk to someone like that even if you were nervous over a date?"

"No. Probably not, but you should still give her another chance."

What would Portia be like on a date? Cool and reserved? What did she do for fun? To relax? What excited her?

"Okay," her voice came out low and husky. She stopped and cleared her throat. Maybe she was as affected by him as he was by her. "So, we should go over any last-minute questions you have."

Rourke tried to focus on the women he was about to meet instead of the one in front of him, but he was totally captivated by the way the shadows played across Portia's skin and hair. He reminded himself the real purpose of being here was not to admire the straight line of Portia's nose or the sensual curve of her mouth, but to give the network their show, pick up his prize money, and keep Nick's butt out of jail. "Do you have any pointers on tonight?"

"Only one, really. We've set up a champagne fountain in the salon. You might want to go easy on it since you're the star."

"Not a problem. I'm not a big drinker." Some of the guys on the set of *The Last Virgin* had complained about the minimal alcohol served. "Why didn't we have a champagne fountain on the last set?"

"This is a different show altogether and the dynamics have shifted. Sexist or not, alcohol flowing freely among lots of men and one woman just doesn't work. But you know sex sells the ratings. You're a sexy man and they're beautiful women, so Lauchmann ordered champagne to loosen things up."

"I manage fine without 'loosening up my dates' with alcohol," he said, just to set the record straight. Then he moved on to her comment that had caught and held his attention. "You think I'm sexy?"

"Of course I do." Her expression remained pleasant and neutral, making him all the more curious as to what was going on in her head. "And that really doesn't mean anything. I consider a Ferrari a work of art. I can admire it, but it doesn't mean I want to drive one."

He didn't need to be a rocket scientist to know this conversation was about much more than a car. And he knew he was going where he shouldn't, but he went there anyway. "What if you were offered a test drive?"

"They only want you to drive if you're interested in buying, and I can't afford a Ferrari."

"What if it was a no-strings-attached test drive?"

"I'd pass. It would only make me want what I know I can't have. I'm a realist."

So was he, but he also had dreams, fantasies. Somewhere beneath that cool cover, surely she had fantasies as well. "And what is it about the Ferrari that appeals to you?"

"The same thing that appeals to everyone else. Beautiful, sexy lines. Perfectly proportioned. Re-sponsive. I've read that it shifts hard and fast, but smooth. All of that power under the hood." Her eyes glittered. "All the women you're about to meet can afford Ferraris, probably more than one."

What exactly were the rules of engagement? And what did it take to shake her up the way she shook him up inside? "What if I want to bring one back to my room?"

"I don't think a Ferrari will fit in here."

So she wasn't shaken, but she did have a sense of humor. "I was asking more along the lines of one of the women."

Portia looked pointedly at the large bed. "That's certainly your prerogative. I believe there's room for all twelve. And of course there aren't any cameras in here."

"How can I be sure there isn't a Minicam with a microphone tucked away somewhere?"

"Because I'm telling you there isn't. You'll just have to trust me on this."

Given the studio's twist on the last show, parading Andrea Scarpini before the world as the last virgin, he'd be a fool to trust the studio or anyone associated with the studio. "So, if I want to bring one of them back here for…privacy…it's okay?"

She glanced toward the bed. "Absolutely."

"And if I bring back a different woman every night?"

"A different one every night or more than one, it's up to you." Ah, she could play the part of cool and collected, but the flush that suffused her neck and face was all too telling. She walked over to the nightstand and opened it. Rourke did a double take. The drawer held several boxes of condoms. "We take your welfare very seriously. If you find you're running low, just let me know."

This was worse than when his parents had put a brown-paper bag filled with condoms in the medicine cabinet when he was in high school and told him it was better to be safe than sorry.

Rourke laughed, both amused and offended. So much for needling Portia to get a rise out of her. He hadn't signed

on for stud service. "I think that's an adequate supply."
Hell, he hadn't run through that many condoms in a lifetime. And twice when he was working out at the gym, his
back had gone out. Running through that many condoms
would probably put him in traction.

"The only rule is everyone has to be willing. *No* means *no*."

"And does that no work both ways? What if one of
them comes on to me and I'm not interested?"

"I suppose you'd handle it much the same as you would
on a date at home."

"Maybe. But at home, I'd have the option of just not calling her again."

"Don't forget you'll be eliminating contestants. Of
course, it won't be as many or as often as it was on *The Last
Virgin*, because we're starting out with fewer people."

"And what if I don't want to kiss any of them?"

Her smile held a tight edge. "I find that scenario unlikely. Surely out of a dozen beautiful women, you'll be attracted to at least one." She glanced down at her clipboard.
"I can't imagine you won't be inspired to share a few kisses
at the Turkish bath or on the terrace."

"Doesn't it make you uncomfortable? Watching people kiss? Listening to intimate conversation?" Rourke
had always been very private and Portia seemed so reserved, he couldn't imagine it didn't make her uncomfortable. God, his palms were sweating just thinking
about facing a dozen women, much less making out
with them.

She shrugged. "We're doing a job. You distance yourself.
It helps if you think of yourself as an actor playing a part."

"I don't suppose you're willing to tell me where there
aren't any cameras other than here?"

"No, I'm afraid I can't do that. It's cheating, plus it
would cheat our viewers at home."

"Do you always play by the rules, Portia?" He knew the answer before he asked.

"Absolutely. Do you?" she challenged back.

"I always have before. I've never wanted something so much that I was willing to break the rules for it, but if I wanted something—" he looked into the depths of her eyes and paused deliberately "—or someone, desperately, if I couldn't think of anything else…"

"That sounds obsessive." A husky note colored her voice.

"I think it's that same fine line that separates love and hate," he said.

She deliberately looked away from him, breaking the tenuous sensual thread woven by their conversation. "Well, let's go meet your bachelorettes and see if you find a woman who inspires you to break the rules."

# 3

"You seem nervous," Portia said to Rourke outside the salon. He might be nervous, but she was relieved to be out of his bedroom and away from that big bed and assortment of condoms.

"Hell, yeah, I'm nervous."

This didn't seem like a playboy to her. "Don't be. They're just women and you're absolutely gorgeous. They'll be falling all over themselves to get to you." She offered the same reassurances that were part of her stock in trade. Ridiculous, really, what an abhorrent thought it was this time.

The set of his shoulders, beneath the dark jacket and crisp white shirt of his tux, was definitely tense. "Turn around and hold this." She handed him her clipboard. Taking a deep breath herself, she lightly massaged his shoulders. She'd never actually done this for any other contestants, but certainly she would have if she'd thought they needed it. It had nothing to do with actually wanting to touch O'Malley because she didn't. She didn't *want* to touch him, didn't want to feel the hard muscles beneath her fingertips. This was nothing personal, this was just her job.

"Where did you learn to do that?" he asked with a low moan of appreciation.

"I've always been good with my hands."

"Oh, Portia."

It took no imagination to hear that voice moaning her

name in bed, her hands on something other than his shoulders... What was wrong with her? Was it the conversation with Sadie? The conversation with O'Malley with its deeper level of meaning? The sensual setting? *Easy, Portia, girl. Get yourself in check.*

"You'll be fine," she said as she smoothed out his jacket. She dropped her hands to her sides.

Pivoting slowly until he faced her, his eyes dark, serious, he bent his head until he was so close she felt the warmth of his breath against her face, and could see the fine lines bracketing his eyes. Oh, God, O'Malley was going to kiss her. And the worst of it was, she wanted it. She wanted to feel his mouth on hers, to test the texture of his lips, to sample in his kiss the heat reflected in his eyes. "Portia..."

At the very last second, sanity prevailed. What was she thinking? Anyone could walk by. Any crew member. And what was he thinking? Did he assume he was such a hot commodity that any woman was fair game? She stepped away.

She took her clipboard from him and prayed he didn't see her hands shaking. She checked the schedule she'd already memorized and glanced at her watch. "Thirty seconds and you're on."

He reached as if to brush his fingers over her cheekbone and longing coursed through her, so intense it nearly buckled her knees. How long since she'd shivered with the heat of a man's touch? How long had she denied herself as a woman? And this was absolutely the wrong man to feel this way with. At the last minute he pulled back and let his hand fall.

Portia licked her dry lips. "It's time for you to go inside."

He shook his head, as if he'd lost track of reality as well. He looked oddly vulnerable and unsure of himself. "I'm—"

"Ready to meet your ladies," she finished for him, still

quaking inside from that near kiss. She had to get them both back on track. "Viewers already love you and these women will too."

Portia turned on the mike that fed directly into the earpiece of Grant Atwood, the show's emcee. "Ten seconds to showtime." She mentally counted backward. Reaching the number one, she opened the door and sent Rourke in, stepping aside so that the camera wouldn't pick her up in the background. O'Malley moved into the room as if he owned it.

Portia had thought all the women were lovely before, but tonight, they were positively stunning. Money couldn't buy happiness, and according to the show's title it didn't buy love, but money certainly bought some kick-butt outfits. Two gowns screamed signature Versace, as well as Vera Wang, Halston and what looked like a Dolce and Gabbana. And the shoes and the jewelry were spectacular.

There was more money tied up in those dresses than she made in a year. Make that a couple of years. Not to mention the accessories. And she'd bet there wasn't a rhinestone on the property. Tara Mitchells wore a pair of Jimmy Choos with a diamond mesh collar that wrapped around the ankle. Paste didn't sparkle like that. Portia's finely cut suit had seemed perfectly presentable…until now. These women were glitz, glamour and designer fashion at its finest and the audience would eat it up. And O'Malley should too, she thought with a hint of cattiness as the women all preened before him.

Grant started the introductions. Portia found a dark corner and observed. Each woman had been instructed not to kiss O'Malley. From a practical standpoint, they didn't need to have their star covered in lipstick and it also gave O'Malley the position of authority. It was all about playing up the harem aspect.

Jacey's camera was rolling and Portia couldn't have asked for a better round of first filming. Despite his earlier pre-entry tension, O'Malley was perfect, greeting each woman as if he were truly glad to meet her, brushing his lips against her cheek as if it were a prelude or a promise of more to come. She knew what it felt like to have his warm breath feather against her skin, to be enveloped in his dark, spicy scent, to feel anticipation quiver through her. But she didn't know what it felt like to have his lips caress her flesh. And thinking this way was sheer, utter madness. Hadn't she just told him that the crew distanced themselves? And whatever this thing, this tension, between herself and O'Malley, surely it would dissipate with the arrival of his women, wouldn't it? Whatever it was that simmered between them was probably just a product of all the hype and the sexual tension conjured up by the situation and the setting. Now he had not just another, but a dozen other outlets for his interest and that suited her just fine. Didn't it?

"I DIDN'T THINK it was possible, but you're even better-looking in person," Carlotta Zimmerman said. Carlotta was the last of the twelve.

Rourke laughed. "Thanks. It's the tux. Even Yoda would look good in a tux."

Carlotta smiled rather blankly, obviously missing the *Star Wars* reference. Oh, well. He bent and pressed a light kiss to her cheek, the same as he had eleven times before. "Thank you for being here. It's an honor to meet you."

Carlotta turned to join the crowd. They were all beautiful. They all smelled good. Looked good. It had actually gone better than he'd anticipated, but he hadn't felt any rush of sexual energy, no slow ribbon of desire curling through him the way he had in the hallway with Portia.

She was tucked in the far-left corner now. He'd been ex-cruciatingly aware of her quiet circumnavigation of the room. In her plain suit, with her hair in the twist she fa-vored, she embodied understated elegance and poise. The other women looked almost garish in comparison.

A waiter offered him a flute of champagne from a tray. He snagged one, sipping. It wasn't his favorite beverage, but it was cold and wet and quite frankly he wouldn't mind a little bit of alcohol to take the edge off, although he wasn't nearly as ner-vous as he had been. Now he had a half hour of mix and mingle.

He had to admit, being the center of all this female at-tention was pretty flattering. Of course, he didn't know any man who wouldn't be flattered by this. Maybe he didn't need Nick's prescribed therapy after all. Maybe this was therapy. Maybe now he wouldn't make a fool of himself the next time he was with Portia and do something stupid like try to kiss her.

"Rourke, why don't you propose a toast?" Lissa Free-man said, curling her arm through his and pressing against his side, as if they were already an item. Lissa's full breasts pressed against his jacketed arm. Oddly, her barely clad bosom didn't send a jolt through him the way Portia's hands on his shoulders had.

A redhead—he couldn't remember her name—slid in front of Tara Mitchells and positioned herself on his other side. Okay, so these two were definitely the most aggressive of the pack. If he remembered correctly, an ex-plicit tape featuring the redhead and her boyfriend du jour had surfaced on the Internet last year. Rourke had passed on watching it, but Jason, two offices down, had gone into a serious state of lust, and would definitely freak when this show aired. The other women sur-rounded him and he almost laughed as he recalled Cindy from wardrobe's earlier shark analogy. They were all dressed to kill.

They all looked at him expectantly. He'd better get on with a toast and quit making bad jokes to himself.

Smiling, he raised his glass. "Here's to a successful show and to all you lovely ladies."

They all touched their glasses to each others' and drank. Rourke tried to sip from his, but it was damn hard to drink without spilling with Lissa attached to his arm like a limpet.

"Now, *I'd* like to propose a toast," the limpet said. She looked at him. "Here's to the beginning of a beautiful relationship."

Well, hell, he'd drink to that as long as it didn't include her, and she hadn't been specific. No sooner had he lowered his glass than the redhead—Maggie, that was her name—not to be outdone by Lissa, piped up. "My turn. Here's to hoping the camera gets us at our best angle."

Apparently now it had turned into a game because Bridget Anders, another contestant, waved the champagne-laden waiter over. "I've got one." Everyone refreshed their glasses. "To long hot nights."

Rourke lost track of who proposed what. He simply raised his glass, laughing as the toasts got progressively more suggestive.

At one point someone actually grabbed his butt and copped a feel. He worked very hard to relax and go with the flow of being the center of attention among very flirtatious, aggressive, beautiful women, but throughout it all, he was always aware of where Portia was in the room. He was, he reminded himself, an actor, but he felt as if he were playing for an audience of one.

PORTIA DRIED OFF and pulled on her terry-cloth robe, hurrying to free up the space. Servants' quarters didn't come with en suite bathrooms and there were six other crew members on site. She gathered her toiletries and knocked as she passed Jacey's room. "It's all yours," she called out.

She heard Jacey's muffled thanks.

Portia closed herself into her bedroom. The past several days on the set had been long and draining. And that hadn't been, she assured herself as she pulled on the shorts and T-shirt that doubled for pajama duty, because she'd had to watch a dozen women cover O'Malley like bees on a honeycomb. That was, after all, why they were here. There were myriad details that had to be overseen each day, and O'Malley was merely one of them. It had nothing to do with the fact that she tossed and turned, exhausted but restless, dreaming disturbing erotic dreams that recapped the days' events but put her center-stage with O'Malley. Small wonder, then, that after a night spent dreaming about him, it felt as if every flirtatious glance, every shared joke, every light-and-easy kiss he exchanged with the contestants was, in fact, meant for her. She'd heard about this happening—being locked on location and losing touch with reality. She could deal with it, of course, but she was becoming mentally and emotionally exhausted.

Even her hard, narrow bed looked welcoming about now. She towel-dried her wet hair. That was the benefit of straight hair and a good conditioner, she didn't have to blow-dry. She'd just brush it and stick it in a twist tomorrow and she'd be set.

She turned down the covers and was just slipping between the sheets when her pager went off. Damnation. What now?

O'Malley. What could he possibly want this close to midnight? Hadn't he had enough attention with all the fawning earlier tonight? She wasn't a night person. She was tired and cranky and he was cutting into *her* time, although as long as they were on location, she was, in effect, on duty 24/7. But she'd had enough of O'Malley for the day. Enough of his dark good looks, his easy charm, even that scent of his that seemed to invade her space when he was around. And she'd definitely had enough of feeling as if she was walking on eggshells.

"What's up, O'Malley?" she asked without preamble. Oy, that was the wrong thing to ask a man who'd just spent three hours with a dozen hot women. "What do you need?" Possibly not the best wording either. Dammit. She gave up.

"I can't…um…get up," he said in a low, strained voice.

She'd have bet her knock-off Prada bag that *that* wouldn't be a problem for him. It was sort of disappointing to learn and sort of gross, too. "I don't need to hear this."

He laughed, still low and strained. "I didn't say I couldn't get *it* up. You don't understand. I can't get up. Literally. I need your help."

"Why can't you get up?"

"What? You think I want to humiliate myself and call you, be a pain in the ass late at night? No. But I can't shoot tomorrow if I'm stuck, now can I?"

Blast. She'd been so relieved he wasn't confessing impotence, she'd missed the filming implication.

"Where are you now?" she asked.

"On the floor in my room."

"What—" Never mind. She find out soon enough. "I'll be right there."

"Thanks."

Because it was business all day, every day, she had work clothes and more work clothes. Somehow putting on a suit to go rescue O'Malley seemed sort of dumb. What the hell? Like he couldn't handle her in running shorts and a T-shirt? She slid her feet into flip-flops and closed her bedroom door behind her. She passed the bathroom and heard

Jacey singing in the shower. Portia grinned to herself. Who would've figured Jacey for a shower crooner? You just never knew. Or maybe she was just under the influence of love. She and Digg were openly an item now. They'd met on the set of *Killing Time* last year. Digg had been a contestant and Jacey was the lead camera. According to the rumor mill, Jacey'd been fired for about half an hour and Digg had damn near got himself kicked off the show. Contestant/crew fraternization wasn't the slickest move for either one of them to make. It had almost cost Digg a million bucks and Jacey her job and reputation.

Navigating the maze of hallways, which were kind of spooky late at night, Portia made a mental note to remember what had happened with Jacey and Digg. Letting herself into O'Malley's room, she stifled a laugh. O'Malley was on the floor, folded over like an envelope.

"You should lock your door."

"I forgot. It's a good thing I did or you couldn't have gotten in."

"I'm scared to ask, but exactly what were you doing?"

"Exercising." He turned his head to look at her. "You know you're dead if you laugh."

It had to be fairly uncomfortable folded over that way, but O'Malley had a devilish twinkle in his blue eyes.

"You don't look particularly dangerous to me."

"Ah, but sooner or later I'll be mobile again."

Okay, so maybe she'd been a bit hasty labeling him safe. Now that she wasn't suffering the heebie-jeebies from the dark hallway and had sort of figured out what was going on with O'Malley, she noticed he was wearing pajama bottoms. And nothing else.

Holy mother of God, his back was spectacular, a physical work of art. All the saliva in her mouth evaporated as heat rushed through her like a wildfire.

She ran her tongue over her dry lips. "How can I help you? I'm not a doctor."

"This has happened twice before at the gym. The trainer got behind me and sort of pulled, slow and steady."

"Okay." Portia moved behind him and swallowed hard. If he'd looked good from the doorway he was positively...orgasmic up close. The light from the bedside lamp spilled across him, burnishing his skin with a golden glow.

"If you can, straddle me and slip your arms under mine."

She braced her feet on either side of his hips and leaned down, hooking her arms beneath his armpits. He was hurt and she was helping, but, God help her, it felt wonderfully intimate to touch the satin of his skin, to smell his scent, to feel the brush of his pajama-clad hips against her bare legs.

"Don't try to pick me up. Just move forward a bit and then straighten me up."

Portia froze, her arms wrapped around his muscular torso, her face near his dark hair, her bra-free breasts precariously close to his muscular back. "I've never done this before. What if I don't do it right?" Not only would she feel bad for hurting O'Malley, but crippling the star wouldn't exactly go over big with her bosses, Lauchmann and Mueller. "I think we should call a doctor."

She untangled herself from him and discovered she could actually breathe again.

"No doctor. You're one of the most efficient people I've ever met. I trust you. This time try linking your hands, just to get a little more leverage."

Once again she wrapped her arms around him from behind. She linked her hands as he'd instructed and pressed them against his broad chest. Masculine hair teased her fingers.

Portia was suddenly, poignantly aware that she hadn't had sex in ten, long, dry years and her nipples were in hard, intimate contact with his back. Thank you, sex drive, for some spectacularly bad timing.

"That's it," he said, his voice more strained than ever.

He must be hurting to suddenly sound so strained, and here she was dithering like a sex-starved idiot. Wait. She *was* sex-starved, only she hadn't realized it until now because suddenly, around O'Malley, all she could think of was sex.

His heart pounded against her hand like a sledgehammer. He'd put his trust in her and she'd help him get some relief. Bracing herself, she tugged forward and then slowly pulled him into an upright sitting position.

"Uh, I need to lie down if you can sort of let go."

Mortified that she'd been standing there pressed against him, she immediately released him and stepped away, putting several feet between them. She was so wickedly strung out just from touching him that the whole distance of the house didn't even seem safe.

"So, you're okay now?" she asked, backing toward the door, desperate to escape O'Malley's appeal.

"I'm sorry to ask, but I need to ice it now." He cautiously climbed on the bed and lay flat on his belly. "There's a fridge over by the sofa, cleverly disguised as an end table. There's some ice in there."

Talk about stark contrasts between her room and his, from communal bath to in-room fridge. She crossed the room to the divan he'd referred to as a couch. Sure enough, the table was actually a fridge. She pulled out the modest ice supply. "Got any plastic bags lying around?"

"There was one but they picked my laundry up in it earlier."

"Hold on a second."

"I'm not going anywhere," he said dryly from his supine position on the bed.

Portia went into the bathroom and looked around. O'Malley's shaving gear, deodorant, toothbrush, and comb were strewn over the bathroom counter, but there were no bags. O'Malley was no neatnik, that was for sure. She grabbed a hand towel.

She had a plastic bag back in her room but that meant going out into that dark hallway two more times than was absolutely necessary. Probably either the kitchen or the laundry center had plastic bags but that also meant wandering around this place in the middle of the night, no thanks, or rousing some of the house staff and that seemed very thoughtless.

She walked back into the bedroom. Come on, she was resourceful. Think. Maybe the bedside table. She pulled opened the drawer and rooted around. No, nothing but a wide assortment of rubbers. She slammed the drawer shut. Whoa. Nah. Sure. Why not? If he ran out, she'd replace them. She re-opened the drawer and pulled out a condom.

"Oh, my God, Portia, this is like a fantasy come true," Rourke began in a choked voice, "but I'm not sure I'm up to this. Wait. What the hell am I saying? The sexiest woman in the universe is standing next to my bed unwrapping a condom. Hell, yes, I'm up to it. I just need to roll onto my back, but you'll have to do most of the work."

It took her hormonally oversaturated brain about a nanosecond to fill in those blanks and imagine herself peeling off her clothes, ripping off his pajamas and climbing on and going for a ride. No, no and no!

"I'm making you an icepack. For your back."

"Oh." He lay there for a second with his eyes closed, then reopened them. "Now would be a good time for a Vulcan mind meld, so I could erase what I just said. As if it wasn't humiliating enough for you to find me that way."

"Unfortunately for you, a true Vulcan mind meld would

give me total access to your thoughts and memories." Dear God, he'd called her the sexiest woman in the universe. The comment went right to her head and all of her other severely neglected womanly parts.

Without thinking she blew gently into the condom to open it. O'Malley watched her and it wasn't pain reflected in his eyes.

It was suddenly incredibly hot in his room. As if a furnace had been cranked, her internal heater was out of control. She packed ice into the penis-shaped rubber. She held it in one hand and put the ice in with the other. Her hand was warm, the ice was cold, and it became increasingly difficult to keep it under control. Damn, why'd she pick a lubricated one?

"Okay, I've already forfeited all my pride today, so I'll just confess that I can't watch you do that." He closed his eyes and immediately popped them open again. "Or, let's just say that I shouldn't."

She should turn her back, go into the bathroom, do anything other than what she was doing. If she were a heroine in a romance novel or a made-for-TV movie, she'd be written right out of the script for standing there and teasing him with her deliberate stroking movements. She'd left her brain somewhere, maybe in that spooky hall. The sexual energy pulsing between them made her feel almost drunk.

"You are a wicked woman, Portia Tomlinson. I think you have a sadistic streak."

"You're watching. Does that mean you're a masochist?"

"That's a distinct possibility where you're concerned."

She tied off the end of the icy phallus. She'd always known that the summer she'd worked kids' birthday parties as a clown and tied a gazillion balloons would come in handy one day.

She admired her handiwork. "Seems a shame to waste

it, but I understand you're in pain. I guess I'm willing to make a sacrifice. Where does it hurt?"

"You don't really want to know, so why don't we settle on my lower back?"

Laughing, she wrapped the ice-packed condom in the hand towel and knelt on the edge of the bed. She placed the bundle right above the drawstring waist of his pajamas. "How's that?"

"It's lower."

She scooted the hand towel against his pajamas, pushing the material down. Actually touching him didn't seem like the brightest move. "How's that?"

"No. A little lower."

She pushed lower still and only found bare skin.

"That's it. Right there."

No elastic band indicated boxers or jockeys, which meant no underwear. Just awesome man beneath those thin cotton bottoms. Suddenly it wasn't so funny. Suddenly it was hard to breathe, hard to look anywhere but at the expanse of gorgeous man-skin in front of her. And suddenly he wasn't just another pretty boy in Hollywood, he was O'Malley who wanted Vulcan mind melts to make her forget he thought she was the sexiest woman in the universe. It would be so easy to go with his misinterpretation. She could open another condom, roll him onto his back, touch him until he was aroused and then she could slide on top of him, take him inside her where she throbbed with an ache he'd started, and stay there until they were both satisfied…. She jumped off the bed like a scalded cat.

"Goodnight," she said, rooted to the spot. The sane portion of her urged her toward the door and sanity. The insane portion held her immobile, drinking in the sight of a sexy, half-naked O'Malley sprawled on silk sheets.

"Thank you. For everything." O'Malley said. "Is it true?" he asked, pointing to her T-shirt.

"What?" Portia instinctively glanced at I Love Nerds printed on the front of her shirt. Danny had given her the shirt for Valentine's Day. Trekkie, Harry Potter addict and fledgling mad scientist, her son took great pride in being a self-professed nerd. "Yeah. My...a friend gave it to me. I do love nerds. I adore them. I live with one."

"I see." The light in his eyes died.

"O'Malley, as far as we're both concerned, none of this ever happened."

Portia scrambled for the door. Nothing in those dark, labyrinthine hallways could possibly be as frightening as the things O'Malley made her want.

# 4

THE FOLLOWING MORNING Rourke presented himself on the terrace at precisely nine o'clock. He hadn't slept worth a damn last night; instead he'd wasted his time replaying his moment of humiliation when he'd revealed to Portia how eager he was to have her in his bed, torturing himself with the memory of her hands on his bare skin, the press of her breasts against his back, and trying to fit together the different pieces of the puzzle that comprised this fascinating woman. And taking heart in the knowledge that she wasn't immune to him either.

She sat at the far end of the terrace where the brilliant California sun wasn't impeded by the vine-laden pergola that cast a diamond pattern over the stone floor. He headed toward her, passing the mosaic fountain that burbled soothingly in the middle of the sun-dappled terrace.

Portia looked up from the notes she was making on her clipboard and offered a bright, impersonal smile. "Good morning. Thank you for being so punctual." He'd noticed over the last several days, much as on *The Last Virgin* set, that she worked hard, possessed infinite patience and was *always* on time.

If today was anything like the rest of the week, having a moment alone with Portia without wardrobe, camera and sound people around would be scarce after their morning briefing. He took advantage of the temporary privacy.

"About last night—"

"You handled yourself beautifully at dinner," Portia interrupted. "Just the right amount of attention to each woman. Have you made a decision?" She smiled and nursed a cup of tea, pleasant and neutral. Obviously the last night he was talking about—that she *knew* he was talking about—was not up for discussion.

Dressed in a suit, her hair in its signature twist, last night truly could have never happened. But it had—even if she was determined to pretend it hadn't. Unfortunately, no Vulcan could save him from his memories of her in his room with her hair hanging about her face in damp strands, sexy and disheveled in shorts and a T-shirt.

He'd been a long way from handling himself beautifully last night. He'd made a total fool of himself. When he'd looked up and seen her opening that condom…it had been like winning the lottery. It had been a moment of revelation, a revelation of how much he wanted her rather than the women he was supposed to choose from.

"Have you thought about who you want to eliminate?" she prompted him again, pulling him out of his thoughts.

*That* was easy enough. "Lissa Freeman."

She opened her mouth, a slight frown tugging at her blond brows and he preempted her. "I'm sure about Lissa and it's not because of the walkie-talkie thing the first day or the fact that she superglues herself to me like a permanent fixture every chance she gets." Rourke gazed past Portia to the spectacular canyon view and the exclusive homes dotting the hillside. "She's made several catty comments to and about the other women. I don't have time for people who feel good about themselves at the expense of someone else." He turned his back to the view and faced Portia, the sun warm against his neck and shoulders. Her scent drifted to him, around him.

"Then Lissa's out." Portia eyed him over her cup rim. "She really pushed your button, didn't she?"

Rourke shoved his hands into his pockets. "I was the someone else more times than I care to recall in junior high and high school." What the hell? Why not tell her? It wasn't as if he could humiliate himself any more than he already had last night.

She raised one delicate eyebrow. "I find that hard to believe."

He shrugged. "My nickname in high school was Rourke the Dork."

"Why would anyone call *you* that?"

"Because it rhymes?" Feeling extremely self-conscious and regretting having brought it up, he leaned against the thick arbor post covered in ropey vines. "I was tall and skinny with pop-bottle glasses and braces to correct a serious overbite. I was a dork, and I knew I was a dork. But I didn't need it pointed out in the hallway or at the lockers."

"That couldn't have felt good." Her voice held a soft note.

Great. He didn't want to be some object of pity. "That was then. The best revenge is living well and—" he gestured to the view beyond them "—here I am." It made a good cover for being here on Nick's behalf.

She nodded. "With twelve, make that eleven, of the world's most beautiful, wealthy women clam-oring for you."

"The dork's revenge."

"Well, you're certainly not a dork any longer." For a second he glimpsed heat beneath her ever-present reserve, sending a prickle of awareness through him. A breeze rustled the leaves overhead and teased a few strands of hair about her cheek.

"Sure I am. The outside may have changed a little, but I'm still the same inside. And that's not a problem for me. I'm fine being a dork." He really didn't want to talk about this any more. He dropped into a chair opposite Portia. "Okay, so Lissa's out of here…"

Portia made a note on her clipboard. "This is a little different from the last show. We'll gather all the contestants together and then you have to tell her."

He winced. "That's not a problem with Lissa, but this is going to get harder and harder. Most of them seem like nice women."

"That's great that you feel that way. Is there anyone in particular you feel like you really clicked with?"

*You.* But he knew as well as he knew his own name that particular answer would send her running out the door, the same way it had last night.

"It's still early yet for that."

"You're not making my job any easier." Her laugh washed over him like a cool brook beneath the warm sun. "There's no one you'd like to get to know better? Find out what really makes her tick?"

His heart thudded heavily in his chest as he looked into her eyes, telling her what he wouldn't voice. *You. I want to know you inside and out.*

"By *better* do you mean her favorite color? The taste of her skin? Her preferred ice cream flavor? The way she looks when she's just waking up and still drowsy? Whether she likes lazy afternoons with a crossword puzzle in front of a fire or a trip to a museum? Whether she prefers early-morning or late-night sex?"

An image flashed through his head of Portia in his bed, her hair fanned across the pillow, her eyes still heavy with sleep but heavier still with desire, reaching beneath the sheet and wrapping her hand around him. His body reacted as if his fantasy were reality.

For the span of a second, he read a reciprocal heat and interest in her gray-green eyes. She blinked and glanced down at her clipboard. "I suppose those would all be considered getting to know someone better." Despite her composure, her voice held a husky note.

Rourke knew a moment of dejection and elation. Elation that for one unguarded moment he'd glimpsed an answering heat, interest, awareness. Dejection that that was all he'd have—a glimpse. And in some weird recess of him, elation that she possessed the honor to walk away from this thing that simmered between them, since she lived with Danny, the love of her life.

Rourke drew a deep breath to clear his head. She wanted him to name someone he wanted to know better, and it couldn't be her. He gave her what she needed. "I'd like to get to know Carlotta Zimmerman better. She seems interesting."

Carlotta was, according to her dossier, actively involved in several children's charities. She seemed the least idle of the idle rich women he could choose from.

Portia looked mildly surprised. "Carlotta? Okay."

"Why does that surprise you?" Nearby, a bee droned in the bower above him.

"She's probably not who I would've picked for you. She's not as…" Portia stumbled.

"As glamorous? As flamboyant?" Carlotta was the shortest and the heaviest of the group.

"Well, yes."

"Do you think I can't look beyond the surface of a woman?" He held her gaze. "Is it just me, or men in general you think so little of?"

"I'm sorry. I've offended you and I didn't mean to." She apologized but didn't answer his question, and the mystery of what made Portia Tomlinson tick merely intensified for him.

PORTIA WATCHED Rourke gallantly divide his time between the women at lunch. Except Lissa, who'd been sent packing, making more than a few choice comments as she flounced out. You could always tell the correct people had been eliminated when they bitched and moaned their way out the door. Nonetheless, Portia'd been surprised that Rourke had eliminated her so early in the show. Lissa's net worth was more than the others' and she was hands down the most beautiful, if you discounted personality and disposition. But apparently personality and disposition counted with O'Malley, which took him one step further from being the boy toy she'd pegged him as.

Portia had gone back to her room after her briefing with O'Malley this morning and doubled up on her vitamins. She was usually healthy as a horse but she had to be coming down with strep or mono or some unnamed malady because she'd definitely felt feverish when he'd run through his litany of questions. Then she'd felt queasy when he'd expressed his interest in getting to know Carlotta better. And following the realization that there was probably more to O'Malley than just a pretty face and hot body, she'd developed a headache. So, she'd rushed back to her room and popped another vitamin pack.

And now, watching him charm his companions, and undoubtedly the viewers when this segment aired, she felt queasy again.

She was definitely coming down with something.

ROURKE ROLLED his shoulders to dispel his tension. They'd scheduled a break between lunch and whatever ridiculous activity they'd set up for this afternoon, and he needed it. He was definitely out of sorts. Eleven women were hanging on to his every word and all he could do was watch Portia, bemused by the way she tilted her head to one side when she conferred with Lauchmann, or Jerry the sound guy or any number of other people with whom she interfaced.

He was crossing the dining room when Jacey motioned him over. "You up for a quick camera lesson?"

"Sounds good to me." It was at least a distraction.

Jacey walked him through the equipment basics and allowed him to pan the room and zoom in on several areas.

"This is so cool, I can see why you love it," he said handing her the camera, his mood definitely improved by the impromptu Camera 101. It was more interesting than a mere distraction.

She grinned. "There are worse ways to make a buck."

Rourke hadn't planned to, but he pulled a move straight from high school and went fishing for information on Portia. "Yeah, but it must make relationships tough, being gone for two weeks or more at a time. I know Portia's boyfriend called the first day we were here."

Jacey did a double take. "Highly unlikely. Portia doesn't do boyfriends."

What the hell? She'd mentioned a live-in…. Was Danny short for Danielle? "You mean she's…."

"A lesbian?" Jacey laughed, which was much more like a bark than an actual sound of amusement. "No, although one of the set designers has a serious crush on Portia and wishes that were the case. As far as I know, Portia doesn't date. She works her ass off and that's about it."

Then who the hell was Danny, the so-called love of her life?

Rourke knew he should drop it, but he seemed singularly incapable. "I thought she lived with a guy."

Jacey's look was as openly speculative as his question. "I don't know. She keeps to herself. I know she has a kid, David or Darrell or something like that."

*He's the love of my life…I live with a geek.*

"Danny?"

"Yeah, that's it, Danny. I grew up with a single mom who worked and it doesn't leave a whole lot of room or time for fun."

Everything clicked into place for him, and Rourke tried shrugging off his obviousness. "I was just curious about her. She doesn't talk much about herself."

Jacey's look said she had his number. "Mmm. That's an understatement. She gets along well with everyone and pretty much gets close to no one. She sorta reminds me of myself," Jacey said with a grin, "but she plays better with the other children."

Rourke laughed again, but the wheels inside his head had shifted into overdrive. Portia had deliberately misled him. Not just once, but twice.

And he'd be very interested in finding out why.

"Geeze, this is really hot. Any hotter and the water's gonna boil," Jacey muttered, steadily filming the afternoon session.

Portia, standing behind the camerawoman, couldn't agree more. O'Malley and the princesses had spent the last hour and a half cavorting in the Turkish bath while discreet waiters served drinks. Watching bikini-clad, semi-drunk women crawling over O'Malley, spectacular in swim trunks, was more than working her nerves, extra vitamin pack or not. She closed her eyes, dropped her head and massaged her temples.

"Holy shit, we've got a catfight," Jacey said. "Hey Portia, are you watching this?"

Portia jerked her head up. Maggie, the socialite whose sex video had surfaced on the Internet, grabbed Carlotta Zimmerman by the hair and screamed, "You friggin' cow, that's where I was sittin'." Maggie slurred her words slightly, but there was nothing wrong with her grip.

Carlotta flailed, trying to get Maggie out of her hair. "Let go, you bitch." She made contact, the slap ringing out in the shocked quiet.

Oh. My. God.

"Whore." Maggie grabbed another handful and yanked again.

"Slut." Carlotta grabbed the front of Maggie's skimpy bikini top and yanked, pulling the top down, leaving Maggie bare-breasted.

Portia stood frozen to the spot.

Maggie lunged toward the other woman, screeching like a fishwife, "We'll show everybody who's a slut."

The censors would have a field day with this. So would the audience at home, filling in the blanks.

O'Malley pushed between the two women. "Easy, ladies." Maggie caught him with a right hook. He worked his jaw, but didn't take a restraining hand off either one of them, pointedly not looking at Maggie's free willies. "Ladies, I'd say this party's over."

Maggie climbed out of the water, stumbling along the way, pausing to pose for the camera. "This is my best side."

Maggie'd passed one too many drinks some time ago.

"Do you think she learned that at her Swiss finishing school?" Portia asked Jacey, coming out of shock mode.

"Oh, yeah. Daddy's dollars at work there." Jacey gave a raucous chuckle. "She could give lessons in the 'hood."

The rest of the women climbed out on the other side, surrounding Carlotta, giving the inebriated flasher a wide berth.

"Un-freaking-believable," Jacey said without taking the camera from her eye.

"Too bad we didn't know ahead of time, we could've filled the pool with pudding," Portia said. "Guess we'll be cutting back on the booze."

"Are you kidding? Our ratings just went off the chart. We just made reality TV history. And I don't think that was the booze at all. I think that was Maggie making sure she keeps a spot on the show."

"You're brilliant and so is she. That kind of stuff doesn't ruin the shoot, it makes it."

O'Malley hauled himself out of the pool, water sluicing down him.

"And that won't hurt our ratings either," Jacey said. "Okay, that's a wrap." She pulled the camera away and turned it off. "Burt's gonna have a freakin' kitten when he sees this." She nodded toward O'Malley toweling off at poolside. "Let's hope our beefcake doesn't come up with a bruise where she decked him."

For as many times as Portia'd referred to him as Boy Toy O'Malley and thought of him as just another pretty face, Jacey's "beefcake" struck her the wrong way. "He should ice it."

She left Jacey standing there and walked over to O'Malley. She felt absurdly prudish in her business suit when he wore only swim trunks and had just been treated to a free show of the best breasts Maggie's dad's money could buy. And his money had bought a big show. "Be sure you ice your jaw."

He shrugged his impossibly wide shoulders and a shiver slid down her spine. "She didn't hit me that hard."

"Better safe than sorry. We don't want to film you with a swollen jaw."

He shot her a look, an expression in his eyes that she couldn't define, but left her feeling flushed and unbalanced. "I'm going to my room to change. Why don't you bring me an ice pack," he said with a curious note of challenge. "I still don't have any plastic bags, but I do have quite a supply of—"

She cut him off. "I'll bring you an ice pack." She was irritable and probably on the verge of some terrible malady and she wasn't one of those simpering women in the Turkish bath. She wanted to tell him to fetch his own damn ice pack, but dutiful fetching topped her job description. Funny, she'd liked her job up until now. "Give me a couple of minutes."

She left him poolside and quickly made her way to the kitchen, where she rounded up a plastic bag and ice. Waylaid on her way out by a positively giddy Lauchmann, Portia was outside O'Malley's room half an hour later.

Her heart thumped wildly at the prospect of being alone with him in his room. Sans cameras. Maybe she'd worked in the business too long, but cameras kept people at arms' length, where she preferred them. She thought about Carlotta and Maggie.

She knocked on O'Malley's door. He yelled that it was unlocked and she let herself in. Locking his door was a good idea. He never knew when a drunk, naked, hostile woman might follow him. It could have just as easily been Maggie, with or without a bikini top, slipping into his room. Portia, however, held her counsel. He was a big boy and he could take care of himself. She might have to fetch his ice, but she wasn't his freaking mother.

He came out of the bathroom, fully dressed, but looking good enough to destabilize her knees. No. She most definitely wasn't his mother. Not even close.

She held up the bag. "Your ice."

He crossed the room and she was struck anew by how gracefully he moved for such a big man. He stopped in front of her and her world became O'Malley—his scent, the subtle rise and fall of his chest, the almost imperceptible sound of his breathing, the width of his shoulders, the blueness of his eyes, the curve of his mouth. Failed by her internal censor, she reached up and plied her fingers along his jaw. Warm, a faint brush of stubble. Her breath caught in her throat. "Does it hurt? Is it tender?"

O'Malley looked as mesmerized as she felt. "It's a little sore."

"Have you ever had two women fight over you before?"

"No." His voice was low and husky, his eyes dark. He tilted his head, leaning into her fingers still cupping his jaw. Oh, God, she was still touching him.

She meant to—really meant to—snatch her hand away, but he was such a beguiling combination of warm skin, rough seductive cologne, not to mention those lovely blue eyes that made her long for things she shouldn't...his taste, his touch.

She had no clue what they'd been talking about. The only thing she knew was that she wanted to kiss him more than she wanted to breathe. There was a list, longer than her arm, as to why she shouldn't, but she couldn't recall a single item on that list. Her urge to kiss him eclipsed everything else.

She slid her hand from his jaw to the back of his neck, her fingers curling into the texture of his thick, dark hair. His eyes darkened and he bracketed her waist with his hands. She pulled his head down to hers, until they breathed the same air. She stepped into him and...an icy cold penetrated her breast.

She jumped away from him, frozen sharply into reality, saved by the melting ice pack intended for her charge. She took another step back, totally appalled that she had almost kissed Rourke O'Malley.

Of all people, O'Malley. As if he wasn't assigned to her. As if she were one of the multitude of women flocking to the Website and chasing him down with panties in hand. At least she was still wearing her panties. Although she would've been pretty willing to peel out of them about two seconds ago.

She shoved the ice pack into his hand and took even a third step back, away from him, seeking sanity in distance. "You'd better ice that jaw."

He obligingly held the ice to his face, and with a distinctly predatory look, stepped toward her, closing the gap between them.

She looked at the heavy drapes lining the window, the brocade-covered chaise, the framed print on the wall of an intimate couple. Better the room's sensuality than losing herself in O'Malley. "That should help," she said, retreating farther.

"I'm already much better," he said, stepping forward.

They played a silent version of retreat and advance until Portia felt the press of the mattress against the back of her thighs and knew there was nowhere else to go. And it was happening again. Her heart pounded and she felt as if butterflies had taken flight in her stomach. A dark, hungry, sensuality stole through her.

"One question," he said, his eyes intense.

She swallowed. "Yes?"

"Why did you let me think Danny was a lover instead of your son? Are you involved with anyone?" O'Malley stood, ice pack to his jaw, his other hand by his side, but the heat in his eyes, the soft sexy timbre of his voice, touched her, wove around her, caught her up in the soft, hot folds of desire's blanket.

How did he know that? Of course any of the crew could've filled him in. Momentary panic assaulted her. She didn't want or need O'Malley interested enough in her to make inquiries. And the worst of it was, there was a smidgen of her, the woman in her that had responded to Sadie's teasing, that was flattered that he'd asked someone.

And *that* simply made her angry with both of them. She called on every ounce of her will to push away the want he aroused in her. His interest threatened her peace of mind and, given their respective roles in the show, was inappropriate. Who was she kidding? He'd asked her why she didn't like him, but she knew in a blinding moment of revelation that she'd been running from this overwhelming attraction since she'd met him.

"That's two questions, not one. You made an assumption I didn't correct. I prefer to keep my private life just that—private." She strove to keep her tone light, but cool and professional. Instead, her voice came out husky with a defensive note.

He tossed the ice pack onto the bed behind her, but still, mercifully didn't touch her. "Your son is the love of your life, the geek in your life, waiting at home for you, isn't he?"

Okay, so she'd hidden behind Danny. She'd sensed his interest and deliberately let O'Malley misconstrue her situation because there was nothing safe or sane about O'Malley's interest and the feelings it aroused in her. "You said one question. I answered that."

"There's no man at home waiting to kiss every inch of you from head to toe until he's drunk from your taste, your scent and the sound of you moaning for him to stop or take you further? There's no one waiting to wrap his arms around you and hold you until you drift off to sleep afterward, is there?"

His words and low tone seduced her and her body responded to the fantasy he wove. Need blossomed inside her as surely as if O'Malley had greeted her at the door, stripped her naked and proceeded to make love to her with his sexy mouth. One of them had to stop this madness.

"Stop. Stop it right now." She looked away from the tender promise of pleasure and passion in his eyes. "What possible difference does it make to you? Why are you doing this?"

He touched her. One finger against her cheek, that drew her gaze back to his and flooded her with heat.

"Because you asked me if I ever broke the rules and I told you only if I wanted something desperately. And I do. You."

# 5

"WHY ME?" Portia looked like a cornered wild creature. A part of him felt guilty for pushing her so hard, but the part of him that recognized her reluctant response to him won out. "You have all those women, not just the eleven in the house, but all those women running amok after you. Why are we even having this conversation?" She raised her chin a notch, challenging him. He dropped his hand to his side and she stepped away so that she was no longer between him and the bed.

Why her? Why not any of the other women? Rourke shook his head. "Hell if I know. It really complicates things and I don't like things complicated. Maybe it's the way you move your head to one side when you're concentrating. Maybe it's the No Trespassing signs discreetly posted despite your friendliness with everyone. Maybe it's the sexy line from your ankle to the curve of your calf."

He scrubbed his hand along the nape of his neck. "I don't know, Portia. I wish I did because it's as if I'm on a damned roller coaster."

Portia's eyes widened but she didn't say anything.

"I feel this energy pulsing between us, I see something in your face, your eyes, and I think you must want me as much as I want you. I find out you don't have a lover, you have a son. But why let me think that? Because you're not attracted to me, but you can't tell me to back off? Because you are attracted to me and don't want to be? Hell, I don't know. I just know I'm frustrated with myself. All of those women, some of them very nice, all of them beautiful, and all I can do is feel your every movement, where you are in the room, what you're doing. Sometimes I even think I catch a whiff of your fragrance."

He didn't dare look at Portia. He didn't know what he'd see. Was she horrified? Embarrassed? And he couldn't seem to shut the hell up. "And I'm damn afraid that Jacey with her all-seeing camera is going to capture it on film so I can be humiliated by mooning over you in front of the whole damn world, or at least the parts able to receive a satellite signal. So, I suppose we're having this conversation because I lie in that bed at night and think about you beside me, beneath me, on top of me. Because I ache for just one kiss, for one moment to hold you in my arms, against me, to breathe your fragrance, your essence. To hear my name cross your lips. Not O'Malley, but my name." He turned to face her then, except she was studying her hands as if they held universal secrets, and he laughed in self-recrimination. "Through no fault of your own, you are driving me mad."

For a man of few words, he'd found far too many. No doubt about it—that qualified as a tirade.

Silence sat heavy in the room, his words settling into the space between them. She raised her head and looked at him. She was neither horrified nor embarrassed. Her beautiful gray-green eyes that usually hid so much hid nothing now. They reflected longing and a measure of despair that brought his heart into his throat.

"I've tried denying it. Disdaining you. Ignoring you. And still I'm attracted to you." Yes! He took a step toward her. She held up a hand to stay him. "And we shouldn't be having this conversation. Nothing can change. We each have a role to play here and this isn't it."

She still wasn't where he longed for her to be—in his arms. But her admission felt like a huge leap forward.

"You're right. But I want two things."

She was already shaking her head. "I don't know."

"Portia, please. I'm dying here. You wouldn't do two little things to save a dying man?"

The resolve etched on her face softened in the slight curve of her mouth. A glimmer of a smile hovered in her eyes. "I don't suppose you'll do us any good if you're dead. What are these two things that I can do to save you?"

"Say my name and one kiss." He spread his hands, palms up. "That's not so unreasonable is it?" Well, maybe it was. Exactly when had he, the most reasonable of men, passed the point of reason regarding Portia? When she'd touched him? When she'd helped him to his bed and unwrapped that condom? When he'd discovered she didn't have a man in her life so surely he stood a remote chance? When she'd seemed to forget herself and cupped his jaw? Was it all of the above or was it the first time he'd seen her on the set of *The Last Virgin* and everything had just been a slow spiral from there?

"That won't solve anything." Portia was much more reasonable than he was.

"No. It won't. But can it make things any worse?" Perhaps she thought she could look at him the same after one kiss. He knew better.

"Rourke." His name rolled off her tongue with a musical lilt, strumming through him, as if he were hearing his name for the first time ever.

She stepped closer. "I know this isn't a good idea." But she slid her arms around his neck, cradling his head in her hands. He wrapped his arms around her, content for the moment to absorb the touch of her hands against his skin and hair, the feel of her in his arms, her sweet scent. He sighed against her hair, savoring each moment, unwilling to rush touching her, tasting her.

"Rourke…" she breathed his name against his neck, her mouth warm and moist against his skin. He clamped down on the desire that gnawed at his belly like a hunger and cautioned himself to take it slow.

Framing her face in his hands, he bent his head and kissed her. At first it was a tentative exploration and then it shifted and changed. Everything deepened. Her tongue met his in an intimate dance of parry and thrust. Hunger replaced tenderness.

Reluctantly he pulled away from her. Breathing had never been such an inconvenience. He was beginning to know Portia. She'd agreed to one kiss. He'd have one kiss and no more.

His chest heaving as if he'd just worked out, his breath still uneven, his body tight and hard, he rested his forehead against hers for a moment, reluctant to give up totally his proximity to her.

"Rourke…" He loved the way she spoke his name. Her face was flushed and her eyes were a soft smoky gray. Her lips were slightly swollen as if she'd just been thoroughly kissed, which she had, and he'd willingly sign on for duty again. This was yet another facet of the woman who so fascinated him.

She stepped away from him and he barely refrained from reaching to keep her. "You are so beautiful, you take my breath away."

She suddenly looked years younger. Flustered. Pleased. Unsure of herself. "You're too kind. It's more likely you just needed to come up for air."

Despite her flippant comment, she raised a hand to smooth her chignon into place and it was shaky. She'd been as affected by that kiss as he had. Her wristwatch alarm went off, shattering the intimacy between them, pulling them back into the reality of their respective roles. "You have to be at the salon in half an hour. But I need to talk to you first."

Rourke knew her well enough to recognize the transition. He also knew there wouldn't be another kiss or even a discussion of that kiss. Portia was back to business. "Go ahead."

"It's time for you to send another contestant home but Lauchmann wants you to keep both Maggie and Carlotta on the show."

He ran his hand over his jaw, neither pleased nor surprised. "Let me hazard a wild guess—it's all about the ratings."

Portia nodded. "It is all about the ratings. That's why we're both here." She crossed to his bedroom door.

Granted, they were here for the show, but the chemistry between them.... "Wait," Rourke stopped her, unable to shake the notion that if she walked out the door without some resolution, they'd lose something invaluable.

Her hand on the knob, Portia pivoted to face him.

"What about us? Where do we go from here?"

"There is no us. There can't be any us." She squared her shoulders. "But if there was, the only place for us is nowhere."

"You're wrong, you know." He looked at her, unwavering. "I'll be there in half an hour, but you need to know every time I look at one of those women, every time I touch her, kiss her, I'm thinking of you."

She fled as if a demon from hell nipped at her heels. He knew because the same demon pursued him.

FOR THE past two days she'd watched O'Malley charm and flirt with his women and she didn't know if it was the power of his suggestion or chemistry or what but all that sexual energy seemed to be directed at her.

Portia wanted to do something she hadn't done in years…plop down and have a good cry. Or bang her head against the wall.

Neither seemed a particularly good option in the middle of afternoon shooting.

For years she'd kept her nose to the grindstone and all of her impulses in check. Now she had almost ten friggin' years of stored impulses exploding inside her, around her, and generally turning her busy but well-ordered life upside down. Yeah, she'd been coming down with something. A raging mother of a case of lust.

And there he was, the inspiration and object of her towering lust, surrounded by ten women all trying to put the make on them. And he wanted her. Cry or head-bang? She simply didn't know, and ignoring it didn't seem to be working.

And today was particularly unnerving. Lauchmann had changed up the day's schedule this morning. He was so pleased with the previous day's filming—according to him O'Malley was exuding a sexual energy that wouldn't quit—that he'd accelerated the schedule to shoot a scene originally planned for later. Today was the day she'd dreaded ever since she'd read the loose scene notes.

O'Malley wore sultan garb and each of the women, outfitted in belly-dance attire, would perform a dance for him and then present herself to him for a question. The salon drapes were drawn and muted lighting bathed the red walls in an intriguing mix of light and shadows. O'Malley sat on one of the low sofas like a potentate. Several incense candles burned, filling the air with exotic eastern scents. Evocative music flowed from a hidden sound system, a rhythmic mix of drums, tambourine and flute.

And damn him to hell, just before he'd entered the room, when she was checking with him on any last-minute questions, he'd reminded her that it was her he wanted performing for him in a harem outfit. Every look, every command, every touch would be for her.

When she'd read the setting notes, it had sounded like a scene straight out of B-movie. It didn't feel that way now. It felt sensual. She felt too aware of her own body. Aware of the swing of her skirt against her legs, the gentle cupping of her bra against her breasts, the insistent ache between her thighs. She was in a state of almost painful want, mired in arousal, which defied reason and logic.

"He's really blossomed on screen. He's gone from hot to really hot," Jacey said, without taking her eye from the camera.

Dear God, she hadn't in a moment of lustful insanity said anything aloud, had she? "Who?"

Jacey spared Portia a disdainful look. "Who do you think? Lauchmann? Of course, Rourke."

Was there a woman alive who didn't fall under his spell? At this point, she was ditching her pride and throwing herself in with the rest of the pathetic women of the world. "He's okay."

Jacey snorted. "Portia, you're either half dead or you're jacking me around."

"Come on, Jacey. Don't you find that get-up just a little over the top?"

A pair of loose, blousing pants rode low on Rourke's hips, an open vest only partially covering his bare, lightly furred chest and muscled belly with its dark V of hair that disappeared under the waistband. An amulet was artfully wrapped around his bicep. No one in wardrobe was going for authenticity. This was all about titillation. He should've looked ridiculous. Instead he displayed just the right hint of arrogance, command and humor that left her body tight and humming.

"You're kidding, right?" Jacey glanced up from adjusting her camera settings. "I plan to beg, borrow or steal that outfit before I go back to New York so Digg can play dress-up. And I think you're lying through your teeth. I think… "

Portia interrupted Jacey, sensing it was better not to know what Jacey thought. She capitulated with a defeated laugh. "Okay, he's really hot."

"He asked me about you," Jacey said.

Ah. He'd found out from Jacey. Not a big surprise. They were operating with a skeleton crew on the technical end. Wardrobe and makeup, however, they had out the wazoo.

"He mentioned Danny. I assumed he'd found out from someone on the set. It wasn't a big deal. He's just one of those people who's curious about other people."

"Uh-huh, and I believe in Santa Claus and the Easter Bunny. It didn't feel that way to me." Jacey shot her another look. They couldn't start filming soon enough to suit Portia. Then Jacey would have to focus on the camera and this conversation would be over. "He's a nice guy, beneath that pretty-boy face. Almost as nice as Digg."

Dammit, that was part of the problem. He *was* nice. And he seemed to have a brain. And personality. And integrity. And regardless of how friendly she and Jacey might get, Jacey was still the executive producer's daughter. The last thing Portia needed was Burt Mueller calling her on the carpet for impropriety. That would be rich, especially from someone with Mueller's past reputation for being a womanizer, on and off the set.

"Yeah. He's handsome, hot and nice to boot. And I'm sure he won't have any problem picking out an equally beautiful, hot, nice woman," Portia added, as much for her own benefit as for Jacey's.

Jacey spared her a sly look. "Oh, I have a feeling he's already found her. I can spot chemistry a mile away. Rourke was hot on the last set, but from the beginning I felt the real sparks were between Zach and Andrea."

Portia tried leading her down another path. "Maggie certainly causes some sparks."

"Hmmph. You and I both know Lauchmann made him keep her in the game so she can threaten someone else into another catfight and drive his ratings off the chart." Once again, Jacey glanced away from the camera and Portia felt pinned by the younger woman's laser gaze. "Ya know, there's one good reason we have rules—so we can break 'em. Digg and I met on a set."

Portia nodded in acknowledgment. "I heard."

"I can tell you heard I got fired for about a day. And no, I didn't get rehired because my old man's in charge. I got rehired because I'm good at what I do and the director was a turd. From what I've seen, you're a workaholic. You could use a little TLC," Jacey said.

Portia couldn't just walk away from the con-versation. They should've been shooting by now. She desperately wished Jerry would fix his sound problems so they could get on with the filming.

"If I thought I did, work would be the wrong place to look for that," Portia said.

"Considering the hours we put in, work's about the only option," Jacey said with a disgusted snort. "You'll be shocked to know I'm a rule breaker from way back. I'm throwing out a wild guess that you aren't. There are times you have to break rules and do it with an attitude. But, unless you're trying to make a statement, the key to breaking the rules and getting away with it is discretion."

Portia was saved from answering by Jerry giving the thumbs-up on the boom mike. "Got it. Let's get this party started."

Carlotta entered the salon through the double doors, her hips keeping time to the music. She swayed and swirled across the room and around Rourke on the divan. She was a decent dancer and Portia knew a moment of stabbing jealousy at Rourke's lazy, sexy smile. And as if he were tuned into her thoughts, he chose that moment to look at her. It may have looked as if he were glancing toward the camera, but his look rocked through her. *Every look, every touch is for you.*

Carlotta ended her dance, bowing at his feet. The music lowered to a background level and O'Malley posed the question he'd been told to ask in a silky, commanding voice that sent shivers down Portia's spine, "If you had me for a night, what would you do?"

"We'd go out to dinner and then maybe some shopping before we went back to your place."

What? Pathetic. If Portia had a man like O'Malley at her disposal for the evening she'd spend her time *shopping?* Carlotta Zimmerman was an idiot with a capital I.

"And would we shop for something *interesting?*"

The way Rourke caressed the last word immediately brought to mind naughty lingerie and massage oils.

"Shoes. I really like shoes. I have a closet built especially for my shoes."

Make that a double idiot. Beside her, Jacey bit back a snort of laughter. Rourke, looking somewhat surprised by her answer, seemed hard-pressed not to laugh as well.

Portia wouldn't spend her time shopping for shoes if she had him for a night. Unfortunately, she'd spent far too much of her time, both waking and sleeping, imagining what she'd do with, to and for O'Malley.

Tara Mitchells came in next. She was tall and willowy but not nearly the dancer Carlotta had been. Portia's mind wandered.

So, why not just go ahead and have a little fling with Rourke O'Malley? Maybe because she had to work with him. Why not just wait until after the shooting and then if they were still interested in one another…. No way. That implied something more long-term, more than a fling and she wasn't about to go there. She knew other single moms whose main focus was to get married or remarried. No thanks. She'd done all right by herself and Danny so far. She didn't have any interest in dating. Not only did she lack the time, she also wasn't willing to open Danny up to a barrage of men coming and going in their lives.

Particularly now when Danny was hungry for a male role model. It was evident in the way he'd glommed on to his grandfather, Portia's dad. But dating didn't mean marriage and she couldn't see herself ever getting to the marriage stage. Marriage meant trusting, opening yourself up to betrayal.

She'd learned the hard way to rely only on herself. People made mistakes and you could cut them slack for that. They weren't necessarily stupid. But when they didn't learn from their mistakes and repeated them, then they qualified as stupid. And Portia was a lot of things, but she certainly didn't want to be considered stupid.

However, this *was* her last location assignment. Rourke O'Malley lived on the other side of the continent. She was southwest, he was northeast. She'd fought it, denied it, all to no avail. He did something for her. In a big way. He was doing something major for her now. Portia had no idea how the whole room didn't know that she'd like to push the other women aside and claim him herself.

The dancing lasted an interminable amount of time. Or

at least it seemed that way to Portia. Not that O'Malley seemed to mind all the gyrating and hip-thrusting coming his way.

Finally, Maggie was the last woman to dance. She stepped onto the back of the divan, bracing one foot on the side and one foot on the back, her crotch poised over his head.

A few of the women gasped, one giggled—probably Carlotta the idiot. The entire thing irritated Portia beyond measure. Maggie shook her tasseled breasts and undulated in time to the music, leaping off the divan as the song ended. She leaned forward, her breasts on either side of Rourke's neck.

"You had a question for me, Master?" she said.

With a wicked grin, he looked up, rather than left or right, which would have put his mouth right next to her breasts, and asked her the same thing he'd asked the other women.

"I'd pretend I was a genie in a lamp and if you rubbed me just right I'd make three wishes come true," Maggie practically purred.

Portia longed for the detachment she'd mentioned to O'Malley. She longed for the woman who didn't stand around, practically aquiver with lust during a shoot. She knew what she'd do if she had Rourke O'Malley for a night. She'd get him out of her system.

Perhaps Jacey was right, there was something to be said for discretion. Tonight, one way or another, there'd be a woman in O'Malley's bed. And she planned to be that woman. If she could beat Maggie there.

ROURKE ROLLED his head on his shoulders. Geeze, he was wound tight. He had a newfound respect for actors. Not that he was Tom Cruise by any stretch of the imagination, but on this "reality" show he was definitely an actor. Lauchmann, the producer, had told Rourke how pleased he was with the shoot so far. He'd reminded Rourke of the proverbial cartoon character with dollar signs in his eyes. According to Lauchmann, Rourke "sizzled" on the screen. Luckily, Lauchmann was clueless that all Rourke's sizzle came from his intense attraction to Portia that seemed to grow exponentially every day. Or hell, maybe Lauchmann knew and was willing to look the other way because he was getting what he needed for his show. Nothing in the inside workings of TV production, particularly "reality" TV could surprise him anymore.

He pulled a bottled water out of the minifridge in his room and took a long, quenching drink, but that didn't cool him down. His heat was internal. Sexual. It was going to take more than water to quell the fire inside him. A knock sounded on his door and he almost groaned aloud. Please, let it be anyone other than Portia. He was so wound up he didn't think he could take one of her debriefings tonight, where he looked but couldn't touch. Where she was near, yet separated by an emotional distance he couldn't seem to span with her.

He crossed the room to unlock the door. Let it be Lauchmann, or one of the wardrobe ladies here to pick up the pants and vest he was still wearing, or one of the maids with towels, or any of the other crew or staff. Hell, at this point, Maggie tracking him down would be preferable to another no-touch close encounter of the Portia kind. With any luck, it wouldn't be her.

He flung open his door. Luck had taken a holiday. Portia, wearing a khaki-green suit that brought out the green in her eyes, stood there clutching her clipboard. Rourke wondered briefly if she even slept with the damn thing.

A wave of desire slammed him. Maybe it was the outfit, maybe it was all the pent-up desire, but he felt reckless, dangerous and he let her see that in his eyes.

"May I come in?" she asked with an underlying breath-lessness. There was something different about her tonight. Maybe edginess was catching.

He knew his smile had a sharpness to it when he stood to the side and swept his arm out in invitation. "What can I do for you this evening, Ms. Tomlinson?" In a perfect world, what she'd like for him to do for her would coincide with what he very much wanted to do for her. But luck had skipped town and it wasn't a perfect world.

"Wardrobe is shorthanded tonight. Cindy Lu is sick. So I offered to help out and pick up your costume," she said looking down at her clipboard, as if consulting a note there.

"Well, give me a minute and I'll get the costume to you and then you can cross me off your list for the evening."

"I thought I could help you with that," she murmured, seemingly fascinated by something on her clipboard.

Okay, he'd misconstrued a situation with her once before and he wasn't about to set himself up again. "How's that?"

"I could help you out of that costume, Rourke," she said, looking up. What he saw took his breath. Naked desire that echoed his own burned in her eyes. This was no cool, shuttered glance, no calm dismissal, no retreat behind a closed door. This was need and passion and all thought fled his methodical, reasoning brain except the singular idea that she wanted him as much as he wanted her and she wasn't presenting a litany of arguments but rather was saying his name in that low, husky tone that nearly brought him to his knees.

"Portia." He reached for her and then pulled back. "If I touch you, I'm not sure I'll be able to stop."

She walked toward him, spanning the gap that separated them. "Maybe I don't want you to." She trailed one finger down his naked chest and he shuddered.

It was his turn to be surprised. "What?"

"I said I want you to touch me and I think I'd prefer if you didn't stop once you start."

He almost asked if she was sure. He almost asked how this would work tomorrow. He almost asked how long she could stay. But instead, he realized none of that mattered. Whatever she was willing to give, he'd take, and, he hoped give even more in return.

"Let me make sure I've got this right. You're offering to undress me and I get to touch you and not stop?"

"That pretty much sums up the situation."

He started to pull her into his arms, but she was holding onto that damned clipboard of hers like a lifeline. "Give me that."

She handed it over and he tossed it onto the coffee table. "I hate that thing."

"My clipboard?" she asked with a laugh as he pulled her hard against him.

"You hide behind it like it's a warrior's shield."

"Maybe I do."

He found the three pins holding her hair in place and pulled them out, dropping them to the floor. Like a shimmering silver-blond curtain, her hair fell past her shoulders. He immersed his hands in the silky mass and buried his face against the fine texture, breathing in her clean, fresh scent. He was definitely a dork at heart. He'd wanted her, and only her, for weeks, and now he had her in his arms and didn't know what to do. He stood, his face buried in her hair, paralyzed by his own want.

"You're exquisite. Fragile," he said.

She leaned back in his arms and looked up at him. "I'll take exquisite, any woman would. But there's nothing fragile or breakable about me. I'm tough."

He traced his finger down her delicate jawline, her throat's slender column, traversing her collarbones and beneath her suit edge to the soft swell of her left breast. Her heartbeat raced beneath his fingertip. "What about your heart?"

She shook her head, her hair skimming the back of his hand. "Especially not my heart. That's not even a remote option. So don't worry about my heart." A hint of melancholy marked her smile. Her professed invulnerability rendered her all the more vulnerable. "But you can carry on with exquisite all day," she said, pressing the swell of her breast against his fingertips.

Rourke didn't know exactly what or who had driven her to lock her heart away so securely. He suspected Danny's father. And he'd find out why later.

Right now, he was going with what he did know. And at that moment, Rourke knew exactly what to do. He knew exactly what Portia needed. She needed to be loved. And he knew just the man for the job.

# 6

PORTIA DIDN'T NEED Rourke to worry about her heart, although it was rather sweet and unlike the men she knew. She needed him to put to bed, lay to rest—every other bad pun she could think of—this restless longing, this incredible ache he'd awakened.

For ten years she'd gotten by nicely without wanting a man. Sex with Mark had been okay, a bit of a disappointment, so abstinence hadn't been such a hardship. She'd been her own island and after all that time, damn it, Rourke came along and made her want and need as she never had before. It stood to reason, if he was the cause, he was also the cure. She'd get this behind her and she'd be good for another ten, maybe even fifteen years.

For a brief second she considered the risk to his heart but then dismissed the notion. From her life observations, men didn't lay their hearts on the line with sex as so many women were prone to do. As she'd done once before. But she'd learned from her mistake.

Portia had waited so long, her hands shook with need as she laced them behind his neck and pulled his mouth down to hers. She greeted him with a hot, openmouthed kiss. All that pent-up sexual energy had her in a flux. She felt as if she couldn't wait another second. But then again, she wanted it to last. She wanted to take it slow, let it go on and on; after all she was saving up for another long haul.

She closed her eyes and lost herself in the sheer joy of their kiss. The taste of his mouth, his heat, the sweet mating of his tongue with hers, the faint rasp of his beard against her skin, his scent, his strength tempered by gentleness.

He raised his head. "I've wanted you since I first saw you on the set of *The Last Virgin*." That left her as breathless as his kiss. "I didn't want to want you." He laughed ruefully. "But sometimes free will doesn't stand a chance." Rourke shifted, raining hungry kisses along her jaw, down her neck, his hands spanning her lower back, pulling her closer, tighter against the length of him. "I didn't stand a chance, once I'd met you."

She, who kept everyone, except her immediate family at arms' length, especially men, felt an intimacy in his touch, a desire for closeness that was alien yet didn't send her running for the door.

Portia pressed closer, reveling in the feel of his body against hers. It was as if his chest had been made for the press of her breasts. "I didn't want to be attracted to you either." She slid her hands beneath his vest, caressing his naked back. "Not even a little bit. You weren't part of my plan." Slick, wet desire pooled between her thighs where the hard ridge of his arousal pressed intimately. Her entire body shuddered at the sensual contact she'd foregone for so long. Actually, she hadn't foregone *this,* because *it* had never been like *this.* "I've fought the good fight, but sometimes surrender isn't giving up."

"I still can't quite believe you're here." Rourke dropped to the loveseat and pulled her down onto his lap, molding his fingers to the curve of her shoulders. "You are so beautiful."

"Hmm. I bet you say that to all the girls," she teased, but a very real part of her needed his reassurance that this was about her. Especially after he'd spent the evening being entertained by partially clad women performing exotic dances.

His blue eyes, like a cloudless sky on a hot summer day, were intense. "There've been far fewer *girls* than you seem to think. And it's not a line. It's the truth. You take my breath. Make me ache."

Given the women he'd been bombarded with, his words were even more meaningful. And with the way his hands and his eyes caressed her, she felt beautiful. And sexy and suddenly young and more carefree than she had since... perhaps ever. "Well, then...thank you."

He brushed his thumb over her cheek. "I've never met a woman like you, Portia. You're special."

God, it should have sounded like a bad line out of a bad script, but the way he said it and the way he touched her, made it poignant. She'd felt special with Mark, Danny's dad. She'd believed that he'd wanted her because she was who she was. But then after she'd wound up pregnant and he'd been so quick to skip out, she'd figured out that it wasn't her at all, but that she'd been vulnerable and available and that Mark had used her. That had been apparent enough when he'd moved on so quickly to the next available, non-knocked-up girl.

But with Rourke, she truly felt special. He had his pick of women and there was something about her, Portia, that floated his boat. He wanted her because she was Portia Tomlinson. And even though she wasn't going for a relationship, it was a nice feeling. *She* did it for him. And, heaven help her, he certainly did it for her.

"I've never met a man like you, either. You're one of a kind," she said.

It wasn't just the fact that he was gorgeous, it was the total package. The way he talked to a person as if they were the only one in the room. His slightly old-fashioned gallantry and courtesy. And beneath that handsome, polished exterior, she saw his geekiness. Weird as it might be to some people, it was even more of a turn-on to her. It made him real. Not so much like getting naked with Michelangelo's *David* or some other model of male perfection.

"I don't even care if you say that to the other men in your life," he said, a light reference to her earlier comment.

"No, Rourke. Only you."

As if her answer gave him immense satisfaction, he dipped his head and breathed a sigh against the base of her throat, his breath warm against her skin. He nuzzled a series of kisses along her collarbone until he met her suit jacket.

He hesitated, his eyes questioning her, letting her set the pace.

She sat back from the hard wall of his chest. "This is in the way," she said, unbuttoning her jacket.

His eyes burning brightly, he slid the jacket over her shoulders. His fingers trailed a line of fire along her bare skin and down her arms. He briefly closed his eyes and then reopened them. "I want to re-member you like this. Beautiful, disheveled, sexy."

Her heart hammered in her chest. "You are the most gorgeous man I've ever seen," she said, leaning forward to press her lips to his bare chest. He was big and broad and well-muscled. Heat flash-pointed through her when she tasted the texture of his skin.

She flicked her tongue against him, finding his flat male nipple. His heart hammered beneath her questing tongue and he groaned her name against the top of her head. He reached around her back, searching for her bra hook.

With a wicked smile—at least she hoped it was wicked and sultry because that's how she felt—she reached between them and unsnapped her bra. "Front hook."

"Once a geek, always a geek," he said with the sexiest smile she'd ever seen.

Still holding her bra together, although it was unhooked, she teased him, "I told you I have a soft spot for geeks. And a hot spot. And something of a wet spot."

She saw a flicker of surprise in his eyes, quickly followed by heat at her sexy playfulness. She'd sort of surprised herself, but hey, she'd made the decision to be here and she wanted to experience it to the fullest.

Despite her bravado, she knew a moment of uncertainty. Her breasts weren't as pert as they'd been at seventeen, the last time she'd been naked in front of a man. As if he were tuned into every nuance of her, Rourke gentled his hands over hers and opened her bra, revealing her.

He didn't say anything. He didn't have to. The look in his eyes said everything. She shrugged out of the bra, the cool air and his hot gaze sliding over her bare skin. Rourke traced his fingers across the slopes. His touch felt wonderful and her nipples peaked in anticipation. She dropped her head back and leaned back, bracing herself on her hands, offering herself to him. He rolled her turgid points between his fingers and the sensation coursed through her, notching up the intensity of the throb centered between her thighs. Instinctively she writhed against the erection pressed against her buttocks and the hands on her breasts. He bent forward and traced a delicate path around her areola with his tongue.

"Yes," she panted. But it wasn't enough. He licked a similar pattern on her twin peak and she arched toward him.

"Tell me what you want. Do you want me to stop? Do you want more?"

She was on fire. She'd never wanted anything as badly in her life as she wanted him to take her in his mouth and assuage the torment.

"Yes. More. Harder." She wasn't capable of saying more than that.

His mouth, warm and wet, closed over the aching crest and she cried out.

It was intensely erotic to be dressed from the waist down and naked above.

He slid his hand beneath her skirt and touched her through the damp satin of her panties. The first tremor of an orgasm shook her. Rourke pushed aside the cloth barrier and his fingers swept her slick swollen fold and the nub beyond, his hard-on tormenting her from behind. His mouth crushed against hers, his tongue mimicking the movements of his fingers and Portia gave herself over to the orgasm that rocked her.

ROURKE, his fingers still slick from her, smoothed his hand over her belly, awed he was here, making love to this incredible woman, and that for the time being he could touch her so intimately, yet so casually.

She looked up at him, her hair spilling over the edge of the sofa, her breasts with their darker tips bared, a satisfied smile curving her lush mouth, her delicious bottom pressing against his erection. All of a sudden Rourke understood why men beat on their chests, why they fought wars over a woman's touch.

"If this was an old movie script, I'd carry you to my bed and finish having my wicked way with you. Ravish you. Isn't that the way it goes? The sultan doesn't want the available harem girls? Instead he wants the fair foreigner," his voice dropped, "and the sultan always takes what he wants."

"I think you've got it right so far." Her voice was low and throaty, her eyes not nearly so slumberous. There was a different kind of glint in them now. He'd definitely turned her on.

"Hmm. And once he has his way with her, she becomes his willing love slave." He ran his finger along the seam of her lips and she took his finger into her mouth, sucking it, laving it with her tongue. The sensation arrowed straight to his throbbing penis and he surged against her buttocks. He withdrew his finger and trailed it down her throat and her chest. "Opening her tender self to his every whim." He caught her nipple between his thumb and forefinger and she ground against his shaft. He continued his journey down her body. "His every desire." He palmed her mound through the layers of skirt and panties.

Panting, her eyes alight with sensuality, devilment and challenge, she sat up and straddled him, her skirt riding up to the tops of her thighs, her sex just out of reach of his erection. "I think that script goes another way." She leaned forward until her nipples teased against his chest, trapping his shaft between her and his belly. "The sultan becomes enslaved by the very woman he sought to conquer." She slowly slid up his cock and he nearly came at the contact, despite the layers of clothing between them.

He dropped his head to the sofa back and caught her hips in his hands, sliding her along the length of him again. And again.

He shuddered, suddenly unable to take any more of her sweet torture. He grabbed her beneath the buttocks, slid her up the rest of his body and stood with her half tossed over his shoulder, her breasts against his back, her woman's fragrance tantalizingly close to his face. He covered the distance to the bed in three strides, ripped the covers back, and tossed her onto the bed. "We'll just have to improvise when we get to that part."

He stood at the edge of the bed, looking at her sprawled against the beige silk sheets. Still watching her, he opened the bedside table drawer and tossed an entire box of condoms on the bed. Not looking away, Portia slowly unzipped her skirt and slid it, along with her panties, down her hips, her legs and dropped them at his feet. She opened the box of condoms, pulled out a foil packet, and opened it. She lay back on the sheets, spreading her legs, giving him the glimpse of paradise he was so hungry for, and wet her lips with the tip of her pink tongue. "Do you prefer Master or Master Rourke?"

That drove him straight over the edge. He dropped the foil square on the bed, shrugged out of the vest and pulled off the pants. She offered him the package and he quickly sheathed himself. Wrapping his hands around her thighs, he dragged her to the edge of the bed and she spread her legs wider to accommodate him.

He could barely think beyond how much he wanted to be inside her. "Portia, I don't want to rush you...I want to make sure you're ready..."

A look crossed her face he didn't understand. As if she were enjoying a private joke. "Rushed? Not at all. I'm definitely ready."

He nudged into her and stopped, savoring the sensation of her tight wet heat gripping him. Portia gasped.

"Are you okay?" he asked.

"Oh, my....yes." She wrapped her legs around his hips, urging him forward with her feet against his buttocks.

It would be so easy to thrust into her, but Rourke kept it slow, easing into her until she was panting and his hands shook. And then it was out of his control because she bowed up, taking him as far into her body as she could, her muscles clenching around him, gripping him.

"Portia..." She felt so good.

"Rourke..."

They performed the intricate steps to the dance as old

as man, the music inside them growing wilder, faster. Portia writhed beneath him like a woman possessed. Rourke held on to his self-control until she cried out with the first wave of her orgasm and then he came with her.

Rourke collapsed beside her, rolling her on her side to face him, still inside her, reluctant to break their connection. She lay very still, her eyes closed.

"Portia?"

She opened her eyes to a lazy half-mast. A sated smile curved her lips. "I've never felt this good before in my life. Now *that* was perfect."

"We *are* pretty incredible together," he said, pulsing deep within her.

Like a curtain-fall at the end of a play signaling to the audience that the suspension of belief was over, her expression changed as reality replaced their lovemaking. She carefully disentangled herself from him, slipped off the side of the bed, and disappeared into the bathroom.

Within a few short minutes, she came back into the room, and gathered her clothes off the floor. He'd hoped she would stay a little longer. A lot longer.

She picked her panties and skirt up from beside the bed. "Don't go," he said.

She paused and looked at him through the sheer material at the corner of the bed. "I have to."

"Not yet." His blood felt thick and hot and it was already starting to pool in his sex again just seeing her naked through the gauzy material.

"I've already stayed longer than I should have." There was a hint of wistfulness and melancholy about her smile. "Have you forgotten that a camera recorded when I came in here? We've already spent too much time *talking*."

She pulled on her panties and slipped on her bra.

"Oh, hell. I did forget."

She zipped up her skirt. "Neither one of us can afford to forget. It's why we're both here." Shrugged into her jacket and buttoned it.

He wanted to say to hell with why they were both here. He wanted to pull her back into his bed and sleep with her by his side through the night. He wanted to wake up with her head on the pillow next to his, her soft body curled into his, and make love to her all over again until she shattered around him again. He gave in to the temptation.

"And what if we said to hell with why we're here?"

"You know neither one of us can do that. You've got a contract and I...well, my stakes are high, too."

"What are your stakes?"

She finger-combed her hair and neatly twisted it behind her head, securing it into place. "It's not just my job. If this goes well, I get promoted to a studio position and that means I'm home with my son."

With each zipper, button, hairpin she became inaccessible once again. It was like unwrapping a Christmas present only to have it taken away and put on a closet shelf where you could see it but couldn't play with it.

Rourke plummeted from the euphoria of great lovemaking to the other end of the spectrum as he considered the weight of their respective obligations. Her son was counting on her and Nick was counting on him.

Dammit. He'd find a way to make it all work. He had to. She was worth it. "When can I see you again?"

She didn't pretend to misunderstand. She shook her head. "I don't know. I should say this isn't going to happen again...."

"No," he said.

She smiled at his vehemence. "But I don't think that's realistic. You know you have to spend some time with one of your candidates when you're not with them as a group."

She picked up that damn clipboard and slipped her feet into her shoes.

Once again, she was so calm, cool and collected and Rourke was frustrated with the situation he'd gotten himself into. Damn it all if he didn't feel like some high-priced man-whore. She could at least pretend that the idea bothered her.

"Doesn't it bother you to know I'll be with another woman?"

She jerked her head up at that. "How can you ask me that? You think I won't go out of my mind thinking of you touching one of them the way you touched me? Do you honestly think I want them to know how you taste? How you feel? Do I want to think about one of them wearing your scent on her skin the way I am?"

Remorse flooded him. "I'm sorry. I'm just frustrated...." He ran his hand through his hair.

"I know. I've got to go." She knelt on the edge of the bed and pressed a hard kiss to his lips. "I'll see you tomorrow morning at nine."

She started to walk away and then turned around, scooping the pants, vest and shoes off the floor by the bed. "Almost forgot these."

He watched his amazing woman walk to the door. His. Definitely his.

"Portia..."

She turned to face him. "Yes?"

"I'm not usually a jerk."

She smiled, her skin flushed, "I didn't think you were."

No. He wasn't usually a jerk, but then again, he'd never been in love before.

PORTIA CLOSED her bedroom door and leaned against it. She'd run into both Lauchmann and Jerry the sound guy on her way back to her room. Amazingly enough she'd managed to carry on an intelligent conversation about tomorrow's schedule without either one of them looking at her any differently than they usually did.

Amazing since she felt as if her whole person screamed *sex*. She felt like sex, from the tenderness between her thighs to the hypersensitivity of her breasts. She smelled like sex. God knows, she still tasted Rourke against her tongue.

She had never, ever suspected sex could be that good. A ten-year hiatus after Mark hadn't been a hardship. But sex with Rourke had been a whole new experience, opened a whole new world to her. Or maybe it was just this first time. Like the first drink of water to a woman who was parched or the first glimmer of spring after a cold winter.

Still leaning against the door, she kicked off her shoes and pulled the pins from her hair. It tumbled past her shoulders and she closed her eyes, picturing the look on his face when he'd taken her hair down. She sighed. She could still feel his fingers in her hair, his breath against her skin.

A knock on her door shattered the moment. Perhaps because she was caught up in him, her first thought was Rourke. He shouldn't come to her room.

She opened the door. Jacey stood on the other side. Relieved he hadn't been that insane, and unreasonably disappointed in equal measure, Portia pasted on a smile. "Hi."

"Can I come in?" Jacey asked.

Gathering her wits, Portia stood aside. "Of course. Come in." She closed the door behind the other woman. "Have a seat," she offered her the ladderback chair tucked in the corner.

"Nah, that's okay." Jacey scrutinized Portia. Maybe it was the discerning eye of seeing things through a lens. Perhaps it was that she looked for details instead of the

whole picture. Maybe it was because women were generally more discerning than men that she saw what Lauchmann and Jerry had missed. Regardless, Portia knew the
instant that Jacey realized she'd just been tumbled by
Rourke O'Malley.

"Oh." A slow smile joined the knowing glimmer in
Jacey's eyes. "You'll definitely be interested in this. I
thought you needed to know we're having some camera
troubles."

Portia reached for her clipboard. "What kind of camera
troubles?"

"Specifically with the camera in Rourke's wing of the
building. Seems we're having a problem with it recording
between nine at night and seven in the morning. It seems
to be looping back on itself," Jacey said.

Great. Like they needed this. "When did you first notice?"

"Today."

"So it didn't record last night?"

"No. There wasn't a problem last night."

Portia looked up from her clipboard. "Well, if you just
found it today, how do you know it won't work until tomorrow morning?" This wasn't making any sense.

"Because sometimes the totally unexpected happens
and short-circuits the wiring we've worked on so carefully." She offered a typical Jacey shrug. "Shit happens. We
may not have that camera working properly before we're
through. And of course if someone," she looked pointedly
at Portia, "were entering or leaving O'Malley's room between those times, it wouldn't be caught on tape."

Click! The proverbial lightbulb went off in her sex-sat-
urated brain. Jacey had fritzed the camera so Portia and
Rourke could have time together. She *was* the original rule-
breaker. "Why are you telling me this, Jacey?" Portia asked,
wondering silently just what Jacey's true motivation was.

Jacey offered her signature shrug, but a look in her eye indicated she knew *exactly* what it was that Portia really wanted to know. "Because you're the associate producer and I thought you should know. Because rules are meant to be broken. Because some opportunities come once in a lifetime." She shifted from one black-booted foot to another. "And I'll have to seriously consider offing you if this ever goes any further 'cause it's so damn stinkin' Pollyannaish, but because everyone deserves to be happy."

Great. Jacey had morphed into a Goth matchmaker and Portia found it incredibly touching that the tough young woman would do this.

"Thank you for telling me. I'll schedule things accordingly. That's good information to have," Portia said. Message sent, received, acknowledged and it was time to change the subject. "Speaking of happy, how's Digg?"

"Lonely," Jacey said with a cheeky grin. "But other than that, he's good."

And Jacey was obviously no fool. She knew Portia had said and heard all she wanted/needed to hear. She opened the door and stepped into the hall. "He's calling me in ten minutes. I'll tell him you asked."

Jacey left and something almost as warm as Rourke's lovemaking embraced Portia. Friendship. She'd discovered a lover in Rourke and a friend in Jacey. It had been a strange—no, that wasn't really right—a magical night. She picked Rourke's costume up from the chair where she'd tossed it and rubbed her cheek against the soft material. It still bore his scent. She breathed deeply. Tomorrow would be soon enough to get it back to wardrobe. Tonight she would pillow her head on his clothes and drift off to sleep with his scent beneath her.

THE FOLLOWING MORNING, Portia hurried along to the study they'd set up as a temporary production office. She and

Lauchmann met each morning before her daily meetings with Rourke.

She was late. She was never late. But she'd slept like the dead last night and overslept this morning. She calmed herself with a deep breath before entering the study. She hated being late.

Instead of being annoyed at her tardiness, Lauchmann looked like the cat with a canary. "O'Malley's bagged someone and I want to know who she is," Lauchmann announced without preamble.

Portia sank into the seat on the other side of the round table. Holy hell. How did Lauchmann know O'Malley had, as he so poetically put it, "bagged" someone? Portia glanced down at her clipboard, taking a moment to carefully school her face into pleasant impassivity. She looked back up at Lauchmann. "What makes you think he's sleeping with one of them already?"

"Empty rubber wrappers." Lauchmann winked at her. "Try saying that six times fast."

"And you know this how?"

"I slipped the maids a couple of bucks to let me know if they found any. There was one the other day—" *ice pack* "—and one this morning." *The real McCoy.* "The man works fast. But I don't have to tell you, this is just the kind of thing enquiring minds, as in our viewers, will want to know. So, it's your job to find out which one of our lovelies has succumbed to stud-boy's charms."

He'd paid the maids to snoop through Rourke's trash? She really, really didn't like Lauchmann. He was a decent producer, but the same couldn't be said for his status as a human being.

Portia crossed her legs and leaned back in her chair, striving for casual and confident. "I don't think he's going to tell. That was one of the things the viewers liked about him so much on the *The Last Virgin*. He's a gentleman with ethics."

Lauchmann peered at her suspiciously and nausea rose. Dear God, if Lauchmann the Crude ever had so much as an inkling….

Portia shrugged and continued quickly, praying Lauchmann was easily distracted. "That's the feedback we got from the Websites." That and orgasm-waiting-to-happen fame. Sister, that woman didn't know the half of it.

He nodded, crossing his hands behind his head and leaning back in his chair.

"If he won't tell, it's your job to find out, P.T." She hated it when Lauchmann called her P.T. "If there's anything women like more than a nice guy, it's a bad boy. They'll eat up an ethical gentleman who's a stud beneath it all. Find out from the women. Ten women, well, nine after today, all chasing the same guy. Whoever's in the sack with him probably can't wait to let the rest of them know she's snagged him this far." He waved his hand in the air. "Don't you women have some kind of intuition thing for that crap?"

Portia resisted a near-hysterical urge to raise her own hand and confess to being bagged, snagged and the culprit in the empty-rubber-wrapper escapade. For once, it might render the ever-disgusting Lauchmann silent.

But the satisfaction wasn't worth her job.

No, it was now her job to try and come up with another woman in Rourke's bed.

# 7

"WOULD YOU like to take a wild guess what my big assignment is today?" Portia asked.

Rourke crossed his arms over his chest to keep from reaching for her. What he wouldn't give for five minutes of uninterrupted privacy so he could greet her the way he wanted to, with a thorough kiss. What the hell? Why not go for broke? A proper good morning would include losing their clothes and discovering one another.

Ah, but he was supposed to be guessing today's mission. He knew what he wished her assignment was. "Let's see, you're supposed to make sure my every need is met and you're here to pick up that list."

It felt good to flirt with her even if he knew he shouldn't. He wanted to position himself in front of the camera and announce to the world at large that she was his and he was going to do his damnedest to make her think of him as hers.

Portia twirled her pen between two fingers. "Better than that."

They didn't exactly have the privacy he craved, but no one else was around. He looked at her, letting her see just how much he wanted her again. "Honey, it couldn't get any better than that."

Aside from an answering flicker of heat in her eyes, she ignored his comment. "Lauchmann informed me you've bagged someone. He knows because he paid the maids to snoop through your garbage. They narked on the condom wrappers."

"You're kidding. No, you're not kidding. He's going through my garbage?" Rourke wasn't sure whether he was more amused or annoyed.

"Not personally. But, yes, he's having your garbage sifted through." Portia rubbed her hand over her forehead as if warding off an impending headache. "I should have thought about the garbage."

All his good humor evaporated. This felt sordid. No way in hell Portia knew that was going on, but he hated she was even involved with a company that ran such a seedy show. "Have you ever considered a career change? You have too much integrity for this," Rourke said.

Her head snapped around. "Most of the time I really like my job, and for the most part it doesn't compromise my integrity," Portia said. "And speaking of integrity, *you* are the one who signed up for this show, not me. When they pay you the kind of money they're paying you to be here, I suppose they figure they own your garbage as well."

He'd pissed her off. He ran a hand over his hair, silently counting to ten, because, damn it, her jibe had hit home. Increasingly, he felt like a high-rent gigolo.

"Did he give you any indication he suspected us?"

"Thank God, no. I doubt I'd be here now."

He thought she was overreacting—Hollywood wasn't exactly puritanical in its outlook. "I can't imagine sleeping with me would ruin your career. I'm sure it's not the first time it's happened."

She recoiled as if he'd struck her, and he realized how his words had sounded.

"Not you, honey. I didn't mean it's happened with you before. I meant the industry in general."

"It does. It's not terribly professional, however."

"Portia, I trust you, and I want you to know you can trust me. I would never do anything to hurt you."

She looked at him without comment, obviously unable to tell him what he needed to hear, that she trusted him. "Lauchmann is going to breath down my neck unmercifully until I give him a name."

"The studio may have bought my garbage, but they don't own me. I've kissed those women, but I'm not going to sleep with any of them. Not to cover you with Lauchmann or for ratings or—" he almost said "or to keep Nick out of prison," but he caught himself in time "—for any other reason. I'll just have to store the wrappers in my suitcase."

"That won't work. I wouldn't put it past him to have the maids count the condoms in your bedside table, just to make sure."

"Are you telling me that I've got this huge supply of condoms and I can't use them with the woman I want to?"

"Lauchmann's antennae are up. So, as long as I'm that woman, no."

"Don't worry about this, Portia. I'll figure something out. I'll take care of it. And yes, you're the only woman I'm interested in using them with. And I can't wait until tonight to convince you."

BEING WITH Rourke was like being a sponge on the edge of a puddle of water. Once she started soaking him up, it seemed impossible to stop. She knew that the puddle wouldn't be there forever. But while it was, she'd become patently incapable of ignoring it.

Tonight it was late, nearly midnight as she made her way through the mansion.

Rourke was waiting for her inside his room.

"Did you enjoy today? It looked as if it was a good time," Portia said by way of greeting, anticipation making her babble.

He locked the door behind her and effectively trapped her against it with his big body. The increasingly familiar heat and warmth and sexual desire shook her.

"I'm having a good time, now," he said in a low, sexy voice. He leaned down and slowly, deliberately, thoroughly made love to her mouth, suckling her lower lip, exploring the tender recesses with his tongue and then upping the pace, his tongue plunging inside, leaving her aching, wanting him between her thighs.

Rourke tugged her blouse free of her skirt and touched her belly and her ribs, and then his big hands were cupping her breasts, kneading, massaging her. He took her nipples between his fingers and lightly plucked and tweaked until she moaned into his open mouth. She arched her throbbing mound against the rigid line of his erection and he ground against her. He tugged harder at her nipples and she felt as if her body were on fire. She reached between their bodies and cupped him, stroking him.

God, she was discovering a whole sensuality and sexuality she'd never known she possessed. And now she was making up for it in spades. Driving her wild. It was as if he got off on destroying her composure. And he could. And he did. And he was a nice guy, both inside and out. And he was a geek. And he was so hot it made her hot.

He'd asked her about fantasies before. And somewhere along the line, throughout the years she'd managed not to think, not to fantasize. But now, since Rourke, she found herself prey to fantasies. She didn't want to think too much about why he'd awakened her fantasies, she only knew he had. And tonight she'd share one and make him wild. She wanted to see the light of reason leave his eyes.

She broke their kiss and pushed him away. "Will you do something for me?"

He didn't hesitate or question. "Yes. Anything."

"I want us to do something for one another."

Apparently that was the right thing to say. His smile was nothing short of wicked and the heat in his blue eyes scorched her. "Tell me more."

"There are rules," she said, her excitement heightened by simply giving voice to her fantasy. She trailed a finger down his chest, past his belly to his belt and felt his muscles contract beneath her fingertip.

"Your rules?"

"Yes."

"And what happens if I break a rule?" He crossed his arms over his chest.

"Then you don't get to play my game."

"I'm all ears."

She glanced pointedly at his hard-on straining against the front of this slacks. "That's not the way I see it."

He laughed, grabbing for her. She danced away.

"Rule number one. No touching each other."

"Is this a game or some subtle form of torture?"

"Maybe both." She walked toward the bed, glancing back at him over her shoulder. "Do you want to play?"

"If it's with you, I definitely want to play. So, rule number one is no touching. What's rule number two?"

"Rule number two is we take our clothes off."

"I definitely like two better than one," he said, laughing. "Okay, okay. How many more rules are there?"

"Only one. You have to do what I tell you to."

He raised a brow, but he was definitely intrigued. And turned on. "Let the games begin."

She swept the coverlet and the sheet back and sank back

onto the mattress. "Undress for me." She leaned back on her elbows. "And do it like you mean it."

"I think being in charge of all those people every day has gone to your head."

She scooted to the mattress edge, her skirt riding up her thighs. "Should I take my toys and go home?"

"Oh, not yet, baby. You and your toys—" his gaze lingered between her nearly exposed thighs "—stay right where you are."

Rourke unbuttoned his shirt and made a production of sliding it off his broad shoulders, flexing his pecs, then slid it down his arms. He tried to shuck it off and it was stuck at the wrists. "I forgot to unbutton the cuffs."

Portia laughed as he worked the buttons free. He was so achingly handsome and sexy and dorky all at the same time.

Laughing along with her, he finally freed himself of his shirt. "Dammit woman, I'll give you something to laugh about." He turned his back to her and did that goofy thing everyone had done at some point in time in junior high when they wrapped their arms around themselves and ran their fingers up and down their sides, as if they were making out with someone.

Portia fell back on the bed, laughing. It was the weirdest sensation to laugh so hard in the middle of being so sexually tense. He turned around, grinning.

The grin faded, to be replaced by a carnal, predatory look. He crossed the room to stand in front of her. She was still sitting on the bed so that put his crotch pretty much at eye level. He reached for his belt and the muscles in his belly rippled and her mouth went dry. She wasn't laughing now. He unbuckled his belt and let it hang. Portia swallowed.

Rourke bent down, his movements slow and deliberate, until his head was between her thighs. Her muscles clenched and she grew slicker, hotter. His nostrils flared, as if he were a wild animal picking up her scent. A dark, wicked smile curled his lips and coiled through her. He braced one hand, big and masculine with its smattering of dark hair, on the bed next to her, oh so close to her thigh, but not touching her. He slid off one shoe and sock and then shifted his weight to repeat it on the other foot. As he straightened, his forehead, nose and chin nearly skimmed her crotch. She could almost feel his warm breath, his heat against her bare thighs and panties. He'd only taken off his shirt, shoes and socks and she was nearly panting.

He dispensed with the button on his pants and then he slid the zipper down, the sound mingling with her raspy breathing. He hooked his thumbs in the waistband and pulled his pants down, moving forward to step out of them, putting his jutting erection, hard abs, and muscular thighs closer. Tantalizingly, temptingly close. His harsh breathing rang in her ears. The smell of him bordered on dizzying—the aroma of male arousal, masculine skin and aftershave.

He pivoted and turned away from her. In one movement, he took off his briefs and she faced the back side of a spectacular specimen of manhood. Broad, muscled shoulders, sculpted back, a perfectly firm, tight ass, and muscular legs. She reached out to run her hand over his well-formed buttocks, jerking her hand back at the last second, remembering her no-touch rule.

"Tur—" her voice was a rusty squeak. She swallowed and tried again. "Turn around, Rourke. Please," she tacked on softly.

He did as she asked and faced her, legs braced, a big, dark, hard man. All humor and perhaps a fine veneer of civility were gone. She might be giving the orders, but she wasn't altogether sure any more that she was in charge. Once again, this time without even touching her, he'd driven her crazy. It was exhilarating and frightening to ride the edge of such intense sexual desire. She wanted to do the same to him, for him.

She looked at his erection and rimmed her tongue around her lips. His cock, sleek and hard, pulsed, reacting as surely as if she'd touched the tip of her tongue to him. He drew a harsh breath but still didn't speak.

She slid off the bed and moved to the foot. "Lie on the bed and I'll undress for you. Would you like that?"

"Very much." She watched, appreciating the ripple of muscles and the sheen of his skin as he stretched out on the sheets.

Portia knew a moment of hesitation. It was much easier to watch than to be watched. But wasn't this part of her whole fantasy, being watched, being wanted for who she was?

She deliberately left her hair up. She knew enough after this week that Rourke liked it down. She'd save it for later. He'd propped himself against the plump pillows on the bed. The bed post and silk drapings cast his face in shadows. She couldn't see his eyes, but she felt the heat of his look searing every inch of her as she bared herself to him until the only thing she was left wearing were her pumps. She left the pumps on because she'd seen more than once how he'd watched her legs and because they made her feel sexy, and right now she was feeling very, very sexy. She raised her hands to her head, aware that it lifted her breasts like an offering, and pulled the pins from her hair. His groan echoed from the bed. Undressing for him left her very wet, very aroused.

"Spread your legs," she said.

"Oh, honey," he murmured as he widened the V of his legs. She climbed onto the bed and crawled across the mattress until she was between his thighs, close enough to feel his heat, but still not touching. Bracing her hands on either side of his head she leaned forward, poised over him, her breasts just out of reach of his chest, his erection nearly nudging her mound.

His warm breath gusted against her face. "What do you think of my game so far?" she asked, her lips close to his ear.

"I'm not sure if I'm going to die of anticipation or of pleasure."

"*La petite mort.*"

"What now?"

She sat up, away from him and slipped back a bit, but still between his legs, on her knees, her legs apart, the air cool against her slick heat. "Now, you sit back and watch. And if you like what you see, tell me. And if you don't, well you can tell me what you'd like to see."

She lightly ran her hands up her thighs, pausing to stroke her belly, and then cupped her breasts. Portia repeated his earlier actions, squeezing and kneading them, plumping them for his benefit. And hers. He fisted his hands in the sheets. "Play with your nipples." His voice was nearly guttural.

She rolled her nipples between her thumbs and forefingers and the sensation went straight to her womb, arcing her back with pleasure. "Like this?"

"Yes. Tell me how good it feels."

"It feels almost as good as your hands on me." She brought her fingers to her mouth, wetting them, and then brushed her wet fingers over her sensitive tips. "And that feels almost as good as your mouth on me."

"Sweet…oh…Portia."

She skimmed her hands over her belly and along her thighs. "Should I touch myself?"

"Yes."

She ran one finger lightly along her aroused slickness.

"I am so wet. Doing this for you makes me so hot. Do you wish you could touch me?"

"Yes."

"I could touch me for you. Would you like me to do that for you?"

"Yes."

She slipped a finger along her wet cleft and moaned at the intensity of the touch, of the situation. "If you want me to do that again, you need to do something for me."

"Anything."

"I would really like to touch you. I'd like to stroke you, taste you. But I can't because we have rules we can't break. So will you touch yourself for me?"

He wrapped his fingers around his shaft and she touched herself. She slid two fingers into herself and clenched her muscles, tightening around them. "This gets me off. I'm so tight and I know this is how it feels to you."

"Oh, baby, you don't know how good it feels when I'm buried deep inside you. And you can't possibly know how hot it makes me to watch you do that."

Aching, raging with a need so desperate she thought she might cry, she added a third finger and worked it in and out of herself in a rhythm that he followed. She found her nub with her other hand and waited until Rourke gasped her name and saw his body go rigid that she relinquished the last vestige of sanity and they climaxed together.

ROURKE CAME OUT of the bathroom after cleaning himself up. Portia lay sprawled across the bed, still naked, obviously exhausted because she was asleep. He'd like nothing better than to crawl into bed with her, wrap her in his arms and spend the night together, but that was a recipe for disaster.

He sat on the edge of the bed. He'd wake her up. In a

minute. Or two. Or five. He studied her in repose. He could look at her a lifetime and never tire of her, from the exotic slant of her eyes—inherited from her Malaysian grandmother as he'd learned this week—to the classic line of her nose, the flat planes of her cheek-bones, the fullness of her lips and the slight pointiness of her chin.

Good God, she'd been on fire tonight. She'd set him on fire. While it wasn't the same as actually making love to her, it had been intensely erotic. He wasn't quite sure when he'd ever been so almost unbearably aroused. And coming from a woman of such immense reserve and compo-sure, it had been all the more titillating.

Unbidden, he wondered how many times she'd played that game before and with whom. There was still so much of her that was a mystery to him.

He had no idea whether her son looked like her. How did she feel about Danny's father? Had she played her game with him? Did she still play with him? Stranger things happened than exes sleeping together. Where did she want to be in ten years? Was there room in her life for him? And he desperately wanted there to be room in her life for him.

He could make it through the next week or so. He could play the reality TV game to keep Nick out of prison and make sure Portia kept her job. He could feign interest in Car-lotta. God knows he'd pretended not to care about being the brunt of jokes often enough. He had that down pat.

It was the aftermath that scared the hell out of him. He wasn't Einstein, but he knew that Portia planned a "have a nice life and good-bye" when this was all over. The catch was, he thought there was a very real possibility that the nice life he craved was with her. While he didn't make enough to bail Nick's ass out of hot water—Nick had "borrowed" a serious amount of moola—he made decent money. Enough so that Portia didn't have to waste herself on mindless shows like this.

How'd he feel about a ready-made family? He didn't know squat about kids, but he did know all about being a geek. He knew from life experience that a geek was a geek was a geek whether said geek was ten, fifteen, twenty-five or thirty. So, he and Danny already had something in common. And they both loved Portia, yet another thing in common.

Rourke felt much less amenable about an ex-husband, but he'd take the bad with the good. Portia being the good, the ex being the bad. And he was jumping way ahead of his game. He had his work cut out for him, convincing her a "them" existed beyond this shoot.

He stretched out beside her and gentled his hand over her shoulder. He loved the soft, satin feel of her skin. Bending, he pressed a light kiss to her lips. "Hey, Sleeping Beauty, wake up."

She blinked her eyes open and offered him a sweet, lazy smile that made his heart sing. "Hey, you."

Then it was as if reality hit and she jackknifed up on his bed. "Oh, my God, what time is it? I didn't spend the night did I?"

He gentled her back down onto the mattress. "Relax. You were only asleep for about ten minutes."

Amazingly, she did relax, curling up next to him. "What did you think of my game?"

He smoothed his hand across her hip. "I think I'd always like to be on your team." He propped himself on one arm. "Portia…" He brushed a lazy kiss across her nose.

"Umm?" She pressed a sweet kiss to his chin.

He smoothed her hair from her shoulder. "Tell me about Danny."

She didn't move, but she withdrew as surely as if she'd rolled away from him. "Danny's off-limits."

A physical slap would have hurt less. He'd just shared mutual masturbation with this woman and she still didn't feel as if she could discuss her son with him? But he couldn't force her to trust him, confide in him. All he could do was respect her decision. But he could still ask other questions. "What about your ex? Danny's father?"

"What about him?"

"Does Danny stay with him when you're on location?"

"He's not my ex. We were never married. I got pregnant and he got MIA." Her cold smile broke his heart. He could only imagine what it had done to hers. "Danny's dad's a crackhead. He wasn't when we were together. Responsibility's not exactly Mark's strong suit. He came by once when Danny was a baby. Not to see the baby—he's never been interested in Danny. He wanted money to score a hit. We haven't seen him since."

It was too goddamned easy to read between the lines. Rourke, not a violent man, wanted to tear the bastard limb from limb. Small wonder that his baby had built Fort Knox around her heart.

"How old were you?"

"Seventeen. I wasn't wild and I didn't sleep around. Mark was my first." Her expression was defiant. As if he might judge her and find her lacking.

"And the bastard just left you to have and take care of a baby by yourself when you were seventeen?"

"Pretty much." There was so much more that she wasn't saying, he could see it in the shadows in her eyes, but he didn't ask. He was almost sorry he'd brought it up. He didn't want to bring her pain, even remembered pain, but it explained so much about her. "I'm extremely lucky that I have a great family. My parents were disappointed but understanding. They've been great. They kept him while I worked and went to night school and still I've felt guilty because we were a financial strain. I don't know what women without family support systems do. And my younger sister Mellina's been great as well. Danny's very much adored by his aunt and grandparents. In fact, they dote on him. And the feeling's mutual."

That he could relate to. His family was close as well. It sounded as if they shared similar backgrounds and he wanted her to know that. "My parents would do the same, and it would be a financial strain on them as well." He really hadn't planned to, but he suddenly found himself confiding in her about Nick.

"So, you didn't come on the last show or this show because you were interested in finding the woman of your dreams?"

"No." He smiled ruefully. "I'm a quiet, homebody kind of guy. I'd have opted for a much less public format. I'm not a player."

She smoothed her fingertips across his chest. "You gave up your privacy to bail your brother out and protect your parents. You're a good man, Rourke O'Malley." The tenderness in her eyes wrapped around his heart and embarrassed him all at the same time.

"You would do the same for your sister if she needed you, wouldn't you?" He knew the answer before he asked the question.

"Absolutely. Tell me more about your family," she said.

Yes! She wanted to know about his family, about him. He *wasn't* just a warm body in her bed. He gave her the abbreviated version of the O'Malleys. She was so easy to talk to. He could spend the rest of his life talking to her... among other things.

"However, they don't have any grandchildren, much to

their dismay. They're just waiting for the day. For some reason they don't consider my dog a worthy stand-in for a grandchild," he said.

She laughed. "Dogs are nice but no, they aren't grandchildren. And there are no grandchildren because…?"

Was she indirectly asking him why he wasn't married? "Because it's up to me and my brother Nick. Nick can't seem to settle on one woman and me, well, I've just been very content with Watson, my miniature schnauzer who thinks he's a person, and my own company."

"Danny wants a dog. They're not allowed in our apartment building," she said. "I've been saving for a downpayment. When I get this promotion, we should be able to afford a condo or maybe even a really small house and I've promised him a dog. A small dog. He doesn't like big dogs, they're intimidating to short, skinny kids."

Asking her outright had gotten him the cold shoulder but she was telling him a whole lot about her son just in general conversation. And he loved it. "Then you ought to look into a mini-schnauzer. Unless he just wanted a puppy, you could even look at a rescue group. I got Watson when his previous owner died. They're great city dogs. But they're smart and need exercise. Of course, if you have a smart kid with lots of energy, that could work out to be a love match. And they're good watchdogs. Very protective of the ones they love. A dog can be great company for a nerd. Dogs don't care how geeky you are or whether you walk around in your socks and underwear."

Portia laughed. "Okay, okay. I'm sold. You've convinced me. You sound like Danny. He'll have to send you a thank-you letter for lobbying his position."

Her laughter died, as if she just realized what she'd said, implied. That they'd be in touch afterward. That Danny was no longer off-limits.

She sat up, the curve of her naked back a study in feminine grace and beauty. "I need to go. It's late and we both need some sleep."

She gathered her clothes and disappeared into the bathroom, returning once again cool and remote in her suit, her hair gathered in a smooth chignon.

But this felt different, because he knew the passionate woman beneath the cool exterior. And she was beginning to know the real him.

# 8

"So, who's in the sack with O'Malley?" Lauchmann asked from behind his desk.

Great. After hours of enduring Rourke being fed—*fed* for God's sake—by the contestants, now she had to put up with Lauchmann grilling her. "I didn't make a lot of headway."

"Well, why the hell not?"

"They have busy schedules and I can hardly walk in and demand to know which one's sleeping with him."

Even Lauchmann seemed to recognize the rationale of that. "I suppose. Dammit, there's got to be a way to find out. The hall camera isn't showing anything. He didn't get any action last night, no condoms in the garbage, so he will tonight. Especially after the food fest with them feeding him with their hands and rubbing up against him." Lauchmann's eyes glittered with the excitement of a voyeur.

Oy. He was maxing out her ick factor. "I'll talk to the ladies again."

"Forget that. I've got a better idea. We're not seeing anyone on the video feed in the hall so they must be coming in through his window."

"Through his window?" Portia almost giggled at the thought of her climbing through Rourke's window. Not that sex with Rourke wasn't worth it. Her temperature went up several degrees just thinking about it. And then lying in his bed afterward, talking about their families.

She'd never known anything like that. It had been wonderful and frightening, because she could get used to it. "You think one of our pampered princesses is climbing through his window?"

Lauchmann narrowed his slightly bulging eyes, which gave him a totally weird look. "Yeah, I do. And you're gonna find out who. I want you to hide in the bushes outside his window tonight and then when she goes in, you go get Jacey and her third eye and the two of you wait in the bushes for her to come back out." He literally rubbed his hands together.

She couldn't help herself. She laughed. "You're kidding."

"You know, P.T., promotions and pay raises go to employees who go that extra mile when a job needs to be done. It'll be great footage and we'll rule the ratings."

Sure. Why not? She could say she had. It wasn't as if she was actually going to catch anyone and then she was a team player. "I want this show to be successful as much as you do. I'll stake out—" she couldn't even bring herself to say hide in the bushes "—his window tonight after I've briefed on tomorrow's shoot."

"I knew I could count on you. Maybe there's more than one of them. Now, that would be *really* hot."

Portia didn't even want to go there with Lauchmann. "I'd better go then. I don't want one or more of his women to slip past me."

ROURKE STRETCHED, his body wound tight. He'd thought filming would never end tonight. They'd had the nine remaining contestants each prepare a dish for him and serve it to him for dinner. He supposed it was meant to be funny because he couldn't fathom that any of them had ever made herself toast. He'd played the game, but it had seemed to go on forever.

Aside from the time they'd had together this morning on the terrace, he hadn't managed another moment alone with Portia all day. And he was aching for her. He needed her. Needed to hold her close, bury his face in her hair, feel her heart beat next to his.

A knock sounded on his door. Anticipation coursed through him as he crossed the room. Finally. He opened the door. Shit. Maggie stood in the hall.

She slipped past him, into his room, without waiting for an invitation. Double shit. "Come in," he said with dry sarcasm as he closed the door.

"I wanted to talk to you privately without cameras and microphones. Your room's not bugged is it?" Maggie plopped onto the couch and patted the spot next to her in invitation.

"No. My bedroom's not wired," he said, ignoring the spot next to her and standing instead. He had to admit he was damn curious as to why she'd sought him out for a "private" conversation. He'd discovered in business that often the best tactic was silence. Most people couldn't stand silence and would speak to fill it. It often garnered more information than asking questions.

Maggie crossed her legs. "You're probably wondering why I'm here."

"The thought had crossed my mind," he said.

She smiled at his dry tone. He had to give Maggie credit. It would've been totally lost on Carlotta.

"I thought maybe we could cut a deal," she said.

She had his attention. Rourke dealt in business deals all day, every day at work. He recognized when someone shifted into negotiation mode. This wasn't personal, this was business. "I'm listening."

"Do you know that whoever you pick gets her own TV show?" *That took care of the twist.* She took one look at his face and smirked. "I can see you didn't. I knew none of those ninnies would have enough sense to cut a deal. They're all hoping to win on chemistry." She rolled her eyes and shook her head.

"Here's the deal. You've got plenty of chemistry, but I don't think it's with any of us."

Maggie was truly a surprising woman. There was more going on with her than he'd ever suspected. Actually, he hadn't thought about Maggie. He hadn't really thought about any of them because Portia'd had him locked up tight from day one. "Okay," he said, neither confirming nor denying.

"So, I want to discuss what it'll take to get you to pick me. I want that show. If it's sex, I don't have a problem with that." She rose, walked up to him, wrapped her arms around his neck and kissed him, her tongue seeking entry while she rubbed her large breasts against his chest. Rourke simply felt mild amusement that she thought he'd find that sexy. He stepped back and firmly held her at arm's length.

She wet her lips. "I don't even mind if you want to make a little home movie."

He shook his head no and she slanted him an arch look. "I think you've got the sex covered. If it's money, name your price."

Rourke put the length of the couch between them. He didn't need any more surprise attacks. "The network's paying me plenty. Why should I pick you?"

"Because I'm no more interested in a love match than you are, tall, dark, and handsome. And all the others, while they want a TV show too, want you along with the show. They want you to want them. I'm the only one who isn't going to cause a stink when we conveniently discover we're incompatible after all."

"How do I know this isn't some studio setup?" he asked. They had dug through his garbage, after all.

"I guess you don't."

"If you want this show so bad, why don't you just have your father buy it?"

"My father's bought my whole life." She smiled. "And I know what you're thinking, 'Spoiled little rich bitch, what a tough life.' Do you have any clue how invalidating it is when your whole life is bought and paid for? I want to earn this on my own. Plus, Daddy will just be mortified to have his daughter with her own tawdry TV show."

She was looking for personal validation through a reality TV show? And she was willing to earn it on her back or buy it with her father's money. Not to mention she was looking to bite the hand that fed her. Hell, he'd bet money Maggie'd leaked that home video that had circulated on the Internet to humiliate dear old dad. Rourke thought she should spend some of her megabucks on a good couch—in a therapist's office. "You know you could always do charity work in some third-world nation."

"That would wreck my manicure." Her smile was deprecating. "So, what's your price for naming me the lucky lady to win your heart?"

At the end of the show, he had to pick someone. And she could get Lauchmann off Portia's back. "You act as if you've seduced me and then when it's all over we go our separate ways and no one's ever the wiser."

"That's all? Didn't you hear me say I'd pay you? I'd willingly screw you." She eyed him up and down like a female wolverine. "It wouldn't be a hardship."

Not even if hell froze over. This chick was nuts. "Not necessary. Just convince everyone else you did."

Like timing straight out of a Greek tragedy a knock sounded on his bedroom door. Portia? What the hell, he wasn't laying any odds. "Excuse me a minute," he said and turned his back to Maggie who had a hand to her chest. He crossed the room and opened the door.

"Hi," Portia said, a lustful smile lighting her eyes and curving her mouth. "Can I come in?" she asked and then peered past him, her smile fading.

"Uh...I was just finishing up—"

Maggie wrapped her arms around him from behind, her hands linked dangerously close to his equipment. "What do we have to do to find a little privacy, darling?" She slid around him, still clinging, ducking beneath his arm. "Oh, hi," she said to Portia, "we were almost in the middle of something." Rourke glanced at Maggie. Her blouse hung open, her hair a mess, her lipstick smeared. "You know, the middle when you get to the juicy part."

He'd just told Maggie to convince everyone they were lovers and she was obviously sealing the deal with an impromptu performance. *No,* his mind screamed. *Everyone but Portia.* But he could hardly say it since that would tell Maggie everything she needed to know. And that kind of information would definitely be dangerous in Maggie's twisted hands.

"Could you come back later?" he asked Portia.

That calm cool that he'd grown to dislike so much because it hid the woman beneath, returned. She offered them both a smile. "That's not necessary. It was nothing that can't wait until tomorrow. I'm sorry I interrupted. Enjoy."

She turned on her heel and walked away, soon disappearing around a corner.

Maggie was still wrapped around him, rubbing herself against him almost unconsciously. "The offer still stands, you know. We might as well finish this the old-fashioned way. The middle is *very* juicy."

It would leave him rock-hard in about two seconds flat if it was Portia saying that and doing that. But it wasn't. And why the hell couldn't this woman take no for an answer?

He reached for her, but it was to button her blouse. "Maggie, you're a unique woman," yeah, she was nuts, "but I think we'd both regret it if this went any farther. You deserve your own show because you think fast on your feet and that was very convincing." Her clothes were intact and he wanted her out of here. He ushered her out the door. "You can be sure I'll hold up my end. Thank you."

She preened, pausing in the hallway. "It seemed like a good opportunity to get the ball rolling. I guess that means we've got a deal."

Yeah, they had a deal and he had a mess.

Fool. Fool. Fool. Portia's footsteps seemed to echo the word along the hall. She knew better than to trust a man. Especially a man who looked as good as O'Malley. Especially a man put in his position. He needed money and he was being pursued by wealthy women. And she'd known there was no exclusivity between her and O'Malley.

No, her outrage was that he'd chosen Maggie, of all people. Maggie who he'd ostensibly wanted to send packing. Brash, crass, lots of money and no class, sleazy Maggie with the juicy middle.

She wanted a shower. A nice hot, long shower. That was what she needed to wash her hands of O'Malley. He was only another bit player in this lousy show and tomorrow was just another day of filming and thank God she only had another six days on this miserable location. And if there was a silver lining here, it was that she could now tell Lauchmann with certainty that O'Malley had "bagged" Maggie Duchanne.

And why did she care? It wasn't as if she and O'Malley

were any part of anything that remotely resembled a commitment. As she'd told him that first day in his room, he could sleep with all the contestants, all at the same time if that's what he wanted and he possessed the stamina.

Who was she kidding? She wouldn't have been any happier to find Carlotta or Tara or any other seminaked woman in his room. She was angry with herself for believing him when he told her she was special. For being gullible after so many years of being careful.

Before she made it back to her room, her pager went off. O'Malley. He'd certainly made quick work of finishing up with Maggie. The part of her that had just found her lover in his room with a half-dressed harlot wanted to ignore the page. The part of her that was paid to be on call 24/7 for the show's star couldn't.

She unlocked her door and toyed with the idea of turning her pager off, but years of conditioning wouldn't allow her such a personal indulgence. Instead, she picked up the phone and dialed his extension. "What can I do for you, Mr. O'Malley?" Not even the slightest quiver marred her cool, professional, even tone. She even managed to inject a friendly note.

"I need to see you. We need to talk."

"Can't this wait until morning, Mr. O'Malley? It's been a long day and surely we can go over any details you need to cover at tomorrow morning's briefing." Her voice was cool and rational, unlike his brusque tone.

"Surely it can't wait, Ms. Tomlinson." He mimicked her formality. "If you're too exhausted to make the trip to my room, I have no problem coming to yours. *But we will talk tonight.*"

You'd think he was the injured party. Of course, the best defense was a good offense.

"I'll be there in a few minutes, Mr. O'Malley." She shot

the phone a bird. *Take that, Mr. O'Malley, and put it where the sun don't shine.*

"I'll be eagerly awaiting your arrival, Ms. Tomlinson."

She left her room, barely refraining from slamming the door, and marched back through the labyrinthine turns to O'Malley's room. For the second time that night, she knocked.

Almost immediately, he flung the door open.

She peered around the doorframe. "Is it okay to come in? I don't want to interrupt another tryst," she said politely, her tone downright solicitous. "Or did you have a break between appointments and thought you might squeeze me in?"

He took her arm and pulled her inside the room, slamming the door behind her. In a second, she found herself pinned to the wall, his arms on either side of her.

"It was not the way it looked," he said before he swooped down and branded her with a kiss that staked his claim.

She loathed herself that his kiss could stir her to instant arousal even though she knew he'd just kissed another woman without benefit of a camera. All her calm, all of her control was swept away by a landslide of anger and passion.

She wrenched her mouth away and wrapped her arms around his neck, fisting her hands in his hair. "I know what I saw," she said and before he could answer she ground her mouth against his, her tongue battling with his.

Rourke broke the kiss. "A little trust would go a long way," he said, unbuttoning her suit jacket. He bent and suckled her breast through her blouse and bra and the sensation pierced the veil of anger surrounding her.

"What should I think?" She dug her nails into his shoulder as the exquisite sensation of his mouth fueled a passion born of ire and betrayal.

He lifted his head and kissed the column of her neck

while he cupped her buttocks in his hands and pulled her hips against him. "Maybe you should think that I was cutting a deal to give you the story you needed for Lauchmann."

She pulled his shirt over his head and threw it to the floor. "It looked like a win-win deal for the two of you." She swirled her tongue over his nipple and heard his sharp intake of breath. She, who was usually so even-tempered and level-headed, was blinded by anger, desire and white-hot jealousy. She wanted to punish both of them. Him for betraying her and her for allowing it to matter.

He unzipped her skirt and pushed it down past her hips. He delved beneath her panties and wrapped his hands around her cheeks, squeezing and pulling them apart and her sex ached for him. "She came to me," he said, his breath ragged, his erection pushing against her belly.

Her fingers didn't fumble as she worked free his belt and unzipped his pants. "That's no surprise. Women can't resist you, O'Malley." Her laughter echoed her bitterness. "*I* can't resist you, even knowing I'm second in line tonight."

He pressed his forehead to hers. "Damn it, Portia, I don't know how to convince you. She wanted to cut a deal so that I would pick her and she'd wind up with the prize show. She offered me both sex and money."

She stroked his erection through his underwear and he shuddered against her hand. "What a surprise. I believe she's free and easy with both."

"I turned her down. My price for picking her was that she let people think we'd slept together. That she'd seduced me. It seemed like an easy answer to get Lauchmann off your back and I don't really care who wins. And in a moment of bad timing you knocked on the door. I swear to you, before I turned my back to answer the door, her blouse was buttoned and her hair was combed."

Maggie *was* calculating and didn't hesitate to cause a scene. "But you had her lipstick on your mouth."

"I told you she offered me sex and I turned her down. I am not even remotely interested in Maggie Duchanne. In fact, the only woman I'm interested in is you. I meant it when I told you that every look, every touch in front of that camera was for you. Cutting that deal tonight with Maggie was for you. For us. If he thinks I'm sleeping with Maggie, then it doesn't matter whether he counts my condoms or checks my garbage. Maggie's just a red herring."

It made sense, but she also felt like one of those pathetic women who wanted to believe anything she was told as long as it exonerated her man. "It looked bad."

"I know. I'd just told her to convince everyone we were sleeping together. I could hardly tell her you didn't need to know. I'd told you I'd find a way to fix this and I did. I need to know you believe me."

Fine lines separated deep emotion. One seemed to mine another. Just as hate was closely akin to love, jealousy and anger shared space with passion. She'd known from the beginning that Rourke was temporary in her life, but it'd been a cold, rude awakening to see him with Maggie and think it was over. That she'd never know the feel of him against her, inside her: never again experience his touch, the taste of his skin, his mouth, his scent. And it galled her to know, even under those circumstances, that she wanted him as desperately as she ever had. "I want to believe you."

She still felt vulnerable, raw.

"How can I prove it to you?"

She needed to prove to herself that she was in charge of herself, of the situation. "You want me to trust you. But how much do you trust me?"

"I trust you implicitly."

IF HE HAD an ounce of pride, he'd tell her he didn't need to prove anything, especially since he hadn't done anything wrong. But, especially knowing her background, he knew trust wasn't an easy issue for her. "I'm at your command. Do with me what you will."

"Anything?"

"Within reason."

"Define unreasonable."

"Nothing immediately comes to mind. How about I'll let you know if we get there."

"Hmm." Something flickered across her face, a look of slight surprise, acknowledgment, sensuality. "What does this house remind you of?"

That was easy. They'd played it up often enough during taping. "A Moorish castle. Harems."

"Exactly. But do you want to know the really interesting part of the house?" she said, leading him to the bed. "It originally belonged to a woman who kept men for her pleasure." She practically purred the last word and it had the same effect on him as if she'd reached between them and stroked him.

He skimmed his hands over her shoulders, lightly touching her breasts. "Do you want me to be one of your men, brought in to pleasure you?"

"Yes." Her pupils dilated.

"I will pleasure you every way that I know how." He bent his head and captured a taut, pink nipple in his mouth and sucked. Her low moan floated over him and drove him to suckle harder. He did the same to her other breast until her breath came in hard pants. She pulled away and pushed him back onto the bed.

"You're willing to let me have my way with you?" Her eyes, more molten silver than green, seemed to shimmer.

He had a pretty good idea of who she was and what she

was about, but he thought he'd better make sure she knew his boundaries. "I'm not into pain."

"Good. Neither am I."

She leaned forward, her hair a pale skein over his shoulders, her breasts teasing against his arm, her breath warm and fragrant against his ear. "I want to tie you to the bed with those cords holding back the curtains. Would you let me put you in bond-age?"

She wanted to tie him up? He'd never tied or been tied. That meant he wouldn't be able to hold her, touch her at will.

"Please. Pretty please, with me on top." She flicked her tongue, warm and wet, against the rim of his ear and he was thoroughly seduced. At that moment he would probably agree to anything outside of cross-dressing or animals.

What did the actual restraints matter anyway? She'd already put him in bondage. A dozen women and all he could think of was her. This. "Yes. Put me in bondage."

She pushed him back onto the bed and he sank onto the sumptuous silk coverlet. She crawled onto the bed after him. Her hair hung over her shoulders, a silvery-blond curtain that teased him with glimpses of her breasts.

She used the silk cords that held the bed curtains in place and quickly bound his wrists and ankles to the four posts, leaving him spread-eagled and the two of them intimately ensconced, as the gossamer curtains shut out the rest of the room. And Portia was on to something because it was incredibly arousing to be simultaneously restrained and so open.

She tied the final knot and turned to face him. He felt as if thick, hot lava flowed through him. Her eyes were hot and glittery; she was as turned on as he was. "Are you comfortable?"

He tested his arms and legs. She'd left a generous amount of play in his silken bonds while still restricting his movements. "Just as cozy as a guy can be, spread-eagled on a bed with the woman he's desperate for just out of reach."

She crawled past his extended legs, her slender hip sliding along his erection with mind-blowing eroticism. She braced her hands on either side of his head and leaned down, veiling their faces in the fall of her hair. Her mouth descended on his in an openly sensual kiss. He unrestrainedly explored her mouth with his tongue, his lips, his teeth. She kissed him back with an abandon that maddened him. More than once he reached to cup her head in his hands, wrap her in his arms, pull her harder, tighter, closer to him. And each time he found his efforts thwarted by the cords binding him.

Longing filled his entire body. He ached for the feel of her satin nipples against his chest, something more substantial than the brush of her hip against his hard-on. He arced his body upward and for the briefest moment felt her body's softness and heat.

Portia pulled away from him. Rourke lost himself in sensation as she stroked his skin, laved him with her tongue, and kissed him all over until he was a writhing, heaving mass of nerve endings. It was the sweetest torture to see her moving over him, naked, but not be able to touch her, only to be touched by her.

The scent of their combined arousal was heady and filled the enclosed area. She leaned past the curtains and plucked a condom from the bedside drawer.

As desperately as he wanted her to sheath him, slide over him and enfold him in the hot, wet folds of her body, he wanted something else even more.

"Wait," he said. She paused, condom in hand. "I need to know that you believe me. If you can't trust me, don't take this any farther."

She wrapped one hand around his shaft and he clenched his teeth. "Yes. I believe you. I trust you." She slid the condom over him with the other hand and he wasn't sure which made him happier, that she trusted him or that they didn't have to stop.

# 9

FIVE LONG DAYS and even longer nights later, Portia finally was back in Rourke's bed, her leg wedged between his, still reeling from the residual tremors of her newfound experience of multiple orgasms.

"That almost made up for the wait," she murmured against the hard wall of his chest.

"Hmm. It's been five days of sheer hell," he said, his breath stirring against her temple.

He'd spent the last five days jetting from one exotic location to another on dates that lasted late into the night. Each night, Rourke and his date of the day had been in a posh hotel with connecting doors, giving him every opportunity for intimacy with that date. And, more importantly, precluding him from any real time alone with Portia. She'd missed the sex, and even more confounding, the times like this, the closeness afterward. She didn't want to think about next week, and the week after, and the months beyond. No, better to concentrate on the here and now.

"You're an odd man to call jetting to exotic locations with beautiful women, dining in five-star restaurants and staying in ritzy hotels sheer hell," she teased him.

He swatted her bottom playfully. "You know good and well it was because I couldn't be with you, but you need to hear me say it, don't you, you little egomaniac."

"I'd hardly qualify as an egomaniac, after watching all

those women do their best to seduce you both on- and off-screen."

His expression grew serious. "I told you from the beginning, it's only you. I took your advice and became an actor playing a part." He threaded his fingers through her hair. "It's funny. When the studio offered me the show, it was simply two weeks that I had to get through. But now that it's almost over, I don't want it to end. And you know the part that I don't want to end? You. Meeting you on the terrace every morning. Waiting for you to knock on my door every night. The way the hair stands up on the back of my neck every time you walk into a room." He laughed. "The only worthwhile things that have happened have been on the terrace and in this room, because those were the two places that I've ever had you to myself."

Her heart knocked against her ribs. This was surely what was meant by making love with words. That was the most beautiful thing anyone had ever said to her other than her son's *I love you*. She swallowed past the lump suddenly blocking her throat. "I'll miss you as well."

"I have a day of down time after tomorrow's wrap-up. I'd like to spend that day with you." He laced his fingers through hers. "A day together without cameras and microphones where I can hold your hand when I want to."

No, no, no. This had been on-location fantasy. That felt too much like a date. And she didn't date. That hadn't changed. She still had her obligations. The rationale that had kept her on course for ten years hadn't changed. "I don't think that's a good idea. We're all under a gag order until after this program airs. And you're a celebrity these days. Paparazzi lurk in L.A. like vultures circling for a fresh kill."

"I know someplace where the paparazzi would never think to look."

She looked at him questioningly.

"Your place. Then I could hold your hand." He brought her hand to his mouth and kissed her fingers. It was gallant and tender and she felt herself waver beneath an onslaught of longing, both his and hers. "I could see where you live. Meet Danny. Maybe you could invite your parents and your sister over. I'd like to meet them all."

God, the sheer, absolute intimacy of letting him into her world scared her senseless. Why couldn't he just tell her he wanted one more day to simply have sex with her? That she could handle. Why wasn't it enough for him?

"I don't see the point. You're a nice guy and we've had a good time together, but I'm really busy and you live across the country and—"

"One day, Portia, please. Just one day out of a lifetime. What could it hurt?"

*Me.* If she wasn't careful it could hurt her. "I don't know that it would hurt anything, but it complicates everything." She shook her head. "And you can't meet Danny. That's one reason I never dated. I didn't want to bring a procession of men into his life."

She saw the hurt in his eyes and hated that she'd put it there. She softened her tone and tried to make him understand. She didn't want to hurt Rourke, but she refused to hurt Danny. "I've seen it happen to so many kids. Their mom starts dating a man, the kid gets attached, the couple break up and the kid is devastated. Danny's already dealt with his father's abandonment. I have no intention of setting him up for further devastation."

He nodded. Solemn. Respecting her concerns and obligations. "Okay. So I can't meet Danny."

"How am I supposed to introduce you to my parents? They're understanding and fairly open-minded, but it could be awkward."

"Friends. You could try introducing me to them as your friend."

Except she didn't have any friends. Especially male friends. She worked and came home. "They're going to ask questions."

He drew a deep breath and she had a feeling she wasn't going to like what he was about to say. "Or you could introduce me as your lover. You're a big girl now, Portia. You're not seventeen and showing up pregnant. You're an adult woman who carries enormous responsibility and does a damn good job of it, but you are allowed a life and that includes a sex drive, honey."

She waffled. Part of her wanted to tell him her life was none of his damn business. Another part of her wanted to rise to the inherent challenge in his words. She didn't particularly want him at her apartment, but it was safer than a hotel, where he was much more likely to be spotted and identified. She was a nobody and the paparazzi didn't hang out at nobody apartment complexes. And it wasn't as if the apartment was really hers or was really personal. It was just a place until she and Danny bought their own home.

And once she ran through all of that rationale, she had to admit it was like standing at the edge of a deep, cold pool and testing the waters with your big toe. What would it be like to have him in her real world?

"I'll have to check everyone's schedule. I believe Danny has a Boy Scout camping trip planned." He missed her when she was gone but, nerd or not, he was a typical nine-year-old boy and after a hug or two was ready to get on with whatever he was into at the moment. And mom's return didn't begin to equal the allure of a scout camping trip. They were so on the brink of having a more normal home life when she got this studio position and didn't have location travel—their own place, a dog and no extended periods of being gone for weeks at a time.

"Thank you. I have this fantasy of spending the whole night with you. Of waking up with you next to me in the morning, your hair on my pillow."

Before Rourke, her full sexual experience had consisted of two times in the back seat of Mark's car. Portia had never woken up next to a man. Never spent the night in a man's arms. Never shared her pillow when morning's first rays slanted through the bedroom blinds. Rourke's words painted such a picture that a frightening longing swept her.

She swept her hand to encompass his room. "Trust me, it's not the Taj Mahal."

He smiled. "It doesn't have to be, as long as you're there." His mouth descended on hers in a kiss so tender it stole her breath, and just possibly a little bit of her heart as well.

THE FOLLOWING MORNING, Portia had a hundred and one loose ends to tie up after they'd filmed the final episode where Rourke selected Maggie and then shot the final interviews. Terry and Jeff were busy disassembling wiring and the various sound components. Jacey and a helper had attacked the cameras. Climbing down from a ladder, Jacey handed the piece of equipment over to her assistant.

"Another reality wrap. Except for putting the show together next week," Jacey said.

"Yep. I'll be glad to sleep in my own bed instead of that brick that doubles for one. When are you heading back to New York?" She'd miss Jacey.

"I'll be here through the end of next week. I thought about flying back to New York for the weekend but Digg's on for twenty-four so I'm staying with the old man tomorrow. He spends every Saturday golfing. Want to do brunch tomorrow? You could bring your kid, if you wanted to."

Jacey had said once that she and Portia were a good bit alike and it was true. They were both loners who tended to keep to themselves, but a friendship had developed between them on this set. During this shoot, Jacey had gone from being a co-worker to a friend. Her abrupt brunch invitation delighted and surprised Portia.

"I can't. Danny's out of town and I…I have other plans." Portia, who kept her distance from everyone, went out on a limb. She reciprocated. "But maybe you could join me and Danny for dinner one night next week."

Jacey looked pleased at the invitation, but not too pleased because too pleased wouldn't be Jacey. "I guess I could do that. When is Rourke leaving?"

"I'm not really sure. You'll have to check with him on that."

"Oh. I was hoping he was your other plans."

Portia couldn't stop the smile that blossomed on her face. "He is."

Jacey grinned. "I knew it."

"He's so great, it's scary." Portia had spent so many years not confiding in anyone, now it was as if some dam had burst inside her and she was spilling her innermost thoughts with Jacey.

"I know exactly what you mean. Digg scared the hell out of me. Still does sometimes. If I was one of those sappy romantics, I might call Rourke your knight in shining armor."

Ha. If Jacey only knew about Nick, the real reason Rourke had appeared on the show. She had no idea. Rourke to the rescue? Was that how he saw her? The thought disquieted her. "I don't want a knight in shining armor. I don't need to be rescued." Being rescued implied a dependency on someone and she'd never put herself in that position. Particularly not with a man. That was foolish.

Jacey barked out a laugh. "News flash. Our men—" *Whoa,* Portia thought. *I wouldn't go so far as to call Rourke my man* "—need to save the day. It's in their genetic makeup. Digg's a firefighter, for God's sake. He donated most of the million bucks he won."

"You do know Rourke's an investment banker?"

"Digg's profession is overt. Rourke is a little more subtle, but it's there in that gallant courteousness that he extends to everyone. Why do you think women around the world are so apeshit over him? He's hot, but so are a lot of guys. It's because they sense that nine hundred years ago he'd be riding up on a white charger to take on the bad guy. That's what makes him really hot."

THE NEXT MORNING, Portia smoothed her hands over her shorts. She was a nervous wreck. A total basket case. He'd be here any minute. Bad decision on her part. She should've never agreed to let O'Malley come. This was different from the anonymity of being on location where she was in charge, where her position and wearing a suit every day allowed for retreat, regardless of whether she'd been naked the night before with Rourke.

Her doorbell rang. For a second she toyed with not answering the door, pretending not to be home. But not only was that a cowardly move, knowing Rourke, he'd camp out on her doorstep and someone was bound to recognize him sooner or later.

She opened the door. Backlit by the bright California sun, he filled her doorway. She'd seen him wearing a tux, faux sultan garb, bathing suits, khakis and button-downs, golf shirts, but she'd never seen him like this. This was the real Rourke and he looked better than he ever had. Worn jeans hugged his hips and a Boston Red Sox T-shirt that had seen its fair share of washings hung loose over his shoulders, the tail out.

The bottom dropped out of her stomach and she had no clue what to say. She felt positively naked without her suit and her clipboard.

He shifted from one foot to another and finally broke the silence stretching between them. "Hi."

"Hi." She needed either to invite him in or tell him to leave. She should really tell him she'd made a mistake and tell him to leave. That would show she still possessed some good sense. "Come in." She opened the door wider. His arm brushed her shoulder as he stepped into her apartment and her whole body tightened at the brief contact. "Did you have any trouble finding it? Traffic can be crazy."

He turned to face her and she leaned against the door she'd just closed. In the span of a single day she'd forgotten how very blue his eyes were, how thick were the black lashes that fringed them.

"No problem at all. My rental car has GPS and you forget, I live in Boston, where traffic is always hell. Getting to Logan airport around rush hour is a nightmare."

She nodded her head. "So, you're here."

He nodded back at her. "I'm here." His eyes flickered over her bare legs, her denim shorts, her cotton top with its scooped neckline, her hair in a ponytail.

He'd seen her naked any number of times, but with just that look, she felt more exposed than she'd ever been with him buried inside her. "Um, why don't I show you around? Trust me, that won't take long, and I can show you where to put your bag." She'd agreed to let him share her room, her bed. What *had* she been thinking?

"Sounds like a plan."

She swept her hand around the room. "This is obviously the den." And the furnishings were all obviously dated and secondhand and she felt slightly embarrassed.

"I've always thought saving my money for a down payment was more important than new furniture, as you can tell."

Rourke laughed, somewhat self-consciously. "I'm an investment banker. The return is much better on real estate than on furniture. I own a condo with a view of Boston Harbor, but Watson's and my favorite chair is an old recliner we inherited when my dad got a new one from my mom to celebrate his retirement."

Some of the awkwardness between them dissipated.

He looked past her. She knew the series of framed black and whites on the wall behind the sofa had caught his attention. He walked over and bent one knee on the couch. For perhaps a full minute he knelt, immobile, studying the photos of her and Danny. Finally, Rourke turned to face her, the tenderness in his face nearly bowling her over. "They're beautiful. I can see you in him."

"He has my flat cheekbones and almond-shaped eyes, but for the most part he looks like Mark." He had Mark's dark hair and blue eyes and when he was concentrating very hard, which was often, he pursed his lips the same way Mark used to. "But he's very much his own person. My mother dabbles in amateur photography. She took a ton of shots that weekend and then mounted and framed those for my birthday. I love them."

"I can see why." He rose, but continued to stand in front of the sofa, looking at the photos. "How old was Danny?"

She smiled, thinking back to the day her mother had snapped the photos. "He was five. My parents treated us to a weekend in Morro Bay to celebrate my college graduation. It was one of the loveliest weekends of my life."

"You both look happy. It's obvious you're devoted to one another."

"I've met lots of single moms who think of their kids as

mistakes. Mark was a mistake, but Danny never has been. He's a blessing. He's the most important thing in my life. I would die for him."

"Mark's a fool and Danny's a lucky kid." He glanced back at the photos and laughed. "I think I wore those exact same glasses when I was about his age. He reminds me a little bit of myself."

Portia knew, somewhere in her heart, without a doubt, that Danny and Rourke would get along like a house afire. Rourke and Danny did share the same coloring and now that Rourke had mentioned it, they both had a way of intensely concentrating on one thing or one person at a time. The resemblance was enough that they could easily pass for father and son. And even thinking that way frightened her. She ignored his comment and walked through the open doorway into the tiny galley kitchen. "This is the kitchen."

He followed her, the space seeming all the smaller with his wide shoulders and scent surrounding her. He leaned against the counter and looked at the professional-quality stainless-steel cookware hanging from a rack. "Those are very nice. Do you like to cook?"

She was truly pathetic. The man was admiring her freaking *pots and pans* and she was getting all gooey inside.

"I love to cook. It relaxes me." She nodded toward the cookware. "A Christmas gift from my parents last year. They're wonderful to cook with. How about you?"

"It's a bit of a passion. I eat better than any single guy I know. That's one of the things I'm looking forward to when I get home. Some kitchen time." His smile held a shade of self-consciousness.

He was so cute when he looked that way, she couldn't help but tease him. "And do you clean up after yourself?"

"I live alone. If I don't do it, it doesn't get done."

He was a nice geeky guy wrapped up in a gorgeous package and he liked to cook *and* he cleaned up after himself. It would be far too easy to fall in love with him and wind up with a shattered heart. She needed to keep it light and easy between them and she needed something to run with. "Do you have any vices?"

"Laundry. I hate to do laundry. I know it's the worst kind of waste of my money, but I send everything out," he said with a sheepish smile.

How could you hold that against a guy? "I don't know anyone who *likes* to do laundry."

Rourke shook his head. "That's because you've never met my mother. If she wasn't scared to drive in the city, I swear, she'd come in and pick mine up to do it."

"She sounds nice."

"She is. You'll like her." His eyes held hers.

Not *you would*, but *you will*. As if it was a given that she'd meet his mother. The thought sent her stomach into a nosedive. And just as she'd done before, she returned to her apartment tour without responding. A small hallway off the den and kitchen housed the bathroom and separated the two bedrooms.

"That's Danny's room," she indicated the closed door but didn't offer to let him look inside. That was Danny's private space and she had no right to share it with someone without his permission. "Obviously the bathroom." She led him into her room, her private sanctuary, her haven. "And this is my room." She realized he was still carrying an overnight bag. "You can put your bag over there," she said, pointing to a spot beside the closet.

He dropped his overnight bag and looked around her room. His assessing gaze seemed to take in everything, from the cool greens and blues of the framed sea abstracts on the wall to her platform bed with its simple coverlet in a soothing aquamarine. "Your place suits you. Elegant but not fussy."

His words pleased her. "Thank you."

The air, the energy between them changed. They were in a bedroom, familiar ground for them.

"Portia, why do you always wear your hair up or pulled back?"

"It stays neat and contained that way." She glanced around the room. "I'm a bit of a neat and organizational freak in case you haven't noticed."

"I did. But I knew that already. You couldn't do the job you do without those traits."

She smiled, inordinately pleased by his observation. "And I bet your place is a bit of a mess."

He grinned. "Guilty. How'd you know?"

"Your toiletries were scattered in your bathroom on the set."

"I'll try not to be a messy guest." He started toward her and her heart began to race. "Can I do something?"

"What's that?" He hadn't even reached her and she was already breathless.

He cupped her shoulders in his hands and she sighed inside at the heat of his touch. Without thought, she caught one of his wrists in her hand and brushed her cheek against his knuckles and pressed a kiss to the springy dark hairs on his wrist.

He half moaned and half sighed. "Oh, Portia…I want to take your hair down."

*Rapunzel, Rapunzel, would you let down your hair so that I can scale your fortress walls and wreak havoc in your well-ordered universe until I and the pleasure you find with me, in me, through me* become *your universe?*

"Rourke, I'd like you to let down my hair."

HOLDING HER GAZE, he worked the elastic band out of her hair. He buried his hands in the mass as it tumbled past her shoulders. "I love your hair. It's beautiful."

He didn't give her a chance to respond. Instead, he did what he'd wanted to do since he'd walked through her door—he kissed her. Her mouth was as sweet, her kiss as potent as he remembered. Maybe more so. His tongue swept the recesses of her mouth, rediscovering her taste, exploring her. She sucked on his tongue and he felt the sensation in his groin. Oh, God, one kiss and he was hard.

He pulled away from her, his breath uneven. Neither said a word, but instead they began to undress. Rourke made quick work of his jeans. He stepped out of his shoes and pulled off his briefs and his socks. Once in a moment of passion, he'd forgotten his socks. Mary, his college lover, had scathingly told him that dress socks on a naked man were not sexy. He'd never forgotten again. He sent a silent thank you to Mary because Portia was looking at him as if she found him quite sexy at the moment.

She'd taken off her clothes and was lying on the bed on her side, propped on one arm, blatantly admiring him. "You could pose for a sculptor."

He was damn glad she felt that way, even though it wasn't a remote possibility. "I don't think so."

"But you're beautifully proportioned." Her hot gaze lingered on his recently lengthened portion and he felt damn near light-headed as all the blood in his body seemed to rush to pool between his legs.

"I could be convinced if you were the one doing the sculpting," he said.

She wet her lips with the tip of her tongue and shifted to her back, canting her legs, her glistening sex beckoning him. "Rourke."

He bit back a groan. When she spread her legs that way

he could barely think, barely breathe, it made him so hot. He could feel the heavy beat of his heart, feel the ache that started somewhere inside him and manifested itself in his throbbing member. The musky scent of arousal hung in the air. He stood still, immobilized by the sheer beauty of her. "You are perfect."

She opened her mouth and he could've sworn she planned to argue with him over his statement. Instead she murmured, "Thank you."

Rourke looked down at her, letting everything he felt show. It was important to him that she know how he saw her. "You're like an exotic goddess who's deigned to reveal herself to a mere mortal."

Okay, maybe he'd spent a little too much time immersed in Arthurian legend and Tolkien before he'd discovered sci-fi. Thank God she didn't laugh at him. Instead there was a glimmer of tears in her eyes. Shit. He'd rather she laughed at him than know he made her cry. Good job, dork boy, take her from lusty to weepy in six seconds or less.

He knelt on the coverlet beside her and spoke without measuring his words. "Oh, baby, please don't cry. I never meant to make you cry."

She blinked away the moisture and smoothed her hand over his jaw. "Rourke, don't make me out to be something I'm not. I'm just a flesh-and-blood woman. I'm not a goddess. And I'm far from perfect, inside or out."

She was perfect—for him. "The way I see it, you *look* perfect." He skimmed his hand down her shoulder, over one rounded breast, down her belly, past the slightly darker blond curls between her thighs, and the length of her leg. "I don't know. You *feel* perfect."

He nuzzled her neck and she dropped her head back with a soft sigh. "You *smell* perfect."

Slowly, deliberately he lowered his head to one perfect

breast with its perfectly tempting nipple and licked her. "Hmm. *Tastes* perfect." He went back for seconds and was gratified by the shudder that swept her and her low moan of appreciation. He raised his head, a teasing note beneath the heat that threatened to consume him. "Ah. I hate to tell you, but you *sound* perfect as well."

"Okay, okay. I give up. I'm the perfect embodiment of womanhood," she said, a sexy glint replacing the tears that had been in her beautiful eyes earlier.

"Hmm. I'm so glad you decided to see things my way." He smoothed his thumb over the fullness of her lips, moving up to the exotic flat planes of her cheekbones.

She slid her leg beneath his, her thigh nudging his heavy erection. She reached beneath her pillow and pulled out a wrapped condom. "You're very convincing." She opened it and smoothed it over his hard sex. He quivered against her hand. "Like water dropping on a stone."

He pulled her other leg over his hip, opening her thighs to him as they faced one another. "Water dripping on a stone. That's not very flattering."

She inched her leg higher, opening herself wider. "You wear me down."

She had no idea. In one smooth thrust, he was buried inside her. "I'd much rather wear you out."

# 10

OH, SHE DIDN'T KNOW when she'd ever felt this good, except maybe every time she was in bed with Rourke.

"I'm ravenous," she said, stretching and rolling out of bed. "I'm going to cook an early dinner. Do you want to help?" She pulled on her shorts and T-shirt but left her hair down and bra and panties off.

"I thought you'd never ask."

He looked like a kid who'd just been handed a Christmas present and her heart flip-flopped.

"You were waiting for me to ask? Since when have you not just gone after what you wanted?"

He grabbed her wrist and pulled her down on top of him, his hands molding to the small of her back. "How hungry are you?"

Laughing she twisted away, "Very. And if you plan to help you'd better get up and put on some clothes."

He raised his arms and pillowed his head on his hands. "No naked chefs?"

He was too sexy for her piece of mind. Even the thatch of dark hair in his underarms sent a shiver through her. She shook her head, her gaze traveling across his broad chest, down his rippled abs, further still to his lean hips that showcased his sex, impressive even when flaccid, surrounded by dark hair, those muscular thighs that tensed to rock-hard every time he came…. Maybe if all she had to do was pop a frozen dinner into the microwave it'd be okay, but serious cooking, where she needed to actually have a clue? No way. "No naked chefs. I'd definitely be too distracted."

Looking extremely arrogant and extremely satisfied with her answer, he stood and pulled on his jeans and T-shirt. He blinked. "Damn. I just lost a contact."

Both of them dropped to their hands and knees and cautiously felt around on the carpet, searching for the lost lens without success. After a few minutes Portia sat back on her heels. "Do you have another pair with you?"

"No. I have a pair of backup glasses but they're…"

"They're what?"

"I look like Rourke the Dork in them."

"Can you see without them?"

He grimaced. "You resemble a Monet painting on a really fuzzy day."

"For God's sake put the glasses on."

"But I'm telling you—"

"Put…the…glasses…on."

"Okay. I'll put on the glasses." He grabbed a contact lens case and an eyeglass case and disappeared into the bathroom. In a minute he was back, wearing a pair of black-rimmed glasses.

Portia took a deep breath. She hadn't been kidding about having a thing for geeks. She'd only thought O'Malley was good-looking before. He was devastating now. "You look like Clark Kent."

He turned a delicious shade of red. "I told you—"

She backed him up to the wall outside the bathroom door and pressed against him. "You don't understand. I have a serious thing for Clark." She pressed a hot, hard kiss to his mouth.

He looked kind of stunned and very sexy when they both came up for air. "I may never take these glasses off."

"As long as you keep them on—" she ran her hand down his body and stroked him through the denim "—later."

He appeared faintly dazed. "Oh, honey, you just say the word and I'll wear them 24/7."

Laughing, feeling young and sexy and carefree, Portia led him to her kitchen. "I thought I'd make a sage- and rosemary-stuffed pork loin, roasted potatoes and fresh asparagus. I went to the market this morning so I'm well stocked. Any preferences, suggestions?"

"What if I provide dessert?"

He was mouthwatering in those glasses and jeans and T-shirt. She glanced at him suggestively. "I was counting on you for dessert."

He grabbed her and pulled her against him, kissing her. "You are a wicked woman."

She kissed him back. "Only since I've met you."

He slid his hands beneath her shorts and cupped her bare buttocks. "Do you have any heavy cream?" He slid one hand between her thighs, his finger testing the wetness that was beginning to gather there.

Her breath hitched in her throat. "Yes. I keep it on hand."

"Ideally it should chill overnight but I could make a crème brûlée."

She gripped his shoulders as he stroked one finger against her. "I like crème brûlée."

His gaze flickered from the bowl of fruit at her elbow to her nipples stabbing against the thin cotton of her shirt. "Or your pears look nice and ripe. I could make a pear tart." He bent his head and dragged his tongue across her nipple, leaving a wet mark on her shirt. "Why don't you think about it while I put on some music?"

She should have protested, but she'd never prepared a

meal in a semiaroused state before. She knew exactly what was for dessert and it was very erotic.

"There's a CD player in the armoire in the den." Her voice was husky, the denim between her thighs wet. "My sister works for an electronics retailer so she gets great deals on equipment. The hip-hop is Danny's and I'd rather skip that. The rest is mine, so anything you pick out is fine."

While Rourke plundered through her CD collection, Portia pulled herself together, decanted a bottle of wine and gathered the ingredients for their meal.

"This is one of my favorites," he said from the other room. She didn't ask, just waited to hear what came on. She immediately recognized the opening chords to a Dave Matthews Band selection.

Rourke stepped back into the kitchen and she smiled her approval. "I love this CD. How about a glass of merlot? I noticed during the filming that you seemed to prefer that." She preferred the richness of reds to whites as well.

"You noticed what wine I prefer and you have it?"

"Yes." Wow. Amazing how a small detail could please him so much. And amazing how it made her feel like an accomplished geisha. She poured each of them a glass and for a while they enjoyed wine, music, aimless conversation and cooking together, and always the potent sexual chemistry simmering between them as they brushed arms while working at the counter, his hip skimming against her buttock as he leaned over the sink.

The song "Crash into Me" came on and Rourke wrapped his arms around her from behind, linking his hands beneath her breasts. "This is how I feel. Like you crashed into me before I knew what happened." His warm breath stirred against her ear, sending a hot shiver down her spine. "That's exactly how I feel around you. Tied up and twisted." Relaxed from her wine, she cupped her hands over his, leaned her head back into the crook of his shoulder and gave herself over to the lyrics, the man, swaying in time to the music.

The song ended and Portia realized she was still wrapped in his arms, her eyes closed. There was something so romantic, so tender, so far beyond mere sex in leaning into him, swaying to the music, that she didn't know how to react. She released his hands and disentangled herself, getting back to business in the kitchen.

"You said you wanted to meet my parents and they're dropping by this afternoon."

Without her asking, Rourke washed the potatoes in the sink. "I'm looking forward to meeting them. Do they live nearby?"

She handed him a cutting board and knife. "Close but not too close, if you know what I mean." She began to mince the herbs. The pungent scents of rosemary and sage filled the kitchen. "I picked an apartment that was in the same school district as their house. Since Danny stays with them when I'm on location, I needed to make getting him to school as easy as possible for everyone. They're dropping off a science project he'd started that's due next week."

"Do they know I'm here?"

"I didn't get that far." Portia stuffed the roast and Rourke stepped over to lend a hand with the kitchen twine. "When you meet my mother you'll understand. She talks fast and she talks a lot." And Portia'd been a chicken. She didn't want to have to explain Rourke. And what if he hadn't shown up? Then she'd have mentioned him when it was totally unnecessary. She washed and dried her hands. "And anyway, I'm an adult. Having a…friend over isn't a big deal." She leaned down and put the roast into the oven. Rourke slid the dish of potatoes in beside it.

Rourke looked almost stricken. "Do you date often? Is there someone special?"

She'd deliberately misled him when they'd first shown up on location. They were far beyond that point, and he deserved better. He deserved the truth. "No. I don't date." She cleaned up the counter and bagged the leftover herbs. "I'm busy and Danny's my priority and men can't handle that. And I refuse to parade a retinue of men through Danny's life. It's not fair to him." She reiterated what she'd told Rourke once before. "He's already had to deal with a dad that doesn't want him. I won't have him dragged into the disappointments of relationships that don't work out for me." That should give Rourke a pretty clear view of what their outlook was and reassure him she wasn't going to chase him across the country.

He propped against the kitchen counter, his arms crossed. "But doesn't that mean you might never find the one relationship that does work for you?"

She shrugged. "My lifestyle works for me now. Very nicely. Just like your lifestyle with Watson works for you."

Behind the glasses, his eyes narrowed and she could literally see the wheels turning. Good Lord, he was impossibly attractive in those glasses with his hair messed, wearing a T-shirt, worn jeans, and bare feet.

"If you don't date, what about sex?"

Portia felt a blush wash her neck and color her face. What was he thinking, asking questions like that? "I don't have any sexually transmitted diseases and outside of that, it's none of your business."

"You know I wasn't asking about STDs." She could see him putting two and two together and coming up with exactly four. "When was the last time you made love before us?"

She turned her back to him, without answering. He slid

his arms around her from behind, enveloping her in his body heat, his scent. "Has there been anyone since Danny's father?" he asked. "There hasn't been, has there?"

The hard ridge of his arousal pressed against her buttocks. He was actually getting turned on at the idea of her not having sex in forever. He brushed his hands across her belly, feathered them over her ribs to cup her breasts. He bent his head, his breath warm against her neck. "Why me, Portia?"

Trapped between the counter and his big, hard body, with his hands on her breasts and his mouth against her neck, she could barely think beyond the feel of him against her.

He nibbled at the nape of her neck and rolled her nipples between his fingers and she grew even wetter and hotter. She didn't have enough…whatever…left to make up a lie. Sexual turn-on as a truth serum. "Because you're across the country. Because it was my last location assignment. And because I wanted you like I've never wanted any man before." The last word ended on an incoherent moan as he ravished her neck.

"Was Mark the only one before me?" He suckled the nerve-rich nape of her neck while his fingers continued to torment her through her shirt. She gripped the edge of the worn countertop.

"Yes." She pushed against him. God, he made her feel so good, so alive, so unlike anything she'd ever experienced before. And it was tacky and crass, but Mark deserved no less, and neither did Rourke. "Mark was the only one. Twice. And it wasn't very good."

"Oh…" he groaned against her neck, unzipped her shorts and slid them down her hips, leaving her naked from the waist down. He turned her around. His face was hard and flushed with arousal. "I may have signed up to bring the dessert, but I know what I'd like for an appetizer."

His big hands spanned her waist and he lifted her to the edge of the sink. Surprised, she instinctively braced herself, grabbing the lip of the counter, her heart thundering. He knelt between her thighs, hooking one knee over each of his broad shoulders, exposing her to him. He parted her with his thumbs and looked up at her, a carnal smile on his face, his blue eyes hot and glittery behind those sexy, black hornrims.

"Something sweet." His warm breath gusted against her and she grew wetter still. "Something ripe and juicy." His thumbs traced her folds. *Please. Please.* "Nectar." He blew gently on her and she almost bucked off the edge. "You." He swiped his tongue along the path of his fingers, the faint scrape of his beard against her inner thighs intensifying the pleasure. She dropped her head back, her "Yes" echoing off the ceiling.

Rourke was a handy man to have in the kitchen.

THE FOLLOWING MORNING, he woke slowly, instantly knowing where he was and who he was with, but wanting to savor the sensation of his first time waking up next to Portia. Because this would be only the first time of many, despite the fact that she'd picked him because he lived over two thousand miles away.

He concentrated on the heat of her naked body pressed against him, the length of her smooth, feminine leg between his, the silk of her hair against his shoulder and chest, her scent that wrapped around him, the fine cotton of the rumpled sheet beneath him, the soft down of the comforter thrown over both of them.

Careful not to disturb her, he reached one arm to the nightstand and groped for his glasses. When he put them on, he found her watching him. "Sorry, I didn't mean to wake you," he said. "I can't see without them and I wanted to look at you. You're just as beautiful as I thought you'd be." He shook his head. "No. That's not true. You're even more beautiful."

A sweet blush washed over her. He could bring her to a rousing, screaming orgasm time and again, but a simple compliment seemed to embarrass her.

"You might need to check that prescription on those glasses when you get home," she said, self-consciously raking her fingers through her hair.

He smoothed a few stray strands from her shoulder as much to prove to himself that this was real and not some dream. He was here in Portia's bed. "Have you been awake long?"

"A while. I'm not used to sleeping with anyone. And you're big." He grinned when she glanced at the sheet tented by his early-morning hard-on. "You take up a lot of room."

"Good thing you're just the right size." He propped himself on his elbow and looked down at her. Drinking in the sight of her. "I think your parents liked me."

They'd dropped by just before dinner the previous evening. Jack and Laela Tomlinson were nice folks who obviously doted on Portia, Danny and Portia's sister Mellina. Portia had inherited her mother's looks and her father's fair hair and reserved demeanor. Although they'd been cordial and gracious, more than once he'd caught the older Tomlinsons exchanging glances. His poor baby was in for the third degree when he left.

She nodded nonchalantly, but he noted the wariness in her eyes. "Everyone likes you. You're that kind of guy."

"I think it's a bonus that they liked me, but I really only care whether *you* like me." He tried to tease the wariness away.

She scraped her fingernail lightly over his belly. "One

would assume that I like you well enough, considering you're naked in my bed."

"Umm. Hold that thought," he said jumping up and heading for the bathroom. If this were one of those romance novels his mother liked to read, he wouldn't have to hop out of bed to relieve himself. But it wasn't and he did, so he made quick work of it. He caught a glimpse of himself in the bathroom mirror. Damn, he looked rough. He needed to shave and his hair was standing up on his head at odd angles. The glasses gave him a mad-scientist look. Make that a naked mad-scientist look. But he was hoping to talk her into for better or for worse and she was definitely getting a glimpse of the worse. He shrugged and hurried back before Portia decided to get up and get dressed.

Luckily for him, she was still nestled under the covers. He slid in beside her, pulling her into his arms. "Now where were we?"

She smiled, her hand curling over his hip. "If my memory serves me correctly, we were talking about you being naked in my bed."

He laughed but inside he felt as nervous as a thirteen-year-old geek with a crush on the pretty girl. If he had a piece of paper, he'd write her a note asking her if she'd go steady with him and give her the yes and no boxes to check her answer. Instead he simply asked her, "Do you like me enough that I'll wind up here again?"

She shifted away from him and propped her back against her pillow. "I do like you, but that's really not a good idea."

"I think it's an excellent idea."

She looked away from him, her fingers absently plucking at the edge of the sheet. "Rourke, let's not complicate this. We've had a good time—" he uttered a protest and she looked at him "—okay, a great time together, but I have obligations and you have obligations and let's just leave it at a good time. Anyway, the show won't air for several weeks and there's that gag order."

Okay. He was going for broke. Laying his cards on the table. "Couldn't we at least talk on the phone? Perhaps see each other every couple of weeks?" He laughed, amazed that now that the time was upon him, he was surprisingly calm. "See, I've got this problem. I love you." Portia's eyes widened and her mouth gaped slightly. "I think I'm one of those love-at-first-sight poor sots because I haven't been the same since I saw you and I'm damn sure I'm not ever going to be the same again."

She slowly shook her head *no.* "Rourke…"

He bulldogged ahead. "And I'm pretty sure you love me, even though I'm even surer you don't want to admit it."

Her chin rose, and he glimpsed a shadow of that cool haughtiness she'd armored herself in from the beginning. "Why would you assume I love you just because we had great sex together?"

Aha. She did consider it great sex. "Because you couldn't make love to me the way you did if you didn't love me. Some women could, lots of women do and there's nothing wrong with that or with them. But that's not the way you're made, Portia." He'd known last night in the kitchen when she'd admitted that there hadn't been another man since Mark. From her comments over dinner, he knew she thought he'd had some caveman response to her having only one man before him, but it was the knowledge that he had to mean something to her that had excited him so. "Otherwise you wouldn't have waited this long to let a man back into your bed, because, honey, we both know you're neither repressed nor frigid."

He wasn't sure if it was the "repressed or frigid" bit, but

it was cute when this elegant woman's mouth gaped like that. He cupped her cheek in his palm. "We could have a good life together. Me, you and Danny. I'm not wealthy, but I do okay. We'd be comfortable enough. And maybe one day we could give Danny a little brother or sister, or both."

She held up both hands and shook her head. "Wait. Whoa. Stop. Are you talking about mar… You mean you'd want to… Let me get this straight…"

He almost laughed at her stumbling around the concept of marriage as though it was something she couldn't give voice to. "Marriage. Married. Wedlock. Matrimony. Yeah, that."

"You don't even know me."

"Yes, I do. And you know me. I know the things about you that matter. I know you're a woman of integrity. A hard worker. Independent. Intelligent. Passionate. A great mom. We both come from similar backgrounds. We both believe strongly in family. We're both very good in the kitchen."

She flushed but patently ignored his kitchen comment. "I don't have any interest in marriage," she said, gazing at the seascapes rather than him.

She didn't have to look at him. As long as he could keep her talking and she didn't just clam up, all wasn't lost. "Why?"

She looked at him then, and he willed himself not to flinch at the starkness of her eyes. "It wouldn't be fair to you. There's a certain amount of trust and vulnerability required for a marriage to work and I can't…I won't go there."

"Let me—"

She cut him off. "I'm not some damsel in distress, Rourke. I don't need rescuing. I don't need to let you do anything."

She damn well didn't need to stay locked up in this fortress she'd built for herself, holding everyone at bay. But he had enough sense to keep that to himself. "I don't want to rescue you. I just want to love you."

"I'm not so sure that those aren't one and the same for you." Okay, so she was a very smart woman. "Jacey says you have a white-knight complex. You have to rescue people and I think she's right." Rather than be offended, he was heartened that she had talked to Jacey about him. She scrunched her knees up beneath the sheet and wrapped her arms around them, becoming a self-contained unit. "Can't you see that I don't *need* to be rescued? I don't *want* to be rescued? I learned the hard way that I can count on my family and I can count on me. It wasn't an easy lesson and I don't plan ever to repeat it."

She'd laughingly referred to him as water dripping on a stone, then so be it. "We'll take it slow. All I'm asking for is a chance to prove that you can trust me, that I'll still love you as much next week as I do now. Probably more."

"I like to think of myself as a person of integrity. How can I take and not give in return? What kind of person does that make me? And you'll get tired of giving with nothing in return."

He reached out and smoothed his hand over the line of her bare back. She was warm satin beneath his fingertips and he felt her quiver at his touch. "That's the thing. It's not a choice. It's a part of me. One of those involuntary functions like the hypothalamus functioning on its own, breathing, my stomach digesting my food and moving it on to the intestines." He caught himself. He'd definitely slipped into total geek mode, but her eyes had softened and she'd loosened her death grip on her knees. "I'm just Rourke the Dork in love with the pretty, brainy girl who sits in the front of the class and doesn't give him the time of day. You're the one with the Vulcan mind meld."

She reached out a tentative hand, her fingers curling around his, her hand small and delicate compared to his large, dark one. "I don't want Danny brought into this. I don't want him hurt if this doesn't work out."

His heart slammed against his ribs. He reminded himself to breathe. Okay, so maybe it wasn't an entirely involuntary function. "Fair enough. This can work, Portia. I just need you to tell me that you'll give us a chance."

She brought his hand, still clasped in hers, to her lips. She pressed a gossamer kiss to his fingers. "Okay. I'll give us a chance."

It wasn't a yes, but it wasn't an unequivocal no either. They were the sweetest words he'd ever heard.

# 11

PORTIA RETURNED the vacuum cleaner to the hall closet, her apartment tidy, organized, everything back in its place. Rourke had left for Boston an hour ago and she had another hour and a half before she had to pick Danny up from his camp-out. She pulled the elastic out of her hair—what the heck, she was beginning to like it hanging loose around her shoulders.

She missed Rourke, missed knowing that she wouldn't see him tonight, or tomorrow morning, or even the day after that. She turned on the CD player, skipping ahead to track seven, "Crash into Me." She was practical, pragmatic, logical. She didn't do silly stuff like moon around, but she couldn't seem to stop herself, and, quite honestly, she didn't want to.

She flopped on the sofa and wallowed in missing him. She closed her eyes and inhaled his scent still clinging to her skin, her clothes, remembering the timbre of his voice when he declared that frightening *I love you.* The blue of his eyes when he'd pulled her to him as he left, as if he couldn't bear to leave, couldn't bear to let her go.

And now he was gone and she felt as bereft as if a dark cloud had rolled in and denied her the sun's warmth. And the damnable part of it was she didn't know when there'd be another sunny day in her forecast.

The phone rang. She answered the portable on the end table without getting up.

"Hi," Rourke's voice slid over her, through her, around her.

She was glad she was alone because she was absolutely helpless to stop the smile that felt a mile wide. "Hi. What are you doing calling me?"

"They're boarding my plane, but I wanted to hear your voice one more time." His voice dropped. "What are you doing?"

"Lying on the couch."

"Are you dressed?"

Laughter burbled up from her at his strained tone. "Yes, I'm dressed." She stepped out on the ledge. "But I'm thinking of you."

His indrawn breath echoed over the line. "I hope it's good."

She inched forward, closer to the scary edge of the precipice. "I miss you."

"Oh, baby. I miss you too." She heard a speaker announcement in the background on his end, the words indecipherable. "Listen, I've got to go or I'm going to miss my plane. I love you, Portia."

"I…uh…I miss you. Have a safe flight."

Another loudspeaker announcement. "Bye."

"Bye."

She clicked the phone off and lay there, floating on a cloud. Things like this didn't happen to her.

The phone rang again in her hands, startling her. She answered it, laughing. "Get on that plane, you insane man."

A short pause on the other end. "Portia?"

Uh-oh. Maybe she'd sign up for caller ID regardless of the expense. "Hi, Mom."

"I take it Rourke has left?" her mother asked with wry amusement.

She'd noticed her mother mentally taking note yesterday when Rourke had mentioned his flight time. Portia braced herself for her mother's inevitable one hundred and one questions. Actually, she wasn't up for this now. "I'm not feeling quite up to speed. Could I call you later?"

"Well, then lie down while you talk to me."

Humph. She should've known her mom wasn't letting her off the hook that easily. "I'm trying to be a good mother and give you some space, but when I see my daughter looking happier than I've seen her in years, I think I deserve to know something about the young man that put that sparkle in her eyes."

Whatever this was between her and Rourke, wherever it was going, it felt too fragile, too new for her to pull out to be examined under her mother's microscope.

"Mom, it's just like I told you and Dad when I introduced you, he just finished two weeks on-site and was having a little decompression time before he headed back to Boston. In Massachusetts. Where he lives. End of story."

"Portia Renata Tomlinson, I am your mother but I'm not a simpleton. Rourke looked at you like you hung the moon. Looks don't particularly impress me, never have, never will. But I recognize a man with a good heart when I see one, and it was easy enough to see that in him. Your father and I discussed it and we'll be happy to have him as a son-in-law."

What? Portia's mouth hung open. She closed it with a snap. "Son-in-law?" What was up with everyone talking marriage today? "You'd marry me and Danny off to the first man who seems interested in me?"

"No. Don't be silly." That was more like it. "But we'd willingly marry you off to the man you're in love with."

Surely she'd heard that wrong. "Excuse me?"

"I said we'd marry you off to the man you're in love with."

"I'm not… That isn't… You're wrong." Portia liked him. Obviously. There was a lot to like about him. But love? Love?

"I'm your mother. I think I know my own daughter."

Portia sputtered. Sometimes her mom was nuts. "I'm me. I think I know me."

Her mother harrumphed her disagreement. "Sometimes it's hardest for us to know ourselves."

"Let's say for one wild moment that you were right. Rourke lives in Boston. You would send me and Danny to Boston? You're all the family my son has. You would tell me to rip him away from all that he knows, all that he holds dear, to live with a stranger?"

"I would tell you that I would rather have a happy daughter in Boston than a daughter only half alive in LA. And I would tell you that it's time for you and your son to build your own family, for your son to see his mother happy, for your son to have a father and know that being a father is more than donating sperm."

That threw her for a loop. "But you met him for half an hour—"

"And it was plenty of time for me to see the most important thing." Her mother's voice thickened, as if clogged by tears. "Mark snatched my bright sparkling daughter from us ten years ago and now your Rourke's given her back."

"She's the ultimate woman. Beautiful, smart, sexy," Rourke said.

Nick smirked, shaking his head. "Man, you've got it bad."

Rourke grinned. "Yeah, I do." Watson wiggled down beside him a little more in the chair.

"And you're giving up your contacts cause she likes the geek glasses?"

Rourke remembered the way Portia had backed him

up against the wall, the press of her lithe body against his, the hungry heat of her kiss. Most definitely he was converting to glasses. "Yep."

"Man, you're going to spend a small fortune flying out there." Sprawled on the leather couch, Nick put his feet on the coffee table, nudging aside an empty pizza box. Rourke was messy. Nick was a slob.

"No, I'm not." He couldn't stop grinning. He gave the chair up to Watson and walked over to the floor-to-ceiling windows that spanned half of the wall and showcased the spectacular night view of Boston Harbor. That view alone had enticed him to buy the condo that had once been a factory. He turned his back on it to face Nick. "I'm going to spend a small fortune moving out there."

Nick sat up straighter and rubbed the back of his neck. "You're serious aren't you?"

"Never more serious in my life."

"But what about mom and dad? Boston's your home. Your family's here." Nick crossed his hands over his belly. "Hell, I'm here and I'm your baby brother."

He nodded. "Yeah, but she's there."

"But you said she's got a kid and the dad's a deadbeat and doesn't support either one of them at all. Do you know how much money having a kid, especially one who's not even your own, is going to cost you?" Nick asked.

For the first time, Rourke questioned the wisdom of having bailed his brother out of his predicament. Nick just didn't seem to get the big picture. "When you love someone, you don't look at them as an investment. When you love someone you give them a check for half a million dollars because you love them."

Nick had the grace to look ashamed. "Okay. So when do we meet this paragon you're forsaking us all for?"

"I don't know yet." He could envision months before he

could talk her into it and even then it'd probably be kicking and screaming.

"You're not like one of these stalker guys who's gone off the deep end are you?"

Nick should've definitely been the one to appear on the show, with his penchant for melodrama.

"One day you'll fall in love and know what it's like to love someone body and soul. To look at them and know you're seeing your destiny."

"I'm happy for you. Truly I am. And you've always been the one to take care of everyone. God knows, you saved me when I was up to my ass in alligators, so I'm telling you now, this woman better treat you right or she'll answer to me."

Maybe there was hope for Nick discovering he wasn't the center of the universe. "You're just sulking. Trust me, you'll love her."

"How can you be so sure?" Nick quirked a dark brow.

"Because I do."

"MONDAY MORNINGS suck and this one sucks even more than usual. We've got a big-ass flop on our hands, boys and girls."

A hard knot formed in Portia's gut at Lauchmann's grim expression. He was a jerk, but he was a jerk with an unerring nose for turning out winning TV programs.

"I spent the weekend reviewing the footage. Forget any promotions—" Lauchmann eyed her directly "—or any pay raises. If we don't pull a miracle out of our asses on this one we'll all be lucky to get a job filming termite mounds in the bloody Sahara. Hell, Mueller's going to have all of our heads." Portia looked across at Jacey, who raised her eyebrows and gave a small shrug. "The studio spent a small fortune on this."

"What's the problem? The filming seemed to be going well." Portia asked the question everyone wanted to, but was afraid to insert into the midst of Lauchmann's tirade.

"The freaking problem, as I freaking see it, is that we freaking lost him. He was hot. You could feel the sexuality rolling off him on the camera. He was really hot, and he was seducing the women of the world. And then he bagged Maggie and that on-screen sizzle was gone."

Except O'Malley hadn't "bagged" Maggie. It'd been Portia. She'd screwed herself out of her promotion, perhaps even her job. Literally.

"What would it take to fix it? What'll it take to save it?" she asked when she could breathe again.

"A damned miracle would be nice. We need to make chicken salad out of chicken shit."

He really was a sorry excuse for a human being. "Could you be a little more definitive?" she asked. What the heck? If she was about to lose her job or any chance of imminent advancement, why not go out with a little backbone? And this was the creep who'd wanted her to hide in the bushes.

Lauchmann shot her a nasty glance. "The first few episodes will rock. We need something to stir the pot for the last half. Some juicy gossip. Some dirt. We'd better come up with something or we can all start packing for Africa."

Portia felt like a sleepwalker waking up. This was the real world. Not some fantasy spun by a blue-eyed, dark-haired man. Promises from O'Malley wouldn't pay her rent, keep food on her table, or clothes on her and Danny's backs. That was her responsibility. It always had been, it always would be. She'd be a fool to watch her job go down the toilet while she clutched some postorgasmic promise from O'Malley. Let the sex cool and he'd reconsider anyway.

"Everyone get the hell out and I don't want to see any

of you until you've got a solution to this total screw-up." Lauchmann dismissed them with a sharp wave of his hand.

She depended on herself. She'd screwed this up for herself, now she'd fix it.

Portia kept her seat while everyone filed out posthaste. Lauchmann glared at her. "What do you want?"

Portia got up and closed his door. "I want to save our collective ass." There was no reason she should feel a kinship with Judas. O'Malley would do the same, wouldn't he? This was business.

Lauchmann sat forward, eyes gleaming. Odd how they reminded her of thirty pieces of silver. "Spill."

This was her job, her livelihood. She opened her mouth. This was her integrity, her self-respect. She could find another job, but if she lost her integrity...and hell no, O'Malley wouldn't do the same. She might not have it in her to be what Rourke wanted her to be, but she certainly didn't have it in her to destroy him and his family. "I thought we could brainstorm."

"I thought we could brainstorm," he mocked her, throwing her a look of total disgust. "Get the hell out and don't come back until you've got something for me."

If she really wanted an exercise in integrity she'd tell Lauchmann to take his show and his job and shove it. But her heroism only stretched so far. She had bills to pay. She got up and left without another word.

Jacey straightened up from where she was slouching against the wall outside Lauchmann's door. She fell into step next to Portia. "What was that about?"

"That was about the dumbest thing I've ever done. How do you feel about filming termite mounds in Africa?"

Jacey shrugged. "I'm not crazy about hot weather and I don't like bugs." She cast a sidelong glance at Portia. "So what was that really about?"

Portia knew Jacey could take the information straight to the top, to Burt Mueller. And it really wasn't her secret to confide. But she needed to talk to somebody, and she considered Jacey a friend. She trusted her.

She led Jacey into her office and pulled the door closed behind her. "I could've saved the show, our jobs. Would you like to thank me now or later for letting you sink with the rest of us?"

Jacey dropped into a guest chair. "I guess I'd rather hear the whole story before I thank you up front."

Portia told her about Nick's embezzlement, what it meant to Rourke's family and the role Rourke played in it. Jacey smirked. "I told you he was a white-knight kind of guy."

Like a classic horror-movie scene, her office door swung open and Lauchmann entered, clapping his hands. "We're back in the game. Good job, P.T. We've got a scandal and a white knight charging in to save the day. Apparently I should've taken you up on your brainstorming offer, 'cause that's a helluva solution." Lauchmann rubbed his hands together, reminding her of a giant insect. Cockroach.

Bile rose in her throat. "That's private information."

"Don't disappoint me. We both know that's good PR. Excellent work." He tossed her clipboard onto her desk. "You left that in my office. Good thing I had to take a piss and was nice enough to stop by with this."

He started out the door and turned around to face her. "You know, I'd have to fire you if I thought you weren't going to share your news with me." There was nothing nice about his smile. "But I'm going to assume you would've told me sooner or later because I really don't want to fire you. Good help is hard to find. In fact, I believe you just earned your promotion." With another unpleasant smile, he left them.

"What a dick!" Jacey said.

Portia couldn't manage more than a nod. Lauchmann was a dick. They had a hit. She had her promotion. She jumped up and ran for the bathroom. She only made it as far as her trash can before she threw up her breakfast.

ROURKE FINALLY gave up after reading the same page for the third time. He put the book on the coffee table and leaned back to listen to his copy of the CD they'd listened to at Portia's place. His head wasn't in a book, it was with her.

Work had been a zoo today. Mondays were always hectic and he'd hustled his butt to play catch-up after two-and-a-half weeks away. Even with his demanding schedule, she'd never been far from his mind. He'd toyed with calling her several times since he'd been home. But damn it, thanks to Nick's comment, he didn't want her to feel like he was some crazy psychopath stalker. On the other hand, he knew as surely as he knew his own name that while she'd promised him a chance yesterday, doubts and fears would begin to crowd her today. And without him to allay those fears, they'd gain the upper hand, and he'd slip back down the slope he'd worked so hard to gain ground on.

He glanced at the clock. Fifteen minutes past midnight. Only a little past nine on the Pacific coast. To hell with Nick, he was calling. He picked up the phone and dialed her number. Cripes. His heart was pounding.

"Hello," she answered the phone, her voice a balm that soothed his soul.

"Hi. It's Rourke."

"Rourke...what are you doing up so late?" She sounded tired. Strained. Agitated.

"Missing you. Were you busy? Is this a bad time?"

"No. No, it's fine. Danny's in bed and I was just folding some laundry."

"Ah, my favorite. Did you miss me today?"

"Yes. I mean, I don't know. I was really busy today. Listen, I was going to call you tomorrow—"

"That's good news—"

"Listen, don't say anything else." He heard her draw a deep breath and knew he wasn't going to like what he heard. "I have something to tell you."

"Okay. I'm listening. But you're not going to tell me anything that's going to change my mind." She really had no faith in his feelings.

"There's a problem." Foreboding knotted his gut. "We had a meeting at work today. Lauchmann spent the weekend reviewing the show. The bottom line was that the second half was a bomb, the part filmed after you and I slept together. Lauchmann told us all our jobs were on the line, that we needed something to save it from being a bomb."

A chill ran over him. He knew what was coming before the words left her mouth. "Let me guess. Lauchmann knows about Nick."

"Yes. He knows." Her voice was barely a whisper.

"How could you, Portia?" Pain, sharp and real, sliced through him and he lashed out. "I trusted you. You of all people should know what it feels like to have a trust betrayed."

"I didn't tell him, Rourke. He overheard me—"

"But if you hadn't been talking he couldn't have heard could he, Portia? I told you that in confidence."

"If I could take it back I would," her voice sounded cool, distant formal, "a thousand times over. But do you want to know the best part of this? I had the opportunity to tell him. I was going to tell him, Rourke. I closed the door and sat in his office and when it came down to it, I couldn't. Not to save my job, not to save the show."

He laughed, bitter, disillusioned. "You know, if you had just called me up and talked to me instead of talking to someone else… I would've probably told Lauchmann myself if it would've meant saving your job."

"So, what's this really about, Rourke? Is it about me betraying you or me taking away an opportunity for you to save the day?"

"Damn it, Portia. It's about trust. I trusted you. Trust—you know, the concept that's foreign to you? Do you still have your job? Did my news get you your promotion?"

"Yes. I have my job and I got the promotion. I told you before I don't need you to come to my rescue."

Her tone, positively glacial, fed his ire. "That's all that matters, isn't it? That you can continue to barricade yourself in your own insular world." He laughed, almost choking on his own rancor. "I thought you were beautiful and brave and a woman of integrity." He closed his eyes, disgusted with himself. He'd failed his parents and his brother. "I was wrong, and now my family will pay the price for my foolishness. I want you to think of what you've done to my parents every night before you go to sleep."

"Are you through?" Was that a hint of tears behind her cool tone?

He thought of his mother standing in line at the grocery store she'd shopped at for years, her family's disgrace screaming at her from every tabloid lining the check-out line, the whispers and the stares that would follow and he hardened his heart to Portia's tears. "I'm almost through, but not quite. You surround yourself with shields. At work you hide behind that damn clipboard. And you hide behind your son. You know, you're so afraid of letting anyone come into contact with Danny. You're afraid to show him to me. Honey, what should really frighten you is what you're turning into."

# 12

PORTIA HUNG UP the phone. Moving like a zombie, she stripped naked and climbed in the shower. Only then did she give way to the tears she'd choked back. At first she cried silently and then great gulping sobs shook her. She curled into a ball of misery on the tiled floor, welcoming the sting of spray on her back. She sat on the shower floor until there were no more tears and the water ran cold.

Rousing herself, she climbed out and dried off. She wrapped the towel around her, leaving her hair dripping past her shoulders. She leaned against the sink and swiped a spot on the steamed mirror. The reflection was watery and murky, but she stared at the woman. Did she know her? Did she like her?

Rourke's words had left her raw and bleeding because in great measure he was right. She *had* cut herself off from everyone. And she wasn't proud of this particular truth, but she *had* hidden behind Danny.

What kind of role model was she setting for her son? Should she show him by example that the only way to go through life was at a distance? Safe, but alone? Was that what she wanted for him when he was a grown man? Alone? An island to himself? Did she want him to view need as a strength or as a weakness? She had only seen it as weakness, but with Rourke it felt like a source of strength. Today, she'd almost made a decision she wouldn't have been able to live with. She'd almost told Lauchmann, willingly, knowingly, to his face. Did she want to stay in a position where that kind of betrayal was valued? Where the reward for wrecking someone's life was a promotion? If she stayed, how long before that corporate culture nibbled away at her integrity until she became another Lauchmann, digging through garbage, real and figurative, to get ahead? She would, thank you very much, prefer filming African termite mounds.

And then she faced the truth that even in this moment of reckoning she'd put off. She loved him. She loved Rourke O'Malley. Beyond reason. Beyond redemption. Whether she wanted to or not. He'd been angry and hurt, but she also knew how much his family meant to him, and exactly how humiliating Lauchmann's revelation would be to those people he loved.

The old Portia would have retreated behind her wall. The old Portia would have been almost grateful that it had come to this, happy for an excuse to amputate the feelings he roused in her, to seek an out and take it.

But she wasn't that same woman. Maybe that was part of the involuntary thing Rourke had tried to explain. No matter what their outcome, she was a different woman. His love had marked her, changed her. She wasn't the same and she couldn't go back to the life she'd had for the last ten years. Nor did she want to.

*We could have a good life together. Me, you and Danny. And maybe one day we could give Danny a little brother or sister, or both.*

She embraced his sweet words and the pictures they conjured. She allowed the fantasy she'd clamped down on to play out in her head. Her and her two geeky guys, Danny and Rourke. And baby makes four? What would it be like to have her belly swollen with a child whose father wanted it? A pregnancy filled with joy and anticipation, rather than fear of the unknown? How would it feel to know she would share all the trials and tribulations of parenthood rather than face them alone?

She had told Rourke she didn't need him to rescue her and she didn't. But it was high time she rescued herself.

Rapunzel had let down her hair and now that she had a taste of what lay beyond the fortress walls, she didn't want to go back.

"SO, IT'S DONE. And it can't be undone." Rourke sat on the edge of the sofa upholstered in a cabbage-rose print in what his mother called the front room, his hands loosely linked between his knees.

He looked from his mother to his father and was stunned at the amused glance that passed between the two of them. "I think I haven't done a very good job of explaining this. Obviously I haven't, because there's nothing funny about this situation. When you go to the store, Ma, it's going to be on the front page of every tabloid. Your neighbors will never look at you the same."

His father gave him a censoring look. "Your ma and I fully understand how serious this is. I can't say that we're very proud that Nicky would do such a thing. We know we raised him better than that, but we're not about to die of shame, the way you think we are. No. Your ma and I think it's funny that you lads thought we didn't know and how you thought you had to protect us from knowing."

Rourke was damn glad he was sitting down. "You knew? When? How?"

"Probably about the same time Nicky confided in you. A man called the house one day," his mother said.

"But if you knew, why didn't you say something?"

"It was up to Nick to bring it up to us. And when a man makes mistakes, he has to learn to handle them on his own."

"But we're family. We take care of our own."

"When you and Nick were little we took care of you when you scraped your knees. Then you got to the point when you took care of your own scrapes. A family sticks together, but ultimately a man has to account to himself for the decisions he does and doesn't make. At the end of the day, he has to be at peace with who he is and what he does. Your ma and I can't do that for you or Nick. You can't do that for your brother."

Rourke nodded. He was finally figuring out that he hadn't particularly done Nick a favor. "I'm beginning to see that."

"There's always been a bit of an inequity in your senses of responsibility. You always had too much and Nick never had enough. Rourke, you've always wanted to rescue things since you were a wee lad. But sometimes rescuing people undermines them. Makes them think they can't do it themselves. Sometimes sinking on his own does a man more good than swimming with help."

He glanced from his mother to his father. "Well, this is going to hit and it'll be up to Nick whether he sinks or swims."

"I believe your brother is made of sterner stuff than you think." His father shot him a loving but censuring look. "Just as your ma and I are tougher than you seem to think."

"And now enough about us and Nick. Tell us about this lass of yours," his mother said.

And he found himself telling them about Portia. Her background, Danny, her parents, everything. Everything except the sex. They were, after all, his parents. "I said something that I shouldn't have. I was angry and hurt. I don't know if she'll forgive me. I was harsh."

His mother smiled at him, soothing him with her calm. "Well, if you love her, and it sounds like that's the case, all you can do is ask."

He was ashamed of the way he'd lashed out at Portia.
He gave voice to his greatest fear. "But what if she won't
forgive me?"

"Then you ask some more," his mother said.

His dad nodded. "Grovel if you have to. And you keep
asking. Trust me son, pride makes for a cold bedfellow."

PORTIA SAT in the coffee shop across from Rourke's apartment building. She hoped he got home soon before she totally lost her nerve. She hadn't called him. What she
needed to say had to be said in person. But nothing she'd
done today had made her as nervous as facing him. Of
course, while important, none of the rest of the day mattered as much as he did. A light rain began to fall, darken-
ing the sidewalk, clinging to the leaves of the tree outside.

A garden of umbrellas blossomed, making it harder to
see the faces of the passersby. What if she missed him? Just
as the thought occurred to her, she felt him, soul-deep, an
instant before she saw him walking down the sidewalk.
Her heart did a slow somersault in her chest—or at least
it felt that way. She was excited and nervous and she wondered if a heart could actually beat out of a chest.

Was he still angry? Was he too hurt, too betrayed to even
give her a chance? What if he refused to let her in? The old
Portia whispered that she could just walk in the opposite
direction, catch a cab and arrive at Boston's Logan airport
early for her flight back. Safe. Familiar. Alone. The new Portia, however, straightened her spine and marched across
the street.

ROURKE TOSSED his jacket and his shirt and tie across the
closed toilet seat and pulled a clean towel off the hook to
dry his hair. His mother had insisted he be home before six
tonight. Something about her having a package delivered

to his house and it couldn't be left at the door. He would've been more curious, possibly paid more attention, if he hadn't been so stinking miserable over Portia. He desperately needed to apologize, but it wasn't something he wanted to handle over the phone. He needed to be face-to-face with her. He couldn't afford a weekday off work, and he could ill-afford the weekend with all the catch-up he had, but Saturday would find him on her doorstep, groveling, trying to salvage something of their relationship from the mess he'd made.

The door buzzed and Watson started barking madly. Towel in hand, Rourke went to the front door. Before he even looked through the peep hole, the hair on the back of his neck stood up. He looked through the hole and for a second thought he was hallucinating.

"Portia?" He threw the lock and opened the door. "Portia? It really is you?"

A thousand butterflies took flight in his belly and he was literally dumbstruck.

Watson sniffed her rain-spattered pumps. "Watson, I presume."

Rourke nodded as the dog lost interest and trotted back into the den.

She took another deep breath, shifting the package in her hand. "Can I come in?"

"Oh. Of course. I'm stunned… I wasn't expecting…"

She stepped past him and he closed the door, turning to face her. She lifted her chin and without preamble said, "I love you."

He had behaved like such an ass. She was so cautious. Surely his head was playing tricks with him. "Say that again."

Her eyes a dark gray, serious, she repeated herself. "I love you."

Galvanized into action, desperate to make it real, he dropped his towel, crushed her to him, and kissed her as if his very life depended on it. Or perhaps that was the way she kissed him. He lifted his head. "Say it one more time."

She smiled. "I love you."

"Oh, God, Portia. I love you so much. I'm so sorry I said the things I did. I was going to show up on your doorstep on Saturday and beg your forgiveness. I thought it was too important for a phone call."

She nodded. Would they always be on this same wavelength? He thought so. "That's why I'm here."

"I'm so sorry. I was—"

"Right. You were right. They needed to be said. I thought I was meeting life head-on but I was simply existing in my tower."

For the first time since she'd shown up on his doorstep, he really looked at her. She looked the same—beautiful—yet, different. A softness had replaced the wariness that had always lurked in her eyes. Her hair fell in a rain-damped curtain past her shoulders. "Your hair is down."

She nodded, almost shy. "I've adopted a new style."

"I like it. It suits you." He slid his hand along her cheek, loving the brush of her hair against the back of his fingers. "You are impossibly beautiful."

"Thank you." She drew a deep breath. "I've got a couple of things to tell you and two things to give you. And I'm really not sure how you'll feel about any of them." She knotted her hands together, uncertainty replacing her former radiance. "You may want to sit."

"Okay." He realized they were still in the foyer and he was shirtless, but she'd seen him in less. Getting dressed wasn't nearly as important as what she had to say. "I'm sorry. Let's go in here." He led her past the kitchen to the den. Neither, however, sat. Watson regarded them from the recliner with dark-eyed interest.

She wet her lips with the tip of her tongue. "First, I need to tell you that I went to see your parents today."

Stupefied, he sat. "You went to see my parents? Here? Today? Why?"

"I wanted to apologize for what was coming down the pike and the role I played in it."

His heart swelled with love, pride and gratitude for her courage, for what it must have cost her. "Oh, honey, they don't blame you. And neither do I." He shook his head at how he'd missed the big picture before, but seeing it very clearly now. "Nick created this mess and I made it worse."

"That's about what they said. They're nice people. Once I got past being so nervous I thought I'd throw up, I enjoyed my visit with them." She smiled, a spark of devilment lighting her eyes to more green than gray. "Your mother showed me pictures."

Rourke felt a dull flush crawl up his face. "Please tell me she didn't show you my graduation picture." He had been at his all-time geekiest. Skinny with braces and glasses. And a bad haircut to boot.

Portia smiled and nodded. "Baby pictures to present day. You were cute."

She had seen those pictures and she'd still told him she loved him? "Ma could've left me with a little dignity."

"She's proud of you."

Eager to shift her attention from those photographs and curious as to what other surprise she was about to throw his way, he prompted her, "You said you had something else to tell me."

"Yeah." Another one of those deep breaths. "I'm about to be unemployed."

What the hell? She was damn good—no, great—at what she did. "Those bastards *fired* you?"

"No. I'm quitting. I'm pretty sure I can find another job. In fact, I dropped by for an impromptu visit at the local PBS station here."

This was better than he'd ever dreamed. But it all felt surreal, as if he couldn't trust any of it. "Here? In Boston? Five blocks from here?"

"It seemed about like that. I got a little disoriented with the cab ride." She reached into the bag she'd carried since she'd walked in and pulled out her clipboard and held it out to him. "I want you to have this. I don't need it an more. But it makes a very effective shield if you're in the market for something like that."

He took the clipboard he'd accused her of hiding behind.

She pulled out something else, a book of sorts. "And I'd like to introduce you to my son. This is a picture album I've kept since Danny was a baby. I thought maybe you could meet him here and then come out for a visit…get to know him…maybe we could all go to a ballgame or… well, something."

Suddenly elation and peace both flooded him. He'd been scared to trust any of this, even her declaration of love, but at this moment, when she offered not just herself, but her son, the person she held most closely, most dear, to him, he knew she was as sure as he was.

"Oh, honey…" He dropped to one knee and took her hand between his. "Portia fair, will you rescue this poor be-sotted white knight? Will you and Danny save me from being a crusty old bachelor who spends his Friday nights switching between *X-Files* and *Star Trek* reruns?"

Her smile illuminated his world. "You have women chasing you and tossing their underwear at you. You just had your choice of the world's wealthiest, most beautiful

women, but you want me to save you from yourself." She
shook her head, as if he amazed her. "Well, maybe we can
cut a deal. I'm in desperate need myself of a white knight.
Not to rescue me, mind you, but to cover my backside."

# Epilogue

"DAD, WHICH WAY would be better to set up the lab table?" Danny asked.

Portia looked up at her two favorite men in the whole world setting up Danny's new lab center in the corner, next to the bank of windows that showcased Boston and its fascinating skyline. Just as she'd anticipated, it had been total adoration from first sight for Rourke and Danny.

Rourke caught her eye and beamed. One of the sweetest moments of her life had been when her son had shyly asked, on their wedding day, if he could now call Rourke Dad. And her strong handsome hunk of a husband, labeled by women around the world as "really hot," had cried. In the three months they'd been married, Danny couldn't seem to say it enough and neither she nor Rourke ever tired of hearing it.

She put down her new clipboard, a gift from her husband. Her production notes for the week's shoot could wait until later. She got up from her spot on the couch where she'd been sandwiched between Watson and Shirley, Danny's mini-schnauzer Rourke had helped him pick out at the rescue center, and wandered over to her two guys. "How's it going?"

Rourke looked up, his eyes shining. "Great. Boy genius here will be blowing up the place in no time."

Danny punched his stepfather in the arm, obviously pleased by Rourke's affectionate teasing. "Mom, look at this." Danny showed her a piece of equipment, which was a total mystery to her.

"Pretty cool, huh?" Rourke asked with enthusiasm.

She had no idea about the equipment, but Rourke and Danny geeking out together thrilled her. "Very cool. This has been some birthday, huh?" She wrapped her arm around her son's thin shoulders.

He hugged her back before pulling away. "Awesome. I'm glad grandma and grandpa were here. I think they liked our place. And I could tell, they liked Ma and Da too."

Rourke's parents had insisted from the beginning that Portia and Danny call them by the names their sons did— they were, after all, family now.

"Yeah, they seemed to get along well together," she said.

"That's an understatement," Rourke said. "My parents are having a blast. They're even talking about buying a motor home so they can travel with Laela and Jack. I never knew they were interested in that kind of thing at all."

Portia laughed, shaking her head. "You? Mom and Dad had never mentioned wanting an RV. Of course they wouldn't have." No, it had taken her getting on with her life and developing her own family to free her parents up to pursue their dreams. Jack and Laela Tomlinson had made the trip from L.A. to Boston to celebrate Danny's birthday in their new motorhome. Moira and Paul had invited them to park it in their yard in Quincey, since Boston's narrow streets didn't exactly accommodate RVs. "I'm glad they like one another."

"Surprised?" Rourke asked.

"Not really."

Danny joined in without looking up from where he was lining up empty beakers. "It's perfect. Grandma talks all the time and Grandpa's kind of quiet. Da likes to talk but

Ma doesn't say much. It all works out." He glanced up
with a satisfied smile.

Rourke slipped his arm around Portia's waist. "That's
one smart kid."

Danny looked up and smirked, obviously pleased at
Rourke's comment. She'd once thought of herself as a sponge
soaking up Rourke. They were a family of sponges now.

Rourke nuzzled her temple and a familiar tingle shot
through her.

"Yuck. You guys are gonna start that kissing business."

Portia laughed. They didn't have make-out sessions in
front of Danny, but she and Rourke were openly affectionate. Her son needed to see how people in love, who re-
spected one another, interacted. She kissed Rourke's jaw.
"I think we just might."

"Double yuck. Can I go up to Jason's and finish this
later? His mom invited me to come over after my grandparents left. I told her I had two sets and she congratulated me."

Jason lived one floor up, and though he was a year
younger than Danny, the two boys were kindred spirits.
"If she invited you…"

Danny was off and running for the front door. "She
did," he called over his shoulder. Two seconds later the
door banged closed behind him.

Portia laughed and threw her arms around Rourke's
neck, all the happiness inside her bubbling over. "This is
the best birthday my son's ever had."

"It *was* good, wasn't it? I think he likes Ma and Da."

Portia snorted, blowing a strand of hair out of her face.
"What's not to like? They spoil him shamelessly."

Rourke grinned and lifted her in a bear hug. "Honey,
I'm so happy. I told you we'd have a good life together."

"Hmm." She ran her hands beneath his shirt, plying her
fingers along the muscles rippling below his skin. A famil-

iar delicious heat stole through her. "That was sweet of Jacey and Digg to take the train up from New York for the party. She's gotten to be one of Danny's favorite people."

Rourke skimmed his hands along her back and her breath hitched in her throat. "Do you think she'll marry Digg before the baby comes?" he asked.

Portia laughed. "Probably. But you know Jacey. It'll be on her terms."

Rourke cupped her fanny and pulled her into intimate contact with his lower body. Moisture gathered between her thighs. He nuzzled her neck. "Remember that little brother or sister we'd talked about for Danny?" he asked.

"Yeah. In a couple of years. Why?" She wanted another child. His. But she also wanted them to have their time first. "You know how I am about schedules."

He slid his hands around her waist and eased down her zipper. Her heart thundered against the broad wall of his chest. His unerring fingers slipped inside her. "If you could work it into your schedule, I thought we could get in a little practice."

She had that dizzying sensation of her entire body tightening and beginning to unravel at the same time. "I could definitely work it in. I've heard practice makes perfect."

\* \* \* \* \*

**SILHOUETTE®**

*Desire™ 2 in 1*

# THE FIERCE AND TENDER SHEIKH
## by Alexandra Sellers

*Sons of the Desert*

His instructions were simple: seek out and return home with the long-lost princess of Bagestan, but when he found her, Sheikh Sharif Azad al Dauleh found bringing her back wasn't nearly as tempting as keeping her for himself…

# DARING THE DYNAMIC SHEIKH
## by Kristi Gold

*The Royal Wager*

Sheikh Dharr Halim was prepared for a loveless arranged marriage to Raina Kahill, yet the more heated their encounters became, the more it became clear that she'd been saving herself all these years…for him!

# *The Crenshaws*
## BRANDED by Annette Broadrick

Jake Crenshaw, her hero, needed her help and Ashley Sullivan began to realise that Jake hadn't spurned her advances because he didn't want her—but because he *did*. Could she make him lose his scruples…so that she could lose her virginity?

# CAUGHT IN THE CROSSFIRE
## by Annette Broadrick

Discovered in the bed of the Senator's virginal daughter, Jared Crenshaw honourably proposed, but suspected he'd been set up. Who would do such a thing and why? He wanted answers…

**On sale from 18th November 2005**

*Available at most branches of WHSmith, Tesco, ASDA, Borders, Eason, Sainsbury's and most bookshops*

*Visit our website at www.silhouette.co.uk*

**SILHOUETTE®** 1105/51b

## *Desire* 2 in 1

## AWAKEN TO PLEASURE by Nalini Singh

Keeping custody of her brother meant Taylor Reid was going to
have to become her former boss's, Jackson Santorini's, bride. And
give him a baby!

## THE SEDUCTION REQUEST
### by Michelle Celmer

When millionaire Matt Conway returned home, he hadn't counted
on running into Emily Douglas—or being asked to seduce her...
again! They had no trouble with passion, but would Matt break her
heart...again?

## *HEAT*
## NEVER NAUGHTY ENOUGH
### by Jill Munroe

She was the perfect executive assistant—until she was hypnotised—
then she turned into a terrible tease. Suddenly sexy workaholic
Wagner Achrom finds his hands full with intimate, naughty items
belonging to his previously proper but invisible PA, *but he wasn't
complaining.*

## WARM & WILLING by Kate Hoffmann

Sarah Cantrell was out of her element when a freak snowstorm
stranded her with Sam Morgan, and she needed a refresher course
on the basics of survival: shelter, heat, food and sex... She could live
without some items, but not without Sam's lovemaking!

**On sale from 18th November 2005**

*Available at most branches of WHSmith, Tesco, ASDA,
Borders, Eason, Sainsbury's and most bookshops*

*Visit our website at www.silhouette.co.uk*

# FREE

## 2 BOOKS AND A SURPRISE GIFT!

We would like to take this opportunity to thank you for reading this Silhouette® book by offering you the chance to take TWO more specially selected 2-in-1 volumes from the Desire™ series absolutely FREE! We're also making this offer to introduce you to the benefits of the Reader Service™—

- ★ FREE home delivery
- ★ FREE gifts and competitions
- ★ FREE monthly Newsletter
- ★ Books available before they're in the shops
- ★ Exclusive Reader Service offers

Accepting these FREE books and gift places you under no obligation to buy; you may cancel at any time, even after receiving your free shipment. Simply complete your details below and return the entire page to the address below. You don't even need a stamp!

**YES!** Please send me 2 free Desire volumes and a surprise gift. I understand that unless you hear from me, I will receive 3 superb new volumes every month for just £4.99 each, postage and packing free. I am under no obligation to purchase any books and may cancel my subscription at any time. The free books and gift will be mine to keep in any case.

D5ZEE

Ms/Mrs/Miss/Mr.........................................Initials ...............................................
                                                                  BLOCK CAPITALS PLEASE
Surname ...................................................................................................................

Address ...................................................................................................................

......................................................................................................................................

..................................................................Postcode ...............................................

Send this whole page to:
The Reader Service, FREEPOST CN81, Croydon, CR9 3WZ

Offer valid in UK only and is not available to current Reader Service™subscribers to this series. Overseas and Eire please write for details. We reserve the right to refuse an application and applicants must be aged 18 years or over. Only one application per household. Terms and prices subject to change without notice. Offer expires 28th February 2006. As a result of this application, you may receive offers from Harlequin Mills & Boon and other carefully selected companies. If you would prefer not to share in this opportunity please write to The Data Manager at PO Box 676, Richmond, TW9 1WU.

Silhouette® is a registered trademark and is used under licence.
Desire™ is being used as a trademark. The Reader Service™ is being used as a trademark.